REBEL OF FIRE AND FLIGHT

REBEL OF FIRE AND FLIGHT

ANEESA MARUFU

Chicken House
SCHOLASTIC INC. / NEW YORK

First published in the United Kingdom in 2022 as *The Balloon Thief* by Chicken House, 2 Palmer Street, Frome, Somerset BA11 1DS.

Library of Congress Cataloging-in-Publication Data available

ISBN 978-1-338-80231-3

10 9 8 7 6 5 4 3 2 1 23 24 25 26 27

Printed in Italy 183

First edition, January 2023

Book design by Keirsten Geise

To Raheem, for teaching me how to fly

1

KHADIJA

The white men looked like birds. Or at least, Khadija thought they did. From her bedroom window they were tiny figures, no bigger than the length of her finger. She studied their bent knees, arms a blur like wings caught mid-flight as their desperate motions brought the deflated silk in their hands to life. Any faster, and she'd think they were the ones about to leave the ground instead of the hot-air balloon.

She was too far away to hear the racist slurs leaving the merchants' lips as they instructed the men to do their bidding, but she could certainly imagine what was being said as their fair skin reddened beneath the hot sun while the silk balloon swelled. And yet Khadija couldn't bring herself to pity them. She envied them. For all their suffering and mistreatment, they still had a better view of the hot-air balloon than she did.

The tip of her reed pen bled black ink across the paper as she sketched the bright globe of the balloon and crisscrossed it with sharp lines, marking each individual panel. She'd seen women in the bazaar sewing the squares of material by hand and stitching the more lavish ones together with freshwater pearls along the seams so that, once airborne, the balloon became a living, flying piece of art. She decided against including the white men in her drawing, or the wealthy merchants hovering close by, ready to leap forward at any moment should their balloons chance an escape with their livelihoods still aboard.

Balloons were unpredictable creatures, after all, whisking men away on the next breeze with almost perfect obedience before becoming greedy and engorged, stuffing themselves with hot air until they burst spectacularly without warning. There were the lazy ones that slumped across the ground like empty carcasses refusing to come alive, and the furious ones with flames so hungry they licked the fabric and set the whole balloon ablaze. No matter how hard men tried, balloons were creatures they could never truly tame. That's why she loved them.

A gentle tap at her door had Khadija swiftly folding her paper in half, causing the wet ink to stick it together. She stuffed it beneath her pillow and wiped her ink-stained fingertips on her shalwar kameez just as the door swung open.

"Yes, Abba." Khadija stood to attention as her father shuffled in. His glasses had slipped down the bridge of his nose, exposing the permanent dents they'd caused from years of wear. Too much time spent poring over paperwork and numbers had reduced his eyesight to that of a fruit bat's so that Abba had to squint even when he was but a few feet from her. His frequent frowning only emphasized his perpetual air of disappointment.

"Ah, there you are, beti!" Abba exclaimed. As if she'd be anywhere else but in her bedroom. His knees creaked as he perched on her bed, brow creasing at the open book Khadija had in her haste forgotten to hide. Its spine was bent back to reveal a picture of a magnificent silver balloon made of a material as sheer and delicate as lace.

She cursed inwardly.

"Are you not too old for storybooks?" Abba picked up the book by its corner as if it was a wet dishcloth.

"It's not stories, Abba, it's history." Khadija quickly freed the book from his fingers. "Stories aren't real. This actually happened."

Abba scoffed. "Pah! You really believe a common jinn kidnapped a princess in a hot-air balloon?"

Khadija winced. The book told the tale of Princess Malika, who, long ago, mysteriously vanished the night before her wedding after her fearless nature had caught the eye of the jinniya Queen Mardzma—the queen of female warriors—or so the story said. The queen sent one of her jinn in a hot-air balloon, disguised as a handsome prince, to seduce the princess. He stole her up into the skies to admire the world below before delivering her to Queen Mardzma's kingdom in the jinn realm, where she was ruthlessly trained to become one of their most heroic fighters. The book contained accounts of a number of her adventures, but the tale of her disappearance had always been Khadija's favorite, if only for the illustration of the silver balloon.

Unlike Khadija, Abba didn't care much for literature depicting women doing things they were not supposed to do. She wasn't sure which part of the story he found most unbelievable: a princess kidnapped by a jinn in a hot-air balloon, or an army of female warriors.

Abba cleared his throat. "Anyway, the real reason I'm here"—he slapped his thighs—"is that I have very good news for you! News you'll be pleased to hear."

Khadija smiled meekly. Abba and she often had very differing views about what they considered good news. Certainly, it couldn't be news as good as fighting alongside a warrior queen.

Still, she had to ask. "What is it, Abba?"

Abba pushed his glasses back to their usual position so that his eyes looked twice their size. "I have finally found the perfect match for my daughter!"

This again. It was always this. Always another match, another potential suitor, another failed betrothal that ended in Abba's sideburns becoming grayer by the day and Khadija spending more and more time in her bedroom, where she could almost be forgotten about, and Abba could pretend the weight of marrying off his youngest daughter didn't still rest on his shoulders.

"He is a fine young man." Abba stroked his beard. "A shoemaker, in fact. Think, Khadija, of all the pretty shoes he could make for you. The neighbors will certainly be jealous!"

Shoes. Really! Did he not know her at all?

"I don't need shoes, Abba. I have enough already." And that was the truth. Their eyes wandered to her dresser and the neat row of shoes beside it—pretty velvet slippers and strappy sandals studded with rhinestones.

None of them hers, of course. None of them ones she'd ever worn. It's not that they didn't fit her. But they were her mother's shoes, collecting dust in the corner of her bedroom. The last time Ammi's shoes had ever been worn felt like another life.

Abba's face fell. His shoulders dropped. Whatever he'd used to inflate himself had just been punctured. "I know, beti," he said, "but I think this could be very good for you. You can't spend the rest of your life in your bedroom reading storybooks."

That stung. He made it sound so trivial. Little did he know there was a pile of sketches under her bed, each one meticulously drawn from hours spent watching balloons take off and land every day. Khadija studied balloons the way one would study birds or wildflowers, and reckoned she knew the anatomy of a balloon far better than the merchants outside.

Girls weren't allowed to fly, but that did nothing to quell her obsession. After all, Princess Malika had flown in a hot-air balloon. All she had to do was get kidnapped by a jinn.

"Most girls your age are already married." Abba shook his head. "Leave it any longer and all the good men will be gone, and you'll be left with someone"—he threw his arms up, as if plucking the right words from the air—"plain. Boring." He fixed his dark eyes on her.

She'd never realized shoes were that interesting to Abba. Khadija dropped her gaze, fiddling with a loose thread on her bedspread until one of the embroidered beads came away. It bounced across the floor. No. They both knew there was nothing grand or exciting about a shoemaker. Her older sister, Talia, had gotten lucky with her husband. A cloth merchant. Now she was busy traversing Ghadaea in a hot-air balloon while he traded in lavish organza and fine crushed silks. But Talia had always had more appetite for marriage. She could stomach it better than Khadija.

"I'm not that old, Abba."

"But you will be. Soon," Abba interrupted. "You're sixteen now. Talia was already engaged at your age, and look how happy she is."

Khadija rolled her eyes. "How do you know she's even happy, Abba? We've not seen nor heard from her in months."

Abba's jaw twitched. A few years ago he would've scolded her for such outspokenness. Now he only sighed, like her candor was a splinter lodged so deeply beneath his skin he had given up trying to rid himself of it.

He rose from her bed, eyes resting on her dresser covered in stacks of glittery bangles meant for girls with far thinner wrists than her. Khadija was reduced to lathering up to her elbows with soap before forcing them on, and that was when she could be bothered to wear them. Then there were the pretty peacock hairpins and jeweled brooches, still nestled unopened in their plush boxes, to decorate her hijab. All gifts he'd often encourage her to wear, all to no avail.

Abba exhaled. "It's almost like you don't *want* to get married, Khadija."

Finally he'd gotten it! And it only took how many years? Khadija crossed her ankles, clasped her palms in her lap, and met Abba's gaze. She felt like a little girl with him towering above her. No matter how old she got, Abba always treated her like she was so little, his youngest child—though she hadn't always been that.

She bit her lip. "I don't, Abba," she whispered. "I really don't."

He winced at her honesty. "I don't know what the matter is with you sometimes!" He threw his head back as if searching the ceiling for answers. "I bet it's all this time you spend alone. Can't be good for you." Abba hummed as if he'd solved the impossible equation that was his daughter refusing to marry. "Have you been sleeping? Any bad dreams? Headaches?"

She knew where this was going.

"You know, the neighbor's daughter was like you. Didn't want to marry either, and Mr. Rashid didn't know what to do about her. It started with bad dreams and then this constant pounding headache." Abba smacked his forehead to emphasize the pounding. "Mr. Rashid took her straight to the physician, and do you know what he said?" He didn't wait for her response. "Jinn possession!" he proclaimed.

"Apparently, it can easily happen to those with weak minds." He tutted and traced his thumb over the ta'wiz around his neck—an amulet consisting of a cloth pouch containing a prayer to offer protection against evil. "Luckily they caught it just in time," Abba continued in his lighthearted manner, as if he hadn't just brazenly insulted her. "The jinn was exorcised, trapped in a copper-and-brass-infused glass bottle, and now the girl is happily married. I believe Mr. Rashid is about to become a grandfather as well."

If it were possible for Khadija to roll her eyes any harder, they'd pop out of her skull and land at her feet. Jinn were shape-shifting spirits residing in Al-Ghaib, a realm hidden to the mortal eye and ruled by various jinn kings and jinniya queens. Most jinn were indifferent to the affairs of mortals. It was unlikely Mr. Rashid's daughter had drawn their interest when, like Khadija, she rarely left her bedroom. What jinn would wish to possess her?

Hunger was the main reason jinn interacted with humans at all. Jinn had a peculiar appetite for corpses, both animal and human. Bodies were never kept long enough to attract them and were cremated with speed. Death was said to pierce the veil between the two worlds, allowing jinn to slip freely into the mortal realm—another reason bodies were quickly disposed of.

"Maybe I should call an exorcist." Abba tapped his chin.

Exorcists were common, though most were frauds, only serving to feed superstition by preying on the most fearful.

"I don't need an exorcist. I'm fine." Though she wished she could say the same for Abba. He'd become increasingly distant over the years, locking himself in his office, where he'd be absorbed with paperwork for most of the day. He thought her ignorant, but Khadija was well aware of the mounting pile of bills and debt letters in his desk drawer. Most likely this was the real reason he wished to marry her off soon, while he could still afford the wedding.

She had to stop this, convince him, before he rushed into something and ruined her life forever. "Just give me more time."

"You've had enough time." His eyes fell to the book on her bed. "All those silly stories you've been reading! Marriage isn't a fairy tale, Khadija. I wish it was, but it's not. Marriage is a matter of convenience, not a whim of the heart."

Khadija rose and circled the bed, as if by putting a piece of furniture between them she could escape this conversation. "Maybe if you let me meet people . . ." She was careful to say *people* and not *boys*. "Then I could find a husband for myself."

Abba scoffed as if she'd just asked for a hot-air balloon as a wedding gift. "A girl finding her own husband? What would the neighbors think of such scandal!" He pursed his lips. "I think it's time you threw that storybook away. Start living in the real world." His words were as brittle as glass. It wasn't like she was expecting a handsome prince to whisk her away in a balloon. Khadija hugged the book to her chest, willing the pages to swallow her. For a moment, Abba appeared ready to snatch it from her. But he didn't.

The book was like Ammi's shoes, from another life. It had belonged to her brother. Hassan had been a natural storyteller, even at his young age. He could read aloud for hours without making a single mistake. Abba had always said he was destined to become a writer or a wazir for the Nawab of Intalyabad if he could afford the airfare to the city. If Khadija thought hard enough, she could still hear her brother's voice reciting the stories, magic seeping across the pages and rolling off the tip of his tongue.

Abba's stern voice snapped her back. "I've been too easy on you, and that's not right. I'm your father. I know what's best."

Khadija's stomach twisted into a knot. She'd always managed to talk her way out of Abba's betrothals, squeezing a few extra months from him. This seemed different. Her time was finally up.

"Put on something nice and come downstairs. He's waiting in the kitchen." With that, Abba shut the door.

2

JACOB

Sticky orbs of semi-cooled glass sat in a line on the counter like a selection of boiled sweets, but Jacob knew better than to touch one. Munir pierced the center of each transparent globe with a white-hot rod, rolling them across a marble slab as he quickly shaped and cooled the glass. Crystal pendants and glass chandeliers twinkled above his head, causing rainbows to swirl around his feet like a kaleidoscope. On the opposite shelf, the copper-and-brass-infused glass vials for the local exorcists glistened a rust-colored orange in the firelight.

Jacob began to count under his breath. Munir was crafting a crystal goblet, or at least trying to. A few more seconds and the glass would be too cool to stick the stem to the base.

He said nothing, of course, as was his place. Munir was not the type to take instructions from his apprentice, let alone admit Jacob might know a thing or two about glassblowing. He had been apprenticed to Munir for not even a year, but already he'd excelled where Munir had expected him to fail. Glassblowing wasn't just about talent and experience. It required patience, working with something so fragile, bending and twisting it into impossible shapes all in a matter of minutes before the glass set solid. It was easy to rush, to produce something careless and sloppy, and that was exactly what Munir was doing.

"Water. Quickly!" Munir snapped, bringing the blowpipe to his lips and inflating a ball of molten glass like a balloon as he worked on the main cup of the goblet before setting the bubble down to cool on the cold marble.

Jacob knew it was too soon for the glass to harden, never mind the stem and base on the side—which would snap apart the minute they were handled.

But he kept his mouth shut. The only reason Munir had selected Jacob as his apprentice was the guarantee that Jacob could never steal his designs and set up business elsewhere like his previous apprentice, who now ran a more successful glass business on the other side of town. People like Jacob weren't allowed to set up businesses. People like Jacob weren't allowed to do much at all in Ghadaea, except blend into the background.

Which meant he was expendable, and so he was forced to hold his tongue even when Munir was butchering his own trade.

Jacob swiftly returned with a bucket. His footsteps caused the glass pendants, talismans, trinkets, and charms people believed warded off jinn to vibrate and tinkle. Perhaps they worked, though that was more likely due to Munir's subpar craftsmanship than anything else.

Munir plunged the ball of molten glass into the water, where it sizzled violently. Flames from the furnace gave his dark skin a crimson hue, his eyes reflecting the fire so that they glowed a hellish red.

They both peered into the bucket. Once submerged, the glass instantly took on a hard, transparent quality. Munir couldn't hide his pleasure if he tried. *Just you wait.* Jacob smiled smugly. *It'll collapse the moment air hits it.*

And it did. The second Munir removed the glass from the water it folded in on itself like melted sugar. Munir growled and launched it across the room, where it smashed against the far wall.

"I'll have to start again!" He rounded on his apprentice with a look of pure fire. There was nothing more embarrassing than making a mistake in front of someone expected to learn from you. "Well, don't just stand there. Get more water!"

Jacob nodded and retreated. He didn't need much convincing. He'd do anything that allowed him a few minutes of freedom from Munir.

Munir turned back to the furnace, his slur following Jacob out the door: "Useless hāri."

The sun dazzled him as Jacob stepped into the heavy heat, past rows of mud-brick houses with orange leopard lilies and red hibiscus flowers dancing in the breeze from their window boxes. Yellow pariah dogs were sniffing through the bins. The air was pungent with rotten fruit and the subtle earthy smell of pine trees. Jacob made off at a steady pace and angled his face away from the midday sun, but it wasn't long before his neck prickled with heat. Those with any sense remained indoors until early evening when it became cool enough to leave their homes. Few wandered the streets, skirting widely around him as if he were one of the dogs rooting through the rubbish.

He was used to it. His white skin and fair hair were evidence that he did not belong among the brown-skinned natives. His ancestors had originated from a place beyond the Himala mountain range, where it was said to be cold enough that when people spoke, their words could be seen in the air. Trade had drawn them to Ghadaea with its wondrous spices and silks, cotton, gemstones, and opium, but it had quickly turned to greed and a lust for power. Their attempts at seizing the land

and all its treasures for themselves had backfired. Almost ninety years later, and the Ghadaeans were still punishing people like him for the mistakes of their grandfathers. They called them hāri now. Unwanted. Stateless. People who didn't belong.

The neat rows of flat-roofed houses soon gave way to dusty shacks and tattered sheets balanced across brittle beams that threatened to blow over at the slightest of winds. Slums—and his home, before Munir had taken him in as an apprentice. In the distance, fields of opium poppies the color of beetroot stretched in all directions, and farther still, the misty blue peaks of the Himala Mountains blurred into the clouds above.

There was only a short line at the well. Jacob slotted behind an elderly man with a constant tremor to his chin. Farther ahead, hāri girls giggled as they bounded through the poppy fields while a cluster of boys lounged against the farming equipment, wolf whistling and flicking pebbles at them. Jacob's insides turned wooden and stiff with longing. He missed this: living among his people—even if it meant returning to long days working in the fields and sleeping outside with the constant risk of being snatched by tigers. It was home. Here, at least, he belonged.

A hand on his shoulder made Jacob flinch until he caught sight of a familiar face. He allowed William to steer him to a patch of yellowing grass.

"Not seen you in a while." William smirked and flopped down beside him, hugging his gangly legs to his chest. He stood a good head and shoulders above Jacob, but he was far skinnier—his tunic hung from his shoulders like it was dangling off a clothes hanger. "How's the life of luxury?"

"Luxury!" Jacob snorted. There was nothing luxurious about dodging Munir's slipper after a poor day of sales in the glass shop, but compared to camping out here with nothing but a moth-eaten sheet to shield against the sun and mosquitoes, it could be a lot worse.

"Must be nice, eating more than one meal a day." There was a bitterness to William's voice that jarred. Jealousy didn't suit him. Not when he had been the one to convince Jacob to accept Munir's apprenticeship.

Jacob's eyes narrowed. "At least you get to live with everyone else. I'd gladly—"

William flashed his palm. "Calm down! I'm only joking." But there was an iciness to the wicked sparkle in his eyes that unsettled Jacob. "Got to milk any advantage you can get in this world. You're getting fed and learning good skills. You'd be an idiot to pass up on that."

Jacob nodded. William was a firm believer in making the best of a hopeless situation. While most of the hāri simply drifted from one day to the next in a daze of constant survival, William still retained his hope that things would change. His spirit crackled with energy that betrayed the apparent weakness of his skinny body. There was a fire about him, an electricity that was both frightening and addictive. That's why Jacob respected him so fiercely. That, and the fact that William had practically raised him. Jacob had been too young to remember his parents before they had been imprisoned, tossed into cells teeming with hāri forced to break the law to survive. He'd never seen them again. William was his mother, his father, his brother, and his friend all rolled into one.

Jacob dug into his pocket and produced a bruised mango. "Got this for you."

William's tongue darted across his lips. His fingers twitched, and Jacob half expected him to snatch it up and sink his teeth into it. Hunger did that to a person, the same way opium made an addict's hands jitter; the sight of food to a starving person made the animal in them come out.

William bit his tongue. "Give it to one of the kids. They need it more."

Jacob ignored him and set to peeling it, sticky juices coating his fingers.

William stopped him with a hand on his wrist. "I'm serious. I don't need it."

Jacob sighed. "You have to look after yourself sometimes, you know." He reckoned he could count the outlines of William's ribs beneath his tunic.

When William shook his head, Jacob relented and slipped the half-peeled mango back into his pocket.

"You want to help us all, then hurry up, fill your bucket, and go." William rose. "The glassblower will be wondering what's taking you so long."

Jacob chewed on his lip. William was right. He could picture Munir simmering by the furnace, but he stayed put, squinting up at William looming above him. "I can spare a few more minutes."

William didn't seem convinced, but he argued no more, gazing toward the distant mountain range and the splatter of fir and cedar trees climbing up the mountainside. "It'll all be different one day, I promise you," he whispered, so softly Jacob wasn't sure whether he was speaking to him or the mountain itself.

Jacob scoffed. "You can't promise a thing like that. It's out of your control." He threw his hands in the air. "It's out of anyone's control."

William's neck twitched. "Is it? Or do *they* just want us to think it is?" He jabbed a thumb toward the colorful market stalls and tents with beaded curtains rattling in the wind. "I wouldn't give up just yet. Things are changing, and when they do, I need to know you'll be ready."

Jacob's brow creased. "What things? Ready for what?" This wasn't the first time William had spoken of change. He was stubborn, refusing to let go of that sliver of hope that things would one day improve. For Jacob, that hope had died years ago. He had finally accepted his place in society instead of clinging to the foolish dream that, one day, hāri would be considered equal to Ghadaeans. There seemed a better chance of Jacob flying before that day ever came!

William didn't respond immediately, eyes still lost to the jagged peaks on the horizon. He lowered his voice. "What if I told you there was a chance we could change all this? Would you do it, even if it meant risking everything?"

Jacob's throat tightened. This didn't sound like William's usual proclamations of change. No. This seemed like more than empty words.

"What are you up to?"

"Just answer the question."

Jacob recoiled. "I . . . I—"

"Still too scared." William sneered. "I mean, I get it. Unlike me, you've actually got a good thing going with your apprenticeship. Why would you want to mess that up?"

Jacob's skin flared.

William pressed a palm to his chest. "But I've got nothing to lose."

Jacob's next words tasted like acid on his tongue. "I'm not scared."

The corners of William's mouth prickled. Jacob suspected there was something William enjoyed about riling him up. Perhaps because it was so easy to do, his anger setting him alight throughout the day so that come evening he'd be scorched with burn marks. William had always told him to channel his rage into something useful, but that was easier said than done.

"Then say yes." William kissed his teeth. "If you're *not* too scared, that is."

Jacob's nostrils flared. "I'm not going to agree to something I know nothing about. Unlike you, I like to think about things before I do them." He bit his tongue, already anticipating William's retort.

Instead, William threw his head back and laughed. "I'm only messing with you!" And just like that, the angry charge of electricity surrounding them dissipated. "You and that big brain of yours always need all the facts laid out." William bonked him on the head.

"Ow!"

"Don't get me wrong, it's good, thinking things through. Shows you're smart." William tapped his temple. "But sometimes there's not always enough time to weigh up all the facts. Sometimes you've just got to act or you'll miss your chance. Bear that in mind, OK?"

Jacob rubbed his head. William was giving him a headache with all this talk.

William twirled abruptly, yanking Jacob up by the collar. "You should get back." He pushed him toward the well. "And make sure to learn everything you can from Munir. Trust me, it'll be useful."

A commotion from the well made their heads snap around. Children shrieked. The crowd scattered.

"What's going on?" Jacob eyed the swinging bucket at the top of the well, except its motions didn't appear to be slowing. If anything, they were growing more frantic until the bucket upturned and a furry lump thudded to the ground.

Then everyone was screaming. Jacob couldn't understand what it was at first, only that it was covered with a swirl of flies. Then the smell hit him, and he backed away with his sleeve over his mouth. There was no mistaking that smell. The stench of something rotten. Decomposing. Dead.

A corpse. A mouse, by the looks of it. And where there was dead flesh there would surely be—

"Jinn!"

William yanked him back, his breath hot against his ear. "Go. Now!"

But Jacob couldn't tear his eyes from the shadow stretching across the ground like spilled ink. Boys chucked rocks at it, but they landed uselessly in the grass, while mothers screamed and swiftly tugged their children inside. The shadow grew, becoming darker, thicker, more opaque until it was no longer a shadow but a swirl of smoke coiled around the dead mouse, flicking its tail and baring its fangs, staring at them with emerald eyes.

A snake. Jacob had heard jinn could shape-shift, the weaker ones often taking on the appearance of snakes and birds, while stronger jinn could shift into cats and wolves. Then there were jinn powerful enough to take the shape of men and women. But he'd never seen one. People made sure of that, ensuring bodies were cremated soon after death. Even animals were burned before their flesh could turn rotten. Weaker jinn were attracted by weaker flesh, mainly animals, while stronger jinn feasted upon larger corpses, specifically human bodies. Some bodies were missed, of course—it was impossible to burn them all—but jinn were always dealt with swiftly, trapped in vessels and buried deep underground or sent back to Al-Ghaib with the help of an exorcist.

"I've got this," William hissed, grabbing a cast-iron pot from in front of a nearby tent.

Before Jacob could snatch him back, William was running at full force toward the jinn, brandishing the pot above his head.

"No!" The word tore out of his throat as Jacob raced after him.

The jinn lifted its head, fangs dripping black, sludgy blood. William skidded to a halt, bouncing on the balls of his feet, eyes locked with the creature.

"William!"

The jinn lunged. William slammed the pot over it and clamped his foot on top. The pot rattled, followed by a wounded hiss.

Jacob's mouth hung open, his tongue turning to cotton wool. "How—"

"The iron." William tapped the pot with his boot. "It can't escape." There was a looseness to his demeanor that Jacob couldn't quite pinpoint. The casual way William removed his foot from the pot, leaned against the stone well, and cracked his neck unnerved him. Almost like he'd done this before.

3

KHADIJA

A murmur of men's voices from the kitchen had Khadija hovering midway on the stairs, hand gripping the banister, the other feeling for Hassan's book. If Abba truly expected her to throw it away, then he didn't know her at all. Toss away all those years of precious memories, as if they'd simply turned rotten like gone-off fruit. How could he even ask such a thing?

Probably the same way he'd asked her to marry someone she did not know nor ever care to know. He did it because it was all he knew how to do. Khadija slipped the book between the folds of her kameez. She'd keep it with her. Keep it safe.

The stairway groaned beneath her weight. She froze, her breath clogged in her throat.

The voices fell quiet. "Khadija?"

She sighed. "Yes, Abba." Khadija emerged into the kitchen, head lowered so that her first sight of the two guests was of their feet.

"Ah, there's my beti." Abba's face lit up like a newly ignited oil lamp. It had always amazed her how quickly he could transform his face when it suited him. Meanwhile, Khadija could barely stifle a yawn, never mind mask a foul mood.

Her eyes remained fixed on the floor's geometric tiles. A few uncomfortable seconds of silence followed as the two strangers drank in her image. One was an older man with a bald head that shone in the sunlight filtering through the window. He had an equally hairless face, not even the hint of an eyebrow. The other was a boy, a year or two older than her. He resembled the other man so clearly it was obvious they were father and son, if their round heads and moon-shaped faces were anything to go by. At her appearance, the boy began fiddling with his thumbs, jittering from one foot to the other. Only then did it occur to Khadija that, like her, he could be an unwilling participant in all this as well. Marriage was for parents, not lovers, after all.

"Khadija has been very eager to meet your son, Mr. Omar." Abba flashed his molars. "Haven't you, Khadija?"

She hadn't even known he'd existed until five minutes ago, but Khadija knew when to hold her tongue. "Yes, Abba."

"This is Mr. Omar's son. Abdel." As Abba gestured to the boy, Khadija noticed Mr. Omar aim a kick at his ankles. The boy immediately straightened up and dropped his fumbling palms to his sides. "He's a shoemaker." Abba beamed. "He has his own stall in the market."

"Very profitable," Mr. Omar chimed in. "Business is booming, and now is the right time for Abdel to consider marriage." Mr. Omar nudged his son. "He can certainly provide for a wife and children."

The mentioning of children had Khadija's stomach shrivel up to the size of an almond. It didn't come as much of a surprise. That seemed the sole purpose of marriage. To produce babies. Still, hearing it aloud made her palms sweaty. She wiped them on her shalwar. Surely she wouldn't be expected to have babies right away. Her sister, Talia, had been married a few months now and there had been no news of a pregnancy. But then there hadn't been any news from Talia since the wedding. She could well be carrying a child by now. The thought of her sister going through something as monumental as childbirth without Khadija by her side caused a tightness in her throat she couldn't swallow down. Would she have to go through the same? Alone.

And without Ammi.

Mr. Omar's voice snapped her back into focus. He'd been rambling about leather sandals and sequined slippers up until now. "Would Khadija like to visit the market stall? See her husband-to-be in action."

Husband-to-be? It was far too soon for that. Weeks, months too soon, in fact. Abba couldn't expect her to make a decision right away. Unless this wasn't her decision at all.

Abba jumped to attention. "An excellent idea!" He was already reaching for his topi on the hook behind the door, donning it and readjusting the tassel so that it wouldn't flick into his eyes when he walked. "After you, Mr. Omar."

Mr. Omar ushered his son into the hallway, where the open front door allowed the late-afternoon sunlight to spill onto the tiles. Khadija couldn't help but bristle as Abdel stole a glance at her before stepping into the street after his father. Abba touched his fingertips to her elbow. "You didn't change," he hissed. "You could've at least put some lipstick on!"

It was Abba looking to impress, not her. And like Abba said, marriage was about convenience, not about lining her eyes with kohl or priming her cheeks with rosewater-scented blush. He couldn't expect her to give up on any hope of romance and still insist she put effort into her appearance. *Talk about double standards!*

Mr. Omar set a strong pace. The sun was not quite as relentless as it had been a few hours ago, and the town was only just coming to life. Qasrah was once a town bustling with trade and architectural splendor, but years of war between the three nawabs, all looking to expand their provinces and seize neighboring lands, had reduced her town to a shell of its former self.

The province in which they lived was in the most northern region of Ghadaea, where the climate was not as sticky with heat like the jungles of the eastern province, nor as arid as the region of the western desert. The Nawab of Intalyabad ruled from his palace made of copper, reaping the benefits of the province's lush vegetation and thriving opium trade. The nawab had installed his soldiers in all the smaller towns to prevent the other nawabs from sabotaging his precious crops, but they came with their own problems—a hefty cost, for one. They were notoriously lazy, lounging in the shade smoking opium, frittering away the townspeople's taxes and generally making themselves a nuisance. Another reason Abba insisted she remain indoors.

They slipped down streets packed with young boys balancing baskets of fruit and fresh flatbreads on their heads, and passed homes with women unpegging the laundry they'd put up that morning to bake in the sun.

Mr. Omar cleared his throat. "Khadija is . . . sixteen, you said."

Abba nodded. "Only just turned sixteen. Still young!" That was a bit of a lie. Her birthday had been seven months ago.

Mr. Omar whispered something to his son, who broke out into a chuckle that ended in a fit of coughing. Khadija felt Abba stiffen.

The higgledy-piggledy maze of tents and flat-roofed houses petered off into an open square as they approached the market. Khadija stretched onto her tiptoes, trying to catch a glimpse of the hot-air balloons teasing her with a flutter of painted fabric behind the stalls.

Abba stuck his elbow in her back. "We are not here for sightseeing," he scolded, yanking her arm as they swerved around a hāri beggar curled on the grass, picking at a sunburn on her cheek.

Khadija dropped her gaze. Though it was common enough seeing hāri wandering the market stalls, begging for food scraps or rooting through bins, they mostly kept to themselves in the mess of patched-up tents and teetering shacks they'd erected just outside of town.

"Filthy hāri." Mr. Omar spat. "Don't know why we still let them hang around. The soldiers should drive them off. They're meant to protect us, otherwise what do we even pay them for?"

Abba guffawed, rather too loudly, causing his topi to flop to the side. "You're absolutely right, Mr. Omar." He shot the hāri woman a look of pure disgust. "But then they're the only ones desperate enough to do the jobs no one else wants to do."

That earned Abba a chuckle from both Mr. Omar and Abdel, with Abdel's turning into a cough and ending with a blob of phlegm landing near Khadija's feet. Too much time spent in the shisha tents, she reckoned. Maybe she'd prefer that. A husband who stayed out most evenings, stumbling in at dawn and sleeping until midday. It would certainly allow her enough time to continue studying the balloons.

Mr. Omar wagged a fat finger in the air. "You've got a good point there. Perhaps we should keep them around, but I definitely don't agree with them being this close to town. Far too close to our women and children for my liking."

Abba nodded, his face suddenly serious. "Of course."

"We should be completely segregated," Abdel chimed in. "The hāri shouldn't be underestimated. They're dangerous. Only a week ago, soldiers found a settlement of hāri a few miles north of here." Abdel shook his head. "The place was sickening, apparently. Corpses strewn across the ground. They'd been practicing sihr, by the looks of it." He cursed.

Everyone reeled. Sihr was the summoning of jinn and was considered forbidden magic. Most jinn were wicked creatures, after all, and required little convincing to cause mischief, especially when it involved spilled blood. Khadija shuddered. Hopefully it was just a rumor, though hāri were known for causing trouble. She had yet to see a hāri who didn't simmer with barely concealed rage. Violence was in their nature. It was in their blood, just like their ancestors.

Abba snarled. "I hope the soldiers dealt with them accordingly."

"Oh, I'm sure they did." Mr. Omar waved his hand distractedly. "Probably turning all the nearby villages upside down as we speak until they find who is responsible."

Abba nodded, his body prickling with a furious heat she could feel from where she stood. Abba detested hāri. Hated them with a ferociousness she wouldn't think possible, if she hadn't witnessed it firsthand, for such a placid man who was forever misplacing his glasses or mixing up the names of the barber and the baker. His rage was raw and unpredictable, lightning in a monsoon. Whenever hāri were mentioned, he became a different person. Seeing him like that, she couldn't help but hate them too, if only for what their presence did to her abba.

Abdel cleared his throat. "There's been an increase in jinn sightings recently. The streets aren't safe anymore. It has to be those cursed hāri. I heard they're planning an uprising."

Most people were quick to call any trick of the light or suspicious shadow a jinn, so Khadija didn't pay much attention to that part. A hāri uprising though. That was different. Even so, she doubted the truth behind Abdel's wild claim. Hāri did not possess the resources or influence for such a thing, not when they were stamped so firmly into the dirt of society, but it didn't matter if his words lacked logic. Abba would still believe him.

Abba scowled. "I've heard similar. A terrorist group that likes to meddle with jinn. Call themselves the Hāreef."

Mr. Omar snorted. "Hāri terrorists! That's impossible. As if they have the organizational skills to plan such a thing!"

Abba's face darkened. His voice crackled. "I know what they're capable of, believe me. They can do some horrific things."

Abba's words lingered above them. Khadija pressed her lips together and swallowed the lump that had appeared in her throat. They certainly could.

Mr. Omar wiped away the droplets of sweat appearing on his exposed scalp. "Khadija has a dowry, yes?"

Slowly, the tedious talk of money and marriage mellowed Abba back down. They'd crossed the market square and were close enough now for her to glimpse the shimmer of vibrant silk balloons peeking through the gaps between the stalls. Her palms tingled, fingertips aching to preserve the image in ink so that she could admire it for weeks to come.

Hāri men were flapping the fabric furiously, forcing the balloons to life. Fire burst into the air in long streams from the balloon's burners as the men quickly inflated the fabric, sweat dampening their shirt collars as they frantically spun the blades of a wooden fan, blowing hot air into the fabric as they encouraged the balloons to inflate. The balloons sucked the air up like hungry creatures until they were full, swollen, engorged, and pulling up off the ground.

Khadija craned her neck farther. A sharp wind had picked up a balloon with green and yellow panels, the vivid colors bleeding into each other the way the sky blends into the edges of the horizon, so that it was impossible to know where one color stopped and the other began. Green like unripe olives. Yellow like sliced turmeric root. So bright it made her eyes sting.

Men scrambled to stop its escape while merchants barked orders from afar. Khadija struggled to hide her envy of the women draped in chiffon dupattas, with painted-on faces and gold nose rings, who stood beside their merchant husbands, most with henna-stained beards, waiting to board the balloon.

Imagine the freedom of owning a balloon. To have the sky literally at one's fingertips.

The green-and-yellow balloon fluttered, tempting her to chase it, spitting fire at the hāri men as they struggled to contain it. Why would it want to spend its life on the ground when it could fly? She knew she wouldn't.

Abba nudged her. "Khadija."

She lifted her head higher.

"Abdel is speaking to you." He spoke through gritted teeth.

Abdel coughed into his fist. "I was saying that jinn encounters have increased sharply as of late. It's really not safe, especially for young women. Jinn are known to be tempted by pretty faces." He cast her a smirk.

Khadija's skin crawled. She'd given him the benefit of the doubt before, but her patience was swiftly evaporating.

"Women should be kept indoors, where they are safe," Mr. Omar butted in.

Abdel nodded. "Absolutely! If Khadija is to be my wife, I want to make sure she's safe. Out of sight."

Indoors? All the time? Permanently? Forever? He couldn't be serious. Khadija faced Abba.

Abba stroked his chin and nodded uncomfortably. "Yes. We want to make sure she's safe."

"Of course!" Mr. Omar exclaimed.

Safe! She'd die of boredom. No. This couldn't happen.

"Of course I could go out sometimes though." Khadija flung her palms in the air. "I'm outside now and there's no jinn trying to possess me."

All three men shot her raised eyebrows. Mr. Omar appeared startled, like he was unaware she had a voice. Abba looked ready to catch fire. She could practically see the smoke curling out of his ears.

She gulped.

Abba laughed it off. One thing he was an expert at was saving face. "Young girls are still so naive. Unaware of how dangerous the world can be." He patted her shoulder.

Khadija's skin started to smolder.

"When you become Abdel's wife you will do as he says, Khadija." Abba's voice held the hint of a threat. "If he wants to keep you safe indoors, then that's where you'll be."

She balled her hands into fists. No. She would not simply trade her bedroom for another, to live out the rest of her days under house arrest. She'd been indoors for too long, watching life pass her by from the windowpane—away from wandering eyes, as Abba would say. What Abba failed to understand, however, was that while men may indeed look greedily upon her if she were to step outside unaccompanied, it did not compare to the insatiable hunger that consumed her whenever she glimpsed the bright circle of a balloon toppling toward the ground.

"Then maybe I don't want to be his wife," she hissed.

Abba stopped dead in his tracks. Mr. Omar and Abdel glanced back. "Everything okay? Did she say something?"

Abba seized her upper arm, plastering on a smile. "She's fine. The heat's just making her dizzy." He drew invisible spirals near his head. "You two walk on ahead."

When Abdel's and Mr. Omar's backs were turned, Abba set upon her like a starved tiger. Khadija struggled to contain the frantic tremor of her wrists. Just like Abba, her rage was building, only she didn't think she had the power to control it any longer. Its heat was leaking from her skin, dripping down her arms, pooling at her feet. She wouldn't have been surprised if the grass started to sizzle where she stood.

"You will not ruin this, Khadija. You will do as I say now."

"You can't make me marry him!" Hot tears sprang from her eyes. She wiped them away furiously.

Abba shook her arm, not hard, but hard enough to convey his anger. Khadija felt something thud to the ground. Both their eyes dropped to the ground.

Hassan's book.

She tried to snatch it up, but Abba was too quick. "I thought I told you to get rid of this book!" He shook the book indignantly. "That's it!" He tugged her down the street. "I'll tell Mr. Omar that you felt unwell so I took you home." Abba was seething. "You are going to marry his son."

"No!"

Heads were turning. They were causing a scene. People started to tut under their breaths.

Khadija knew how much Abba hated scenes.

He yanked her past a market stall where chefs were frying samosas in bubbling oil, his grip so tight on her arm she was afraid it would bruise.

"And no more reading stories!" Abba shook Hassan's book one last time and shoved it into the depths of the cooking fire.

Khadija screamed like he'd set her skin alight. She wrangled free and shoved her hands into the flames, trying to save Princess Malika's face before the fire licked it to dust. The skin of her fingertips blistered.

Abba hauled her back. "Enough!"

Khadija desperately clawed off a singed page and hugged it to her chest. A crowd had formed now, and the chefs were staring, wide-eyed.

Abba spun her around.

And there it was again. That glimmer of colorful fabric. Green and yellow. Fluttering.

Abba lifted himself to his full height and crossed his arms. "We're going home." He turned and stomped a few steps, expecting her to follow.

But her feet remained rooted, chest hammering. Khadija couldn't take her eyes off the balloon.

Another harsh wind lifted the balloon into the air. The hāri men skidded across the ground, yanking on the ropes as they fought to stifle its escape, but the balloon refused to be dragged down.

It spoke to her. Words hidden in the crackle of its fire that only she could hear. It whispered. Taunted. Teased her with the brightness of its fabric that made her eyes blur, the color was so vivid. And all at once, her restraint crumbled. She was nothing but a hungry spark lapping at brittle firewood.

A flame flying across the grass. Sandals smacking the ground. Her scarf billowing out behind her like a pair of wings. She was every caged bird seeing the sky for the first time and realizing that the pain of squeezing through the gap between the iron bars did not compare to the agony of spending a life having never tested its own ability to soar.

"Khadija!" Abba's voice was lost to the thrumming of the blood in her ears. "Come back. Now!"

But she'd already gone too far. The burned page of Hassan's book crinkled against her chest as she ran.

I can't stay inside forever.

The balloon broke free of the men's grasps and shot upward. Three feet. Five feet. Floating higher with every second. Her thighs burned as she increased her speed, eyes locked only on the balloon.

"Don't you dare disobey me, Khadija!"

She jumped.

There was a moment in the air when Khadija wasn't connected to anything. Totally free. Weightless. Airborne. Then her fingers scraped the edge of the basket. She felt herself lift.

Floating felt a lot like falling, but in the opposite direction. Her insides jumbled and hastily rearranged themselves. Her stomach turned to lead. She looked down.

"Khadija!" Abba cupped his hands around his mouth.

But she couldn't let go now.

Her arms throbbed. The balloon was like a wild horse. Threatening to throw her. Refusing to be tamed. It took all her strength to pull herself up to where she toppled over the edge and landed in the basket with a thump.

"Khadija!" Abba's voice sounded distorted, as if it was coming from underwater. She peered over the edge and instantly felt like vomiting.

He was already so small from up here. "Please come back, Khadija!" His voice shrank into nothingness.

Buildings, bleached to the color of bone, became the size of her fingernail. The spidery tendrils of the Ravi River running through the length of Qasrah became a thin blue line as if she'd sketched it with a reed pen. A landscape of rolling hills, lush green against the harsh white of the cotton fields, unfolded below. Up and up she went. Khadija pressed a hand to her mouth, because if she didn't she'd scream. There was no going back down now. And despite her fear and her rage and all the emotions in between, there was only one thing she knew for certain: She didn't want to touch the ground again.

4

JACOB

Water sloshed over the sides of his bucket as Jacob struggled to keep up with William, who was trampling through the opium poppies.

"Go back to Munir. He'll be waiting for you," William called back to him.

Waiting. Jacob scoffed. More like he'd be heating up his poker in the furnace to aim a swipe at him when he returned. Jacob flinched. The longer he left it, the crueler his punishment would be, and yet that didn't stop him hurrying after William and the cast-iron pot tucked under his arm.

"Just tell me what's going on."

William didn't respond. Jacob growled. They were much farther out now, past the stretch of blooming poppies with their violet petals whispering in the soft breeze, and on to the immature poppies still contained in their sticky bulbs. There was the odd hāri farmer in the distance, lacerating each bulb to collect the white, oozing substance used to make opium, but otherwise they were alone.

William abruptly spun, his neck covered in a slick shine of sweat. He set the pot down with a thud. The jinn inside hissed.

Jacob refused to take his eyes off it. The silence stretched on like the tick of a clock that had just skipped the last second, before William finally said, "Fine. What do you want to know?" His voice was breathy, like if he tried to speak any louder his words would snap in half and be lost to the wind.

Jacob wanted nothing more than to walk away and pretend this had never happened. He looked back toward the slums. The crowd of hāri inspecting the well for any more dead animals had mostly dispersed, but surely their screams must have caught someone's attention? Jacob squinted, expecting the flash of soldiers with their steel swords and green uniforms to appear on the horizon, followed by the sharp sting of gunpowder that always reminded him of fermented eggs as they loaded their muskets and took aim.

The punishment for sihr was death. The Ghadaeans meticulously ensured anything dead was burned long before it had a chance to rot, even animals. Every morning and every evening, the Burners made their rounds, covered from head to toe and bearing long poles with a hook at the end so they could sift through bins and comb alleyways with relative ease, searching for any sign of something dead, then setting it alight before it rotted to the point of attracting a jinn.

Except they'd missed one this time.

"How did you know what to do? Everyone else was terrified, but you—"

William crouched beside the pot. "It's easier if I show you."

"Don't open that thing!" Jacob recoiled. "Are you insane?"

Jacob couldn't deny the chasm that had steadily formed between them since he'd accepted Munir's apprenticeship. Before then, they used to talk of everything and nothing, empty wishes and hollow dreams. Perhaps Jacob's absence had affected William more than he liked to admit. Jacob had never stopped to ask how William was managing without him. Maybe he should have.

"It won't hurt me." William tugged at a string around his neck to reveal an amulet carved with an eye. Jacob had never seen him wear this before. William traced his thumb over the emerald-green iris. "Do you know what this is?"

Jacob shrugged.

"It is the eye of Bidhukh. The jinniya queen of magic." William paused. "And our savior."

Jacob shook his head, trying to spill William's words from his ears. "Please tell me you've not been practicing sihr."

William teased the lid of the pot open slightly. "The jinniya queen has been watching us. She's seen how the Ghadaeans have made our people suffer." William spat. "And she sympathizes. She wants to help."

Jacob's arms shook with the urge to lash out, knock the nonsense out of his friend with a fist to the jaw. If William was to be discovered practicing sihr, every last hāri in the village could be killed. If one of them was found guilty, they all were.

"Are you even listening to yourself?" His voice rose. "You're risking everyone's lives by doing this. You realize that?"

"I know it sounds crazy." William's gray eyes, which always reminded him of rain clouds, were now crackling like a storm was coming. "I didn't believe it either until I saw it for myself."

"Saw what?"

William smirked, a wild look to his face that made Jacob's palms sweat. "This jinn will not attack me, not when I have this." He twirled his amulet between his fingers. "It knows I serve its queen, and so it will serve me as well."

Then William lifted the lid.

A forked tongue and a flash of green eyes lashed out. Jacob shrieked. William simultaneously clamped a hand over Jacob's mouth while dangling his amulet with the other. The jinn locked its eyes on it, hissing, thrashing its tail.

Then it retreated, its smoky edges shimmering in the sun, thick and black like the smoke curling out from the hookah pipes. It looked insubstantial enough that if Jacob aimed a kick at it, he imagined his foot would pass straight through, and yet the sharp point of its fangs made him think it could easily wound him if it wanted to. The jinn-snake let out a deep hiss, its edges blurring as it changed shape before morphing into a crow. The crow cocked its head, flashing a twinkle of an emerald eye before disappearing into the sky. William's hand dropped from Jacob's mouth as it disappeared toward the mountains. He turned to him, his eyes sparkling. "See."

Jacob thought he'd vomit.

"Don't worry. It was only a weak jinn. I'm still practicing how to control stronger ones."

"Who taught you this?"

"They're called the Hāreef." William tucked his empty pot under his arm. "They're hāri just like us, allied with the jinniya queen, who allows them command of her jinn. With their help, we won't have to be afraid anymore. The Ghadaeans will be afraid of us." William grinned widely. "That's why I'm going to join them."

Jacob staggered under the weight of what he'd just witnessed. His mind flickered like a compass needle struggling to find north. William had done a number of reckless things over the years, always dancing along the edges of the law. He'd pickpocketed soldiers, swiped food from market stalls, and even fried fish in broad daylight, a crime punishable by death—Ghadaeans were strict vegetarians, fearing the smell of cooking a dead animal would surely attract a hungry jinn. Yes, he'd been reckless, but Jacob had always been secretly impressed by William's bravery. This wasn't brave though—this was stupid.

Jacob shook his head. "This is wrong."

"This is our only chance of freedom!" William rounded on him. "Aren't you tired of all this?" He waved at the flimsy shacks of the slums in the distance. When Jacob didn't immediately respond, he chuckled darkly. "Let me guess, you're just happy carrying on like this. As if this is all we'll ever be in life."

"Of course I'm not happy," Jacob snapped.

William ground his teeth. "But you must be happy enough with how things are if you're not willing to do anything about it."

Jacob tightened his grip on the handle of his bucket. "If you get caught, you're dead. You know that, right?"

"I'd rather die knowing I at least tried than live knowing I could have changed things and didn't."

Jacob's breath caught in his throat. William didn't mean that. Surely. In the slums, hāri came and went with the changing seasons, there one minute, gone the next; there was nothing permanent about the people around him. That was something Jacob had grown to accept. Except when it came to William. The thought of William wishing his life away stung Jacob in a place he couldn't quite describe.

Jacob huffed and threw his head back. The sun was more than halfway across the sky now, and the distant hum of the village slowly coming alive reached them from all the way out here. Munir would be fuming. He really needed to get back.

William seemed to read his mind. "Go if you want."

Jacob ran his hand across his face. There was no swaying William when an idea had already consumed him. "There's nothing I can say to convince you, is there?"

William shook his head.

Then there was nothing left to say. "Just promise me you'll be careful."

William grinned. "If you promise to meet me in the opium fields tomorrow night. Then you'll see for yourself what I'm talking about."

Jacob wanted no part of this madness. "I think I've seen enough."

William shrugged. "Suit yourself." He turned and marched off into the fields.

Jacob watched William's figure shrink into the distance. He'd come around. William wouldn't just leave him. Not after everything they'd been through. He'd been misled, but he'd see sense soon enough. Sihr would bring William nothing but certain death. Jacob bit his lip and dug his nails into his palms. He couldn't deny that something in William's words had resonated with him.

You must be happy enough with how things are if you're not willing to do anything about it.

The thing was, he wasn't happy. He *did* want to change things.

He didn't have to go back to Munir. There was no one around to force him. He could leave—go with William. Munir would find a new apprentice. Jacob was expendable, after all.

His friendship with William was not. It was the most precious thing he owned, and he was allowing it to slip through his fingers. Jacob swallowed the achy soreness in his throat. Instead of listening to William, or at least agreeing to find out more, he'd watched him leave, too scared to hear the truth. He was a coward. And now he was all alone. Jacob roared, lashing out at the purple poppies, snapping stems in his rage.

What he needed was answers, and there was only one way he would get them. He'd have to meet William tomorrow night. He needed to see for himself how far into this madness his friend had slipped, and whether he was willing to fall with him.

5

KHADIJA

An hour had passed. Maybe two. It was quiet up here, the only sound being the creak of the balloon's ropes in the wind and her erratic thoughts slamming against her skull. Khadija groaned. What had she been thinking? Had she even *been* thinking? Clearly she hadn't, but there was no going back now. Qasrah was long gone, the ground below a distant smudge of green with blotches of yellow wheat fields as the balloon settled on its own direction, following the meandering Ravi River toward the distant haze of the Himala Mountains.

She was stuck up here, probably forever, and yet Khadija couldn't bring herself to care. The cloudscape was too beautiful. From the ground, clouds seemed gray and flat, but up here she could appreciate the way shafts of sunlight sliced through them, creating prisms of light that turned the clouds pink, lilac, and tangerine. Some were only thin white wisps that floated past her with speed, while others were darker and denser, heavy with moisture, but luckily for her there seemed no possibility of rain. It was the height of dry season, the perfect time for ballooning. Had she decided to steal a hot-air balloon during a monsoon, then it would have been a totally different story.

Khadija closed her eyes, allowing her body to become accustomed to the gentle back-and-forth sway of the balloon like it was a creature breathing, and she was merely encased within its lungs. There was something euphoric about being up here—it made her dizzy, her legs like stringy noodles, so that she had to grip the edge of the wicker basket to steady herself. She was flying! Khadija sucked in a breath. Even the air tasted different. Cooler, cleaner.

Of course, there was always the elephant in the balloon to sink her back to the ground. She couldn't return home. Abba would lock her away indefinitely, jinn possession being the only explanation for her madness. The exorcist would be over in no time.

Khadija dug her nails into the basket's edge. Abba would be the laughingstock of the village: the man with a shame for a daughter. People would avoid him in the streets. Mr. Omar and Abdel had probably spread the gossip far and wide by now. *Well, let them talk.* Khadija huffed. It served Abba right for choosing such a mismatched betrothal for her, as if he'd just thrown the two of them together the way one would fling wet clothes along a washing line. No thought. No consideration for their obvious differences. Just boy, girl, marriage. She supposed that's all Abba knew marriage to be. His marriage to Ammi had been similar. Of course he'd loved her, in his own way, and then she'd died—and she'd taken Hassan with her, leaving a gaping hole in Khadija's family. With Talia gone too, Khadija was now all Abba had left.

Guilt made her tongue taste rancid. There was no going back. Anyway, she didn't even know how to.

The balloon wasn't filled with much. Her guess was that the merchant it belonged to had just unloaded his wares. The burner dominated the basket, shaped like a tandoor oven with a tall cylinder that pumped hot air through the balloon hoop and into the heart of the balloon. Below the burner was a metal canister with a tap and a small candle flame hovering above it. She'd seen similar canisters for sale in the market, filled with propane gas that squealed when ignited. There was a glass dial with a flickering needle that swayed back and forth, never settling on a number for long. She wasn't sure what its purpose was. Her eyes followed the long tube filled with water attached to the dial. The surface of the water rippled with the motions of the balloon.

Now the balloon was full and floating of its own accord, the tiny candle flame dancing in the breeze. Beside it was a wooden propeller that could be manually turned, which forced hot air into the swaths of silk panels, stained green and yellow like autumn leaves that were just beginning to turn.

There was a portable cooking stove and a tinderbox, a sack of uncooked lentils and another filled with rice, all secured with ropes to the deck. Above her head, the thick ropes of the balloon's rigging attaching the fabric to the basket creaked and swayed in the wind, begging to be pulled, but she didn't dare risk it just yet. There was a box of instruments tied to the deck that Khadija assumed were used to navigate. She'd seen similar objects being crafted in the bazaar—precarious metal devices with dials, and bits that twisted and spun. Khadija had rummaged through, but other than a rusty telescope, she had found nothing of use. For all her fascination with balloons, she was ill prepared for what was actually involved in flying one.

She sipped from the water gourd she'd found and cast her eyes to the white cloud of birds on the horizon. Abba would never forgive her. She squeezed her eyes shut.

But I would never have forgiven Abba if he'd agreed to lock me indoors forever.

She couldn't have won either way. Khadija tried to lose herself in the clouds' wispy flicks and milky swirls, like brushstrokes painted across the early evening sky. She still had hold of the single burned page she'd managed to salvage from Hassan's book. She gripped it tightly, afraid it would blow away, and traced her fingertips over the curve of the letters as she sounded them out.

Khadija could read, albeit poorly, though it was more than most girls her age. That was thanks to Hassan. Not once had he teased Khadija for asking her younger brother to read to her. He'd never been unkind like that. Hassan hadn't a single cruel bone in his body.

Instead, he would pull out a sheet of paper, set down an inkpot, and draw letters for her to copy. That was until Abba found out and ordered him to stop. "Boys and girls are not the same and they never will be," he'd said. "They do not do the same things or lead the same lives." Khadija sighed and stroked her finger across the drawing of a man peering through a telescope at a starry night sky. A small smile graced her lips.

She remembered that part of the story from the picture alone. It was Hassan's favorite part. Princess Malika had just been discovered missing and the palace was turned upside down in search of her. The people hadn't slept in days. The nawab, the princess's father, was busy declaring war on his neighbors, accusing them of the abduction of the princess. It was the clever wazir who suspected something more. He searched the skies, trying to read the stars to reveal the location of the missing princess. The jinn bewitched the hot-air balloon with a silver light so that it appeared like the moon, but the wazir was not to be fooled and told the nawab that it was a jinn that abducted Princess Malika. The wazir was Hassan's favorite character, probably because he'd wanted to be one, while Khadija's had been Princess Malika, or perhaps the jinniya Queen Mardzma. Any of the women in the story, who were obviously leading more exciting lives than her.

Until now.

Khadija pressed the page to her chest, her throat tightening. Now the book was lost forever. Angry tears pricked her eyes. How could Abba do that to her? A pit of grief opened up in her stomach, so deep even she couldn't see the bottom of it, and yet she couldn't bring herself to hate her father. She pictured him sitting at home, head in his hands, asking what he'd done to deserve such a disobedient daughter. Would he slip into despair, waste away, refuse to eat? He'd miss next month's tax payments without her to press him about it. Soldiers would come knocking at the door, toss her poor abba into the street like the other paupers declared bankrupt.

And it would all be because of her.

Khadija picked at the blisters forming on her fingertips and paced the deck of the balloon, eyes flickering up often to scan the sky, as if expecting someone to pursue her. So far, no one had.

The day was transforming into evening. The amber circle of the sun was rapidly toppling over the edge of the land, and the sky was stained with blotches of pale blue and indigo. The temperature was plummeting, and her teeth started to rattle. She hugged her elbows. The thought of being so high up when night fell made her knees buckle. Would it be better to land? She glanced over the edge. A long way down. She retreated, her head spinning. No. Landing did not seem like a good idea.

And there was no way of telling where she was going.

A gust of air caused her thin shalwar to flap around her ankles. Khadija shivered. Another sharp wind. The orange glow of the burner flame flickered . . .

And then puffed out. She was plunged into darkness.

Khadija felt herself drop.

Her throat constricted. She stumbled across the deck, her elbow smacking the edge of the wicker basket. Tears pricked her eyes. Then she looked up.

The balloon was collapsing in on itself, its material no longer taut but blowing flimsily like a flag in the wind as it deflated.

She sank like a stone. Her stomach backflipped. She grasped the ropes for balance and flung herself toward the burner. Her fingers shook as she felt for the gas canister, turning the tap until she heard the squeal of pressurized gas escaping, and the smell of gas stung her nostrils.

The balloon continued to drop.

Khadija fumbled for the box of matches in the dark, struck a match, and brought it toward the burner. The gas sparked to life. She grasped the wooden propeller and turned it furiously the way she'd seen the hāri men do it. The fire roared in satisfaction, but Khadija refused to slow her movements, sweat quickly appearing across her brow. As the propeller gained speed, it began to fan the hot air into the deflated balloon. The material puffed up like a peacock.

Her descent slowed, then stopped altogether as the balloon became engorged. Khadija didn't dare let go of the propeller until the balloon became so swollen it was threatening to burst at the seams. She twisted the gas tap for good measure so that the fire crackled, and a stifling heat flooded the basket. That should do it. She withdrew to the other end of the deck and slumped to the floor.

Maybe she'd made a mistake. Maybe Abba was right, and she was naive. A stupid girl who should've stayed indoors. Now look at the mess she'd gotten herself into. Khadija hugged her knees to her chest and allowed herself to come apart. Her shoulders shook, overcome with wave after wave of violent sobbing. Here she was, living out her daydreams in a hot-air balloon, and all she could think about was the life she'd left behind on the ground.

6

JACOB

Jacob was up at the first sign of dawn, his neck sore from a night on Munir's kitchen floor with a sack of garlic bulbs for a pillow. The kitchen was littered with shards of glass that looked like hailstones. Luckily for him, Munir had taken out his frustration with him on the glasswork instead. Word of a jinn being spotted in the hāri slums had already reached the glassblower's ears when Jacob finally returned yesterday. He'd managed to use it to his advantage to explain his unusually long trip to the well. Of course, he'd been careful to omit any details of the situation to avoid arousing suspicion.

Jacob rose and set to sweeping up the glass, then tended to the coals in the furnace, flipping each one when they developed a white dusting of ash so that the fire glowed a hellish red. When the furnace was lit, Jacob quietly left the workshop with his empty bucket in hand. He stepped out into the early morning.

The sky was duck-egg blue with splotches of pink, and a crescent-shaped moon hung overhead, unaware of the night's departure. The air was cooler, and the village slept peacefully, the only sound being the bleating of skinny goats as they fought over the few patches of shade. Jacob liked this time of day best, when the world had not yet woken and he could wander the streets unseen. Like a ghost. Like he wasn't really there. Like his skin didn't make him stand out the way it did. In the mornings, Jacob didn't need to hide.

As he approached the slums, his eyes rested on a shack with a red sheet balanced across two crates—the shack he'd shared with William before Jacob had moved into Munir's home. But it was empty. In all the years Jacob had known William, his friend had never been an early riser. It could only mean that he'd never returned last night.

Worry made his lungs feel like a lump of coal rattling against his ribs. William was stupid. He'd put the life of every hāri in the village at risk, and what was it even all for? Jacob tried to spark his rage to life, but the flames fizzled out. William was just doing what everyone else was. Trying to make his life that little bit less hopeless. He couldn't be angry at him for that.

A rukh cawing overhead stole his attention. He squinted. The bird was so high up it appeared normal size, but Jacob knew that, up close, the bird would dwarf him with its six-foot wingspan. He watched the rukh loop through the air, sunlight catching its feathers as if they'd been dipped in oil so that the bird shimmered multicolored.

That's when a flutter of green-and-yellow fabric caught his eye. Jacob shielded his brow from the sun's rays.

A hot-air balloon was tumbling toward the ground like a falling leaf. Balloons very rarely landed in Sahli. He'd see them flying overhead, so high they could be mistaken for birds.

But this balloon was getting lower, so low now that it was scraping the tops of the sleepy buildings. Maybe it was empty. Abandoned. Why else would it land here? Jacob scanned the deserted streets. The village seemed unaware of its visitor. He bit his lip. Munir wouldn't rise for another half hour at least. There was no harm in looking. He made for the balloon at full force, his empty bucket banging against his thigh.

Please be abandoned.

A little head poked out of the wicker basket. Jacob skidded to a halt and cursed. Of course it wasn't abandoned. He'd never be that lucky.

The balloon was close enough now he could trace each of its ropes. The fire was flickering weakly in the burner, and the material was no longer taut, growing slack as the air escaped. A figure was bustling around the basket, clearly struggling. There was a muffled curse before the occupant tugged on a rope and shrieked. A perfectly round hole the length of his arm appeared at the very top of the balloon, opening neatly like a blind. The parachute vent. Jacob only knew that from overhearing a conversation between two traveling merchants in the bazaar of the precariousness of the parachute vent. Excellent for a quick descent, but it was easy to lose control with such a sudden drop in altitude. "Definitely not a rope to be pulled idly." The merchant had chuckled, spitting out a date kernel. "The side vents are a much safer option. They let the air out gradually."

Jacob watched the hot-air balloon crumple, its material folding in on itself as the basket smacked the ground. He winced. If the balloon had been even ten feet higher, the force of that landing would've snapped the basket in two. Whoever was flying this balloon clearly didn't know what they were doing.

The balloonist writhed beneath the deflated fabric like it had swallowed them. Should he help? Again he scanned the streets. Empty. No one. Jacob glanced at his bucket. He couldn't afford to anger Munir again today, and he'd already wasted enough time.

That's when a figure emerged from the fabric. A girl, only a year or two older than him. She hurled herself over the basket's edge and collapsed onto the grass, panting.

Jacob gaped at her.

She caught his eye and jumped to her feet, dusting the dried mud off her knees.

They stared each other down.

"What are you looking at?"

Jacob quickly dropped his gaze. He knew better than to gaze at Ghadaean women. That alone could earn him a stoning. He turned to scurry off.

"Wait!"

Jacob's head snapped around. She was scrutinizing him, as if assessing his weight. Jacob buckled underneath her gaze. He was unused to such interactions with Ghadaeans. Before Munir, Jacob reckoned he had never directly spoken to one, certainly never had a conversation.

"Where am I?" Her voice cracked at the end, and she erupted into a hoarse fit of coughing, as if she hadn't drunk for days and the insides of her throat had turned to parchment paper. He knew that feeling.

Jacob stuttered. "Sahli . . . miss. You're in Sahli, miss." His eyes remained fixed on a little rock by his feet. Hopefully that was all she wanted.

He heard her curse under her breath. Jacob's eyebrows rose. Girls certainly weren't meant to curse like that, not Ghadaean girls anyway, but then, Ghadaean girls weren't even allowed to leave their homes unaccompanied, never mind fly hot-air balloons. He glanced back at the deflated balloon, expecting another figure to emerge. No. She was alone.

The girl's head twisted back and forth, taking in the cluster of bright tents around them. She grabbed a fistful of material and hurled it above her head as if she thought she could simply throw the hot-air balloon back into the sky. The material fluttered briefly, protesting such a rude awakening, before collapsing into a saggy heap. That hot-air balloon certainly wouldn't be in the air any time soon.

She faced him, lips parted. He knew that look: the look that often accompanied a slur or an upturned nose or a blob of spit landing across his cheek.

He's a ḫāri. That's what her look meant. It was too early for those looks. Jacob turned.

He left the girl quietly cursing as she attempted to stretch the deflated fabric out along the grass, but it was all twisted and knotted up, far too large for a single girl to manage. However, that wasn't his problem. He had enough of his own.

Jacob made for the slums, though he couldn't help stealing glances back at the girl. She looked around sixteen. Seventeen at the most. Jacob knew he looked young for his age. At fifteen his limbs were just starting to stretch out like a beanstalk's, but it was his skinniness, his waiflike legs and spindly arms that made him appear weak and childlike.

There was nothing weak about this girl. Her body crackled with frustration as she fought to get the balloon in the air, huffing with the fury of electric storm clouds. She reminded him of the kettle Munir heated on the stove, its insides bubbling, boiling, its whistles turning into shrieks. The girl's arms rose and fell as she flapped the material. People would start rising soon, and by the urgency of her movements it was clear she knew that too.

There was a simplicity about her. Most Ghadaean girls decorated themselves in glitter and gold, and wore patterned scarfs that they knotted in complex structures on their heads. The girl was pretty plain in comparison, and he couldn't help but wonder if the reason for it was an unplanned flight. Not that it was any of his business.

As he neared the well, the soft creaking of broken beams and unstable shacks swaying in the morning breeze comforted him. Hāri children slept among the dust. The few who had risen were congregating at the well.

Jacob approached. The young boy who had to stretch on his tiptoes to reach the lever to wind the bucket up the well gave him a brief, weary smile. For him, it was the start of another long day, exacerbated by hunger and thirst. Already, life with Munir had turned Jacob soft. How easy it would be for Munir to toss him back onto the streets, where he'd resume this type of existence. It was a prospect he constantly prepared for.

With his bucket full, Jacob turned to leave. That's when a figure lingering in the poppies caught his eye.

His chest felt like it had been carved open with an ax.

William.

Water splashed against his toes as Jacob hurried over. He stopped in front of William, gnawing the edges of his lips, not knowing quite what to say or where to begin. "You okay?" His eyes fell to the sack filled to the brim with cut poppies. "What's that for?"

"Don't ask questions you're too scared to know the answer to." William selected two poppies and knotted their skinny stems together. One snapped. He tossed it away, retrieving another. "You made it very clear yesterday you didn't want anything to do with this. Unless you've changed your mind." Beside his boots was a growing chain of poppies knotted together like a rope. Jacob struggled to imagine what that could be for, though he had a sinking feeling it was sihr.

"We should talk."

William continued to loop and thread the stems together. "I've already told you everything you need to know."

Jacob huffed. "I get not wanting to live like this. I get wanting things to change. I get all that." He sighed. "But what I don't understand is, why jinn? Couldn't you find another way to help our people, something that isn't so"—he struggled for the word—"dangerous? You could get everyone killed with what you're doing, William."

William shot him a look with eyes as gray as freshly forged steel. "*Why jinn?* I thought it was obvious: Jinn are the only thing that Ghadaeans truly fear."

Jacob couldn't deny he had a point. "And why is it that the first I'm hearing of any of this is yesterday when you literally had a jinn in your arms? I thought we told each other everything." Jacob couldn't disguise the wounded note to his voice.

William shrugged. "You would have stopped me. Better to tell you after I've got everything figured out." He held two poppies up to the light, comparing their length. "Look, are you still coming this evening or not, then? You won't get another chance. This is it."

Jacob ran a hand through his hair. He couldn't deny the spark of curiosity flickering like a match inside of him. It couldn't hurt to listen. He was not as easily led astray as William, and he reckoned he could recognize a pack of lies.

"I'll come, but that doesn't mean I'm agreeing with any of this." He gestured at the chain of flowers, now long enough for William to wrap around his neck like a noose.

A smirk spread across William's lips. "I knew you'd come. You just needed some convincing." Jacob couldn't help but allow his anger to melt. William had always been good at swiftly brushing arguments away with the back of his hand when it suited him.

"This is serious though," William added. "The Hāreef are coming tonight to recruit new members, and they only want the best. You can't just show your face. You need to impress."

"Wait. I said nothing about joining them!"

"Not yet. But you will when you see them. Trust me." William's eyes sparkled with that same energy Jacob had always admired, and secretly envied: hope—something Jacob had never really had. He wondered if that was because, unlike him, William had known his parents before they were killed; while Jacob held merely an empty space where his parents should be, William's grief drove him. It could easily swing back and forth between a furious rage and a brilliant spark of optimism. Jacob imagined how it could feel—almost euphoric—to allow hope to consume him like that.

He sighed, relenting. "Impress them how?"

William stroked his chin—a habit he'd grown accustomed to, as if by rubbing it enough times he could will the facial hair to start growing. "Well, I've been practicing how to command jinn with the amulet they gave me." He fiddled with the string around his neck. Jacob stiffened. "But you could tell them about your glassblowing."

Jacob's brows knit together. This was not what he had in mind when he'd agreed to accompany William this evening. "Do you think they'll care about that?"

William nodded. "Of course! Not many hāri can do that. They'll definitely be interested."

Jacob's mouth formed a thin line. Sometimes he wondered why he still stuck by William when he caused him this much trouble. Jacob's cheeks tinged with guilt. But William was all he had and it was better to have someone who drove him crazy than nobody at all.

"Okay." Jacob glanced over his shoulder. "Well, I should get back." He stared at the stagnant water in his bucket. "Did you see the girl in the hot-air balloon earlier?"

William's neck twitched. His head snapped up. "What girl?"

"Just some Ghadaean girl with a hot-air balloon." He shrugged. "She landed in the center of the village."

William's ears pricked up. "Hot-air balloon. Here?"

"Yeah. Did you not see it? It's a big one as well, and she came in it all on her own."

The corners of William's lips upturned. The flowers slipped from his fingers. "Okay," he whispered smoothly. "Change of plan."

Why did Jacob have a bad feeling about this? "It's not anything illegal, is it?"

"Depends how you look at it. But you don't need to worry about that. All you have to do is something small. Easy, even."

If this was what it took to stop William from abandoning him, then so be it. Jacob nodded. "What do I have to do?"

"Go back and talk to that girl. I'll figure out the rest."

7

KHADIJA

"Get up, will you!" Khadija gave the balloon another furious flap. It collapsed into a heap. She slumped against the basket and wiped the sweat from her brow. It was no use. She was stuck here. Khadija studied the empty streets of Sahli. She vaguely remembered Abba mentioning a potential suitor from the village, but he'd been swiftly turned down once Abba realized Sahli was even poorer than Qasrah. She eyed the colorful tent flaps for any signs of life. A girl traveling alone was bad enough, never mind with a stolen balloon . . . She swallowed uncomfortably. Her water had run out as well.

Khadija bit her lip. Getting out of sight seemed the best idea, but that meant abandoning her balloon.

Her balloon. She scoffed. She really had no right to claim it, but somehow it felt like hers. Discarding it was such a waste, especially after all she'd risked in taking it, but if she couldn't get it in the air in the next half hour, she'd be spotted and the soldiers probably alerted. It was written all over her face that she was a runaway.

Khadija thrummed her fingers on the basket's edge. *Such a stupid idea!* Abba was right. Her head was obviously filled with so many stories that she'd forgotten reality. Girls weren't supposed to steal hot-air balloons and go off on adventures. Why? Because they got stuck in strange villages with nowhere left to go and no one around to help. What a boring story that would be.

Khadija glared at the green-and-yellow fabric. *Thanks for nothing.*

She stormed off, her legs wobbling uneasily at first, unaccustomed to the ground's solidness. She wondered how long it would be before someone claimed her balloon as their own. She huffed. Let them. It had done nothing but cause her trouble anyway. *Stupid balloon!*

The smack of sandals against the sunbaked ground caused her to jump. Two figures emerged between a row of tents, panting. Hāri boys. She paid them no attention until one of them whistled at her as if she were a domesticated cat. Her jaw dropped. Who did they think they were?

The boys approached. One looked about her age, tall and lanky with dark hair and a long, skinny nose. The other was younger, fairer, with hair like strands of gold and cheeks that were badly sunburned.

The boy from before. He was carrying a bucket with water splashing up the sides.

Khadija folded her arms. "What?"

The older boy bent over, hands on his knees, wheezing. He looked ready to collapse. "You want to . . . hide your . . . balloon. Yes?" He spoke through gasps. "Before . . . anyone sees it?"

She pursed her lips. "What's it to you?"

The older boy shot her a look with eyes like a silver storm. She startled, surprised by his brashness. Most hāri wouldn't dare meet the eyes of a Ghadaean. The younger boy seemed to know his place, because he kept his eyes firmly on the dirt.

The older boy regained his breath and rose to his full height, a good head above her. "It just seems like you'd rather not be seen out here with a balloon. All on your own."

Khadija shrugged. "Why do you care?" She stared both boys down, hoping to burn holes through them. She knew better than to trust a boy so easily. Especially a hāri boy.

The younger boy with the bucket tugged on the other boy's arm. "Come on, William, let's just go. Before someone sees."

William shrugged him off and squared his shoulders. "It's stolen, isn't it?" He smirked. "I can tell."

Her cheeks flushed.

"Don't worry." He flashed his open palms. "Doesn't matter to us." His steel-gray eyes traced over her balloon. He licked his lips. "Just seems such a waste to leave it here. We can hide it for you if you'd like."

Hide it. More like steal it for themselves. "And why would you do that?"

"We obviously wouldn't do it for free."

Khadija dug her nails into her sides. "Well, I don't have anything to give you, so you might as well go away!"

"You don't have to give us anything right now. Think of it like a debt. You'll owe us for later."

She didn't like the sound of that.

"We can hide your balloon for you," William repeated. He inclined his head to the younger boy, who was busy kicking a stone back and forth across the grass. "Jacob knows a place you can get some breakfast, and then afterward you can think about how you'll pay us back. After all, you must be hungry."

Oh, she was. Thirsty too. But she didn't like the look of William. His chin jutted outward like the precipice of a rock, giving his face a sharpness, as if he'd been carved from glass. One unwise move and he'd surely slice her in half.

William burst out laughing.

Khadija's rage began to bubble, boiling inside, spilling at her feet. How dare this boy laugh at her!

"Come on!" he goaded. "What've you got to lose? We're hāri, after all. You could easily call the soldiers on us and they'd string us up, no questions asked. If anything, we're the ones who need convincing to help you. You're getting a good deal out of this."

He did have a point. She was the Ghadaean.

Khadija peered at the sky. The sun had risen farther during the course of this conversation. She was running out of time. She rocked back on her heels. "Fine. Hide my balloon."

William flashed her a wicked grin. "Yes, miss." He approached the balloon, tentative at first, like it was a magnificent beast, while the younger boy trailed behind with his bucket. "Jacob can take you to get breakfast."

She eyed Jacob suspiciously. He still hadn't lifted his head, shoulders curled in on themselves as if he wished to sink straight into the ground. He really posed no threat to her.

Khadija nodded stiffly.

Jacob's eyes flickered up. He turned and set off down the street. Khadija had to hurry to keep up with him, shooting William a look of daggers over her shoulder, but William was too busy stuffing the balloon fabric into the basket to notice.

If he stole it, what did it matter? She was going to abandon it anyway.

Khadija followed Jacob as they weaved through empty streets where market stalls were yet to open. Goats with droopy ears rifled through the rubbish bins. The village stank of gone-off fruit and manure.

He stopped outside a home without a door, which allowed the air to breeze in and out at its pleasure. Jacob removed his dusty sandals and stepped inside. Khadija hesitated before doing the same. Pots and pans hung from the ceiling, and heavy sacks were lined up against the far wall, brimming with rice, lentils, flour, and onions. Amber light spilled onto the tiles from a half-open doorway and the smell of fire lingered in the air.

Jacob waved at a chair and placed the bucket on the floor. Khadija remained standing. The boy hesitated, chewing the inside of his cheek as he reached for a copper jug and poured a cup of water, sliding it across the table toward her. Khadija drank quicker than she could blink. He wordlessly took the cup and refilled it. Again, she drank. She could feel Jacob's wary gaze, as if she was an open flame that could at any moment erupt into a roaring fire.

He retrieved a plate covered with a tea towel, revealing a stack of freshly made parathas. He folded one on a plate with chipped edges and placed it beside her before disappearing into the other room. The sight of fresh dough stuffed with spiced potatoes made her salivate. Khadija scoffed it down, too hungry to eat like a woman.

Once she had eaten and drunk her fill, as if on cue the boy returned. He took her empty plate and wiped it clean, placing it on a shelf beside a cluster of garlic, which filled the room with a powerful smell that threatened to cling to her clothing.

Once that was done, Jacob jittered around the kitchen. Khadija was busy thinking of something to break the silence.

Footsteps from deeper in the house caused them both to startle as the door swung open. A Ghadaean man appeared in a long bed shirt and loose shalwar pants. He jumped, stubbing his toe against the doorframe. He clutched his foot and rounded on Jacob.

"Who is this?" The man had a splatter of burns across his cheek as if he'd been working with hot oil, and thick, dark eyebrows that exaggerated the whiteness of his eyes.

Jacob cowered in the corner. "She was all alone outside. She hadn't eaten . . ." His voice trailed off. "I thought I should help her."

The man approached, with a raised palm, causing Jacob to immediately flinch. A pang of sympathy washed over Khadija.

The man stopped abruptly and turned to her then. Her heart started hammering. He shot her an unnerving smile, bringing his hand to his chin as his gaze swept over her, tracing the contours of her face, drinking in the richness of her skin. She shifted uneasily.

"That's very kind of you, Jacob." He ruffled the boy's hair, his eyes not once leaving her. "Are you . . . alone, miss?"

She hesitated, but there seemed no point in lying. It was obvious she was, or else she wouldn't be standing in his kitchen. Khadija nodded.

The man must have noticed her discomfort because his voice softened as if calming a frightened bird. But she was not a little bird.

"Then you are our guest. My name is Munir." He brought a palm to his chest. When Khadija didn't immediately respond, he asked, "And yours?"

"Khadija," she whispered reluctantly.

Munir snapped his fingers. "Jacob, get Miss Khadija something to eat."

Jacob rushed to the stack of parathas.

"Thank you," Khadija quickly interjected. "He's already given me food and water."

Munir's eyes flickered over the thin material of her kameez. "Would you like some fruit, then? Dates?" He rummaged through his pockets and thrust a coin toward Jacob. "Go get some fresh fruit. The market should be opening now."

Jacob nodded and hurriedly escaped through the open doorway, refusing to look back.

She was alone with Munir now. Khadija burrowed her nails into the seat of her chair and tried to steady her breathing as a rope of fear coiled in her belly, twisting, curling, tightening itself into a knot. She pressed on her abdomen.

Munir filled a pan with water and set it on the stove, humming to himself. He sprinkled a handful of tea leaves into the water, followed by a cinnamon stick and cardamom pods.

"Chai?"

She shook her head.

"You've been traveling, yes?" He smiled at her. "You must be tired."

Right now, alone with this man in his kitchen, the last thing on Khadija's mind was sleep. Her body was tired, exhausted even, but her mind was racing, counting all the windows and doorways, familiarizing herself with the escape routes. She jittered on the edge of her seat.

Munir didn't wait for her response. "You can sleep in my spare room if you'd like. Come." He gestured deeper into the house. "Rest for a while. Jacob won't be long with your fruit." He chuckled, twirling the ends of his beard. "The boy runs fast."

His laughter unnerved her, but Khadija followed, more out of fear of what he'd say if she refused. She didn't wish to know what he'd be like if his mood were to flip. She followed Munir down the hallway, her footsteps echoing loudly against the tiles. An open doorway to her right revealed a glassblower's workshop, where a furnace simmered in the corner and glass trinkets dangled from the walls. The whole room sparkled. She gasped.

"Pretty, isn't it?" Munir peered at her, gaze sweeping across her body. Up and down and back again.

Khadija nodded nervously. He tugged open a door and ushered her inside. "If you need anything at all, don't hesitate to call me."

Khadija hurriedly slammed the door in his face, not daring to breathe until she heard Munir's footsteps retreat.

Her heart was in her throat. Now what? She eyed the little room—a simple bed with cotton sheets, and a tiny window. Outside, the heat was already growing thicker as the day progressed. It would be suicide trying to leave in such heat, especially without any water. She pitied Jacob for having to go outside for her. Khadija supposed it couldn't hurt to stay a few hours longer. Just thinking about the heat from the balloon made her dizzy.

A copper wind chime hung above the window—supposedly there to alert her if a jinn were to enter. The air was like a stagnant pool, however, and the wind chime made no noise. Khadija lay as still as possible atop the thin sheets. Moving would only make her hotter. She closed her eyes, listening to Munir's movements throughout the house. The clang of pots and pans, then later on, the tinkle of glass. He was in the workshop. She eyed the door. It would be easy enough to leave now. Unless he'd blocked the door from the other side. She rose swiftly and checked the handle, but the door swung open, and she sighed with relief. She was just being paranoid. Abba's voice recited in her mind: *You can never be too cautious when it comes to men, beti. Always better to be extra vigilant. Always question their motives.*

She scoffed. Maybe it was about time she questioned Abba's motives for being so eager to marry her off to what appeared to be a boy he'd literally picked up off the street. A stab of guilt melted her frustration as she pictured Abba sitting beside the window all night, watching the sky for her return. He'd probably do that again tonight, and the next, and the next. She wondered how long it would take for him to realize she wasn't coming back, and then how long for his heart to shatter. Khadija slumped on the bed. She was too exhausted to wreck her insides with guilt.

The heat slowly consumed her, and lucid dreams swam across her eyes. She dreamed she was in Hassan's storybook, hurrying up and down marble corridors lined with rose-petal-topped pools as she searched for the missing Princess Malika. Hassan was there too, in the courtyard, twisting the end of a telescope as he gazed at the night sky for answers.

Then a voice like wind chimes, a flurry of notes that blended seamlessly together in a song that forced her eyes upward. Hassan followed the creature with his telescope as it looped across the sky in a flutter of opalescent feathers that shimmered silver and lilac. She would've thought it simply a bird if not for the voice carrying across the night. Khadija gasped. It was a peri, a creature of the heavens that was mostly birdlike, save for a human face and body that ended in delicately pointed talons and wings that were said to be fashioned of pure starlight. Peri only appeared at night underneath a full moon, to sing, their harmonies guiding the souls of the dead that were free of sin to Heaven. Khadija tore her eyes from the sky to Hassan, still fiddling with his telescope, oblivious to her.

Look at me. Please. She made to go to him, to hug him, to squeeze him, to beg him to tell her a story one last time so she could hear his voice again, but then the dream dissolved.

Khadija awoke, shaking. The room was dark, and it was cooler now.

How long had she been asleep? She shifted onto her elbows. Her back was sticky and covered in a cold sweat that made her shiver. Shadows lingered in the corners, and the wind chime tinkled an eerie tune. She wiped the sleep from her eyes.

Glass shattered.

She jumped, knocking her elbow on the bedpost.

More glass. Then screaming. It was coming from the other room.

Khadija rose and yanked the door open. Shards of glass littered the hallway like confetti. The door to the workshop was half-open, allowing the blood-orange light coming from the furnace to illuminate the tiles.

Another yelp that turned into whimpering. She rounded the corner.

Jacob was cowering on the floor, both arms shielding his face as Munir poised over him with a glass bowl. "You are starting to be more trouble than you're worth, häri!"

Jacob dragged himself across the tiles, slicing his palms open on the glass. Khadija winced. Munir put an abrupt end to his retreat by launching the bowl, where it shattered just inches from Jacob's head. He screamed.

Khadija's hands balled into fists. No one should treat a child that way. She stood, frozen by the doorway, as Munir reached for a white-hot poker resting in the furnace.

"Perhaps I should darken that pale face for you." He twirled the poker in the air.

Her body stiffened. Khadija didn't need to think. She swung her arm.

She had never struck a man in all her life, so when her fist connected with the side of Munir's head, Khadija was surprised that her power was enough to stagger him. The poker clattered to the floor. He grunted but recovered quickly, closing in while nursing a lump on his face. Khadija backed away.

"That was most unladylike, Miss Khadija." His eyes lit up with a wicked sparkle as his stare raked across her body.

Her back hit the wall. Khadija's breathing hitched. Her ears were ringing with all the blood rushing through them. "Leave him alone."

What she had hoped would come off as brave instead came out a shaky plea. Munir cackled. "Taken a liking to the boy, have you?" He snarled. "Really, miss, I did not have you down as a hāri sympathizer." The glassblower approached her, sniffing like a bloodhound, as if he could smell her fear. "We'll have to force that compassion out of you somehow." He cracked his knuckles.

A yell made both their heads snap around. Glass shattered. Munir hit the ground.

Khadija's heart was beating so fast it hurt. A dark puddle pooled around Munir's head. Shards of colorful glass were sticking out of his forehead. She counted down the seconds, expecting him to move. He never did.

"I think he's dead," Jacob whispered, hands trembling, sending a wave of shadows rippling across the wall.

Khadija squeezed her eyes shut, trying to calm her breathing. *OK. Calm down. Just breathe. He's probably not dead.*

She opened her eyes.

Munir's body was still there.

What was she supposed to do with it? She daren't touch him. Maybe he would wake up.

Maybe he wouldn't.

She tried to will herself to check if he was breathing, but her body refused to move. Bile rose up her throat.

Khadija made for the door and staggered into the hallway, sucking in a deep lungful of air. She leaned her forehead against the wall. Ragged breathing was coming from behind her. Once she had battled the urge to vomit, she returned to the workshop—a room bathed in amber light, its shelves filled with glass orbs while swinging chandeliers twinkled above her head. It was a pretty sight, if not for the murder.

A roar that barely sounded human made her spin and duck as Jacob hurled another bowl at the wall, where it exploded in a shower of glass. He reached for a vase.

"Stop it! You'll draw attention." She attempted to grab his arms.

Jacob flinched, chest rising in shallow shaky breaths. "The soldiers. They'll kill me!" The color drained from his face, allowing Khadija to trace each purple vein across his eyelids. His head darted from left to right, scanning the room, as if expecting soldiers already to be climbing in through the windows. His eyes were a bright, vivid blue. Bluer than anything she had ever seen.

Khadija tried to deny it, but he was right. They would kill him. As for her, she might be able to talk herself out of it. They'd still put her on the first balloon straight back to Abba though. No, she couldn't let that happen.

Hiding the body would be difficult. Too many neighbors, too many eyes that could catch a glimpse of their dragging a body down the street. And besides, she didn't have the stomach for that. Which left only one option. "We have to leave before someone notices he's . . ."

Jacob clutched the vase to his chest but didn't throw it. She watched how he hugged it close for comfort. Or was it to protect himself from her?

Khadija didn't know what else to say. In a single moment she had risked everything for him. She'd done it without even thinking, and in turn he'd done the same for her. They were strangers and already circumstances had bound them together, whether they liked it or not.

She chanced another look at Munir's body. The puddle of blood had doubled in size. She retched. They needed to leave. "Where did your friend hide my balloon?" Jacob didn't reply. She sighed. "Look, we don't have time. We need to go." She made for the doorway. "Tell me where."

"Near the bazaar," he blurted. "William said he'd hide it in an alley near the bazaar."

She nodded. Sahli was a small village—the balloon shouldn't be too difficult to find. Jacob dropped his gaze.

"Okay. Let's go."

"You go on ahead," he said. "I need to get William."

She scowled. She didn't like the idea of him tagging along. Khadija looked Jacob up and down. Could either of them be trusted? They were hāri, after all.

She clenched her jaw. It wasn't like she was any safer with her own kind. She shuddered. At least they were boys and not men. She could handle two boys, as long as she kept her guard up and they maintained their distance. Besides, she couldn't launch the balloon on her own. "OK," she grumbled.

Jacob hesitated, then followed her out of the workshop.

"I'll see you soon?" Khadija said uncertainly.

He refused to meet her eyes. "Sure." Then he disappeared into the street, and Khadija allowed herself to steal one last look at Munir's house before stepping after him.

8

JACOB

Jacob stuffed his hands in his pockets to stop his wrists from shaking. Drops of Munir's blood stained his sleeves. He'd done it, without even thinking. All it had taken was that wicked grin spreading across Munir's face as he had backed the girl into a corner.

It was amazing how a single moment could change everything. Now he really did have no choice but to meet the Hāreef with William and pray that they'd take him in. Perhaps they could offer him some protection when the soldiers inevitably discovered Munir's body.

The fruity smell of shisha filled the air as Jacob weaved through the streets. The village of Sahli was alive with hookah pipes as Ghadaeans celebrated the sun's retreat across the sky. Men blew smoke rings while children sat at their feet squabbling over pistachio-flavored barfi. The women huddled in groups farther away, chuckling quietly to each other. Afraid to laugh too loud.

Jacob proceeded to the hāri slums. It would be nightfall soon, and the first sprinkling of stars were appearing beside a banana-shaped moon. He needed to hurry. His eyes couldn't help but flicker to the old barn near the slums where William had really hidden the girl's balloon. It was a clever hiding spot, relatively abandoned save for the odd goat.

The bazaar, on the other hand, was on the opposite side of the village. She would never find her balloon. A pang of guilt threatened to chew up his insides. She'd helped him, put herself at risk, all for a boy she barely knew. A hāri boy. He brushed aside his feelings before they forced him to turn and go back for her. Was she a hāri sympathizer like Munir said, or just a girl who despised violence? Or perhaps, like him, she'd merely acted impulsively and would have done the same whether it had been him or a dog suffering Munir's wrath.

Either way, he couldn't go back for her. She'd be all right on her own. She was a Ghadaean, after all.

When he reached the slums, Jacob scanned the poppies for William. The slums were unusually quiet for this time. Perhaps, after the incident with the jinn, the hāri were taking no chances in drawing any more unnecessary attention.

A movement from the corner of his eye made Jacob's head snap around, but it was just the wind making the shacks and brittle beams sway from side to side. He hugged his arms to his chest.

Something tugged on his shirt collar. Jacob yelped.

"Shh!" William clamped a hand over his mouth, an impish glimmer to his eyes. "Come on."

Jacob pressed his palm to his chest to prevent his heart from bursting through his rib cage and followed William through the poppies. The only sound was the snap of stems beneath their feet and the ragged puffs of their breathing.

When they were a safe distance away from the village, William threw a cursory "You all right?" over his shoulder.

"I think I killed Munir."

William stopped dead in his tracks. "You what?"

Jacob relayed what had happened, expecting a slap around the face. Instead William's chest bobbed up and down, laughter spilling out of his throat.

Jacob gritted his teeth. "It's not funny!"

"Oh, it is." William hummed with amusement. "Glassblower by day, murderer by night." He nudged him with his elbow. "That'll certainly impress the Hāreef."

Jacob's teeth crunched together.

"Which is a good thing, since you'll have to join them now."

Jacob nodded. He supposed William was right, though he sounded a little too smug about it for his liking.

"And the girl." William faced him. "She won't find her balloon, will she?"

Jacob shook his head. "No chance."

"Good. Balloons are like gold dust. Offering it to the Hāreef will surely better our chances."

Jacob tried not to picture the disappointment on the girl's face when she realized he'd lied. They carried on.

In the distance, orange torchlights danced in the evening breeze. Voices carried across the air, soft and low like the hum of an insect's wings, as they approached a clearing in the field where the poppies had been harvested, their blunt stems protruding from the ground like severed limbs. William sped up. "They're here. Do as I say. Don't say anything stupid."

Jacob bit his tongue. If either of them was going to say something stupid it would more likely be William. This whole thing was stupid. But it was either this or deal with Munir's body—and the Ghadaean girl. He squashed down his guilt and trailed William as he emerged into the clearing.

Figures in white cloaks hovered in groups, breaking off into clusters. A hot-air balloon was tethered to the ground, its silk globe stippled white and pale blue so that when airborne, he imagined it would blend seamlessly into the cloudscape. Its burner was turned low, emitting only a faint haze of light so that the basket just brushed the tops of the flower petals, and was all but invisible until he stood a few feet from it. Jacob's palms prickled with a familiar excitement, similar to the feeling he had when Munir retired to bed and Jacob was left alone in the workshop to craft whatever he pleased. Opportunity. Anticipation. It sparked his insides with a delicious warmth that trickled down his limbs and thawed the numbness in his toes.

For a moment, he almost forgot about the sihr. He swallowed the sickness rising in his stomach. With Munir dead, this was his only option now.

William pointed at a figure in the center of the group with a long crimson tendril of hair escaping from a heavy hood, fluttering in the breeze, hair the color of blood. "That's their leader. It's her we have to impress."

"Her?" Jacob wasn't sure why out of everything that surprised him.

William nodded. "She's the one who gave me this." He traced his thumb over the amulet around his neck. "They're here to recruit new members. More hāri on their side means a better chance of changing things."

"What things?"

William flashed his teeth. "Everything. Society. The world." He marched ahead. "Come on. I'll introduce you."

Jacob's knees suddenly felt like they were made of paper, but he willed his legs to follow William. There were around fifteen figures; those dressed in white seemed to be the Hāreef, but there were other hāri he'd seen in the slums as well: an older man with a horrid scar on his cheek and an ax hanging from his hip, a woman with a dainty face sitting cross-legged with a selection of daggers laid out on a blanket, and a young man who looked about nineteen with a thick book tucked under his elbow. Jacob's eyebrows rose. Most hāri, like him, could not read. It seemed the Hāreef were after more than just brute force. They wanted intelligence, talent, something out of the ordinary. Something they could bend to their advantage. But what use could they possibly have for a glassmaker's apprentice? The young man with the book met Jacob's eyes and gave them both a brief nod. William inclined his head and beckoned Jacob over.

The wisp of red hair escaping the woman's hood danced in the wind like a ribbon as they neared, and Jacob had the urge to catch it. William cleared his throat. "Excuse me." He sounded younger, and Jacob realized it was because he was nervous. He didn't think he'd ever seen William nervous before. His stomach tightened. If this woman made William nervous, maybe he should be nervous too.

The woman spun, and the first thing Jacob noticed how tall she was, taller than most of the men. "William. You came!" Her teeth dazzled pearl white in the darkness.

"Of course." William puffed out his chest. "And I brought my friend. The one I was telling you about." He gave Jacob a shove. "He's a glassblower."

Jacob stumbled forward.

"A glassblower," she purred. Her voice was like sticky honey, and Jacob thought he'd melt under her gaze. He chanced a look up and was startled by two emerald eyes, the greenest eyes he'd ever seen.

"Nice to meet you, miss," he stuttered.

There was a pause where even the wind seemed to still. Then the woman threw her head back, a soft chuckle escaping her lips. "So polite." She ruffled his hair. "You may call me Vera," she said, hooking her finger under his chin, lifting his head for her inspection. "What's your name?"

"J-Jacob."

"Beautiful name," Vera whispered.

His breath stuck in his throat so that Jacob could only croak out a thanks. No one had ever complimented his name like that before.

Vera twisted his face left and right, but there was a gentleness to her actions. "You want to see our people happy, without fear, living the way we want?"

He nearly collapsed into her words. Didn't every hāri want the world she described? But such a thing didn't even seem possible. And the means she was using . . . sihr. Jinn. Was it worth it? Jacob pulled his chin free of her grip.

Vera's brow creased. She was much older than him, her porcelain skin edged with crow's feet and laughter lines that gave her face a softness that even her bloodred hair couldn't tarnish. "You have your doubts," she said matter-of-factly. "You would be a fool not to." Vera clicked her fingers, and a man appeared with a fold-up stool, which he plonked on the grass. She perched herself on it. "First, let's see what you can do. Then we'll talk about your doubts."

Did she mean for him to put on a performance for her? How was he supposed to blow glass in the middle of a field? Jacob glanced at William, begging him to save him.

William stepped forward. "I've been practicing with the amulet, like you said."

Vera nodded, a movement to the left stealing her attention. Jacob followed the direction of her eyes. A woman was unloading from the hot-air balloon crates that rattled with glass vials. Not just any glass, he realized, as the torchlight revealed the familiar amber tinge of copper-and-brass-infused glass. He swallowed.

"Care to demonstrate?" Vera said to William as she waved the woman over and selected a vial made of brass-tinted glass—the kind Jacob and Munir often crafted for the village exorcists. He'd seen only empty ones before, but this vial contained a black swirl that swam beneath the glass. Jacob frowned, curiosity drawing him closer until he caught the flash of jade-green eyes. He gasped. There was a jinn in there.

This was a mistake.

Jacob tugged on William's sleeve. "Don't do this," he whispered as Vera peered into the black depths of the vial.

William wrangled his hand free. "Shut up!" he hissed.

"We should go back."

William jabbed him in the ribs, stepped forward, and took the vial. Jacob doubled over. "Don't," he croaked.

But William had already smashed the vial beneath his boot. The jinn sprang to life. There was a furious growl, and then a wolf made of smoke stood before them with eyes as green as Vera's, saliva dripping from its fangs.

Jacob's throat closed. "William!" This was stupid! He shouldn't have come here. He shouldn't have listened to William.

"This one's bigger than the snakes and birds you've been practicing on, William. Let's see how well you do commanding a more powerful jinn." Vera's gaze swept from William to Jacob. "Don't be afraid. Like us, this creature is a loyal subject of the jinniya Queen Bidhukh. It is our ally, not our enemy. It just needs to be told."

William's hands were shaking as he reached for his amulet, the eye of Bidhukh. He dangled it in front of the jinn. "I serve—"

The jinn snapped. William jerked his hand back.

Vera straightened up. "Come on. More vigor." She clapped, the sound muffled by her crisp white gloves. "Demand its obedience!"

William's grip tightened on the chain of his amulet so that his knuckles turned white. "I serve your queen." His voice rang across the field as clear as the peal of a bell.

"Say her name," Vera instructed.

"Bidhukh. I serve Queen Bidhukh."

The wolf growled, a deep hum that caused the ground to vibrate. William stood firm. "You will serve me as you serve your queen. She commands it."

The wolf jerked forward. Jacob yelped, reaching his hand out to snatch William back before the creature's fangs locked around his ankle, until the jinn settled on its hind legs and licked its paws, staring dutifully at William.

Vera grinned. "Very good, William."

William glowed with pride.

The other hāri soon came up to demonstrate their talents. The man swung his ax, slicing poppies with a desperate fever while Vera watched, masking a yawn with her glove. Jacob couldn't take his eyes off her. The way she commanded so much respect from the hāri around her, who waited on her every call, every click of her fingers. She didn't even have to raise her voice. Always, her tone remained soft, barely above a whisper, so that those around had to strain and lean in rather than dare ask her to repeat herself.

The woman with the knives was next, whipping around as she

released them into the night, where they pierced individual petals on the poppies, before bowing like a performer. William nudged him. "Glad you came?"

But Jacob's insides felt like they'd been splattered with a mortar and pestle the closer it got to his turn. The young man with the book was stuttering over the first sentence now. "How am I supposed to show her I can blow glass?"

William rubbed his chin. "Have you not got anything to show her? Anything you've made?"

His first thought after killing Munir hadn't been grabbing a vase to show. "No! Quick. It's almost my turn. What am I supposed to do?"

William shrugged. "You could tell her about the hot-air balloon we've got, I guess."

The young man's jilted words filled the air, gaining speed as he grew with confidence, eyes skimming over the page of his book as he recited a recipe for chickpea pilau.

"Stop!"

The man's last word died on the air. Jacob's head turned, wondering who had interrupted, until he realized it was Vera, her voice worlds away from the softness of before. She stood so quickly her stool toppled over as her gaze rested on the distance.

"Fire," she breathed.

Jacob followed her line of sight to the orange flames licking away at the poppies. The crackle of fire and the sharp sting of smoke drifted over, followed by the thud of boots and the slice of metal as swords were drawn. His heart stopped.

"Soldiers!" Vera reached for the crate of glass vials, smashing the lot against the ground. The air swirled with jinn just as the glimmer of swords tore through the flowers. A group of ten Ghadaean soldiers came into view, the green sashes around their waists marking the soldiers as belonging to the Nawab of Intalyabad, one of three nawabs all reigning over different regions of Ghadaea. They were close enough that Jacob could make out the royal symbol etched on the copper hilts of their talwars.

"The terrorists are here!" the soldiers roared, loading gunpowder into the matchlock firearms attached to their wrists. The first few hāri collapsed with bullet holes studded against their cloaks.

Then the jinn sprang to life. Black tendrils rippled across the grass, spinning, swirling, morphing into shape. Green eyes appeared.

"Jinn!" The soldiers slashed through the air, but their talwars passed straight through the jinn. A jinn the shape of a cat pounced, while a snake made of smoke and shadow wrapped around the legs of a soldier and brought him to his knees, before coiling around his neck and hugging him to death. A hāri finished him off by sinking a sword into his side. The soldier collapsed.

"Queen Bidhukh wishes Ghadaean blood to be spilled tonight!" Vera revealed her amulet. "Obey her wishes." The edges of the wolf blurred as it started to shape-shift before it rose on two legs and stretched itself to its full height. A jinn the shape of a man.

"Come on!" William yanked Jacob up, dodging a blade as it whirled toward them. A dagger sliced through the air from behind them, sinking into the soldier's throat. He slumped just as the hāri woman with a fistful of daggers bounded over, ripping the blade free of his neck. Jacob felt sick.

A blade hacked through the rope tethering the hot-air balloon to the ground, and it started to drift up into the night, cutting off the Hāreef's escape . . . and Jacob's too. The human-shaped jinn rubbed its hands together, creating sparks, sparks bursting along its fingertips before erupting into a violent green flame that devoured the nearest soldiers. This was jinn fire, hotter than any other heat source known to man. Burned flesh stung Jacob's nostrils.

Then they were running back through the poppies, William dragging Jacob so hard he thought his fingers would pop out of their sockets.

Three soldiers blocked off their escape. They skidded. Swords clashed, and one of the Hāreef collapsed, his white cloak stained with blood. The boom of muskets filled the air.

A sweep of white fabric descended on them. "Get behind me!" Vera pushed them back.

Two soldiers approached. Blades flew. Jacob hit the ground face-first, his mouth filled with poppy petals. William crumpled beside him, hands pressed to his side, a red stain blossoming across his tunic.

Jacob screamed. "William!"

He pressed on William's abdomen. William shrieked and batted his hands away. There was blood everywhere. Jacob's hands were covered. *No.* This couldn't be happening. This wasn't supposed to happen.

More swords clanged. The soldiers grabbed Vera's throat and kicked her in the shins. She roared.

William squeezed his hand, chest rising in quick shallow breaths. "It's OK . . . Jacob," he wheezed.

But it wasn't OK. It would never be OK if William were to—Jacob shook his head. He couldn't think that. William had to make it. They were a team. "Come on. Get up!" He attempted to lift him. William groaned and slumped to the ground like dead weight. Jacob refused to give up.

"I can't." William yanked at his amulet and pressed it into Jacob's palm. "You have . . . to go."

"I can't!" Jacob's voice cracked in half. "I can't leave you. I *won't* leave you." He flung William's limp arm across his shoulders and tried to lift him. William slid to the ground like a sack of coal.

"You must." The color was rapidly draining from William's face. "Join them. It's the only way . . . you'll be safe."

Jacob's wrists were trembling as he struggled to lift William again, until a hand on his arm stifled his efforts. Snuffed them out like a candle flame. All hope evaporated. *He's not going to make it, is he?*

"Listen to me, Jacob." There was a desperation to William's voice he'd never heard before. "Promise me you'll join them." His nails dug into Jacob's skin, hard enough to draw blood.

Jacob didn't trust himself to speak. He nodded.

William's face relaxed slightly. He pushed Jacob away. "Now go. Go to . . . our balloon."

Jacob's face crumpled. "William—"

Vera had freed herself from the soldiers' grips, driving a spear through one of them, painting the purple poppies red. The soldier collapsed. She slashed at the other, forcing him back.

William lurched to the side as pain racked his body. Jacob gripped William's shoulders to steady him. "Go," William spluttered again, spraying spit across Jacob's face. His eyelids began to close.

"No! Don't leave me. Don't you dare leave me." Jacob shook him.

William groaned. "Go."

Then the life slipped out of him, like a pebble dipping below the surface of the water. Gone. Empty. Extinguished.

Dead.

Jacob shook him again, knowing it was useless. He brought a hand to his mouth.

He's gone.

Vera yanked Jacob up before he had a chance to touch William one last time and dragged him through the field. Flowers whipped his face. They were running back toward the village. Jacob could see the roof of the barn where the balloon was hidden. They burst from the poppy fields and into the slums, now a wreckage of broken shacks and children's screams as soldiers tore through each dwelling, setting it alight, watching the flames with hungry eyes. Hāri ran in all directions.

Vera spun, blocking an oncoming spear aimed at Jacob's side. The soldier collapsed as Vera lacerated his throat. She turned, and her eyes traced over Jacob: bright green, like jinn's eyes. She reached for his chin, held it steady, and this time, Jacob didn't pull away from her.

"Join us." There was a steely hardness to her voice, nothing like the soft hum of before. "Do it for William. Do it for them." She gestured at the children screaming for their parents, the old woman with a broken nose where a soldier had rammed the hilt of his blade in her face, the men who were furiously trying to salvage something from their fire-ravaged homes.

Heat flooded his insides. He couldn't have spoken even if he'd wanted to. All he could do was let himself burn.

Vera's hand dropped from his chin and her grip tightened on her blade. "This shouldn't have happened." She lifted her sword, eyes fixed on the bodies littering the ground. "You want answers. You want justice. But more than that, you want revenge." Her lips curled over her teeth. "Meet us in Intalyabad in three days' time, in the rose gardens at nightfall." Her green eyes twinkled. "And you'll get your revenge."

Then she disappeared into the field and was lost to the sound of death and swords.

Jacob could only run. Far away. He didn't think he'd stop running until his feet bled, until none of this was real. His sandals smacked the ground as he tore through the slums, weaving through the streets beyond, his vision a blur of tears.

Jacob burst into Munir's house. "Hello?"

She was gone. Of course, she'd already left. Why had he even come here? But he'd chosen not to go to the barn. Suddenly Jacob wasn't so sure he could fly the balloon alone. He studied the amulet William had given him. Sihr. Forbidden magic. Jacob shuddered and slipped it into his pocket. His shoulders shook. His lungs ached.

Glass crunched in the shadows. "I'll kill you!"

Jacob screamed as Munir emerged from the hallway, a shard of glass sticking out of his left eyelid. He charged. Jacob retreated around the kitchen table. Munir circled.

"And then I'll throw you into the furnace," Munir hissed. "Watch your filthy hāri skin burn!" He flipped the table, sending pots crashing to the floor. He lunged.

Jacob shrieked and jumped, Munir's fingers just scraping his arm. Jacob kicked out, but Munir was quick, catching his ankle. He dragged him deeper into the house.

"Get off me!" Jacob writhed, scratching Munir's face, but his grip remained strong.

A wooden stool cracked against the back of Munir's head. Munir slumped to the ground. A hand pulled Jacob up and tugged him into the street. They were running.

"Stop them!" Munir screeched, clutching a bloody nose. Soldiers' heads turned from the other end of the street. Munir stabbed a finger in their direction.

The soldiers clattered in pursuit.

They didn't slow, not even for a second. He caught a flash of brown skin and almost tripped over.

The Ghadaean girl. She'd come back. For him.

She turned to face him, still running. "Where's my balloon?"

9

KHADIJA

Khadija forced Jacob to run faster as they dodged bodies and bloodstains that made her mouth fill with sour bile. Why were the soldiers doing this? Killing hāri so blatantly in the streets. Even soldiers were not normally that bloodthirsty. Jacob whimpered, and Khadija wished she could cover his eyes. They needed to find her balloon and get out of here. That was if it was still here. *Please let it still be here.*

"The barn," Jacob puffed beside her. "It's in . . . the barn."

"You better not be lying again!" she snapped. "You told me it was near the bazaar."

Jacob yanked her in the opposite direction, and Khadija had no choice but to follow. "I'm telling the truth this time. Just trust me!"

As if she ever could. Khadija doused her anger before it erupted into a roaring flame. If he was lying again now, they'd both die. He was their only way out of here.

Soldiers' boots thundered behind them. Figures in white cloaks blocked the path ahead. Khadija caught a glimmer of green fire licking away at the buildings. She skidded to a halt. Jacob turned sharply and hauled Khadija against the nearest wall.

The white-cloaked figures were terrorists: the ones Abdel had been telling Abba about—the ones who summoned jinn. Her throat closed up. She spluttered, eyes never leaving the swirl of smoke that took the shape of a woman. A jinniya. She'd never seen one before, but Khadija had read enough stories to know what jinn looked like. The jinniya approached a building, and a stream of green fire left her lips, swallowing the house and reducing it to cinders. Khadija quickly turned her face away from the heat.

Then soldiers and terrorists collided in a flurry of metal and high-pitched screams. "Come on!" Jacob broke into a sprint. Khadija stole a final look at the jinniya and the green flames dancing from her palms, before running after him.

The barn stood peacefully, unaware of the carnage at its doorstep. Skinny goats nestled in the hay beside broken beams scattered at the barn's entrance. Heavy tools swung from hooks along the walls. The barn was stacked with crates filled with jars of a sticky white substance that Khadija instantly recognized to be harvested opium resin.

Jacob pulled the basket of the balloon out from behind a stack of crates, and Khadija rushed to assist him, keeping one eye on the street. She grabbed a rope and tossed another to Jacob. They dragged the balloon into the night, trampling poppies as they reached the safety of the field. Khadija grasped the material, laying it flat on the grass the way she'd seen the hāri men do. It had taken five men to inflate just one balloon. Her chest tightened. What if they couldn't get it in the air? She swallowed her fear back down. There was no other option. They *had* to get it in the air.

Even when deflated, the balloon still looked majestic. Its bright colors lit up the darkness, keeping her fear at bay. Khadija clambered inside the basket and twisted the tap of the gas canister until she heard that familiar squeal of gas escaping. Then she grasped the matchbox beside the burner and sparks struck a match. Orange sparks lit up the night, but the burner did not catch alight. She tried again, hands shaking as she brought the quivering match as close to the burner as she dared. The flame caught the gas fumes and erupted into a violent blue fire.

"Grab the balloon!"

Their arms rose and fell, furiously flapping, forcing the balloon to life. The fabric rippled, but it remained a heap of saggy material.

Khadija increased her speed, and Jacob was forced to match her, both of them now lifting their arms as high as they could in an attempt to inflate the balloon. The material swallowed the air up only to breathe it back out and fall slack in their fingers. Khadija left Jacob with the deflated fabric and grasped the handle of the wooden propeller beside the balloon's burner. Her shoulders burned as she frantically spun the propeller, guiding the hot air into the balloon.

Men's shouts filled the air.

Their motions grew more forceful. The balloon swayed drunkenly, too lazy to raise its head. The basket trembled as the balloon strained to lift its weight.

"You can fly, can't you?" Jacob panted.

Khadija didn't answer.

"I mean, you've taken off before, right?"

She tried to ignore Jacob's doubts, but they washed over her like a storm. What if they couldn't take off? Then what would they do?

Jacob was tiring quickly. He waved his arms in a final burst of energy, and the balloon sprang to life, escaping his grip and swelling up. Khadija quickly yanked on a rope, feet skidding across the ground as she fought to prevent its escape.

Jacob looked ready to collapse with relief, but they weren't safe yet. Green uniforms flitted past. Shouts carried across the air. Soldiers. They had to go.

"Jacob! Get in the balloon."

Jacob clambered inside the basket, his weight just enough to prevent the balloon from leaping into the night. "Come on," he called over to Khadija.

Khadija calculated her next move carefully. The basket was three feet off the ground. She would have to release the rope and jump before the balloon shot up and left her.

She planted her feet wide apart, bending her knees, readying to jump.

"The soldiers are coming!" Jacob yelled.

The barn's doors burst open as soldiers tore through, heads snapping around as they scanned the field. Swords slashed at the nearest poppies.

She released the rope. Air whooshed as the balloon leaped into the sky.

And Khadija jumped. The basket tilted sharply with her weight. She clamped her eyes shut, sinking her nails into the basket's edge, not daring to breathe, until two hands grasped her arms and pulled her over the edge. She toppled into the basket and collapsed on the deck, shaking. Khadija was aware of Jacob hovering awkwardly above her. She allowed herself a few more seconds to recover before shooting to her feet, busying herself with the balloon, examining the gas canister and checking that the ropes were secured tightly. As the balloon continued to ascend, the true destruction of Sahli became apparent. Flames tore through the village below.

Khadija rounded on Jacob, hands on her hips, ready to unleash her fury. If she hadn't thought to go back for him, they'd both likely be dead. Her skin sizzled.

But Jacob's attention was not on her. It was on the fires below, the orange shapes dancing across his face. He had a haunted expression, like he'd witnessed something he shouldn't have. Images of the hāri littering the street scorched Khadija's mind: nothing but empty faces to her, but to him . . .

Faces of friends. Loved ones. She paled. Something no one should have to see. A wrangled cry escaped his lips then, until Jacob was heaving.

Khadija recoiled and furiously turned away, unsure what to do. Maybe it would embarrass him if she were to stare. She glanced at him. No. She couldn't just ignore it.

"Jacob?" Her voice was soft. "It's OK. Just breathe."

He grunted in response, but her words seemed to have an effect on him. She repeated them again and again like a mantra, her voice as smooth as silk, until she noticed his breathing begin to steady, his breaths growing deeper.

Her rage melted into the night. "I never got to thank you," she whispered. "Earlier. For Munir."

Jacob shrugged. "It was nothing. You saved me first, remember?"

But it wasn't nothing to her. She didn't want to ask, but she had to know. "Your friend . . . ?"

"William." Jacob's voice cracked at the end. His jaw tightened. "Gone."

She nodded, not sure if any words of comfort would sound sincere leaving her lips. "We're lucky we managed to get away before the terrorists . . ."

Her voice trailed off as a fiery heat seemed to consume Jacob's features. He folded his arms, squaring his shoulders, ready to unleash his rage. "It's the *soldiers* who killed him, not the *Hāreef.* They're the real terrorists." His arms shook, struggling to contain clenched fists.

Khadija didn't know what to say. She watched him warily like he was an open flame, ready to push him over the edge of the balloon if he were to strike out at her. But his anger soon fizzled out, replaced by a shaking that started in his wrists and traveled up his shoulders until his body was trembling. Then, as Sahli became nothing but a smudge along the black horizon, like a dam bursting, his face crumpled. Jacob wept.

Dawn had barely broken when Khadija arose the next morning. Jacob's sniffles and choked sobs had kept her awake all night. But she hadn't tried to comfort him again. What could she possibly say to lessen his grief?

The sky was a blank canvas, not a single cloud across the horizon. It would be a hot day, even hotter up here where they were at the sun's mercy. She peered over the edge. They were hovering, with barely any wind to push them along. She could pick out only the outlines of terracotta rocks and the faint blue smudge of the Ravi River. The rest was a blur, no hint of civilization. Qasrah, her town, was far behind them now, and so was Sahli. She shuddered at the image of all those dead hāri sprawled across the grass. The soldiers. The terrorists. Abba and Abdel had been right about one thing: It was certainly dangerous out here. Maybe she *should've* stayed indoors.

Khadija glanced at Jacob's sleeping figure curled up on the deck. He looked much younger in sleep, almost innocent, though she hadn't forgotten how he'd tricked her. He'd had no qualms about taking her balloon and leaving her even after they'd saved each other's lives. She mustn't forget that.

Khadija checked the balloon's burner, a habit she had assumed every few hours after the near disaster of her first night in the balloon. The fire was steady and the gas canister released a constant stream.

She eyed her meager supplies. When she'd been unable to find the balloon after searching Sahli's small bazaar, she'd swiped what she could from an idle market stall, refilled her water gourd at the well, and returned to Munir's home. It had felt wrong stealing, but she supposed that after stealing a hot-air balloon, a few pieces of fruit couldn't hurt. How long they would last between them was another question, but it was too early for such thoughts.

By mid-morning, Khadija had managed to use the portable lavatory when the urge to go had become unbearable and was nibbling her way through half of their supply of dates by the time Jacob awoke. Her tongue had a sickly sweet aftertaste to it. Jacob just stared at her with red-rimmed eyes as if he'd forgotten she existed, then rolled over.

Khadija opened her mouth, but the words were stuck in her throat. She had never been very good at comforting people when they cried. When they were younger, Hassan would always burst into tears over the slightest of things—perhaps he'd used the wrong colored pencil to color the grass in his drawing and had ruined the picture, or because Ammi had scolded him for not finishing his vegetables. He'd storm up to his bedroom and bury his tearstained face in his pillow. Khadija had always made sure to make herself scarce whenever her brother was throwing a tantrum, but up here in the balloon there was nowhere to hide from Jacob's grief. It weighed the balloon down.

When it became clear that Jacob intended to do nothing but lie there all day, Khadija rose and slid the water gourd toward him, careful not to cross the invisible line that they seemed to have carved across the deck since last night. Her side. His side. How long could they keep that up?

The water gourd bumped his foot. Jacob jumped up and shot her a glare, his blue eyes reflecting the fire so that they glowed red. Khadija looked away, scalded.

Jacob pulled the stopper off the water gourd and glugged it down, water dribbling across his chin. Khadija bit her lip to prevent herself from chastising him. *We need to be careful with that water. Who knows how long that'll last?* She held her tongue. She didn't know him well enough to scold him. When Jacob was finished, he wiped his mouth on the sleeve of his tunic and slid it back to her, mumbling, "Thanks."

She nodded, and that familiar awkwardness threatened to swallow them. "Would you like some fruit?" She produced a mango from the sack, and Jacob's face lit up. She rolled it across the deck.

He snatched it up. Sticking his thumbs into the mango so that juices squirted across his arms, he began to peel the skin away, revealing sticky yellow flesh. He dug his teeth into it with a satisfied groan. When he was done, Jacob didn't toss the mango stone over the edge like she'd expected. Instead, he wiped it clean and slid it into his pocket. Why would he keep something like that?

He seemed to read her thoughts because he said, "I don't like throwing things away. You never know what might come in handy." He lifted his red eyes to meet hers. His voice was hoarse from a night spent crying.

She nodded awkwardly. "I suppose so." Jacob made to roll back over, shutting himself off from the world. "So what do we do now?" she asked.

He shrugged. "You tell me. It's your balloon." When Khadija didn't respond, Jacob snickered. "Oh yeah, I forgot, you stole it, didn't you?"

Blood rushed to her cheeks. "You tried to steal it too!"

"I guess we're both as bad as each other, then."

Hardly! She didn't like being compared to him. A hāri boy. She ground her teeth.

Jacob wiped the sweat from his brow and peered over the edge. "You know we're not moving, right? You planning on cooking us alive up here?"

She huffed. "Sorry, but I can't control the weather. It's not my fault there isn't any wind."

Jacob rolled his eyes. "It's probably because we're so high up. Drop the altitude a bit and see if we catch a wind current. That should push us along."

His nonchalance as he ordered her around was surprising. Even Jacob seemed taken aback by his words because he quickly dropped his gaze. "I mean, it might be a good idea," he mumbled. "Probably be cooler too." His shoulders folded in on themselves as if he'd suddenly remembered his place.

It made her cheeks tinge with shame. "How do I make the balloon go down?"

Jacob pointed to the panels of material on the side of the balloon. "The side vents." His eyes traced the ropes, determining their purpose, before his gaze rested on a rope just above her head. "If you pull that, they should open, and it'll let some of the air out."

Khadija didn't like the sound of that but she got to her feet. Taking a deep breath, she tugged the rope.

Nothing.

Jacob snorted. "No need to be scared! Pull it a bit harder."

Khadija shot him a death glare and yanked it. Two panels on the right side of the balloon flipped open, exposing a gash in the material. The balloon started to tilt.

She shrieked.

"Do the other side. You need to balance the balloon!"

Khadija pulled the second rope beside her, and the left side of the balloon opened. The balloon righted itself. They started to sink.

Jacob licked his finger and stuck it in the air. Khadija watched him intently, her grip on the ropes so tight her fingers were starting to hurt.

A cool breeze tickled her face. Jacob nodded. "That should do it."

She released both ropes, and the side vents closed. Their descent halted, and the balloon began to drift to the right. The wind was pushing them along.

Khadija folded her arms and regarded Jacob with raised eyebrows. "How did you know that?"

He shrugged. "You end up overhearing a lot of things when people are always pretending you're not there. I guess being hāri has its advantages."

Again, that familiar shame made her bite her lip. What could she say to that?

"We should probably figure out which way we're going, otherwise we could be floating around in circles up here." Jacob traversed the deck, stopping a few inches behind the invisible line that marked his side and her side. He pointed at the wooden crate of useless navigation tools and oddments that she'd barely given much look at. "What's in there?"

Khadija lifted the lid and produced a strange object that looked like it could spin. "Just junk, really. I don't know what any of these things do."

"May I look?"

Khadija chewed on the inside of her cheek to stop a smirk from forming. "Sure."

He hesitated before crossing the invisible line. Jacob knelt beside the wooden box, pulling out various things, muttering to himself. His fingers curled around the battered old telescope Khadija had fiddled with before, all to no avail. He smiled triumphantly, bringing it to his eye.

"I wouldn't bother with that thing," Khadija grumbled. "I think it's broken. Everything's too blurry."

Jacob twisted the lens of the tube. "No. Works fine. See." He handed it to her.

Khadija used the telescope to focus on the ground. He was right. She could pick out individual trees and bushes with perfect clarity. She gasped. "How did you do that?"

Jacob fiddled with his thumbs. "You just have to twist it to get it to focus." He rummaged through the box. "I'm not sure what the rest of these things do. Probably stargazing equipment, but what we really need is a compass." Jacob rifled through the box again and groaned. "Which we don't have. We don't even have a map! We're flying blind."

The thud of Jacob plonking himself on the deck cross-legged made her jump. He began emptying his pockets.

"What are you doing?"

Jacob didn't respond until he'd finished lining all the contents of his pockets into a neat row. "Right, so here are our materials." He gestured to a pile of what Khadija could only describe as useless bits and bobs: odds and ends she couldn't imagine ever having a use for. Empty pistachio shells, a spool of thread, and a shard of bright blue glass. She noticed how his voice was less hoarse. Even his demeanor had changed. His shoulders were no longer slumped, and his eyes didn't appear quite so puffy. Focusing on a task seemed to keep his grief away. Khadija knew the feeling. The months following Ammi's and Hassan's deaths had been a blur of activity, her mind not daring to rest for too long a period, afraid what thoughts would plague her during its silence. Abba had been the same, allowing paperwork and numbers to consume him, while Talia had immediately turned her thoughts to marriage, probably thinking it her only escape from the grief that had burrowed into the floorboards and oozed into all the furniture.

Jacob eyed his materials intently, sorting them into piles. Khadija soon realized the larger of the two piles consisted of objects that were useless. Even the mango stone made an appearance, before that too befell the same fate. What remained was a considerably smaller collection of potentially usable items.

He rummaged through the pile again, mumbling to himself. A craftsman hard at work. It reminded Khadija of the little sculptures Hassan used to make out of coconut shells and river reeds. He'd make entire villages out of them, complete with tiny people with date-kernel bodies, until Abba had laughed at him. "Stop wasting your time with arts and crafts, beta. You are a boy. You should be practicing your letters and numbers. Leave this to the girls." Then Hassan had stopped making his sculptures. Abba had always been very good at invalidating their interests. He had clear-cut definitions of what boys and girls were supposed to do. The two never crossed over as far as Abba was concerned.

Jacob eyed a silver hairpin, twisting it around his fingers for what felt like the hundredth time before bending it backward, flattening it into one long piece. He stabbed the hairpin in her direction.

"I can use this." He set it aside. "But I need something that floats." He dug through his pockets again despite knowing full well they were empty. His eyes locked on the water gourd, and she passed it to him. Jacob yanked the cork out, but instead of taking a sip, he stabbed the cork with the hairpin and rubbed it against the hem of his tunic, slowly building a static charge. She watched him curiously. Her childhood had consisted of learning how to cook and clean, facing giggles from Talia, who had always shown more aptitude for such duties. Khadija remembered Ammi's eyeroll and her huff of frustration every time Khadija burned the daal, followed by Ammi instructing her to scrub the pans—the only thing she seemed incapable of messing up.

Meanwhile, Abba had taught Hassan to read, believing him destined to be a wazir. Hassan had taught her in secret, but Khadija didn't want to learn in secret. What use was learning if she was forced to hide what she knew? It seemed to her the only reason people learned things was to show off how smart they were, like how Hassan had always favored books with long, complex words that showed off his reading prowess. Khadija's throat ached as she felt for the last crinkled page of Hassan's book in the folds of her kameez.

Just like she had wished to be a boy so that she could learn, she wondered how many times Jacob had wished to be a Ghadaean.

After concluding the hairpin was well and truly charged, Jacob reached for the metal pan beside the portable cooking stove and, much to Khadija's annoyance, filled it with water.

"What are you doing?" Khadija attempted to snatch the water gourd. "We can't waste water!"

“I just need a bit,” he whined.

Satisfied he’d wasted enough water, Jacob popped the cork into the pan and studied it intently. Khadija couldn’t help but watch as well.

The cork spun a few turns and settled. Jacob traced the length of the hairpin with his fingertip. “The north-to-south line.”

She struggled to hide a smile. How had he done that? “But which way is which?”

Jacob settled on the mango stone and a twisted nail as his next choice of equipment. He hammered the nail into the mango stone with the butt of the telescope and placed his creation in the center of the deck. Then he marked a notch into the deck where the nail’s shadow ended and settled back on his heels.

Khadija wasn’t sure if it was their similarities in age or the sudden movement as Jacob flicked his fringe out of his eyes that reminded her of Hassan. Had Hassan had a fringe? She racked her brain. How long had his hair been? Had it fallen over his left or his right eye? What had his hair been like? Had it been as poker-straight as Talia’s, or did it fall in loose waves that tangled at the ends like her own? It was one of the harshest realities of losing a loved one. Not just grieving the loss of the person, but the loss of their memory over time. That was a constant grief; every day, his image became blurrier, her memories of him fainter. He would’ve been around Jacob’s age by now, the age where boys start losing the childish roundness of their faces, their limbs stretching out like beanstalks. If he hadn’t . . . She swallowed the tightness in her throat.

Khadija glanced at Jacob’s creation, blinking away the excess moisture. “Is that it?”

“It takes a while.”

After thirty minutes or so, Jacob re-marked the top of the nail’s shadow and joined his two marks together. He traced the direction with his fingertip. "The sun travels from east to west, so that makes *this* way north." Jacob carved an arrow into the deck and tossed the scrap piece of metal away. Satisfied.

Though his efforts were admirable, Khadija wasn't so convinced. "You're assuming the balloon won't spin."

Realization dawned on him. Jacob huffed. "Well, it's better than anything you've come up with!"

She supposed he had a point. At least now they had a sense of direction, albeit somewhat inaccurate, but it was still better than nothing.

"Now what?" she asked.

Jacob shrugged. "Means nothing unless we know where we are and where we're going. We need a map."

Khadija peered over the side of the basket. There was nothing but sky across the horizon. No sighting of civilization. How long could they really stay up here, flying aimlessly?

By late afternoon, they were both sprawled across the deck, passing the water gourd between each other, taking tiny sips.

Jacob growled and rolled over, smearing his sweat across the deck. "It's so hot!"

Really! She hadn't realized. Khadija grunted in agreement.

Jacob staggered to his feet and paced the deck.

"Doing that will only make you hotter. You need to stay still." Her words slurred together.

He plonked himself back on the deck. "Easy for you to say. Your skin doesn't burn like mine does."

It doesn't make me heatproof! Khadija eyed the back of his neck, which was rapidly reddening. She winced. It looked sore. She was lucky her shalwar kameez was loose and thin, shielding most of her skin from the sun.

She closed her eyes, allowing the heat to claim her. Whether she slept, she wasn't sure. By early evening, the sun was hanging so low that the sky had developed a pinkish hue, and it was cool enough for her mind to function. Khadija rose and tended to the fire. Navigating a balloon was a lot like caring for an infant. She slept only in short bursts, feeding the flames every few hours.

Jacob turned her way, his lips cracked with thirst. "So why'd you steal it, Khadija?" he croaked. "Did you think it'd be fun flying a balloon?" His voice was laced with sarcasm.

Heat rushed to her face. "Maybe I stole it for the same reason that you were going to steal it," she snapped. "To escape."

Jacob perked up. He pushed himself onto his elbows. "Escape what?"

Those familiar iron gates surrounding her mind slammed shut, bolts creaking as they were locked, the key tossed away. It was an action that occurred so frequently it functioned of its own accord, powered by a little switch in her head and a trigger-happy finger that was spooked by any remotely personal question. She shrugged. "I don't have to tell you."

He rolled his eyes. "Suit yourself."

They spoke very little after that. Khadija gazed at the setting sun as it tumbled over the horizon. The sky was a blanket of navy with a silver crescent moon that had risen to celebrate the sun's departure. She glanced at Jacob. He was fiddling with his makeshift compass, oblivious to her. She doubted he'd bother her that evening, but still. Abba's words rang in her ears. *He's a boy. He can't be trusted.* Best not give those wandering eyes any excuse to stare.

Khadija rose and rifled through the sacks and crates. Jacob watched her wordlessly. She settled on combining the sack of dried beans with the uncooked rice so that she was left with an empty piece of material. Khadija unpicked the stitches with her nails until the sack unfolded into a large sheet of fabric. She flung the sheet across a horizontal rope above her head and readjusted it so that it split the deck in two like a curtain, shielding her from view.

Khadija stepped back to admire her makeshift privacy curtain. That should work. She stole a glance at Jacob. He wasn't the only one who could make things. Khadija smiled smugly and slipped behind the sheet, settling down on the deck for the night.

10

JACOB

Jacob's dreams that night were plagued with thoughts of William. When he awoke, he felt raw all over, as if he'd had a layer of skin ripped off. He glanced in Khadija's direction, but she was hidden behind her curtain. He could hear the gentle hum of her breathing.

Jacob studied William's amulet, the eye of Bidhukh, tracing his thumb over the emerald stone in the center. He shuddered. Tossing it overboard would be the safest thing to do, but he couldn't bring himself to do it. It was sihr, something he'd always known to be wrong. Evil. But William had given it to him, made him promise to join the Hāreef. He'd said it was the only way. Jacob's body began to boil, a fire starting in his stomach and spreading outward until it reached the tips of his fingers and set his hair ablaze. When Jacob closed his eyes, all he saw was red. William had deserved so much more than the life he'd been handed. Hungry nights spent lying on sunbaked dirt. Forgotten. Abandoned. Jacob shook his head. What kind of a life was that?

It was a life William had been desperate to change. He squeezed the amulet. And now it was up to Jacob to change it—if not William's, then his own, and the lives of countless other hāri. He slipped the amulet back into his pocket. Maybe it was what was needed. Something big, drastic—a huge change, and big changes didn't come easily. He knew that. They required force and commitment, something powerful. Maybe William had been right. Maybe sihr *was* the only way.

It still scared him. The whole idea scared him, but he couldn't float around in the sky with a Ghadaean girl forever, pretending the world below and its problems did not exist. At some point, he'd have to land, and then where would he go? Who would he become?

The Hāreef seemed his only option.

Vera had said to meet the Hāreef in Intalyabad, the home of the northern nawab, in three days' time. She'd said he'd get his revenge. They could use someone like him. Jacob tried to steady his hands, but his fingers still jittered. Big cities weren't the safest of places for hāri. Most hāri chose to stick to the outskirts in little villages and minor settlements where it would be easy to pack up and move if things got rough. Big cities meant more soldiers.

What did he have to lose though? Only his life, as if that had ever been worth anything.

Khadija awoke an hour later. He could see the outline of her shadow silhouetted against the drape as she rose. She tugged down the curtain. "Morning," she whispered.

He grunted in response. There was no use being too friendly to a Ghadaean. They'd be parting ways soon enough. But first, he had to figure out where they were, and how to get the balloon to Intalyabad.

Breakfast consisted of the remaining fruit, which had started to brown in the sun, but it tasted fine. As for the water, Khadija kept that close to her, and whenever he asked for a sip, she watched him like a hawk with her dark eyes, scolding him if he drank too much. He held his tongue. All that effort escaping Munir only to end up serving another Ghadaean!

Not for much longer.

Jacob rifled through the box of navigation equipment. There had to be something in here. Something he'd missed. Jacob tossed a miniature globe covered in tiny numbers and astrological symbols to one side, along with a brass astrolabe and armillary sphere. All devices used to chart the course of the sun, the moon, and the stars—the Ghadaeans' preferred method of navigation. There was something half-hidden at the bottom of the box that he'd overlooked before. He pulled out a burgundy leather tube and shook it. Something rattled inside. It was hollow. Jacob tugged on the end, snapping his fingernails. It wouldn't budge. He wrapped his teeth around it.

"Need any help?" Khadija cocked an eyebrow.

Jacob scoffed and passed her the tube, a smirk prickling his lips. If he couldn't open it, then she surely couldn't. Jacob crossed his arms.

Khadija shoved the tube into the crook of her elbow and yanked the top off in one swift motion. A roll of parchment paper landed on the deck.

Jacob's ears burned. He snatched the paper up and unrolled it, refusing to meet Khadija's eyes. He'd been outmatched by a girl! If William had witnessed that, he wouldn't have let Jacob forget it any time soon. His shoulders dropped. *William.*

It appeared to be a very basic map, scrawled with a piece of charcoal that had left black fingerprints and smudges along the edges of the page.

Khadija's shadow appeared. "A map!" she exclaimed. "Finally some luck!" They studied it in silence, neither appearing to make sense of the loopy scrawl and dotted lines gracing the page.

Jacob huffed. "Not sure it's of much use though." He shoved the map in Khadija's direction.

"Can you read?" Khadija glanced at him.

The most experience Jacob had with words were the neatly labeled jars of colored powders that Munir used to tint the glass different shades. He would study the shape of the letters whenever Munir's back was turned but had failed to master a single word. He shook his head in defeat. He was supposed to arrive in Intalyabad in less than two days, but despite the compass and the map, he still couldn't figure out where they were. He'd never get there in time. Jacob's fringe flopped over his eyes as his head lowered in dismay. Vera had clearly overestimated his abilities.

Khadija traced the map with her fingers. "My brother taught me a few letters." She wasn't much taller than him, but it was the way she held herself that made her appear older, much older than him, though he doubted the age gap was that big. "We're running low on water," she hummed. "Maybe it would be best if we land."

Jacob shook his head, glancing at the expanse of grass below. "Probably not a good idea. There's nothing down there." So far, they had seen no other balloons in the sky. Balloons were a common sight, used not only for trading but in the construction of tall buildings, or tethered to the ground to act as guard posts providing aerial views of a city. They were used in combat, and for celebrations and festivals, where they'd often throw flowers and colored powder to the revelers below. But there had been nothing. Not even the sight of a postal balloon.

Jacob stared at the horizon, words mulling in his head. How to convince her? He would need her help to get to Intalyabad. He shifted uneasily. "Where is it you want to go?"

She shrugged and got to her feet, smoothing the creases from her kameez. "I don't know. I thought about going back home."

He smirked. "You mean the place you ran away from?"

Khadija's mouth parted. He quickly swallowed his remaining laughter, disguising it as a cough. Khadija didn't look convinced. It was easy to forget his place up here. Sometimes he'd catch himself talking normally to her, like they were equals. Like he was a normal person. Then he'd remember who he really was and wish he could steal his words back.

But Khadija only sighed. "You're right. I can't go back."

"Why not?" Jacob tried to mask his curiosity. Why was he so interested in the life of a Ghadaean? Who cared what her struggles were? She surely didn't care about him.

"Well, for starters, I stole this." She gestured at the balloon. "And I disobeyed my abba." She shook her head. "If I ever did go back, they'd probably accuse me of jinn possession and lock me up." She rolled her eyes.

Jacob paled. He'd thought only hāri were accused of meddling with jinn.

She read his expression and frowned. "Thought you were the only ones without freedom, did you?"

Jacob lowered his gaze, focusing on the mango stone with the nail protruding from it, which he'd repositioned in the sunlight. He marked the edge of its shadow. In half an hour the shadow would've moved enough for him to make the second marking. "So don't go back. Go somewhere else. Start a new life." He met her eyes.

Khadija averted her gaze as if uncomfortable with the eye contact. "How?" She threw her arms in the air. "I'm on my own. I have no money and a stolen balloon."

Jacob scratched his chin. "I mean, you don't have to tell people it's stolen."

She chuckled. "Girls aren't meant to fly balloons on their own. They'll know it's stolen."

"Then say you weren't alone. Say you were flying with your husband and he fell overboard."

She burst out laughing. "I guess I could say that," she hummed. "But still, no money." Khadija flashed her empty palms.

Jacob pursed his lips. His next words rolled off the tip of his tongue as easily as if he'd rehearsed them. "Then go somewhere you can make money. A big city. Someplace you can lose yourself in." He studied Khadija's face as she soaked up his words. "You could be whoever you want to be in a place like that."

Her eyes sparkled. Jacob caught himself staring. He had always assumed all Ghadaeans had eyes as black as ink, but in the sunlight he realized Khadija's eyes weren't black, or even brown. They were amber.

"Do you know a place like that?" she whispered softly, as if afraid to break the magic of his words.

Jacob grinned. "I sure do."

Once they'd figured out roughly where they were, and Khadija had sounded out the name *Intalyabad* on the map, they set off in earnest for the city.

The rest of the day and the morning of the following one passed with broken conversations and plenty of awkward silences, but they were sprinkled with a few genuine moments. Jacob had never expected to have much in common with a Ghadaean, and certainly there weren't many things he and Khadija could talk about, save one thing. Balloons. While Jacob had always been interested in the engineering elements of ballooning, Khadija had a more dreamlike fascination, spending most of the time sketching the cloudscape or the silky yellow-and-green skin of the balloon above their heads onto the back of the map, labeling her sketches to depict the balloon's anatomy.

Jacob pointed across the horizon. "Look. We must be getting close."

Hot-air balloons dotted the sky, bearing their colors proudly. There were balloons made of silk and crushed velvet, balloons studded with pearls and feathers, and balloons crumpled on the ground stained with blood and sporting large tears in their seams. Some were landing while others shot up into the air, disappearing across the horizon.

Pastures peppered with fluffy cotton and paddy fields of rice stretched as far as the eye could see. There were olive trees and grape vines climbing up garden trellises, and little birds he'd never seen before soaring up from the bushes.

The Nawab of Intalyabad's copper palace stood in the heart of the city. Its curved domes and tall minarets studded with jewels stretched into the sky, dwarfing everything else around it. The palace sparkled so fiercely in the sunlight it looked ready to catch fire.

Jacob gasped. They'd made it.

11

KHADIJA

A cluster of colorful balloons were up ahead, the nearest embroidered with gold leaf and opals that sparkled in the firelight from the burner so that Khadija was unsure whether it was a balloon or a floating chandelier. She gasped. Never had she seen a balloon as beautiful as this before. Another farther ahead was decorated with peacock feathers that fluttered in the breeze like wings as it sank into a gentle decline beside a balloon that in place of a basket supported a long rowing boat complete with oars that seemed to wave at her. Her eyes zipped left and right, furiously taking it all in and burning the balloons across her memory so that she could paint them later. This moment, right here. She wished it could last forever.

Hāri men yanked on ropes as they guided the deflating balloons to the ground underneath the harsh gaze of soldiers. The sight of their green uniforms and curved swords made her feel sick.

They'd discussed this part in great detail, conjuring a story extravagant enough to convince the soldiers that a Ghadaean girl traveling alone with a hāri boy was nothing out of the ordinary.

Earnest footsteps thudded across the deck. When Khadija lifted her head, Jacob was leaning over the edge, bent at the waist, swinging back and forth as he hungrily drank in the new sights and smells of Intalyabad. Even Khadija had doubted their ability to navigate, and yet somehow, they were here. It made her insides tingle just a little. *See. I can do things.*

"Look. They've got cotton fields and fruit trees. I can even see the bazaar from here. It's huge!" The basket's edge creaked underneath his weight.

She quickly yanked him back. "You'll fall!" she scolded, her eyes refusing to leave him until he had planted both feet firmly on the deck.

"I told you I could find it." Jacob's mouth twitched into something resembling a smile. Khadija was amazed by how it transformed his face. She decided against telling him that, through the night before, she'd dropped the balloon's height to catch the current of air blowing toward the north after discovering they'd been floating, unmoving, for a number of hours.

Jacob turned to her, a sparkle in his eyes. "You could easily start a life here."

She clasped her hands together to stop them from jittering. "I guess." She couldn't deny her nerves. All her life she'd lived confined to her bedroom. What would it be like to be alone in a big city like this? How would she fare? It was exciting and yet terrifying all at once. Khadija took a breath.

I can do this.

Jacob was busy twiddling his thumbs. "I guess we should say goodbye."

She hadn't given much thought to that part, too consumed with what she'd do the second she arrived in Intalyabad. She nodded, unused to long goodbyes. "I guess so."

Jacob grasped a rope and inclined his head. "Good luck."

"And you."

He tugged the rope, and the balloon declined. A whoosh of air tickled the tops of their heads.

"I think we have to land over there." Khadija pointed toward the landing bay, where deflated hot-air balloons were sprawled across the grass like empty carcasses.

The balloon swayed as they brushed the tops of the acacia trees, close enough to snatch at the leaves. Her head swam with a flurry of crickets and chirping cuckoo birds. They neared the landing bay, which had been cleared of trees. The basket grazed the ground, bouncing then striking the ground again. Khadija grabbed a rope to steady herself before they came to a halt beside a group of women in purple lehengas.

Soldiers circled them. Jacob moved closer. Khadija stood tall. Nervousness would only make the soldiers more suspicious. This was going to have to be some performance. She opened her mouth, ready to speak the story they'd rehearsed through the night.

"Show me your flight pass, miss." A soldier with a thick raised scar across his eyebrow gave her a sour look.

She stuttered. What was a flight pass? Jacob looked to her with the same blank expression. Their story had failed to include this part.

Keep calm. Khadija exhaled, refusing eye contact. "Erm . . . my husband fell overboard during the night." She faked a sob. "He had all our documents." She pulled off what she hoped was a convincing tremble of her lower lip.

The soldier tutted. "Fell overboard? My condolences."

The soldier beside him disguised a chuckle with his fist. "He must have been a foolish man. It's a miracle you made it here in one piece." He smirked. "I didn't know women were even capable of flying." The soldiers around them jeered. Heat rose to her face, but she kept her cool. *Don't give them a reaction.*

One of the soldiers pointed at Jacob. Jacob shrank back like the soldier's finger was a loaded weapon. "Unless he didn't fall. Perhaps he was pushed instead."

Khadija stammered. This wasn't good.

The soldiers exchanged grins. "That does make more sense." The soldier leaned in, giving her a whiff of stale tobacco. "Or perhaps you pushed him, miss. Maybe you planned to run away with the hāri."

This wasn't good at all. Khadija stole a breath, focusing on the part of the soldier's eyebrow where the hair no longer grew. Sweat appeared along the back of her neck. "I would never do such a thing."

"Oh, really?" The soldier was clearly enjoying her discomfort. "We'll see about that," he hummed.

Khadija sank her teeth into the insides of her cheek. This was a stupid idea. As if they, a girl and a hāri boy, thought they could simply walk into the city spouting such a ridiculous tale as this!

"Traveling without the necessary documents holds a fine of five hundred gold coins." The soldier clicked his tongue against his front teeth. "And I'm guessing your money went overboard along with your husband."

Khadija clenched her jaw.

The soldier continued. "With the recent terrorist attack on Sahli, the nawab is taking extra precautions to ensure no unauthorized hāri enter Intalyabad." His eyes locked on Jacob. "The boy will have to come with us."

He couldn't be serious?

But he looked it.

Jacob started to tremble. Khadija instinctively stepped in front of him. "And where will you take the hāri?" She wasn't sure why calling Jacob a hāri so blatantly made her feel uncomfortable, but it did. Had she not spent two days in his company, she would have thought nothing of refusing him the privilege of a name and reducing him to the only thing that mattered—the color of his skin—but after sharing a journey together, it didn't feel right just to dehumanize him the second they touched the ground.

"He will be questioned to see if he's working with the Hāreef."

Khadija gulped. She knew what questioning meant. She'd seen enough hāri strung up underneath the hot sun, whip marks crisscrossing their backs. Sometimes, they'd be left there for days until they either confessed to their sins or they rotted in the sunshine. She glanced at Jacob. Would they really do that to a child? Khadija recalled the hāri children in Sahli lying facedown in the dirt. She shuddered. Of course they would. No. She couldn't allow that to happen. Even if it did risk her own freedom, she was the Ghadaean. It was time she flexed the muscles her privilege allowed.

"I can assure you he's not one of them." Khadija clawed at the air for her next words. She was thinking off the top of her head now. "He's a mute—he cannot speak at all. Questioning him would achieve nothing."

The soldier appeared stumped. His brow furrowed, causing his scar to bulge. He gritted his teeth.

She had him. Her face gave nothing away of the pounding of her heart against her ribs, so loud she was certain the soldier could hear it.

Khadija prayed the rumors of soldiers and their laziness would work in her favor. She eyed the copper archway with its border of miniature metal roses crafted from enamel and gold inlay. A steady stream of bodies passed beneath it. All they needed to do was lose themselves in the crowd.

The soldier's eyes narrowed. "There are other ways of determining if he's working with the Hāreef or not," he stated flatly. "You would do well finding a new hāri . . . and a new husband." He snickered. "It would be much simpler for you."

Khadija ground her teeth, eyes darting to the city's entrance. She was in touching distance of Intalyabad, and with that came her new life. Freedom. Something that only featured in her daydreams. Here, she could become the new Khadija, reinvent herself. Become the girl she was supposed to be. Her brow furrowed. But she wasn't quite sure who she was supposed to be. Khadija looked to Jacob. She did know one thing though. She had more integrity than most, even if that did make her foolish. She was no traitor. "I do not want a different hāri."

The soldier's gaze turned icy. "If you aren't willing to give him up, I suppose you'll both have to come with me." He flashed a sickly half smile. Satisfied. He had won. "Put the fire out."

Her breathing hitched. She clamped her mouth shut to disguise the tremor of her jaw. The copper archway sparkled, tempting her with its ebb and flow of people. This was her last chance to slip away.

Khadija exhaled. No. *I can't just abandon him.* She wouldn't even be here if it wasn't for Jacob. *If this is the consequence of loyalty, then so be it.*

She did as instructed. Her eyes met Jacob's. "It's going to be OK," she whispered, and smothered the flames. The balloon crumpled in on itself, and Khadija and Jacob struggled to catch it before it swallowed them. The soldiers made no move to help.

They balled the fabric up, stuffed it beside a barrel, and hopped over the edge of the basket. Jacob leaned toward her. "Should we follow him?"

"We don't have a choice," she mouthed.

Jacob's voice wobbled. "But they'll—"

"Hurry up!" the soldier snapped, and they both fell silent.

Khadija stepped onto the grass. The soldiers sneered at Jacob, laughing as his legs buckled at the ground's lack of motion. Khadija glanced at her balloon. It would probably be the last time she saw it: the balloon that had both liberated her and turned her life upside down. It seemed fitting that she lose it in such unfortunate circumstances when it had entered her life in a stroke of sheer luck to begin with.

They wove through the crowd of balloons, past clusters of wealthy merchants and hāri men unloading heavy barrels and crates. The hāri stared at Jacob only briefly before hurriedly dropping their gaze. Khadija winced at the bruises and burns across their bare backs. Would the soldiers do the same to Jacob? Her chest tightened. What would they do to her?

They followed the soldier and then another, this one with a long beard and curly mustache, up a set of stairs cut into the stone walls. Their walk was shadowed by huge banana leaves. Birds flitted through the trees. All around them was the sweet smell of fruit and the trickle of running water, but Khadija had no time to soak in the beauty—her mind was busy trying to conjure up a story elaborate enough to talk them out of this, but she kept drawing a blank.

They shouldn't have come here. Why had she listened to Jacob?

They could've gone anywhere, in fact, and he had chosen here of all places. She should've known better. Instead, she'd let Jacob's fantasies sway her so that she'd forgotten the danger that revolved around big cities. Khadija barely paid any attention to the colorful pavilions with their geometric tiles, or the streams of Ghadaeans milling through the streets like a flock of angry sheep. Jacob's head flicked from left to right, overwhelmed with the bright colors and vivid smells of Intalyabad. The soldiers took a sharp right into a shaded street where that telltale green flag with its copper sun shimmered in the breeze. The flag of the northern nawab.

They turned and melted into a crowd of old men carrying goats, and ladies draped in pretty dupattas with groups of children trailing behind. The street was a patchwork of colorful garments and silks, wobbly rickshaws pushing through the throngs of people, and gold-studded palanquins dividing the crowds.

Khadija eyed the back of the soldiers' heads. They could try and run away, disappear into the crowd. No. It was too risky.

The street widened into a large square.

"Justice for Sahli!" Pots and pans clanged together, and people stomped their feet.

"We want justice for all of Sahli's victims!"

"How can the nawab justify slaughtering the innocent?"

"Punish those who are actually guilty!"

Khadija stood on her tiptoes. Soldiers circled a group of hāri, prodding them with their spears, herding them away from the crowd, but the hāri weren't deterred.

"We are not part of the Hāreef! We will not be punished for their crimes!"

There must've been over a hundred of them, shouting and waving banners, disowning the Hāreef's crimes. She had never seen hāri act like that before. Drawing attention to themselves, all in a bid to rinse the blood off their hands, as if society would finally accept them if they did. She pitied them. Terrorists or not, they were still hāri, and that in itself was too big a crime.

The soldier scowled. "What do they think this will achieve, hmm? They think we'll forgive them? Let them live for now. Ghadaean women and children died because of them. Sahli was burned to the ground! I say we burn them all!"

Khadija shuddered as bloody images of Sahli flashed across her mind. Many people had died that night, hāri and Ghadaean alike. It was no surprise the nawab was taking action, stifling the hāri even more than before. What was a surprise was this. Protestors. Brave or foolish, she wasn't sure, but it was a sight to behold either way. Until the soldiers grew tired of their antics. Then Khadija didn't wish to witness what punishment awaited them.

She eyed the protestors. Old. Young. Hāri of all description. Khadija was drawn to the odd brown faces dotting the crowd of protestors. She did a double take. There were Ghadaeans among them.

No. That couldn't be right. Surely they had found themselves mixed up among them in all the commotion. They couldn't be supporting the hāri, could they? Was that even allowed? But they were shouting and brandishing banners just like the rest of them. The only thought she could muster was . . . why? Why go to all that trouble for a hopeless cause? Unless they believed fighting for hāri freedom was no longer hopeless.

The soldiers noticed them too and cursed. "Look. Our own kind among them. Traitors!"

The soldier swore. "They call themselves the Wāzeem. Hāri sympathizers. Fighting for equality or something like that." He burst out laughing.

"Equality!" The first soldier guffawed. "Why? A cow and a rat will never be equal, no matter how hard you try. You could feed the cow the same amount as the rat, and watch it starve, or you could feed the rat the same amount as the cow and watch it gorge itself to death. Either way, one of them ends up dying."

Khadija bit her tongue at the soldier's cruel analogy. Racial equality was surely more complex than that, but it would take far more than shouting in the streets for the Wāzeem's voices to be heard. The Wāzeem were just as powerless against the three nawabs as the hāri, never mind the rest of society. How could they expect to change the minds of thousands of people just by shouting?

Both soldiers chuckled. "Of all days to protest, they had to choose the day of the royal wedding." The soldier tightened his grip on his sword. "Anyone gets out of line, I have no qualms with slicing off a few heads."

Khadija paled. They weaved through the crowd. Soldiers circled the protestors, boxing them in, but they made no move to attack—there were too many of them. Ghadaeans spat and shouted slurs from behind the safety of the soldiers, but the protestors overpowered their voices.

"We are the Wāzeem. We want justice for all!"

Jacob lifted his head, eyes lighting up. They shared a look. Khadija reached for his shirtsleeve, gradually slowing her pace, allowing the space between them and the soldiers to grow.

Horns blared and heads turned as a wave of glitter and gold burst through the streets. The soldiers pushed the protestors farther back, but that only made them louder.

Bodies pressed together. Khadija quickly gripped Jacob's hand, afraid to lose him. His palm was sweaty as he squeezed hers in return.

"The Nawab of Intalyabad has returned with his new bride," the soldier mocked from farther away.

"Is that the third or the fourth one now?"

"I've lost count—there's been so many royal weddings."

"He certainly is a lucky man."

An entourage of horses with coats the color of freshwater pearls emerged. Generals with gold pins studded into their giant turbans sat proudly atop their horses, followed by six men balancing a palki across their shoulders. The palki was decorated with red and orange flowers and draped in sheer layers of the finest spider silk. A palki like that could only hold a royal bride.

The crowd flocked closer. Children jumped and gasped, trying to catch a glimpse of the bride. Men followed the palki, dressed in elaborate sherwanis with heavy dhol drums slung across their shoulders as they banged their dagga and tilli sticks against the double-ended drum. Festive music flooded the streets, shattering the gravity of the protest as the crowd erupted into song and dance.

Khadija's cheeks burned. She was embarrassed watching them. Surrounded by all this civil unrest, royalty still had the nerve to parade their wealth, and the Ghadaeans were loving it.

The street burst into applause as a man dripping in gold appeared atop an elephant. He wore a bejeweled crown that refracted the sunlight and dazzled the crowd. A garland of bright orange marigolds hung around his neck and was framed by a salt-and-pepper beard. His appearance screamed overindulgence, not in a gluttonous way, but in the gleam of the thick rings adorning each finger that caught the light when he waved, and in the plump smoothness of his cheeks, which were still stained with the faint yellow of a turmeric mask, no doubt applied the night before. He was a man who clearly had too much of everything.

It was the nawab. Sitting on his decorated elephant with his head so swollen with his power, the nawab was blind to his protestors. The Wāzeem grew louder. Angrier. People started to push and shove. Khadija's arm stretched as Jacob was pulled away from her. She kept her grip strong. She was not going to lose him.

A flash of white caught her eye. Both their heads turned. A pair of white cloaks with their hoods drawn were making their way through the crowd.

Khadija's eyes met Jacob's.

They could only be one thing.

The crowd was ignorant, consumed by the music. The white cloaks pushed their way to the front of the procession. She caught sight of a long box, which they shared the weight of between them.

Something was going to happen. Something very bad. Khadija backed away, pulling Jacob with her. The soldiers hadn't noticed them leaving, distracted by the sight of the nawab as he waved to the crowd, flexing his muscles and twirling his golden talwar, which looked better suited to a mantelpiece than a battlefield.

The terrorists approached.

The soldiers nearest to the nawab were suddenly suspicious and reached for their scimitars.

The box swung back and forth.

The soldiers were alert now, drawing their swords. The terrorists released the box. It landed on its side, and the lid slid off.

Not a box, she realized. A *coffin.*

The crowd paused.

Khadija heard the screams first. The musicians stopped their music, and the nawab's waving hands dropped in midair. Khadija caught the glimpse of a body lying across the ground—a swirl of maggots and flies feasting on its face. A curl of black smoke danced across the ground, morphing into the figure of a man.

They've summoned a jinn! The crowd exploded. Laughter turned to screams. People trampled over one another as they struggled to escape.

"Jinn! It's a jinn!"

A large man bashed into her. Khadija fell to the ground. Jacob's hand slipped from her fingers.

Confused screams engulfed her. "The Hāreef are attacking!" a woman shrieked.

Heavy feet trod on her back. Khadija clawed at people's legs, using their momentum to pull her up. The crowd carried her forward. Then there was the unmistakable sound of glass shattering as more jinn materialized. Snakes. Birds. Cats. Wolves. A jinniya with a long skirt that swirled like coiled smoke was crouched by the corpse next to the man-shaped jinn, black sticky blood dripping down her chin. Khadija heaved and backed away.

Swords slashed, and startled horses whinnied. She saw the nawab topple from his elephant, and then she was sandwiched between the crowd and a building.

A screech that stung the insides of her ears made the crowd swiftly split in two as a cat made of shadow took a swipe with its claws at the nearest ankles. Emerald eyes turned her way. All the air left her lungs as the cat hissed, crouching on its hind legs, readying to pounce.

The jinn sprang forward. Khadija screamed and covered her face as a flash of metal lurched toward the creature and yanked it back midair. She peered through her fingers at the jinn writhing on the ground, a copper whip wrapped around its neck. The jinn disintegrated in a puddle of smoke.

A hand clamped down on her arm and tugged, so hard she thought her shoulder would dislocate. Khadija was too shocked to fight it. The stranger pulled her against the wall and out of danger. Khadija tried to focus on her savior, but her eyes landed instead on the copper whip dangling from their waist.

"Come on." The voice was warm and deep with a pair of dark eyes to match. Khadija could do nothing but follow as the stranger led her through the chaos.

12

JACOB

Jacob crashed into a market stall stacked high with crates of colorful lentils. The flimsy structure buckled beneath the force and soon there was a pileup of twisted limbs. Khadija was pressed against a wall farther away, wedged behind a mess of sweaty bodies and terrified faces.

Jacob's eyes searched for the flash of a white robe or the black swirl of a jinn. The Hāreef were here just like Vera had said. But she had failed to include why. Now it was obvious. They were after the nawab.

Suddenly a hand curled around his arm. Jacob tried to wrangle free. He spun around. The sight of Khadija calmed him, until he saw the tall Ghadaean woman by her side. He tensed.

"Come on!" Khadija yanked him forward.

Then Jacob was being dragged through the crowd like a river reed caught in a flowing stream as they followed the Ghadaean woman. He was pulled down a narrow alley with stained-glass windows that turned the ground below multicolored. Jacob struggled to keep up as they burst through a beaded curtain into a terraced house. Tiny beads smacked against his teeth. Sunlight filtered through the sheer fabric covering the windows, creating a whirl of bright patterns on the ground, and the air was foggy with smoke and the smell of sickly sweet fruits mixed with tobacco. Hookah pipes had been abandoned, their coals still glowing amber. Jacob twisted his hand free of Khadija's and staggered, banging his thigh on a coffee table.

Khadija rounded on the Ghadaean woman. "Who are you?"

She didn't look much older than Khadija, and when she spoke, her voice was deep and smooth like the strum of a sitar's strings. She was dressed head to toe in armor, with a chiffon scarf covering her hair. The thin material looked almost out of place next to the stiff leather she wore, but it was the copper whip coiled around her belt that stole his attention. He'd seen whips like that before, spun from copper thread that could slice a jinn in half, but only ever dangling from the waist of an exorcist. And as far as he knew, only men could be exorcists.

"Trust me, you do not want to be out there right now." She flicked back a curtain drape with her forefinger, and a slice of sunlight spilled into the room, followed by high-pitched screams. Jacob took in the little room with its worn couch that had a deep gash exposing the fluff inside, and the coffee table with mug rings burned into the mahogany wood.

Khadija bristled. "I said, who are you?"

The woman faced her. Jacob noticed Khadija's posture deflate. There was a power behind the other woman's stance that reminded him of reinforced glass.

"I am Anam. And you?"

"Khadija. And this is Jacob," she said warily, waving in his general direction. "Why are we here?"

"Forgive me if I was mistaken, but it looked like you needed help." She gestured to the doorway. "You are of course free to leave."

Khadija gnawed her lip. Jacob's eyes flickered to the door. A beaded curtain at the other end of the room rattled, and a hāri woman appeared.

"Anam. I thought that was you." Her hair was cropped to the scalp. If she was surprised by Jacob and Khadija's presence, she didn't show it. "New recruits?"

Anam shrugged. "Found them in the street."

The woman's lips curled. "That's where the best recruits are." She slumped on the sofa, causing some of the stuffing to pool out. "How did the protest go?"

The back-and-forth exchange between Anam, the Ghadaean woman, and the hāri woman had Jacob's mouth hanging open. They spoke as if they were equals. Friends, even. He'd never seen that before.

"It was going well before the Hāreef arrived. Now it is chaos out there," Anam tutted, flicking the curtain drape back and glancing anxiously out at the street. "The nawab is in grave danger."

The woman shook her head. "I knew the Hāreef's forces were getting stronger, but even I didn't expect them to make an attempt on the nawab's life. Not so blatantly as that."

"Was it an attempt on his life though? Or were they simply trying to scare us—show us how powerful they have become?" Anam mused. "My guess is they wanted a spectacle, and they certainly got one."

Jacob couldn't deny the irritation that prickled his skin as the two conversed without so much as a glance his way. Khadija appeared to be thinking the same as she crossed her arms and huffed. Who were these people? And why did they know so much about the Hāreef?

Jacob cleared his throat. Both heads snapped around.

The hāri woman looked at him properly for the first time. "I'm sorry, the two of you must be confused. I am Myra." She placed a palm to her chest. “And you’ve met Anam. She makes up one third of the Wāzeem’s Council.”

“The best third,” Anam chimed in.

Myra chuckled.

The Wāzeem. Jacob thought back to the protestors he’d glimpsed, the ones shouting about equality. Justice. He’d thought them mad. He still wasn’t sure what to think now.

“You aren’t with the Hāreef?”

Myra’s eyes widened. “God, no!” She pursed her lips. “The Wāzeem want equality. Fairness. A better world for both races. The Hāreef just want violence. Destruction.” She gestured to the window. “Like you witnessed out there. What will all of that achieve, except further brutality against our people? Violence only sparks more violence.”

Jacob fiddled with his shirtsleeve. The Hāreef were about more than just violence, surely. If war was all they wanted, why had Vera bothered to recruit those with talents beyond skills in battle? Like him—though he supposed glassblowing would serve a purpose in containing all her jinn. “And how can you make the world fair?”

Myra smiled. “A good question.” She rose from the couch and beckoned him over. Khadija was still hovering by the doorway like she was seconds away from bolting out the door. “Why don’t we show you?”

Jacob crunched on another samosa. Khadija sat opposite, dusting pastry flakes from her lips. The long table they sat at seemed far too large for the two of them, and never mind the feast laid before them that could feed the belly of every hāri in Sahli, but so far no one had joined them. He’d already piled his plate up twice, and now he was smearing his finger in the leftover raita. Their eyes met briefly, and Khadija dropped her gaze. He could feel the awkwardness between them, as if neither had expected their time together to extend beyond reaching Intalyabad. He didn't have to be here, of course. He could leave.

And go where? The sky was darkening. The screams from outside had quieted so that the only sound was the clatter of soldiers as they trampled through the streets in search of those responsible for ruining the nawab's wedding day.

Khadija scrunched her nose. "What do you think about the Wāzeem?"

What did he think about a group of Ghadaeans and hāri working together? It would have sounded ridiculous if he hadn't seen it for himself. The Wāzeem didn't seem real. Like at any moment the charade would shatter and they'd turn on one another. Anam and Myra had led them through their network of terraced houses, where members of the Wāzeem slumped in beds or pored over maps or practiced swinging mugdar clubs at targets. There was an even mix of both races, and they seemed to get on under Anam's instruction. Two other Ghadaeans, she explained, made up a trio called the Council, which led the Wāzeem. One leader each from the three provinces of Ghadaea. Anam represented the north. The other two, both men, the eastern jungles and the western desert.

It sounded unreal, laughable, and yet he couldn't deny the small spark that flickered beneath his skin at the thought of it.

"I never realized there were Ghadaeans that opposed the treatment of your people." Khadija's gaze wasn't fixed on him but instead staring at the space above his head, as if a world where his people weren't so violently mistreated was playing before her eyes. "I think it's a nice idea," she hummed.

Nice idea. He scoffed. Breakfast in bed was a nice idea. A cool bath at the end of a hot day was a nice idea, but reducing the struggles of his people to something mundane, something that could easily be fixed with simply a *nice idea*. He could've slapped her. "I'm sure it sounds *nice* to you." His words were brittle. "How my people are treated doesn't affect you in any way, but for me, this"—he gestured to the empty room—"this is like a tease. A way of saying we know it's bad how hāri are treated, and we want to help, but we're only willing to help a little bit, not enough to inconvenience ourselves. Not enough to actually change anything," he spat.

Khadija bristled at his tone. "Is that what you really think?" She sounded wounded more than anything. Jacob's anger melted into bitter remorse.

Anam's approach put an end to their conversation as she sat on the bench next to Khadija, biting the corner off a samosa. "We have beds if you would like to rest." She dipped her samosa in the mint chutney. Jacob couldn't help but study her. She was out of her armor now, plainly dressed, her wrists free of jewelry or adornments, and yet there was a regal air about her. Whether it was because of her manner of speaking or the way she sat poised on the bench, back perfectly straight, shoulders square, he wasn't sure. Jacob's eyes were drawn again to the copper whip at her waist. Was she a warrior? A killer. Did she kill on the Wāzeem's behalf? She'd made it very clear earlier that the Wāzeem were peaceful, exercising nonviolent protests and negotiating with Ghadaean leaders to get their point across. Jacob had tried to ask what progress they'd made so far, but she had cleverly evaded his question.

In short, it meant nothing. Of course it did. Why would the nawabs listen to a group of protestors? Their voices held no real weight, even with a few Ghadaeans backing them, so how could they really expect to change society? They seemed hopefully delusional to him, and though he wished he could believe in their cause, he couldn't. William would have laughed in their faces if he were here.

Jacob balled his hands into fists under the table.

"Yes. I would like to rest." Khadija rose, refusing to meet his eye. Anam led her into an adjoining room and returned a few minutes later.

"The men rest in the room opposite." She pointed to a closed door.

Jacob nodded, something inside him fluttering at being called a man.

"You are not from Intalyabad." She said it like it was a fact and not a question.

Was it that obvious?

"If you were from here, you would have left by now. The fact that you have stayed means you have nowhere else to go."

Jacob's jaw clicked. "Do you want me to go?"

"Not at all," Anam said without meeting his gaze as she selected another samosa. "What do you think about us, now that you have heard our cause?"

"I think you severely underestimate how much Ghadaeans hate us."

Anam smirked. "I understand why you would think that."

When Jacob scoffed, Anam's thick eyebrows rose. "You think us naive?"

"I think I'm just a bit confused why you would even care about us being treated equal. How does it benefit you? Do you get paid to do this or something?" Even Jacob was surprised by the brashness with which he spoke. A few days ago, he wouldn't have dared speak to a Ghadaean with that much heat behind his words. Whether it was the time he'd spent with Khadija, or witnessing William hacked down before his eyes, he found his tongue no longer clogged in his throat like it used to when in the presence of a Ghadaean.

"No, I do not get paid. If anything, I have sacrificed more by being here."

"Then why do it?"

"It is what's right."

Jacob wasn't sure he bought it. Everything came at a price. Kindness was not free. Why would she disrupt her otherwise normal life, make it harder, all for a group of people who weren't even hers?

Anam seemed to read the thoughts as they crossed his face. "And I love my country. I love my city. I have seen what this racial tension is doing to my home. The increase in violence on both sides. I do not like it."

He wondered what it felt like to have such a fierce pride toward a location. Jacob had lived all his life in Sahli and yet it did not feel like home. Even watching it burn to the ground, it was only a cluster of buildings at the end of the day. Intalyabad was magnificent of course, beautiful, but it too was only a selection of wonderfully crafted buildings.

"Do the protests actually do anything?"

Anam pondered his question. "To an extent. More soldiers deployed to manage our protests means less on the streets to terrorize innocent hāri like yourself."

"And what else?"

"How about this . . ." Anam leaned in. "We have another protest scheduled for tomorrow at the temple where the nawab usually conducts his morning prayer. You should come. You will see firsthand how effective our protests can be."

Jacob shrugged. "I don't know."

"There is nothing to fear. You will be perfectly safe, and even if you do not believe wholeheartedly in our cause, at least do it to see more of this wondrous city. The temple is quite beautiful, and the rose gardens are exquisite."

Jacob perked up. *Rose gardens.* Could they be the same gardens where Vera had instructed him to meet her? It had been three days since then, which meant it was tonight that they were supposed to meet. Jacob brushed his fingers over William's amulet in his pocket. "Is the temple far?" He tried to make his voice sound as nonchalant as possible.

It seemed to convince Anam. "Not far at all." She rose and drew the curtain drape, pointing at a structure which, in the dark, was only the faint outline of a curved dome surrounded by minarets. "Just there. We leave early though."

Jacob chewed his lip. "I'll probably rest now. You know, so I'm up early."

Anam nodded. "That is a wise decision."

Jacob swiftly traversed the room to the door where the men slept. The soft hum of snores greeted him. There were five beds, only two occupied. Jacob chanced a look at Anam, who gave him an encouraging nod before the door clicked shut. His eyes fell to the open window and the flutter of the curtain. He pulled it back to reveal a trellis with climbing flowers hugging the stone wall.

Fifteen minutes later, and after a lot of stifled curses, Jacob was stepping off the trellis and into the quiet street. He kept the temple's dome always in his sight as he turned down a series of dimly lit streets. The distant shouts of soldiers sped him on. He stuck to the shadows until the temple came into view, surrounded by manicured gardens topped with orchids and beds of thorned roses. Jacob jumped the low wall and scanned the gardens.

His breath came in a short, shaky puff. The Wāzeem couldn't give him the change his people desperately needed, but perhaps Vera could. Though he still had his reservations about her use of jinn, she stood a far better chance at evoking real change than a group of Ghadaean outcasts and a poorly organized protest.

His feet padded on the soft grass as Jacob delved deeper into the garden, startling at every flicker of a shadow, every creak of a tree branch waving in the evening breeze, until he saw a telltale white cloak and something else, something that made his heart stick in his throat like toffee.

Jacob stumbled backward.

Two heads snapped up, their whispers dying on the breeze.

"Well, who do we have here? An eavesdropper." It was Vera. He could tell by the bloodred strand of hair escaping her hood.

"I do not like eavesdroppers," the figure beside her rasped. Its voice was like charred cinders and the crackle of flames.

Jacob gulped, his feet tingling, urging him to run. "No." He stood his ground. "I'm not an eavesdropper." Jacob stepped into the silver cast of the moon. "It's me. Jacob. You asked me to come here."

A flash of recognition spread across Vera's face. "Jacob," she breathed. "You came. I knew you would."

The figure beside her grunted. "You think this child can be of use to us?"

Jacob's eyes flickered to the face of the man by her side, only it wasn't quite a face. It was a face carved from smoke attached to a thick neck with two ram's horns protruding from its head. He stood over a foot taller than Vera, shrouded in armor that was white hot—the piercing white of a poker left in a furnace to turn bright red before its edges shone a brilliant white with heat. His armor looked hot enough to scald with a single touch. His eyes were not the vibrant green of a jinn's but the deep orange of hungry flames. This was no man at all. This was a creature far worse than any jinn he'd ever seen.

Jacob bit his tongue as he fought the urge to scream.

"He is a very talented child, Sakhr." Vera's teeth shone like pearls in the dark. "If what I hear is true, he can craft a vessel of glass to keep even a shaitan like yourself contained."

A shaitan was a demonic spirit and a creature of Hell, far more powerful than a jinn. Jacob's eyes flickered to the horns protruding from Sakhr's scalp, thick enough to gouge his eyes out with a single blow. He shuddered. Jinn was one thing, but demons! What had he gotten himself into?

Sakhr scowled. "Nonsense! I am far too superior to be trapped in mere glass." His hand rested on a blade the length of Jacob's leg, simmering with a fiery-red heat that bled into a white-hot tip. "I will slice off the head of any human that tries to contain me."

Jacob dug his nails into his palms. He shouldn't have come here.

"Easy, Sakhr." Vera chuckled. "Let's hear what the boy has to say." She faced him. "The fact that you have come here means we want the same thing. Change. To undo all the wrongs that have been done." Her beautiful face distorted into something ugly. "Your friend William."

Jacob's skin burned at the mention of his name.

"There are so many like him. So many have suffered at their hands." Her voice had a serrated edge. "These things. These tragedies. They end now." Vera's words ignited something in Jacob, a flame that couldn't be extinguished. A heat that fired up his limbs, made his blood rush, his muscles pump. It was a warmth that seeped into his very bones and refused to cool down. Jacob realized it was *hope*—something he hadn't allowed himself to feel for years. Vera had given him hope.

"How?" he whispered. "How will they end?"

Vera beamed. "It will become clear soon enough, but first, I want to tell you a story." She nudged him playfully. "You're not too old for stories, are you?"

He shrugged, suddenly forgetting how to use his own tongue. *Say something. Idiot!*

Vera smiled. "Good. This story doesn't have a happy beginning, or a particularly pleasant middle, but the end has yet to be written. Maybe, with your help, we can make it a good one.

"I started out life like most hāri. Poor. Afraid." Her words were like acid. "I never knew my father, but I remember my mother well. She was a selfless woman. Kind. Loving. Even when we had nothing she still found a way to share it with me. I watched her die." Her voice caused the roses to curl in on themselves. Jacob didn't dare breathe.

"The sacrifices she made for me right up until her death, I will always be grateful for. She taught me how to hide my skin, how to keep my eyes down so that I could live among the Ghadaeans. I lived like that for years, hiding, scavenging what I could. I promised myself I'd never bring a child into this world. No child should be forced to live that kind of life." Vera's eyes grew glassy with moisture. "But sometimes things don't always go the way you think they're going to.

"When I had my son, everything changed. Life wasn't just about survival anymore. It was so much more than that. Being a mother taught me what it meant to walk around with your heart beating outside of your body." She thumped her chest. "Seventeen years I managed to keep him, my heart, safe. And then one day, my heart stopped beating." Her hand dropped to her side.

Jacob swallowed, consumed by her words.

"They beat him." She snarled. "They beat him to within an inch of death . . . and then they burned him." Her voice cracked. "I watched my only son go up in flames."

Images of Vera's son ablaze danced across Jacob's vision. So cruel. So heartless. His insides began to bubble and boil. Not even an animal deserved to be treated in such a way. But he was no fool to think that these things didn't happen.

"That day changed me. It taught me that it's no use having anything good in this world when it can simply be snatched away." Her hand closed around thin air. "That's when I began practicing sihr.

"Even I was scared at first. We've been spoon-fed stories of forbidden magic and jinn. The number of hāri who have been accused of necromancy or witchcraft and burned to death made me so sure that I'd get caught." The flames from the distant oil lamps flickered across Vera's face. "But I didn't get caught. I found the jinniya Queen Bidhukh instead, and if it's one thing she hates, it's the plight of those who are misunderstood. After all, she is the daughter of Iblis—perhaps Bidhukh is the most misunderstood jinniya queen of them all."

Jacob reeled. Iblis was the angel who was cast out of Heaven for refusing to bow to man, claiming humans were made of but simple clay and were inferior to his divine being. He was burned for his rebellion and became the creator of Hell. Iblis commanded the undead and all demonic creatures, like the shaitan before him. Most jinn chose to follow him too—though jinn were neither inherently good nor evil, their loyalty was easily bought with spilled blood, which Iblis had in no short supply. Queen Bidhukh, the jinniya that the Hāreef held so dear, was his daughter. Jacob wasn't sure what to do with this information.

"With her help we will finally undo all these wrongs."

Sakhr spoke then. "And in exchange, you will do as the queen wishes." His words held the hint of a threat that had Vera furiously nodding in agreement.

"Of course!" She dipped her head. "I will always be a loyal subject of the queen."

"You are wise . . . for a human," Sakhr sneered.

Jacob's eyes darted between Vera and Sakhr. Could he trust a demon? Vera seemed to. Vera's son, just like William, had lost his life far too soon. He'd lost it for no reason. He'd lost it because he was hāri, and just like him, Jacob would lose his life too if he wasn't careful. Something needed to change, and Vera was giving him that chance. He pictured himself shedding his old life, like a snake discarding its skin. He could become something new. Something worthy of a better future.

Jacob stole a glance at Sakhr again. But would he really side with a demon?

Maybe it didn't matter either way. Maybe there were more demons spilling hāri blood right now than all the shaitan in Hell.

He nodded. "I understand."

Vera's eyes sparkled. Her clap was muffled by her white gloves. "You are a smart boy. That's why there is something you can do, actually. For me. And when you've completed this task, you will be part of the Hāreef."

"Me?" Jacob stuttered. His mind was suddenly blank, the only coherent thought he could string together being that this was what William had wanted of him. He had promised.

She opened her arms wide, like a flower embracing the sunshine. "Oh yes, but first I need to know I can trust you. The last thing I want is your talents going to waste." Her face twisted. "You know, there are some hāri out there who have sided with the Ghadaeans! Our own kind have betrayed us by joining them to fight against us. They call themselves the Wāzeem."

Jacob's mouth turned dry.

Vera frowned. "Little do they know the Ghadaeans are only using them to do their dirty work. They'll kill them the first chance they get." She fixed her eyes on him. "But I know you're not stupid enough to do that, are you?"

He certainly wasn't stupid. Anyone who knew him well enough knew Jacob prided himself on how much he knew. Even Munir couldn't argue that he wasn't clever, even if he *had* tried to throw him in the furnace. Jacob shook his head, his fringe flipping from side to side. Something had seemed off about the Wāzeem right from the start, and he clearly wasn't the only one who thought that.

His agreement earned him a smile from Vera. "Can I trust you, Jacob?"

"Yes."

Vera enveloped him in a hug. "Then welcome to the family."

13

KHADIJA

Khadija missed the last rung of the trellis. There was a moment where she hung, suspended, before she collapsed to the ground in a heap. She quickly righted herself and hurried off in the direction she'd watched Jacob disappear down from the window. A part of her felt silly running after a boy in the dark. If he wanted to leave, then he could. There was nothing stopping him. No obligation that he had to stay with her at all, and yet she couldn't deny the sting his absence left to her pride. Was she not even worthy of a goodbye? After all she had done for him, was their friendship, as fragile as it seemed, not worth at least a brief farewell?

His earlier words chewed at the corners of her mind. *How my people are treated doesn't affect you in any way.* It caused her skin to itch, as if her clothing were made of sandpaper; the more she dwelled on his words the more uncomfortable she felt, and that only made her guiltier. She'd hated the hāri nearly as much as Abba had, but there was only so much hatred she could feel before her insides were scorched and her mind numb from the heat. So she'd avoided thinking about them, and that had served her well. How hāri were treated did not affect her life . . . until now.

But with Jacob, things were different. There was no revulsion crackling in the back of her throat, no stone-cold indifference masking her face. She wasn't sure what to call it, only that it was something she could no longer willfully ignore.

Khadija darted down the stone path. In the dark, all the streets looked the same, oil lamps sending shadows dancing up the sides of buildings. The chink of metal up ahead made her dash behind a low garden wall, crouching down just as a trio of soldiers appeared, the smell of liquor clinging to their uniforms. Her breathing hitched. This was ridiculous! She should go back. Nothing good could come of a girl wandering an unfamiliar city in the dark.

Khadija glanced down the street where Jacob's little figure had been only moments before. Her curiosity got the better of her. She rose.

"Bit late for a walk, miss."

Khadija jumped out of her skin.

The nearest soldier sneered, while the other two were wobbling farther back as they supported each other with shaky legs.

"Are you lost?" A slow grin spread across the soldier's face. "Where do you live?" His words were a jumbled slur.

Khadija backed away, her skin already prickling. Fear pooled in her stomach. Her eyes darted to the men's hands, the twitch of their fingers, the hungry sparkle of their eyes, and the lewd smirks on their faces. Cold dread trickled down her spine.

"I'm not lost." Her voice cut off at the end like she'd run out of air. She sucked in a breath, trying to slow the pounding of her heart.

The soldier took another step. "No." He paused. "You look like you're running away."

Khadija could already feel phantom hands clawing at her skin. She flinched.

"Perhaps I can help."

"I'm fine." Her words were so faint even she could barely hear them. Khadija cleared her throat. "I'm fine," she said again.

"Are you sure?"

"She said she's fine." A voice from the shadows made everyone's heads whirl around.

The soldier's hand shot to his talwar. "Who's there?"

Footsteps padded on the pebbled walkway. Khadija could just make out the outline of a figure, but nothing more.

"I said." The soldier drew his sword, and his two drunken companions followed suit. "Who's there?"

The figure stepped into the light. The orange glow from a lantern lit up his milky-white skin, and a pale glimpse was all it took for the soldiers to pounce. The figure twirled, pulling out a blade, a simple dagger half the length of the soldiers' talwars.

But the soldiers were drunk and clumsy, and the hāri swiftly had the first two on the ground in a tangle of legs.

The soldier roared. "Dirty scum!"

Metal clanged like the chime of a gong. The hāri staggered, then spun out of reach as the soldier's blade lanced through the air. Khadija studied the soldier's footwork, his lack of balance, waiting for the right moment when, in his fury to strike the hāri, he'd plant his feet poorly.

Khadija pushed. The soldier went down easily, his head smacking against the cobbles.

For a second, she and the hāri simply stared, their ragged breathing filling the night air. Seconds passed. The soldier refused to move.

The hāri faced her. "If you're running away, then I'd do it now."

Khadija didn't need telling. She ran.

Back down the street, she clambered up the trellis and through the open window, sinking to the floor in a fit of jittering. She squeezed her eyes shut, the image of the hāri etched across the back of her eyes. How long she stayed like that she wasn't sure. It was only when her limbs became heavy with sleep that she dragged herself into the nearest bed and flopped down on the mattress before her world turned a welcoming black.

Khadija awoke to the creak of floorboards and the soft puffs of controlled breaths. Her eyelashes fluttered open. It was morning now, amber rays slicing through the window and splitting the room in half. All the other beds were made. She rolled over.

"Sorry, did I wake you?" Anam was perched on one leg, palms pressed together above her head in a perfectly balanced tree pose. "I cannot start the day without yoga."

Khadija rubbed the sleep from her eyes, memories of the night before flooding back. She shot up. "Is Jacob still here?"

"In the other room." Anam exhaled and transitioned into warrior pose.

So, he didn't run away after all, Khadija thought, but the knowledge left more questions than answers about the real reason why he had sneaked out last night.

"We will be leaving for the protest soon. You may come with us, if you like. Jacob is."

Khadija rubbed her elbows, suddenly cold. She had no desire for any more run-ins with soldiers today. Not after last night. Her mind couldn't help but wander back to the hāri. Why had he helped her? The more time she spent in Intalyabad, the more confused she was. Back in Qasrah, hāri and Ghadaeans very rarely mixed. Their homes were segregated; they shopped in different markets and walked the streets at different times of day. But here, the Wāzeem lived among each other, though she doubted the rest of the city did similar. She still wasn't sure what to make of it. It sounded moral, selfless, righteous . . . in theory. But was it realistic, and more important, was it actually making a difference?

"I think I'll stay here."

Anam's chest deflated in a long steady stream. "Are you sure? We might not be back for a while. You will be here on your own."

"I don't mind being on my own." It would give her a chance to figure out her next move. She was stuck in Intalyabad now. Maybe she could look for work, find somewhere else to stay that wasn't with a group of illicit people. She could even see what had become of her balloon.

"Suit yourself." Anam rolled up her reed mat, swirled her long plait into a bun, and tied her headscarf. "Come eat with us." Then she left.

Khadija rose. She'd slept in her scarf, and pins were digging into her scalp. Khadija retied it, then smoothed out the crumples of her kameez before following Anam.

The long table she'd eaten at the night before was now brimming with hāri and Ghadaeans, men and women, old and young. She spotted Jacob perched on the edge of the bench nibbling on salted pistachios. It took all her restraint to prevent herself marching over and aiming a kick at his shins bobbing under the table. Their eyes met. Khadija slipped down beside him. Anam pulled up a stool and reached for a pitcher of thick, frothy lassi.

"Sleep well?" Anam turned to Jacob.

He nodded.

Khadija stifled her snort, and then her stomach growled as she spotted homemade halwa puri. She dug in, reaching for seconds, and thirds. It had been too long since she'd had a home-cooked breakfast like this. She and Abba usually rose at different times, helping themselves to the kitchen and eating alone. Ammi had been the one to cook breakfast, usually rising at dawn to prepare a spread of dishes that gradually enticed each member of the family downstairs one by one as the smell of semolina steeped in buttery sugar syrup and the sizzle of frying puri filled the house.

"We will be leaving shortly." Anam nudged Jacob. "Make sure you are wearing something easy to run in. No valuables. Nothing that could identify you in case it is dropped."

Jacob shrugged. "I don't have anything valuable anyway." But Khadija noticed his hand hover over his trouser pocket.

Myra appeared at the other end of the room and beckoned Anam over.

"Excuse me." Anam pressed a napkin to her lips and rose.

Khadija could feel Jacob staring at her. Once Anam was out of earshot, she rounded on him. "Where did you go last night?"

Jacob fumbled, the beginnings of a denial fresh on the tip of his tongue.

"Don't lie! I saw you climb out the window."

"Just . . . went for a walk." He sipped his lassi, leaving a frothy ring on his upper lip.

She didn't buy it. Not even for a moment. "At night? In a city you've never been to before? And after the attempt on the nawab's life yesterday?" Her voice became shrill. "Are you stupid?!"

Jacob slammed his glass down. The conversation at the table died.

"I don't have to explain myself to you," he hissed. "We're not family." His voice lowered. "We're not even friends."

That remark was like something sharp sliding between her shoulder blades. Khadija stiffened. No. They weren't family, though she felt there were similarities between Hassan and Jacob that had her unconsciously slipping back into the role of a big sister—a role that had lain dormant for so long it physically ached. Jacob was right. As for being friends, clearly they weren't that either.

Khadija sighed. "Fine. Whatever."

She waited for the eyes to stop staring and the conversations to pick up around them before she asked, "Why are you going to the protest?"

"I want to see what it's like."

"It'll be dangerous."

Jacob rolled his eyes. "Everything's dangerous for people like me."

Khadija didn't know what to say to that.

"I didn't expect you to come anyway." His voice had a sharpness she wasn't used to. "The Wāzeem are protesting for hāri rights. Not something that has ever really concerned you, is it?"

His words were a slap to the face. Khadija bristled. Why was he so bitter all of a sudden?

"Of course it has." But even as she said the words aloud she knew it to be a lie. Jacob was right. The troubles of hāri people had never been of much concern to her. Maybe they should be. "You know what." She set her glass down a bit too forcefully so that the cutlery rattled. "I'm coming."

"Don't bother." Jacob pushed his plate away. "You're not proving anything by coming."

Khadija gritted her teeth. Had he forgotten the days they'd spent in the air together? How about all she'd risked with the soldiers when they'd arrived in Intalyabad? She could have easily left him to deal with them alone but she hadn't. And he wasn't even grateful.

"I'm coming," she repeated more sternly.

Jacob's brow creased with frustration. "I'd prefer it if you didn't."

"And I'd prefer it if you didn't tell me what to do," she snapped back.

Anam soon returned, and then they were preparing to leave. It was amazing what a change of clothes and a splash of cold water to her face could do for her mood. The women's room was a whirl of activity as hāri and Ghadaean women twirled around each other in a bid to get ready. Khadija couldn't help but study them, searching for a similar trait that they all shared, but there was nothing. They were all as different as could be, and yet they had found something to unite them. A common purpose.

The door creaked as Anam entered, and Khadija noticed something in the room shift. Most of the women carried on as normal, save two Ghadaeans who were still dressing. They hurriedly ducked down, dressing swiftly while crouched behind their beds so that they were mostly hidden from view. Khadija noticed another woman act similarly, quickly throwing on her scarf and tying it without waiting for the little square mirror balanced on the dresser to be free. The three women left just as Anam perched on the end of a bed to change her shoes, her jaw set at a stiff angle. Khadija noticed her tug on the laces a bit too forcefully.

"Ready?" Anam's tone was clipped, not the pleasant hum Khadija was becoming used to.

Khadija nodded. She thought about questioning the other women's behavior, but wasn't even sure how to word it. She certainly didn't want to overstep, so instead she said, "I can imagine it must make some people nervous, getting ready for a protest."

Anam jeered. "Nervous? No. *You* are nervous. They were just disgusted."

Khadija startled. She hadn't expected Anam to openly admit to noticing the women's harsh gazes, but already in the short time she'd known her, Khadija had gotten the impression that Anam had a bluntness about her. She was honest, perhaps too honest in saying exactly how she felt. Khadija liked it.

"Do you not get on with the other women?"

"Most of them do not mind." Anam sighed. "Of course there are always the ones who do. I suppose my presence still makes them uncomfortable."

Khadija's brow creased.

Anam caught the confusion on her face and let out a single laugh, but it was sharp and tuneless. "There is something bittersweet about meeting new people like you." Anam smiled, though it was more a sad upturning of her lips. "It is comforting knowing that your first impression of me is of a normal woman." She paused. "But it is often soon followed by the . . . shall we say, *not*-so-comfortable feeling of having to explain myself."

She sounded exhausted, like it was a line she had repeated so many times to so many new faces that the words were now thick and heavy, stuck in her throat.

Khadija stopped her before she could continue. "You don't have to explain anything to me." She squeezed her arm reassuringly. "You have been kind and welcoming to me, and that is my first impression of you. You certainly don't make me feel uncomfortable."

Anam's eyes sparkled. "Thank you, Khadija." Her gaze flickered to the door. The room had emptied long ago. "We should go."

The Wāzeem left in clusters of twos and threes, turning off in different directions so as not to arouse suspicion. Khadija watched Jacob and two other hāri men disappear down the street. Ghadaean and hāri members roamed the streets separately before reuniting as a group at the temple where the protest was to be. There was nothing more suspicious than hāri and Ghadaeans walking the streets together.

Anam motioned for Khadija to follow, and together they stepped into the morning sunshine. The temple was up ahead, glittering in the sunlight like it was covered in fresh rain. Anam kept a swift pace, turning down streets as if she could walk the city blindfolded, all the while gesturing to various buildings as she admired the architecture, or pointing out the best shops to purchase clothes or where the top bargains could be found. Pride leaked out of her voice. It was clear Anam loved her city.

"Have you always lived in Intalyabad?"

"Only for the past year, since I joined the Wāzeem. I am from Daevala originally."

The seaside capital of the eastern province. "Daevala must be beautiful."

"Oh, it is, but even the most beautiful cities can become ugly when filled with the wrong sort of people."

"Is that why you left?"

"Partly." Anam dipped down an alley. "And to escape my family. They were, shall we say, displeased when they realized I would not fit into the mold they had been trying to stuff me into."

Khadija knew exactly how that felt. Being yanked and pulled, squished into a shape that her body refused to fit into until eventually all she could do was shatter. "I left my family too." She chewed her lip. "Although with everything that's happened since then, I'm not sure I made the right decision." It felt good talking to someone about this. Anam was easy to open up to. There was nothing judgmental about her gaze, just pure, unadulterated honesty.

Anam nodded. "I doubted my decision too at the start. Wondering whether it would have been easier to stay and go along with all their theatrics." She threw her arms in the air. "But I could not. I physically could not. It was like being forced to hold my breath underwater. No matter how long I remained under, I could not help but come back up for air."

Anam had succinctly put into words exactly how it felt to be locked in her bedroom all day, gazing at the hot-air balloons from afar. It had felt like drowning.

The Wāzeem were regrouping at the bottom of the temple's bronze stairway. Khadija's village had contained temples with separate areas for men and women to pray, although none had been as extravagant as this. It was beautiful, and yet it confused her. Did one really need to be surrounded by such finery to pray?

Khadija scanned the crowd for Jacob. Soldiers were positioned at the main entrance. Her chest tightened.

"The nawab is inside. When he emerges, our protest will begin."

"I'm surprised he left the palace today," she said. "After yesterday."

"Nothing comes between the nawab and prayer. Even an attempt at his life," Anam responded. "If you stay in the middle of the group, you will be fine."

Khadija stretched onto her tiptoes, trying to catch sight of Jacob.

There were about fifty of them, all pressed tightly together. Excited whispers spread up and down the group like a hot breeze. Everyone seemed to tingle with electricity. It was contagious. Her earlier fears melted into the ground.

Soon the temple doors opened, and a flash of gold appeared. Then the Wāzeem came alive.

"Hatred breeds violence!"

"Hāri are people too."

"Actions not appearance determine guilt!"

Voices fought over one another. Anam's voice boomed beside her. The Wāzeem were shouting unrestrained, whatever they felt like saying, whatever came to mind. Khadija wanted to scream too, but she wasn't sure what to say. What could she say about hāri mistreatment? Did she even have the right to scream about it when she had never cared, never really questioned it before? She thought back to Sahli and the atrocities she'd witnessed there. It was more a repulsion to the violence rather than the rage of injustice that filled her, but she allowed the feeling to sweep her up. She thought about Jacob, how despite their differences they had managed to find something up in the balloon that they both shared. Their desire for freedom had prevailed over everything else that drove them apart. She clung on to that, allowed it to fill her lungs, until she was inflated, bursting like a balloon. She screamed.

Everything poured out at once, a jumbled mess of words that didn't make any sense, but the feeling it gave her was exactly how Anam had described it. It was coming up for air after years spent below the water.

The soldiers herded the group back to make way for the nawab. Bodies pressed against her from all sides. That's when Khadija caught the familiar glisten of blond hair slipping away from the crowd toward the rose gardens. She jumped for a better view.

Jacob.

Khadija called for him, but her words were swallowed by the noise. She pushed through the mess of bodies and limbs. Every time she moved, the crowd grew tighter.

Something black overhead caught her eye. She glanced up just as a swarm of crows shot into the sky. Only they weren't just crows—and the shouts that were quickly transforming to screams weren't just ordinary screams.

Khadija's stomach plummeted. It was happening again.

The crowd swiftly dispersed all at once. Khadija stumbled forward as crows with emerald eyes burst through the rose gardens.

Soldiers stabbed the air with their spears, but they passed uselessly through the jinn. A bird flew past. Khadija covered her head as the creature flew over, a swirl of smoke and charred feathers.

"Khadija!" Anam seized her arm. "It is the Hāreef. We have to run."

She glanced at the rose garden again, praying Jacob would appear from the bushes. A flurry of white made her head spin around just as a figure tackled the nawab. The crows surrounded the pair, warding off the soldiers with a snap of their beaks.

"They have captured the nawab!" Anam uncoiled her copper whip and lashed at the nearest crow. It erupted in a puff of feathers. "Follow me." She tore a path through the crowd, and Khadija made to follow when a hand tugged her in the opposite direction. She tried to yank herself free until she glimpsed a familiar face. Jacob. Then she was running with him.

14

JACOB

Jacob dragged Khadija through the rose gardens. He had to get her out of there. Drop her somewhere safe. Jinn cawed overhead, and his stomach soured with sickness at what he'd done. But it had been easy. Vera had left the vials for him concealed beneath a rosebush, now littered with glass and crushed petals where he'd trampled them beneath his boots. His fist closed around William's amulet. All it had taken was a glimpse of it, and at his command the jinn had swiftly turned their attention to the protestors.

Khadija puffed beside him, but she followed without restraint. The gate at the other end of the gardens was in sight. He could leave her there, tell her to run, then go back.

That was until a familiar white cloak with a streak of red hair escaping from its hood appeared at the exit.

Jacob skidded.

Khadija yanked him back. "It's them."

A flash of copper skin and glittery gold appeared beside Vera. The nawab.

Jacob's heart was in his throat. He pushed Khadija back. "Go the other way."

She tried to pull him with her but he shoved her off.

"Come on, Jacob!"

Jacob glanced at Vera again. He caught the gleam of her sword pressed against the nawab's throat. Then a fiery heat tickled the back of his neck, followed by the charred smell of something burned.

Khadija shrieked. Jacob spun as Sakhr appeared behind them, his white-hot blade swinging from his hip. "Not bad, human boy," he cackled. His red eyes rested on Khadija. "Who is this?"

Khadija backed away, eyes darting between him and Sakhr. "Jacob . . . ?"

Jacob's mouth fell open but no words came out. What words could explain this?

Sakhr knelt beside a sewer grate and tore the bars off. The metal melted at his touch. "In," he rasped.

Jacob paled. Khadija's shallow breaths beside him were growing faster with every second. "Let her go. She doesn't have anything to do with this."

"In!" he roared, and Jacob dipped into the sewer tunnel, refusing to meet Khadija's eye as she followed him down. His boots splashed into foul water, and then darkness embraced them, the only light being from the flames coming off Sakhr as the shaitan led the way. Behind them, the tunnels reverberated with the nawab's whimpers as Vera dragged him along.

Even after yesterday's attack and the increased number of guards, Vera had still successfully captured the nawab. After all, nothing could protect the nawab against jinn, and that was where the Hāreef's power lay, Jacob realized.

The tunnel stretched deeper until the stench of moldy water

transformed to moist dirt. The orange glow of a lantern lit the way ahead, where the tunnel branched off as Sakhr turned to the left. Voices carried across the stale air until the tunnel abruptly spat them out into a cavern that reminded him of the hollow eye sockets of a skull that had been picked clean. Furnaces glowed in the far corners, causing shadows to flitter and bounce across the walls as if the cavern were alive. There were many hāri practicing with drawn swords or stacking glass vials filled with the black swirls of jinn into crates. Hāri women sat sharpening arrowheads while men dragged bodies into piles—one pile of animals and the other of humans. Some had been dead awhile. Others still dripped trails of fresh blood. Nearby, crates of wilted flowers were being swiftly knotted into long chains.

Everywhere he looked there was death.

Khadija was muttering prayers beside him, and Jacob considered stretching his hand out to meet hers in a feeble attempt at comfort when she shot him a glare with eyes that threatened to burn holes through him. He dropped his hand. She wasn't supposed to be here. What had he done?

Sakhr spun and clapped. White sparks erupted from his palms, causing the cavern to swiftly fall silent. All eyes, human and emerald alike, were on Vera as she dragged the nawab to the center and hurled him to the floor.

Jacob didn't breathe, eyes glued to the spectacle of the nawab dragging himself across the rock floor, smearing mud across the gold hem of his sherwani. The crowd erupted with laughter. Jacob's gaze flickered to Khadija. How long would the nawab steal everyone's attention before the Hāreef realized there was another Ghadaean among them?

"Let this serve as a message to the rest of the Ghadaean royalty."

Vera stomped on the tail of the nawab's sherwani, putting an end to his escape as she addressed her audience. "No amount of gold, no number of soldiers, will ever keep you safe." A sharp scrape of metal split the air as she drew her blade.

The nawab whimpered. "Maybe we can come up with a deal? I have gold. Lots of it."

"We do not care for all the gold in Ghadaea!" Vera bared her teeth. "There is nothing you could possibly offer us that is more valuable than your death."

The nawab's jaw trembled. Jacob pressed himself against the wall as if he could pass straight through it, away from here.

"You terrorists are all the same. You think by killing me, you are somehow saving your people from oppression." The nawab's voice shook. "When all you've really succeeded at is guaranteeing the death of every last hāri. We won't stop until your kind is wiped from this world like the dirty, disgusting taint that you are." The nawab's mouth curved into a snarl. "You're just giving us the perfect excuse to slaughter all of you."

Sakhr's roar made Jacob's heart slam against his rib cage. "Come on! Enough talk. Do not keep the queen waiting." He set his flame-filled eyes on Vera.

Vera raised her sword and in one clean sweep sent blood spraying across the rock. The nawab's body slumped to the ground.

Jacob retched. Khadija screamed. The crowd burst into howls of bloodthirsty approval. Sakhr silenced them with a growl that sent the rock vibrating beneath his boots. The shaitan brandished a silver hand mirror with an ornate handle, far too delicate for his thick palms. The surface of the mirror swirled as if there was a layer of fog trapped within it. Jacob held his breath as he watched a face slowly form across the mirror's surface.

"My queen." Sakhr dipped his head. "It is done." He raised his arm and sent the mirror shattering beside the nawab's lifeless fingertips.

Jacob sprang back as smoke rippled out from the fragments of glass. A shadow danced across the ground, spinning, swirling, until the figure of a woman appeared to take shape. She was white-hot like Sakhr, with a blazing crown of green fire and a dress that whirled like the blackest part of the ocean. The hem trailed along the rock floor, ebbing and flowing around her ankles like the tide soaking up the beach, tipped with white sea foam that made the air taste salty, while the bodice was embroidered with pearls, shells, starfish, and shark teeth.

The room gasped. Then everyone dropped to their knees. Jacob quickly followed suit. Even Khadija sank to the floor beside him and buried her face in her palms.

Vera cleared her throat. "My queen." Her voice quivered. "I offer to you the flesh of a king, the blood of a royal, the corpse of a nawab for you to feast upon."

"A nawab," the jinniya queen rasped. Her voice made all the hairs across Jacob's arms stand upright. "You have done well, Vera." Queen Bidhukh glanced at the body by her feet with eyes as green as sea moss. The flames of her crown made of jinn fire flickered with hungry approval. While Sakhr radiated a fiery warmth, there was no heat radiating off the jinniya queen. It was a cold, dead flame, as cold as the bottom of the ocean. Bidhukh was the jinniya queen of witchcraft, magic, and all things sihr, with a jinn kingdom that inhabited the deepest parts of the ocean—according to the stories Jacob had heard.

Vera glowed at the queen's praise. "Thank you, my queen."

"And, as promised, in exchange for your service, *my* end of the deal." Queen Bidhukh snapped her fingers and a green flame appeared. She threw it at the ground, where it grew into a coil of smoke with two emerald eyes.

Vera wailed.

The figure that stood before them had the charcoal skin of a jinn, but its body was far more substantial than the smoky outlines of the creatures Jacob was used to seeing. This jinn was a fully formed man, down to the muscles that twitched in his cheeks as he flexed his face and the sparkle in his green eyes as they caught sight of Vera.

Vera flung her arms wide, ready to embrace the jinn, when two slippery wings unfurled from his back. Her arms dropped. She stuttered, "C-Caleb?"

Queen Bidhukh flashed her pointed teeth. "He has been of much use to me, your son, so I took the liberty of bestowing on him a gift." She gestured to his silky black wings, which when held to the light exposed a web of tiny veins connected to a skeleton that reminded him of sunlight piercing through the thin, transparent material stretched across wooden kite frames as they leaped across the sky.

Queen Bidhukh smirked. "Why wish for a simple, mortal son when you can have an ifrit instead?"

Jacob tensed as he studied the man before him. An ifrit was a powerful winged type of jinn, far stronger than the common jinn.

And this ifrit was Vera's son. The one she'd said had burned to death.

Vera's voice cracked. "Is it really you, Caleb?"

"Yes, Ammi." The ifrit's voice sounded like the splutter of fire mixed with burned cinders.

Vera let out a wrangled sob and pressed her hand to her chest, as if trying to prevent it from splitting open. "You've come back to me. Finally you are home where you belong."

The ifrit approached and ran a finger across Vera's face. She hissed, tears springing from her eyes, but she didn't flinch even though Jacob heard skin sizzle. A burned line marked Vera's cheek. He winced.

"I am home, Ammi."

Vera's composure collapsed.

Jacob glared at the pair of them. Mother and child. Human and ifrit.

Queen Bidhukh grinned. "Death has certainly changed him. It has made him stronger." She crouched by the nawab's corpse. "Now. My feast awaits." Queen Bidhukh sank her teeth into the nawab's throat.

The sound of human flesh being ripped apart made Jacob gag. He looked away. When the jinniya queen was finished, she licked her lips. "The blood of a mortal royal." Her mouth dripped black blood. "Just the blood I needed." She faced Vera. "You will be seeing much more of me now, thankfully without that wretched mirror." Glass crunched beneath her foot as she gestured to Sakhr with a flick of her wrist and flashed the ifrit a wicked grin. "Until next time, Caleb." Then the jinniya queen erupted in a brilliant white spark and was gone.

Conversations soon picked up around them as the cavern resumed its previous activity, but there was a hushed atmosphere now, and no one dared approach Vera and her ifrit son, or the shaitan picking through the nawab's remains. Jacob couldn't help but steal glances at Vera's son. Ifrit. Whatever the creature was, the jinniya queen had brought him back to life, but not as the boy Vera would have known. Would she still love him though, exactly as she had before? Vera was clawing at her son now, trying to plant kisses upon his charcoal face. He swiftly dodged her efforts. "Don't, Ammi. I'll burn you."

"I don't care," she whispered.

Then Khadija yanked him by the elbow. "You're one of them. This whole time! You're a terrorist."

Jacob shook his head fiercely. "No . . . I . . ." he stuttered, "I can explain." But what could he say? How could he possibly explain the sticky bloodstain where the nawab's body had been, now only a finger bone and half a cracked jaw remaining? Last night, Vera had made everything sound so simple as she weaved a new world before him with her words—a world where there was no fear, no hate, no violence. She'd said that freedom didn't come easily, and that there was a price for everything. Was it such a tragedy that the nawab was dead? After all, there were still two more nawabs remaining.

Khadija had called them terrorists, but she was wrong. They were *freedom fighters*. This wasn't about mindless killing. This was about putting right what had been wrong. But of course, Khadija wouldn't understand that. She'd never understand. She was a Ghadaean. That's all she'd ever known, and that's all she'd ever be.

Khadija backed away from him, eyes darting anxiously to the hāri around the cavern. Most hadn't spotted her, and the ones who had were flashing her wicked grins, no doubt wondering what violent end would befall her. "I trusted you." Then she spun and came face-to-face with Vera!

Vera's cheeks were still wet with tears that made her green eyes sparkle. "Who is your friend, Jacob?"

Khadija shrank back, but her head remained high. "He is not my friend," she spat. Jacob tried to meet her gaze, but it was a staring contest he couldn't win.

Vera cocked an eyebrow. They were red too. "Is that so?"

Jacob's stomach dropped. "No. Wait." He jumped forward. "She's got nothing to do with this. She's nobody. She's—"

"She's someone who has seen far too much," Vera purred. "Take her away."

"No!" The word escaped his lips before Jacob could stop it.

A hāri man seized Khadija's upper arm. She struggled out of his grip. "Jacob!"

He didn't know what to do. Jacob turned to Vera, who was doing nothing to hide her smirk while she inspected her white gloves for bloodstains.

Khadija's gaze was hotter than the heat radiating off of the ifrit. *"Terrorist!"* she spat at Jacob.

His lips parted but no words escaped.

"I think you'll find it's your kind who are the terrorists. All the innocent lives lost in Sahli, they were because of your kind, not ours." Vera's face had turned to stone. "And we prefer the term *freedom fighters*." She looked Khadija up and down. "Ghadaean," she hissed, her voice filled with so much contempt she managed to make the word sound like a slur.

Vera clicked her fingers, and a hāri man with dark hair hanging limply across his face like two curtains disappeared down the tunnel with Khadija in tow, much to the amusement of the hāri onlookers. The cavern erupted into wolf whistles.

She'd trusted him, and he'd failed her. Shame washed over Jacob. "You won't hurt her, will you?" He glanced at the empty spot where Khadija had been. They were from completely different walks of life, traveling down paths that were never meant to cross each other. It had been a stroke of fate that had brought them together, but that had long since faded. Who knew what Vera had in store for Khadija? And it was all because of him. He should have ditched her earlier. At least then she would be safe.

Vera patted his shoulder. "I do not harm without good reason. Not like the Ghadaeans do." Her face contorted at the word.

Jacob wasn't sure whether to be relieved or not. Khadija had done nothing to warrant harm, so presumably she would be safe, for now. He eyed Vera. Could she be trusted? He'd just witnessed her butcher the Nawab of Intalyabad and feed his corpse to a jinniya queen. Their conversation from the night before rippled through him, pushing the doubts from his mind. He'd made the right choice, of course he had. The nawabs embodied all the greed and hatred in Ghadaea. Get rid of them, and they were one step closer to being free.

William had said he could trust the Hāreef. He'd said it was the only way he'd be safe. And Jacob had promised to honor his wishes. His hands quivered.

"Caleb. There's someone I'd like you to meet."

Jacob watched Vera's ifrit glide toward them. Up close, he could feel the heat, like he was standing beside an open flame. Jacob stepped back.

"This is Jacob, a new recruit of ours. With his help this morning we were able to capture the nawab." Vera beamed down at him. He shifted uncomfortably underneath the ifrit's hot gaze.

"You have made a wise choice siding with us." The ifrit nodded his approval.

"He is a wise boy indeed, or so I've heard." Vera nudged him playfully. "A glassblower. Reminds me of you, Caleb. You were quite the craftsman at his age too." When she spoke, her eyes sparkled like she was reliving a time where her world had been different. Simpler. A world where she didn't have to assassinate a nawab and ally with a jinniya queen. Maybe it was as simple as that. Fighting for a life where hāri were not forced into situations that demanded they do impossible things. Instead, they could just be.

The ifrit—*Caleb*—scrunched his brow. "I am far from that same boy, Ammi." His gaze dropped to the needle-thin claws protruding from his fingertips.

Vera's smile dissolved. "Queen Bidhukh . . . she has changed you—"

"She has blessed me," Caleb corrected. "I would still be trapped in Hell with her father, Iblis, if she hadn't bargained for my soul."

Iblis, the scorned angel and creator of Hell where all lost souls wound up, was also the father of the first jinn, like Queen Bidhukh. Jacob's earlier repulsion of Caleb began to dwindle. If he had to choose between spending the afterlife in Hell or in the jinn realm of Al-Ghaib serving Queen Bidhukh, he knew what he'd rather do, even if it meant accepting a pair of wings.

Vera's face twisted into something poisonous. "I promise you, I will put an end to the darkers for what they did to you!" Jacob had never heard anyone refer to Ghadaeans as *darkers* before. He tested the slur on his lips, but it didn't feel right. It felt hateful. It felt like something he wouldn't say.

Vera tore her attention away from Caleb to face Jacob and stooped down to his eye level. She was a tall woman. "And to William too."

Jacob swallowed the tightness in his throat.

"Darkers will never understand our suffering, Jacob, no matter how hard you try to explain it to them." Her voice was so soft, so reassuring. It was the type of voice that could soothe crying infants or lull children to sleep. It was the type of voice that could easily befriend you. "But *I* understand you. *We* understand you." She dug her nails into his shoulder.

Vera turned to address the entire cavern. "Their leaders took my son away from me!" Her voice was shrill. "Only seventeen years old, and they'd decided he'd lived enough life." She was shrieking now, body shaking, barely able to contain her suffering. "It's taken me years, but finally I've been able to undo the wrong that was done. I've brought him back." She clasped Caleb's hand in her own. Jacob watched her white glove blacken. Vera held on for as long as she could bear before yanking her burned hand away.

Jacob stole a glance at Vera. She had brought back the dead. He wasn't sure how to feel about it. He had never known his mother, but he'd heard a mother's love was eternal, endless, passing through time and space with no clear beginning or end. He'd always thought it impossible to love someone that much, but now, watching the way Vera admired her ifrit son, he realized there must be some truth to it. His chest ached. How different could his life have been if he'd grown up surrounded by a love like that? But there was no use for such thoughts now. Instead, he simply said, "You must have missed him."

Vera pressed her palm to her heart. "Like an arrow through my lungs." She traced an X across her chest with a fingernail. "Now . . . I feel like I can breathe again."

Jacob swallowed. No one should be forced to go through life carrying that much grief. Her son had been not much older than him when his life had been stolen from him. Jacob felt his insides catching fire. Just like the Ghadaeans had stolen William.

"You can change things?" he whispered, afraid to break Vera's spell.

She nodded, eyes glittering. "I've just killed a nawab. I've raised the dead. I can do anything." Vera's gloved hands curled into fists. "Remember, you can't change an old system. First you must break it, then forge a new one, and that's exactly what I intend to do. I'm going to break them like they've broken us for years."

Jacob mulled over her words. Like William had said, Ghadaea needed this. Something big. Something that would change things indefinitely.

Vera stood, addressing the room. "Decades of hāri torment will finally come to an end."

The terrorists—no, not terrorists, freedom fighters—murmured in agreement.

"All these years the darkers have been beating us, burning us, watching us suffer. No more! We are hāri. We do not burn easily!" Vera raised her voice, thumping her chest.

The crowd mimicked her, their voices rising. "We are hāri. We don't burn easily!"

And Jacob found himself joining in, his skin tingling with electricity as their voices melded together. Finally he'd found his people. He was home.

15

KHADIJA

Khadija pressed her forehead against the iron bars and forced down the rage clawing its way up her throat. It was easy to lose her head down here. The lack of water didn't help.

He's betrayed me. He's left me here to die.

Filthy hāri boy!

Khadija kicked the bars and let her anger simmer. She needed to think. The hāri man had made sure to dangle the key in her face as he left. "You're not leaving that cage alive," he'd hissed.

Khadija had no doubt about it. She'd end up just like the nawab if she didn't do something. She squeezed the bars until her knuckles threatened to protrude from her skin. Abba had been right. He was always right. She should never have left. She should never have trusted Jacob. She should never have stolen that balloon.

It didn't matter now. Abba would never know his daughter had perished in a cage, surrounded by terrorists, her body left to rot. Khadija could feel her throat tightening. Her breathing quickened, shallow and shaking, until she thought she was suffocating. She scrabbled at her neck. *Calm down. Breathe.* She sucked the air in through her nose, a long slow breath. Damn that Jacob! *He played you like a fool. He used you. And you trusted him.* She was naive. Ignorant. Stupid.

But it was herself she was angrier at. She'd allowed that boy to worm his way into her heart, disguised as a very different boy. A boy she'd convinced herself that he resembled, with his ability to fashion a compass out of a mango stone and his knowledge of ballooning, when in fact they were nothing alike. Her brother would never have done this to her.

Khadija closed her eyes. The memory she'd spent years burying was threatening to resurface, only this time she didn't fight it. She let it spill out of her until it was a pool of waist height and rising rapidly. A pool of anger and grief and hatred and shame, rising until it was at her throat, and Khadija thought she'd drown in it if she didn't box it away again.

The waiting had been the worst part. Waiting for news—any news, good, bad, it didn't matter. Any news that would stop her mind from conjuring false realities of what could have happened to them. Those three days of waiting had been the worst, and then the bodies had been found, and by then it had been a relief just knowing that the waiting was finally over.

Until the grief had kicked in, along with the knowledge that Ammi would never get to cook in that new cast-iron pot she'd bought at the market that day. It was probably still at the bottom of the ditch where they'd been found. Hassan would never come home to read her that story like he'd promised her that morning either. Time had stopped for them, snuffed out like a candle flame. A book that wasn't finished. The sentence just ends . . .

They said hāri men did it. A revenge killing, or mindless violence, or something that had led them to justify beating a woman and child to death and leaving their broken bodies in a ditch. Ammi had a swollen face. Her scarf had been ripped off. Hassan had a broken arm.

After the grief had passed, there'd been anger. Bright, vivid flames of anger that had lasted years until they'd eventually lost steam, having burned her insides raw. The only thing that remained now was the hatred. It had been just as virulent as Abba's at one point. Spitting at hāri in the street had been a form of healing for both of them, even if its edges were tinged with shame and the knowledge that she couldn't blame them all. She could try, of course, but it would only torture her more that way. Now the hatred was still there, but it was only a small part, a part she was ashamed to even admit to herself, but it was there, in the darkest corners of her mind. It still leaked its poison.

It was easy to hate Jacob, and a part of her did. It was much harder to admit that, deep down, she understood, even sympathized. Deep down, she probably would have done the same had she been him.

Khadija rested her cheek against the cold iron. "I can't do this," she whispered.

"Yes, you can."

Khadija shrieked, head snapping from left to right, searching for the voice in the dimly lit tunnel. No one. She was going mad.

A figure emerged from the darkness carrying an oil lamp. It was a hāri boy. A terrorist.

Khadija backed away. "Get away from me!"

The boy approached, heedless of her warning, and placed the lamp on the ground. The flames momentarily danced, sending long shadows across his face. And it was a familiar face. He looked her up and down in turn.

The boy from last night. The one who had saved her from the soldiers.

"You?" His eyebrows rose, and then his lips turned into a smirk. "When I told you to run away, this was the last place I expected you to turn up."

Khadija sank her teeth into her tongue, hard enough to draw blood. He was making a fool out of her. Him. A hāri. Her pride wouldn't allow it.

"I thought you might be thirsty." He pulled the stopper out of a water gourd.

Khadija didn't move. "No, thank you."

The right side of his mouth curled up, only a fraction. *Is he laughing at me?* Khadija growled. "Just leave me alone, hāri." She fired a spitball by his feet.

She'd expected him to retaliate, but his face hadn't moved. It was like he was carved from stone, but there was a warmth in his eyes that softened the harshness of his jawline, made the deep sockets of his eyes appear less sunken. His eyes were the color of amber.

"Ghadaean," he said flatly.

Khadija furrowed her brow.

The boy smiled. "Well, now that we've established what we are, would you like a drink?" He shook the water gourd, allowing the water inside to slosh around. Just the sound of it made her throat ache.

Khadija stared at him. He'd shaken off her slur, batted it away as easily as one would swat a fly. She'd expected so much worse. Anger. Violence. But nothing. It made her own anger fizzle out. "Why are you giving me this? I'm going to die anyway."

The boy's face darkened. He replaced the stopper on the water gourd. "Seems you've already made up your mind, then."

Khadija scoffed. "You think I *want* to die here!"

"You've already given up." He retrieved his oil lamp, bringing it closer so that it lit up her face. His eyes traced over her features. He looked a similar age to her or slightly older. Seventeen, perhaps. "Goodbye, Ghadaean." He turned to leave.

Khadija growled. "I have a name, you know."

The boy threw his head back. "I'm sure you do."

That was it. He didn't say anything more. The seconds of silence stretched on until it became awkward. Khadija stuttered.

He grinned and ran his hands along the sides of his head. It was shaved closely, almost to the scalp. Khadija imagined it would feel like the bristles of a brush.

"I have a name too." He paused. "Or would you prefer to call me hāri?"

He was taunting her. Toying with her as a hunter would with its prey. "Do you enjoy this? Laughing at people before they're about to die."

"Not in the slightest."

Khadija was taken aback by the seriousness of his voice. Her lips parted, ready to respond, when a high-pitched wail shook the walls. She winced. It was like the scratch of a bird's talons against metal. It stopped, making her ears ring with the absence of the noise. Then again.

"What is that?" They both listened. It was a creature screaming, she realized. There was something ethereal, inhuman about the noise. No person could scream like that, contort their voice so that it held so much tortured pain. Tears pricked her eyes.

"What are they doing to it?"

"I don't think I want to know."

Another screech made her feel physically sick. "The poor creature."

His features softened. "What do you think it is?"

Khadija tried to focus on the noise, but it was too painful to listen to. "I don't know, but it's definitely not human, and it's not a jinn. It must be something benevolent. Angelic, even."

The boy hummed. "What do you know of angels?" His voice was barely a whisper so that Khadija had to press her cheek against the bars to hear him.

"It cannot be an angel." She shook her head. "An angel is too powerful for even the strongest of jinns to capture, and they don't meddle with our human affairs like the jinn either. I don't know of anyone who has ever seen an angel."

She focused on the noise again, its high-pitched keening like the peal of a bell mixed with breathy moans of anguish that sounded like wind chimes. The creature had a beautiful voice, and yet it had been twisted into such an ugly sound.

She knew what it was: an angelic creature that guided the souls of the dead to Heaven with its voice alone. She thought back to her dream of Hassan searching the skies with his telescope as silver-winged peri shimmered and sang across the night. "A peri."

The boy folded his arms, clearly impressed. "I wasn't sure before, but I think you're right."

"But . . . why?" Her voice cracked. She didn't know why she was so repulsed by the peri's screams. A peri was part bird, part human, but it was their voices they were most treasured for. Many balloonists throughout history had sought to capture them—to no avail—waiting for the night of a full moon, for it was only under moonlight that peris chose to sing. Then the balloonists would ascend to precarious heights in an attempt to seize the creatures in their nets. Peri were treasured among angels as more than just songbirds, however. They were considered their companions.

And the Hāreef were torturing one. Khadija's insides flared to life. The Hāreef were terrorists. They had summoned jinn, assassinated the nawab, and yet this seemed beyond all of that. This was mindless cruelty against something innocent.

He shrugged. "Vera wouldn't waste her time like this. Only someone who enjoys inflicting pain for the sake of it would do something like this."

Khadija pictured the winged ifrit the jinniya queen had conjured from an emerald-green flame. She shuddered. A creature that had existed only in books before, but nothing about this was a fairy tale. This was a living nightmare.

The boy's neck twitched at another scream.

"Then you are a monster for joining them," she seethed.

His jaw clicked. "I don't agree with this."

"You only agree with summoning a jinniya queen to kill the nawab!"

He shook his head. "I don't agree with that either."

She scoffed. "Then you're clearly in the wrong place."

He approached the cage. Khadija stepped back. The boy slipped the water gourd through the bars so that it landed by her feet.

Khadija glared at it.

His lips prickled. "You're right. We're both in the wrong place, but I know you're not going to die down here," he whispered. He walked off.

Khadija smacked the bars like a wild animal. "Wait!"

He didn't turn as he disappeared down the tunnel, leaving her in darkness.

Khadija huffed and kicked the bars. She retrieved the water gourd and pulled the stopper, glugging it down. The water trickled out, and something metal pressed against her lips. She peered into the water gourd, feeling the metal with her fingers. Khadija pulled it out.

It was a spoon. He'd given her a spoon.

16

JACOB

The fire crackled in the center of the cavern as hāri gathered around, dishing out steaming plates of meat that had been cooking on a rotisserie. Jacob sat awkwardly on his own, picking at the meat. He had never eaten something dead before. Every time he brought a bite to his lips, he pictured the crack of joints and the ripping sound of flesh as the jinniya queen feasted on the nawab's corpse. He gagged and set his plate down.

His mind kept wandering back to Khadija, and fresh guilt sloshed in his belly. Their arrangement had never been permanent. They'd never promised anything to each other, and yet there had been something unspoken between them. He wouldn't call it friendship, but it was something. He recalled the days they'd spent in the air. Up there, they both seemed to shed parts of themselves the higher they went until they were no longer hāri and Ghadaean. They were merely Jacob and Khadija. But of course, they had to come back down eventually.

He didn't like the idea of Khadija trapped underground, surrounded by members of the Hāreef. It had been his intention to help her escape the chaos of the protest, not lure her into imprisonment. Jacob wasn't sure why he cared so much. *She's not one of us.* Perhaps it would be good for her to see with her own eyes what the Hāreef were really about. They weren't terrorists. They were freedom fighters. Justice seekers. Preservers of the innocent. With that thought, he pushed the guilt from his mind.

A slender hand on his shoulder made him jump.

"Here." A hāri woman passed him a water gourd. He gulped it down.

"Thanks."

"I'm Sara." She crouched so that the fire lit up her face. Jacob couldn't stop a gasp escaping. He looked away, ashamed by his reaction. *Does it pain you too much to look? Imagine her pain.* He forced himself to meet her eyes, but his gaze kept wandering across her cheek, the side of her nose, the corner of her lips, down her neck. He traced the thick scars, the way her mouth was turned permanently downward, how her left eye no longer closed properly. She stared back with tortured eyes until he couldn't bear to look any longer. Burned. Disfigured. Mutilated. The pain was too great to comprehend.

"They did this to me."

Jacob chanced another look, this time hoping to keep his expression neutral, but as his eyes swept over the blotches of pink where her skin had been burned raw, focused on the area where her left eyebrow no longer grew, watched the skin stretch so tightly as she spoke that he thought it would tear, Jacob couldn't stop the heat rising up his throat, his rage boiling, spilling out.

Who would do that to another human being? What monster would do that?

Sara seemed to read his thoughts. "It happened when I was not much older than you." She gazed into the fire with faraway eyes, reliving the fury of its touch. "You know, I used to be pretty before this." Even her words were bitter and burned. "According to the darker women I was *too* pretty. I was distracting their husbands, they said." She tore her eyes from the fire to face him, but the shadows of the flames still danced across her skin. Impatient. Craving the day they'd finally consume the rest of her. "So they did this," she whispered. "They burned me like they burn their corpses."

His skin prickled with the scorch of her burns. He clenched his fists. When he thought of all the lives ruined or cut short because of the Ghadaeans and their hatred, Jacob couldn't comprehend the extent of the horrors caused by their hands. And it would never stop. These things happened every day.

"Don't forget what they're capable of. Even the girls aren't innocent." Sara pulled her hood over her face, hiding her suffering beneath it. "And remember, no matter what they do to us, we are hāri. We don't burn easily."

Jacob mulled over her words, the same words Vera had encouraged them all to chant earlier. His whole life he'd been conditioned to believe that hāri were weak, inferior, ill-suited to Ghadaea—from their inability to conquer the country, which had been their initial intention, to the fairness of their skin, which blistered beneath the hot sun. Yet today he had met not one but two hāri who had suffered the wrath of Ghadaeans and survived. Sara had been burned, in the same way the Ghadaeans set corpses alight, and still she stood. And as for Caleb, he had been burned also, burned to death, and yet he had returned as an ifrit. Vera's words were not only an affirmation that Ghadaeans would continue to oppress them, to hurt them, invalidate them, even kill them, it was the promise that they would refuse to burn no matter how cruelly they were set alight.

Vera soon reappeared with her son by her side, and the crowd immediately fell silent while she spoke of change, painting a new world before them with her words. A world where there was no oppression. No fear. No death. No suffering.

But interwoven with her words was Ghadaean fear, Ghadaean deaths, and Ghadaean suffering. A twisted parallel world that made him itch with excitement. Was it wrong to revel in another's suffering? The Ghadaeans had been doing it for years. Perhaps it was his people's turn now. Something to even the score, a short burst of bloodshed, and the past would be forgiven, the slate wiped clean and the world could start again. It didn't seem so bad when he thought of it like that.

When Vera's words drew to an end, the crowd cheered and wolf whistled with approval. Jacob clapped in earnest. Then red hair was forcing a path through the crowd, making a beeline toward him. Jacob swiftly stood at attention as Vera appeared with Caleb as her shadow.

"Enjoying yourself so far?"

Jacob's head bobbed up and down.

"Good." Vera flashed her teeth. "It's time we put those talents of yours to use."

"As long as he has no plan of trapping me in any of his creations." Caleb appeared, with his arms the color of slate crossed tightly over his chest.

Jacob gulped.

Laughter spilled from Vera's lips. "I see you've not lost your sense of humor."

But there was nothing humorous about the ifrit's face to Jacob.

Caleb flexed his talons. "The boy likes to befriend darkers. While his skills as a glassblower are indeed useful, can he be trusted, Ammi?"

"You mean the girl?" Vera tapped her chin. "I am interested where you managed to find her."

Then two pairs of green eyes were upon him. Jacob could taste the salty layer of sweat appearing on his upper lip. "She's from Qasrah. She had a hot-air balloon." He fumbled for what else to say before finally he blurted, "She means nothing."

Vera beamed, satisfied with his answer. "See. He is a loyal member of the Hāreef." She clicked her fingers, and Sara reappeared. "Take him to the workshop."

As Sara steered him away by his shoulder, Jacob caught Caleb's glare. How a creature made of fire could have a stare so cold was beyond him, but it sent his insides twisting into a knot. He'd have to be careful from now on. No more thinking about Khadija, he scolded himself. He needed to prove himself, and she'd only distract him.

Jacob didn't release his breath until they were out of sight as he stumbled after Sara in the dark, being led down a network of tunnels that merged into a cavern with a low ceiling. His nostrils tingled with the familiar smell of melted glass.

The furnace was double the size of Munir's, with three hāri men tending to the flames, twisting sticky glass into vials. Rows of empty glass vials were stacked in crates on every available surface, next to bars of solid copper that glowed orange in the firelight. A heap of brass candelabras, dinner plates, and trinket boxes were being swiftly melted and dripped into molds to set on the floor due to the limited counter space. The result was a workshop that was chaotically overcrowded, and yet the methodical way the three men worked around each other, stepping over hot molds while simultaneously blowing glass bubbles and flipping ash-covered coals in the furnace, only gave Jacob the impression of a well-organized operation. One he was itching to be a part of.

A tremor of excitement coursed through him. Here, he could be useful. Here, he belonged. Sara motioned one of the men over. "Marcus. This is Jacob. Vera said he could be of use to you."

Marcus looked him up and down. "You blow glass?" His voice was gruff from hours spent breathing in ash, and he had burn marks splattered up his bare arms.

"I've been apprenticed for nearly a year," Jacob said, not bothering to hide the smugness leaking from his voice.

"Then let's see what you can do."

Marcus brought his hammer down against a sheet of copper with a clang that made Jacob's teeth rattle as he flattened the once-solid bar into a layer of foil thin enough to tear between his fingers. Jacob studied his movements as Marcus then began sandwiching the copper foil between sheets of semi-cooled glass, firing each layer in the furnace with a meticulous precision that put Munir's sloppy handiwork to shame. While Jacob had watched Munir fuse glass with copper and brass before, never had the results been as breathtaking as the array of infused glass on the counter that ranged from the deepest burnt umber to hues of ocher and russet.

"Why go to all this trouble if jinn can be trapped in iron and lead?" Jacob brushed his fingertips against the cool surface of the finished glass vials. They were beautiful, and having witnessed every step involved in their creation, it irked him that their sole purpose was to be smashed.

Marcus set down his hammer. "Not all jinn are made equal, as I'm sure you know. A jinn that can only take the form of a bird or a rat could be contained in iron or lead, no problem. But for a stronger jinn—one that can take a human shape, for instance—iron and lead is not enough. That is why we use copper and brass." He gestured to the empty vials with his charred glove. "We infuse the glass with these metals so that they can be easily smashed."

Jacob soaked up his words. "Could you trap an ifrit in one of these?"

Marcus's booming laugh made Jacob jump. "I hope you're not getting any ideas," he chuckled. "It would be useless anyway. Ifrits are one of the highest classes of jinn, like marids; they are far too powerful. And as for a jinn royal"—Marcus wiped the slick film of sweat covering his forehead with the back of his glove—"I don't think a material exists that could trap a jinniya queen."

"So the higher jinn are happy for us to trap the lower jinn in glass?"

"It seems that way, but I ain't surprised. Jinn are vain, and there's nothing that vanity loves more than power. As long as we have no intention of trapping them, they're happy to watch their lesser counterparts be contained."

Jacob nodded. It made sense. His fingers unconsciously hovered over William's amulet, now hot against his skin from the heat of the furnace. "But what about this amulet? It can command jinn."

Marcus dug underneath his tunic collar to produce an identical amulet, studded with the green iris of Bidhukh. "It can command lesser jinn, but nothing stronger. As for what material this is"—he stroked the "eye"—"even I don't know the answer to that."

Jacob thought back to how he had commanded a swarm of crows to descend on the Wāzeem's protest simply by flashing the jinn his amulet. He ran his thumb across the green jewel in the center. He'd assumed it was an emerald up until now, but as he tilted his palm, allowing the jewel to catch the light, he realized he'd been mistaken. The green stone swirled and danced beneath the firelight the way morning mist coats the grass.

"It's not an emerald."

"No." Marcus shook his head.

"Or jade. Or peridot, malachite, aventurine, serpentine . . ." He tapped his chin. "Or any other green stone I can think of."

Marcus raised an eyebrow. "That's an impressive knowledge of precious stones you've got there."

Jacob tingled at the praise. Though he'd worked mainly with glass previously, some of Munir's more expensive pieces had required gemstones. "Then where did the stones come from?"

Marcus shrugged. "All I know is Vera was given the amulets by Sakhr as a gift from the jinniya queen. If I were to hazard a guess, I'd say the stone wasn't from our world at all."

"It's from Al-Ghaib!" Jacob gasped, tracing his fingernail across the crude edges of the stone, as if it had been part of a larger stone and hastily snapped apart. "Have you tried crafting with it? Maybe if you melted them together, you could—"

Marcus put an end to his musings with a firm shake of his head. "No. Vera wants me to blow glass, so that's what I do, and that's what you should do too." He leaned in. "A word of advice: Do as she says and you'll go far."

Jacob nodded and tucked his amulet beneath his tunic collar.

Marcus raised his hammer. "Let's get back to work."

Hours passed unnoticed as Jacob slowly earned Marcus's trust until, by the end of the day, Jacob was blowing glass and stretching it out like strings of melted sugar as he twirled the hot glass into shape. He enjoyed repetitive work like this. It was the type of work that silenced the mind so that he was aware only of the motions of his fingers. It was calming, and not having Munir leaning over him ready to strike if he made a mistake gave him a new sense of confidence while he worked.

It wasn't until Sara returned and beckoned him over that Jacob set down his tools and became aware of the cramping in his wrists. Jacob approached Sara, wrists clicking as he rotated the stiffness from them.

Sara's lips were upturned into what looked like a smile. Her thin skin seemed on the verge of tearing from the motion. "Marcus is impressed with you. He is not easily impressed." She clapped his shoulder. "Well done."

Jacob fidgeted at her praise, wiping the sweat that had pooled in the hollow of his neck.

"Vera has set another task for you."

"She has?" He couldn't hide his excitement if he tried. With so many hāri under her wing it would be understandable for her to soon forget him as he blended into her ranks.

"We're going outside." She pointed at the ceiling. "Let's get you ready."

In fifteen minutes Jacob was following a group of hāri through the tunnels and up into the city. It had taken all his effort to tear himself from the comfort of the workshop. Down there, surrounded by fire and glass, he had felt safe, at home. Outside, he wasn't sure what to expect, and the uncertainty chewed at his insides as he neared the surface. He wrapped the cloak he'd been given tighter around himself. It was long on him, and the crisp white hem had already muddied where it trailed in the dirty water. Jacob drew his hood as they emerged through the sewer grate into an alleyway, not the entrance in the rose garden he'd previously used.

"Vera wants anything made of brass and copper to be brought down to the workshop," Sara instructed.

Jacob couldn't imagine the workshop being overcrowded with even more crates of brass and copper ready to be melted down and dripped into molds. He'd lost count of how many glass vials he'd crafted that day, though he was certain Vera had hundreds of empty vials waiting to be filled. He paled at the thought of so many jinn. It had been easy to overlook that while his mind had been consumed only with bending and twisting molten glass, but outside, the knowledge struck him like a harsh gust of wind. It was clear Vera was planning another jinn attack. One far bigger and deadlier than the attack on Sahli.

Hāri dispersed in different directions. Sara took his elbow and steered him to the marketplace, where the shops were shuttered for the night. "You're with me, new boy." She thrust a linen sack his way. "I'm expecting you to be good at this," Sara grunted as she kicked the first stall in, shattering the wooden boards. "I usually just toss in anything that looks metal and shiny." She rifled through shelves stacked with rolls of vibrant cloths and silks. She swiftly moved to the next stall.

Jacob hovered close by with his empty sack.

"How has your first day been?" Sara snatched two necklaces from their display case—one copper, the other made of gold. At Jacob's word she bagged the copper and tossed the gold. "Can be a lot to take in at first, but you'll settle in just fine." Sara swiped a brass figurine of a leopard. "Although I wouldn't get too comfortable in the tunnels. We won't be there much longer."

"Won't we?"

Sara shook her head. "Vera's certainly made the most of the tunnel network. It spreads beneath the entire city. It's how we learned the nawab's routine so that we could pick the best moment to strike." Her eyes sparkled in the night. "But with him gone now, it's best we leave Intalyabad while we still can. Vera has big plans for her jinn army."

"A-army?" Jacob stuttered. So, he'd been right, but it was still difficult to stomach that many jinn descending on a city at once.

Sara abruptly yanked him into the shadows as the chinking sound of soldiers neared. Her hand felt rough and bumpy in his palms, like wax that had melted and cooled.

Voices carried across the air, closer than he'd expected. Sara nudged him and pressed her lips to his ear. "I'll lead them away. You get back to the tunnels."

He didn't like the idea of Sara risking herself for him, but the sound of metal drawing nearer made him bite his tongue.

"You know the way back?"

He nodded, not trusting himself to speak. Jacob dug his nails into the linen sack. *Come on. I have to prove myself to them.* He swallowed down his fear.

Sara patted his shoulder, then swiftly disappeared around the corner, purposely knocking over a ceramic tea set.

Soldiers roared, and then Jacob was running, his sack of goods rattling by his side. It was a mad dash across the shadowed marketplace, the only noise he was aware of being the thrumming of his blood in his ears. A streak of white caught his eye as Sara fled into the night, her white cloak trailing behind, before Jacob emerged into a deadened street. He skidded to a halt and pressed himself against a wall. His heart was hammering.

Jacob shut his eyes and listened. Listened for the distant thud of soldiers' boots as they trampled in the opposite direction. Listened for Sara's screams as she was inevitably found, but the metal footsteps petered off instead, leaving only silence.

Jacob focused on steadying his breathing and opened his eyes. He was in an unfamiliar street lined with peach trees and ornate benches crafted out of stone. His head swiveled left and right. It could be either way. He settled on a direction and walked as fast as he dared while trying to muffle the jingle of brass and copper in his sack. Down a twist and turn of streets and back again, retracing his steps, starting over, with his chest tightening the longer he spent wandering the streets. At every corner he expected soldiers to be waiting. Every shadow caused him to flinch. Even the sigh of the wind made his muscles stiffen.

A familiar row of terraced houses abruptly came into view. The Wāzeem's headquarters.

His stomach tied into a knot as he pictured Khadija trapped underground. *But she's a Ghadaean.* That she was, but somehow it was easier wishing for their downfall when they remained faceless. Nameless. But Khadija had a face and a name. He growled. *Stop thinking about her. She means nothing.*

But she had done nothing to deserve her capture. Nothing except misplace her trust in him. Jacob scanned the empty street. He needed to get back to the Hāreef. He glanced at the Wāzeem's block of terraces. The sooner Khadija was out of the way, the sooner he could throw himself all-in with the Hāreef without thoughts of her chewing at the back of his mind. According to Sara, the Hāreef would be leaving the tunnels soon. Would they take her with them, or leave her there, or maybe something worse?

It was that thought that had him powering up the steps. Jacob unclasped the white cloak from his neck and dropped it in a nearby bush along with his sack. If the Hāreef found out about this . . . Jacob conjured an image of the ifrit, Caleb, his palms ablaze with furious green jinn fire. He shuddered.

They wouldn't find out. He'd make sure of that. Jacob tentatively knocked.

Nothing.

He hopped from foot to foot, then tried again. There was a sliding of bolts from within, and then Anam appeared. Her mouth formed a ring. "Jacob. Are you OK?"

Jacob nodded, wishing he'd planned his next words. "They took Khadija. The Hāreef."

Anam cursed. "I knew it! When you both disappeared at the protest this morning, we thought the worst." She attempted to tug him inside. "Come inside."

Jacob withdrew. "I can't."

Anam eyed him. "Why?"

He really should have thought this through. "She's underground in a tunnel network." He backed away. "The entrance is in the rose garden."

"Jacob . . ."

"Just . . . make sure she's OK." Then Jacob fled into the night, ignoring Anam's calls after him.

Even with his heart pounding, his chest felt lighter. That was it. He and Khadija were even. He had done all he could for her, and now he could push her from his mind and focus on what really mattered. The Hāreef. And avenging William.

17

KHADIJA

Khadija wiped her brow. Her fingers were cramping up. The hole was only a foot deep. It needed to be a lot deeper than that for her to slip underneath the bars. Useless boy gave her a spoon! Couldn't he have given her a shovel instead?

He could've given her nothing. He could've left her there to rot like Jacob had, and yet he'd chosen to help her. Her. A Ghadaean, which he'd taken great pleasure in reminding her of. Khadija cracked her fingers and resumed digging. She wasn't going to wait around to ask him why. She had a hole to dig.

But her mind kept traipsing back to Jacob, half expecting him to appear sobbing down the tunnel, explaining this was all just a misunderstanding.

But he never appeared.

If he wanted to be friends with terrorists, then fine! What did she care?

But a part of her did. She wasn't sure of her reasoning behind it. Not having him to rely on meant that she was all alone, and that thought did scare her, or was it something else? Something niggling in the back of her mind. Something that found a sense of familiarity in the way his face lit up when he learned something new, or how his eyebrows scrunched together until they became one whenever his mind was mulling over something tricky, or the way he flicked his fringe out of his eyes as he concentrated on a task. Perhaps it was the way he could appear so smart when it came to hot-air balloons and stars and glass and navigating and whatever else Jacob knew, but then at the same time he could appear totally lost. She supposed there were similarities, but Khadija chose not to dwell on them too much. It did no good comparing Jacob to the dead.

They're not the same. He's gone. He's never coming back. Jacob can never replace the gaping hole in your heart.

A flame in the distance caused shadows to frolic across the walls. Khadija hastily shoved the spoon behind her back and stood in the hole. A figure came into view. It was the same boy. Unless he had a shovel, she wasn't interested.

His hands were empty.

"What do you want?"

He didn't respond, just assessed the hole she was standing in. His eyes widened until they were practically popping out of his skull. "Is that all you've done? It's been an hour."

Khadija's cheeks flamed. "You gave me a *spoon*," she hissed, holding the bent spoon to the light.

The boy smirked, a crooked half smile. "Bet you would've preferred a knife."

So I can sink it into your throat!

He crouched beside the bars and reached into his white cloak, producing a piece of metal that Khadija almost mistook for a knife, until she realized it was another spoon. He plunged the spoon into the dirt.

Khadija scoffed. "Don't you have something better to dig with? Or do they only trust you with the spoons?"

He chuckled, a soft hum vibrating in his chest. "Actually I work in the kitchens. Spoons are the only things I have access to."

Khadija's brow creased. "Didn't you have a sword last time?" She thought back to the night they'd met, when he'd challenged three drunken soldiers.

He shifted uncomfortably. "I . . . erm, lost that."

She laughed. "You're a pretty rubbish terrorist, then."

His eyes fixed on hers, suddenly serious. Khadija bit her lip, afraid she'd said too much.

"I'm not a terrorist."

Her face twisted. "Of course not. You're a . . . what do you call it? Freedom fighter."

He shook his head. "I'm not one of those either." He began scooping out chunks of dirt and flinging them over his shoulder before stabbing the spoon into densely packed soil with enough force to bend the metal out of shape. He huffed. "You're right. This does take ages."

Khadija studied him.

He lifted his head, the fire from the oil lamp illuminating the sharp points of his cheekbones. "I'm not here for the reason you'd think."

"Then why are you here?" She breathed. "Why are you helping me?"

"I—"

A shrill shriek from the peri made them both wince.

"You and that creature have something in common," he finally whispered when the wailing had died down to a continuous moan. "You don't suit a cage."

When the moaning became a high-pitched sob, Khadija could take it no longer. She didn't know birds could cry like that, and it made her want to cry too. "We have to help her."

"I think our main concern is getting out of here." He stabbed his spoon in her direction. "It would only waste time trying to save her."

Khadija crossed her arms. "I don't care." She stiffened as the peri's long-drawn-out sobs came to an abrupt silence. Somehow, that was worse. "I'm saving her. You can help if you want."

The corners of his lips upturned. "You're not really in a position to make demands when you're stuck in a cage."

Khadija gritted her teeth. She would be stupid to ever trust another hāri boy again, but she was in a cage, and there weren't many other options presenting themselves. She would not make the same mistake with him as she had with Jacob. That she was certain of. Her chest ached with a heaviness as if her lungs were full of water. Grief hurt, but betrayal wasn't far behind, and somehow Jacob had managed in the short time she'd known him to inflict her with both. For that, she didn't think she could ever forgive him.

"But I could use your help," the boy added. "The world out there is not kind to my people."

She pursed her lips. "The world out there is not much kinder to me either."

A flash of recognition turned his amber eyes a fiery copper. "Soldiers are attracted to anything that makes them feel powerful. They just like feeding their egos."

He wasn't wrong. The soldiers in Qasrah had done nothing but doze in the sunshine, flittering the townspeople's taxes away on gambling and drink. "Why did you help me that night?"

"Seemed like a good idea at the time." He hummed. "Now knowing you've just ended up here anyway makes me think you have a death wish." He snorted. "Or you're just extremely bad at taking care of yourself."

She growled. "I can take care of myself."

He picked up his spoon. "Then prove it. Start digging."

They dug in silence. Her on one side of the cage. Him on the other. He kept shooting glances down the tunnel before sinking his spoon into the dirt and sending a chunk flying across to the opposite wall. Khadija huffed and scooped hers into a tidy pile.

He looked across, amused. "No need to be neat about it."

Her eyebrows rose. "I'm thinking more on the lines of leaving the least amount of evidence. Look." She pointed behind him. "You've left dirt everywhere. Someone will easily notice that."

He shrugged. "You missing from that cage will probably be the biggest giveaway anyway." His eyes flickered to meet hers. "Hopefully by then we'll be in the sky."

"They have balloons?"

He nodded. "My plan is to take one—but I can't fly a balloon on my own." He glanced her way. "You know much about flying?"

Khadija struggled to hide her smirk. "A little." She paused. "But we're saving the peri first."

He was quiet so long she thought he wouldn't answer. Then finally he nodded. "Fine."

They continued to dig, allowing the silence to stretch between them. The boy started humming. How she hated humming. "I'm Darian, by the way."

Khadija nodded, not bothering to offer her name in return. What use was getting to know him?

The following silence was awkward to say the least. Darian resumed his humming. "So why are you in here? The Hāreef don't usually take prisoners. Well . . . alive prisoners."

She sighed. "Not that it's any of your business, but I was betrayed, actually."

His eyes widened.

"Betrayed by someone who I thought was like me." Her face darkened. Her next words came out like a hiss. "But we're nothing alike, in fact." Khadija stabbed her spoon into the ground. The metal twisted backward at a ninety-degree angle.

"Was this person a hāri by any chance?"

She nodded, not daring to speak for fear her voice would give her away.

Darian rolled his eyes. "Then, please don't take this the wrong way, but what made you think you were anything alike in the first place?"

His question surprised her. It sounded a lot like something Abba would say. Heat rose to her face. "OK, I get it!" She threw her spoon down. "You think we're a completely different species. Yeah, we're different." She stared at the hole, searching for the right words. "But some things must be the same."

Darian cocked his head, as if amused by her naivete. "Like what? Name one thing you and that hāri who betrayed you have in common."

Her eyes narrowed. "We both wanted to escape our lives. We both lost people we cared about." Her voice dropped to a whisper. "We saved each other's lives when we didn't have to." When Khadija lifted her head, Darian was staring at her intently. "Is that good enough for you?"

He dropped his spoon and stepped back. "Perfect."

She locked her jaw.

Darian smirked. "I think you'll be able to fit under this."

Khadija eyed the hole. It wasn't much of a hole, more like a ditch underneath the bars, barely two feet deep. It would be a tight squeeze.

"Quick—we don't have much time. Most of the Hāreef will be sleeping, and the rest have gone outside searching for copper and brass, but they could be back soon. Go headfirst," he instructed.

Khadija swallowed her rage and flattened herself against the ground, tilting her head to the side. She grasped the bars and tried to slip her head underneath. "I can't."

"Yes, you can." Darian grabbed both her arms and pressed them deeper into the ground.

She felt herself slip beneath the bars, the iron grazing the side of her cheek. Then her head was through completely. The iron bar was pressed against her neck, threatening to choke her. Darian tugged her arms, yanking her through, while Khadija used her legs to push her body. As the iron passed over her chest, Khadija jolted to a stop. She was stuck.

Her chest tightened.

Darian crouched down, furiously digging, flinging giant clumps across the floor. "Go on, try now."

She winced as the iron bar pressed against her belly, and then she was through. Khadija got to her feet and brushed the dirt from her kameez.

"Come on." Darian was already marching down the tunnel, hugging the walls, keeping his head low. Khadija trailed him.

"You need to do everything I say. All right?"

Khadija raised an eyebrow. *He wishes.*

Footsteps bounced off the walls. Khadija tugged Darian back just as a figure appeared. A terrorist—a man, judging by the height. "Now what?" Her voice was barely a whisper.

Darian peeked around the corner, then flattened himself against the wall. They were far too close for her liking. Close enough for her to smell the sweat and soil clinging to his skin.

Footsteps approached. "Get ready," he murmured.

Just as the terrorist rounded the corner, Darian stuck his leg out. The terrorist yelped and crashed to the floor, his hood slipping back. It was a spindly man with sunken cheeks and a ponytail. Tall but waiflike. They could take him.

Darian hurled himself at him, landing a punch. The terrorist staggered back with an "oomph!" before aiming a kick at him. Darian rolled to the side. Khadija yanked the man's ponytail and smacked his head against the wall. His eyes rolled back, and he slumped to the floor.

Darian whistled, hands on his hips. "Nice work." He shook the terrorist by the shoulders, making sure he was completely out cold before undressing him. Khadija blushed and looked away, feeling slightly shameful. Darian slipped the man's cloak off and shoved it toward her. "Here. Put this on."

Khadija stretched the material out. "It's enormous!"

He snickered. "Would you prefer to wear mine?" His eyes sparkled wickedly.

The nerve of this boy!

Khadija huffed and shrugged the cloak over her head. It dragged along the floor and the sleeves were far too long, but she drew the hood, feeling more confident now that she was dressed like one of them.

Voices rebounded off the walls as they walked, traveling back the way she'd arrived. Khadija pictured the large cavern filled with terrorists and jinn and dead bodies. There was no way they could walk through it and expect not to be noticed. Even with her dressed like one of them, surely someone would catch a glimpse of her skin? Her heart sped up.

"Keep your face covered."

They emerged into the cavern, mostly empty now, the dying embers of the cooking fires casting the cave walls a deep crimson. There were only a few terrorists sparring in the far corner. Khadija couldn't help but glance at the sticky bloodstain where the nawab's corpse had once been. She swallowed hard.

They reached the opposite end of the cavern undisturbed, where they found themselves lost down a series of tunnels and dead ends that forced them to retrace their steps, drawing suspicious glances from a group of terrorists they'd encountered for the fourth time.

"Don't you know where you're going, or have you never left the kitchens?" she hissed.

"I've not been here that long," Darian snapped as he turned a corner, emerging into a smaller cavern with a cloth roof, which sent dappled moonlight swimming about their feet. Khadija counted ten balloons, all different colors with the material laid flat across the ground, ready to be inflated. Three terrorists on the other end of the cavern were stacking barrels against the walls. Khadija dropped her head, tugging her hood over her face, but the terrorists paid little notice to them.

Darian scanned the cavern and marched toward a balloon that appeared to be made from spun gold with ropes interwoven with gold thread and a balloon hoop of a gold so pure she feared it would melt with the heat. Tiny beaded pearls were sewn across the seams of each shimmering panel and studded along the polished banisters framing the basket. It was a balloon far too regal for the damp cave that held it captive, and Khadija was itching to free it, as if, like the peri, it was a caged bird aching to see the sky. But it was too flashy, too obvious, she thought . . . even so, it was the smallest balloon there, and probably the easiest for two people to fly.

Darian leaned near her ear, the thin fabric of her headscarf the only thing stopping his lips from brushing her skin. Khadija withdrew. "Do you know how to light a balloon?"

She nodded.

He stepped into the gold balloon. The wicker basket was filled with crates of rice as well as cooking supplies and tools for navigation. A thud made their heads snap up, but it was just the terrorists slamming the door behind them. They were alone now.

"Light the balloon. I'll figure out how to open the ceiling. Then we'll get the peri."

Khadija nodded, and they set to work. Darian leaped over the basket and began brushing his fingers against the walls. If they couldn't open the ceiling, their escape would be ruined. Khadija focused on lighting the balloon, but the peri's shrieks kept stealing her attention. They were much louder. The peri must be close, and by her breathy screams she must be weak, possibly close to death. If she stood any chance, they needed to get her under the moonlight as, like the peri, the moon was celestial. They were one and the same: just as jinn were creatures of fire, peri were beings of the heavens.

She twisted the gas tap and retrieved the flint stones, scratching them together to create sparks. The burner roared to life with a bright orange flame. She grasped one end of the sheer gold material and started flapping. It reminded her of how she and Jacob had forced the hot-air balloon to life back in Sahli. Her mouth soured. And now she was leaving him here to be consumed by whatever twisted tales Vera was feeding him. But what choice did she have? He'd chosen his side. Now she had to choose hers.

She tired quickly but kept raising her arms as high as she could, demanding the balloon to breathe. Khadija puffed hard as a flash of moonlight bathed the cavern in silver. She squinted but didn't slow her pace as the ceiling opened like a blind, revealing the night sky. Darian returned with a smug grin and, grabbing one end of the balloon, joined her in flapping.

"Almost . . . there," Khadija heaved as the balloon came alive, swallowing the air and puffing out until the material was almost taut. "Spin the propeller." She pointed at the wooden fan blades inside the balloon. Darian grasped the handle and spun frantically.

Luckily, the balloon was small and easy to inflate. Soon, it was lifting off the ground. Darian threw a rope out and leaped from the basket, securing the rope to a post beside the balloon. The hot-air balloon struggled to escape but remained hovering above the ground. He flashed her a grin. "Nice work."

18

JACOB

Dawn was only a few hours away when Jacob finally stumbled through the sewer grate back to the Hāreef's tunnels after trudging aimlessly through the city's streets for longer than he cared to admit. It was a relief to be back, but with it came a jittering in his wrists that he struggled to conceal. What if they knew what he'd done? What if someone had seen him speaking with Anam?

Nonsense. No one had seen. But the knowledge did nothing to ease his trepidation. Jacob turned down empty tunnels that reminded him of hollowed-out wind chimes until the familiar smell of hot glass welcomed him. He entered the workshop.

"Ah, there he is."

Jacob froze, eyes scanning the workshop for life. Marcus and the other hāri had long since retired to sleep. A rustle of fabric from the corner made his head snap around as Sara rose from the stack of crates she'd been perched on.

"Decided to take a little detour?" There was a sharpness to her voice that made his insides twist into a knot.

No. She couldn't have seen. He'd made sure of that.

"So where could possibly be more important than the Hāreef?"

Every muscle in his back tensed, waiting for her accusation of betrayal. But none came, only her look of suspicion. His posture loosened slightly. She hadn't seen, he realized, only suspected. "I got lost," he mumbled.

Sara folded her arms. "Lost your cloak as well, did you?"

He cursed. In his haste to flee from Anam he'd left it discarded in the bush. "I didn't want the soldiers to catch me wearing it."

"Let me guess, you lost the brass and copper we collected as well?"

Jacob chewed on the inside of his cheek. "It was . . . making too much noise when I ran."

Sara tutted, unconvinced. "All I'm hearing right now is excuses. Do you think Vera cares for excuses?"

Was he supposed to answer? Jacob kept his mouth clamped shut.

"Seems Vera misjudged you." Her tone was biting. "You may be good at blowing glass, new boy, but you'll need to do more than that if you want to impress her. When we leave in a few days, we won't be taking the workshop with us. Maybe we won't take you with us either."

No. They had to take him. He had nowhere else to go. "Wait! Please. Just give me one more chance—"

Sara's snort cut him off mid-sentence. She'd been so nice before, the sudden change in her jarred him. Maybe no one was nice unless they had to be.

"That's not up to me, I'm afraid." She waved him over as she left the workshop in a swish of white material. "Vera has another task for you, and you've kept her waiting long enough. Hopefully, this one you don't screw up."

Jacob nodded meekly as he followed Sara through the tunnel network, the only sound being the pad of their footsteps and the crinkle of

Sara's cloak. He rubbed his eyes and forced himself to focus. He wasn't sure how long it had been since he'd last slept, but he fought the hazy fog that was beginning to make his limbs feel heavy, his eyes stiff and hard like balls of lead. This was it now. He had to prove himself. Whatever Vera asked him to do, he'd do without question. He'd always known befriending Khadija would come back to bite him, and yet he didn't regret telling Anam where Khadija was. He wasn't sure what Anam would be able to do, but it pushed the responsibility of Khadija's safety away from him. He didn't need that weighing on his mind.

As they turned down a series of tunnels, a moaning like the somber sigh of the ocean striking the shore made all the hair on his arms stand upright. It fell still, followed by a sharp, shrill scream that stole all the air in his lungs. "What is that?"

Sara made an abrupt left and struck the first closed door with her fist. A murmur from within, and she pushed it open. "Find out for yourself."

As the door swung open, another piercing scream had Jacob clamping his palms over his ears. He peered through the open doorway.

"Is this really necessary?" Vera's voice, but it was laced with concern, though not for him.

What he saw made Jacob's lungs drop into the pit of his stomach. Vera's once-white cloak was now studded with burn marks, but that didn't stop her reaching toward her son, worry etched across her face. Caleb dodged her advance, conjuring a green flame with a snap of his fingers, and slipped his hand between the cage bars, brushing his fingertips against the wings of a creature that was both woman and bird, and beautiful. Charred feathers stung Jacob's nostrils. The bird-woman shrieked and drew her wings back, the edges of her silver feathers singed black.

Bile rose up his throat when Jacob realized what she was. He'd heard stories of peri and their beauty, but they did not compare to seeing one up close. Who would do this? What monster would do this?

The ifrit sneered. "It's what she deserves, Ammi." He smacked the bars. The creature whimpered.

"Where's your pretty voice now, peri?" Caleb hissed. "The pretty voice that never sang for me when I died. I was forced to wander lost." He flashed a set of fangs. "Until Iblis found me and took me to Hell!" Caleb's forearms burst into flame. Jacob flinched.

The peri covered her delicate face with what remained of her wings. "Not everyone can hear our song—"

Caleb roared. "What did I do to deserve Hell? What did I do wrong?"

Vera stepped between Caleb and the cage, blocking the peri from view. "You did nothing wrong." Her voice carried years of heartbreak in each syllable. "The peri doesn't know what she's talking about." Vera kicked the cage. "I know you were a good boy. You don't need to do this—"

Caleb swerved around Vera and once more thrust a burning palm into the cage. The peri screamed. "I don't *need* to do this—but it certainly makes me feel . . . satisfied."

Jacob winced. Vera stuttered. It was strange seeing a woman who portrayed such confidence fumbling over her words. "Is it Sakhr who put you up to this? That bloody demon—"

"Sakhr was the one to capture the peri." Caleb smirked. "On my request."

Vera sucked in a breath.

"It seems we have an audience." Caleb whirled around, his leathery wings fanning out behind him.

Jacob gulped.

"What are you two doing here?" Vera barked.

Sara straightened up, clasping her hands behind her back to disguise their jittering. "You said you had another task for Jacob." Already she was backing out the door.

Vera's gaze fell to him, and Sara took the opportunity to flee down the hallway. Jacob's eyes flitted from Vera to the peri in a pile of her own blackened feathers. His mouth went dry. "Is there anything you need me to . . . do?"

Vera raised an eyebrow. "There is, though I'm hoping you will have this done far quicker than the last task—"

Footsteps hammering down the tunnel stole everyone's attention before Sara's face reappeared in the doorway. Vera rolled her eyes. "What now?"

Sara keeled over. "The rose garden entrance has been overrun," she wheezed.

"What?!" Vera was already striding toward them, casting a worried glance over her shoulder. "I'm sure you'll find another time to do . . . whatever this is." She beckoned Caleb over. The ifrit shot the peri a bloodthirsty grin before following. Jacob quickly dived out of his path.

Vera stormed down the tunnel, Sara and Caleb not far behind. Jacob cast the peri a final glance, and she stared back with tortured eyes. Then he stumbled after Vera.

"How many soldiers?"

"They're not soldiers."

Vera shot Sara an incredulous look. "Then who are they?"

"I think they're the Wāzeem." Sara's voice was lost to the clang of metal as hāri spilled into the tunnel, all with swords bared. Vera charged forward and was swallowed by the crowd. Jacob glimpsed fighting up ahead, and then the tunnel became so packed it was difficult to breathe. He shrank back as hāri pushed their way to the front. Caleb appeared ablaze, a bright green spark in the darkness, and the bodies swiftly parted as he marched to the front where Vera's red hair was just visible whipping around her like a bloody halo as she engaged in combat.

Jacob retreated. He wasn't sure what he'd been expecting when he'd spoken to Anam, but certainly not this, and not so soon. His breathing became shallow. If Vera were to discover what he had done, she would never forgive him. And if any of the Wāzeem were to spot him, and to call him by name, that would be the biggest giveaway.

It was that thought that sent him dashing in the opposite direction.

19

KHADIJA

Whimpers like the melancholy hum of a lost insect's wings guided her as Khadija sped through the tunnels.

"Sounds like it's coming from this direction." Darian made a left and stopped behind the first door, where the whimpers had transformed into weeping that made her own throat ache. Khadija hastily pushed the door open. "Oh my goodness!" She gasped. "What have they done to you?"

The peri was sobbing into her wings, pearlescent talons clawing uselessly at the heap of charred feathers beside her. Feathers that had once been a lustrous silver were now a deadened black. Acid pooled in Khadija's stomach. "They're monsters," she breathed as she approached the cage.

The peri's lilac eyes snapped up, and she shrank to the far corner, folding her patchworked wings over her face.

"It's all right," Khadija soothed, slipping her arms through the cage bars. "We're trying to help you."

Fat tears ran down the peri's cheeks, making the tips of her white lashes sparkle with wetness. "My wings . . ." She lifted the mess of twisted bones and snapped feathers that replaced her arms, then dropped them back down with a thud. Khadija's eyes fell to the bald patch on the side of her neck where part of the silver crown of feathers adorning the peri's head had been mercilessly plucked to expose gray skin. Khadija's knuckles curled around the iron bars.

"We should hurry." Darian's firm voice sliced through her rage.

Khadija nodded. "Find a key."

There was rustling from behind as Darian rummaged through the barbaric tools on the table. Then the creak of the door opening made her whirl around.

"Looks like we've got company."

A familiar figure appeared in the doorway. Her eyes narrowed. "Jacob!" No. He couldn't have. She glanced at the peri's tattered wings. He wouldn't do this. He wasn't a monster.

"Khadija," Jacob stuttered.

Then she saw red. "You did this!"

Jacob shook his head firmly. "No. I'd never!" He held his hands up. "I just wanted to see if she was all right."

Khadija growled. "Does she *look* all right?" As if in answer, the peri wailed like the dying notes of an instrument. The three of them winced at the sound. "Look at what they did to her, and you've chosen to side with them."

"I . . ." Jacob ran a hand through his fringe. "This isn't what they usually do. This was Caleb—the ifrit—not the Ḥāreef."

"I can't believe you chose *them* over the Wāzeem."

"The Wāzeem are your people, not mine."

"They want equality for both races."

Jacob snorted. "That doesn't exist! You can't change an old system without breaking it first."

Khadija spluttered. "Are you even listening to yourself?" These were not his words. "You've been brainwashed, Jacob."

Jacob's jaw clicked. "You're the one who's brainwashed if you think what's been done to that creature is any different to what your people do to mine." He stabbed a finger at the peri. "But I'm not expecting you to understand. Why would you want to break a system that suits you so well?"

He'd stolen all the words in her throat. Khadija could only stand there, stunned, until the grating sound of metal brought her back as Darian slipped a key into the lock. "We don't have time for this," he said over his shoulder. The cage door groaned open. "Is he coming with us or not?"

As if she'd ever allow him anywhere near her again. "No. We don't need him." Khadija joined Darian and reached a tentative hand toward the peri. Balancing her limp wings across their shoulders, they staggered toward the door. "Don't think about stopping us." She threw Jacob a glare as she sidestepped him, her arms burning underneath the peri's weight.

Khadija didn't turn at Jacob's next words. Instead, they pinned her in place like a blade burrowing into her ribs.

"Just go, and don't come back."

Then she and Darian dragged the peri around the corner, and Jacob was no more. The peri's breath was hot against her neck as they limped back through the tunnel as fast as they dared. Behind, the distant clang of metal seemed to follow them. "What is that?"

"Think the Hāreef have bigger problems than a missing peri right now," Darian puffed as they emerged into the balloon cavern with the open ceiling, where their hot-air balloon was hovering patiently, tied down by a single rope.

A slice of moonlight split the room in two. "Get her into the moonlight."

Together they guided the peri into the silvery light. The second the moon's rays bathed her skin, the peri came alive again, her feathers shimmering the way sand twinkles in the sunlight, not a hint of black burns remaining. She flexed her wings, broken bones cracking back into place, and turned to them with eyes that glistened like actual stars. "Thank you." Her voice was like raindrops tickling the surface of a flowing stream.

Khadija gasped. The peri was indeed beautiful, the most beautiful creature she had ever seen. The books did her no justice at all.

"Tell me how to repay your kindness." The peri fixed her lilac gaze on her.

Khadija shook her head. "There's no need to."

The peri's wings flickered to life, impatient to be among the stars. "If you ever need my help, please call for me. My name is Tahmina." Then, with a flutter of feathers, she was gone, leaving nothing but a silvery trail of moonlight in her place.

Khadija could only stand there, stunned, until Darian's voice snatched her back to the present. "We should get going too." Darian turned to the gold balloon. "That boy. Was he the one you meant? The one who betrayed you?"

Khadija's fingers curled into a fist. She nodded.

Darian hummed. "At least he had sense enough to let us leave without a fight."

He *had* let them go. But that did not excuse what he'd done. The side he'd chosen. "Let's go," she grunted.

Darian began fiddling with the rope tethering the balloon to the ground when the chiming of metal made them both stiffen. Whatever was happening out there, it was getting closer. Shouts spilled across the walls of the cavern.

Khadija clambered inside the basket and made for the burner just as figures in white cloaks poured into the room in a twist of combat. Blades scraped together. But who were the Hāreef fighting? A familiar face brandishing a curved sword and a copper whip caught her eye as she made a stab at a woman with bloodred hair.

Khadija's breath caught in her throat. "Anam!" It was the Wāzeem they were fighting, she realized.

Anam spun, ducking as Vera swung for her neck. "Khadija!" Her dark eyes traced over her, then shot to Darian beside the balloon, still in the white cloak of a terrorist, but instead of hovering uncertainly at his attire, her gaze fell to his face. A flicker of familiarity. Then she yelled, "Go!"

Khadija dug her nails into the basket's polished banister. "We have to help them."

But Darian had already unsheathed his blade and made a swipe for the nearest terrorist.

"Got out of your cage, did you?" Vera approached, her sword hanging from her hand like a metal limb. "I'm impressed. Seems you're not as useless as you appear." Her face twisted into a scowl.

Khadija stiffened. Vera advanced. Her eyes swept to Darian. "And who are you? A traitor? Sided with the darkers now, have you?" Moonlight glinted off the hilt as Vera brandished her blade. She swung and Darian ducked, swerving low then spinning, jumping back as she aimed a stab at his chest.

Khadija spun around the basket and squatted down, searching for a weapon. She grabbed a crate of rice and sent it hurling toward Vera. It smacked against the side of her head, spilling grain everywhere. Vera went down. She roared. Her blade skidded across the floor and Darian dived for it. Vera grabbed his ankle and yanked him back before Darian stilled her efforts by sinking an elbow into Vera's ribs. The two rolled across the ground in a knot of limbs as they fought to reach the blade. Vera was clearly trained, her movements quick, her jabs striking true, but Darian fought with a burning hatred in his eyes that gave power to his strikes. Khadija didn't know a simple kitchen boy could fight like that, or with that much rage coursing through him.

Vera landed a punch on Darian's jaw. Khadija heard his teeth grind together, and then Darian's eyes rolled back and he was still. Vera made for the sword again but slipped once more on the rice. Anam appeared, her blade arcing down, aimed at Vera's neck. Vera knocked her to the side and wrapped her hands around Anam's throat. Eyes wild, she dug her nails in and started to squeeze.

Khadija leaped out of the basket and retrieved Vera's sword. Her gaze flickered between Darian sprawled unmoving on the floor and Anam's puffed-out cheeks, which were beginning to tinge purple.

She didn't need to think. Khadija sank the blade into Vera's thigh!

Vera howled, and for a moment, everyone paused. Then the terrorists sprang to life, all swords pointed at Khadija as they zigzagged around the maze of deflated balloons in the cavern toward her. Khadija kicked Vera's injured leg. Vera cried out in pain and buckled, smearing blood across the ground.

Khadija then ran to Anam's side and yanked her up. "Come on!" They made for the balloon, each grabbing one of Darian's arms and dragging his limp body across the ground. Together, they hurled him into the basket. Terrorists were gaining on them from all angles—the remaining Wāzeem fighters were either busy fending them off or lay on the ground, dangerously still.

She was mere feet away from the balloon when a pair of hands caught her. She shrieked, kicking back wildly. Anam tackled Khadija's attacker to the ground. "Go!" She shoved a palm in the middle of Khadija's back. Khadija smacked into the wicker basket, then hurled herself up and over. "Anam!" she called out.

Anam had managed to fight off her attacker, but she had a nasty cut on her bicep that spurted blood whenever she moved. Khadija reached for her just as Vera appeared from the corner of her vision, charging, red hair billowing out behind her so that she resembled a lioness with a bloody mane. A screech like a bat in the dead of night made everyone turn just as a pair of inky-black wings appeared at Vera's side.

It was the ifrit, his palms aglow with green jinn fire, loathing simmering in his emerald eyes, which were fixed on Khadija.

"You dare to strike my ammi!" The ifrit took flight. Khadija ducked just as Anam leaped into his path, her copper whip cracking against the stone floor. She lashed out, whip licking the ifrit's cheek. The ifrit hissed but continued to power toward her. "It will take more than mere copper to stop me!"

Anam's next motions were a blur as she simultaneously dropped her whip and dived into the satchel strapped across her chest, producing something that looked flimsy and fragile, something that would snap apart at the faintest of touches. It was a line of flowers with their stems knotted together to make a chain. Something a child would wear around their neck. It surely had no purpose here in battle, and yet Anam laid it across the ground in front of the balloon.

The ifrit was closing in, near enough to slash the gold material with his talons. Khadija stretched a hand to Anam. "Come on!"

Anam raised her sword. The ifrit reached the chain of flowers and was immediately hurled backward with a growl that sent Khadija's teeth rattling—it was as if the flowers were a boundary of barbed wire that he could not cross. As if, like copper and brass, the flowers were a substance that would wound him.

The tip of Anam's sword punctured the ifrit's wing. The ifrit howled and flung the sword aside with a jerk of his wing, the force of the deflection knocking Anam sideways. Anam swiftly regained her footing and faced Khadija. A decision flashed across her face, quick, cold, and calculated.

"Anam!" Khadija called again.

Anam's blade sliced through the rope. The balloon containing Khadija and Darian, still out cold on the deck, leaped into the sky. The cavern shrank, and then she was soaring over Intalyabad, buildings shrinking to the size of her thumbnail in a matter of seconds. The basket groaned.

"No!"

Khadija's wrists refused to stop shaking. The whistle of air as she ascended snapped her into gear. They were going too high. The air was thinning. Khadija stumbled over Darian's body in her haste to grasp the tap of the gas canister, twisting it until the shriek of gas escaping was only a soft whistle. The balloon leveled. She hid her shivering in the floaty sleeves of her kameez.

Anam. She'd left her there to die. Khadija bit down on her tongue until she tasted blood. She had to go back. She had to save her. But she knew it was hopeless. What could she do?

Anam had sacrificed herself for them.

She scanned the balloon. There were sacks and crates of supplies, mostly food and, thankfully, a couple of large, full water gourds. She eyed a chest where golden astrolabes and navigation devices rattled together. Then her eyes rested on Darian. His chest was rising and falling. He would have appeared to only be sleeping if it wasn't for the dark stain coating his hair. Khadija grabbed a water gourd, tore a strip off of one of the burlap rice sacks, and crouched down to clean the wound. He didn't even flinch. He was completely gone. Who knew when he would wake up? Or if he ever would.

Khadija was not the sort of person who stared at faces, but with his eyes closed she found herself tracing his features, the curve of his eyelashes, the way his jawline met his exposed neck, more uncovered flesh than she knew what to do with. She hastily backed away, heat rushing to her face.

She stared into the darkness, her knuckles bone-white as they curled around the smooth ivory banisters at the edge of the basket. How long she stood there, she wasn't sure. When her eyelids became droopy with sleep, Khadija finally lay on the deck and let exhaustion claim her.

The next morning, Khadija awoke to banging. Her eyes snapped open. Darian was crouched by the wooden box of navigation tools, tossing metal devices over his shoulder, rather too heavy-handedly. The cut on his head had scabbed over, and there was a purple tinge showing the beginnings of a bruise around his left eye. But he was alive, and that meant she wouldn't be forced to fly the balloon alone, and that thought was reassuring.

He glanced her way. "Morning."

Khadija sat upright, promptly checking her headscarf was still secure. The balloon groaned as Darian padded across the deck and tugged on a rope that had been woven with gold thread. She craned her neck back and gasped. Glimpsing the gold balloon in the cavern was nothing compared to being encased within its shimmering fabric, listening to the rustle of the sheer material as the balloon breathed, each breath causing the beaded pearls bordering each seam to dance in the morning rays. She blinked rapidly, her vision streaked with colored blobs. Khadija peered over the edge. Intalyabad was long gone, the horizon dotted with yellow wheatfields and bright green pastures. The balloon was caught in a steady wind current that tickled the tip of her nose, and by the way Darian bent over the map spread across the deck, the direction they'd settled on was no accident.

"Where are we going?" She tried to disguise the tremble to her voice. She couldn't really trust him, and now that they were alone he might decide he had no further use for her. Khadija backed away until her hip bumped the edge of the basket, feeling suddenly claustrophobic. Who was in charge here? Whoever was would be the one who got to decide which way the balloon was flying.

"I figured we'd better put as much distance between us and Vera as possible."

Khadija hummed. He was avoiding her question.

"An—" Darian cleared his throat. "Your friend. The woman."

Anam. "She didn't make it." Her voice was barely audible.

Darian scratched his head. "That's a shame." He turned back to the box of navigation tools. "How did you know her?"

Khadija had to bite her tongue to prevent herself from blurting out everything she knew of the Wāzeem. She couldn't trust him. He used to be a terrorist. Could still be. Either way, the less he knew about her the safer she felt in his presence.

"I didn't know her very well. She helped me when I came to Intalyabad." Her voice quivered. "She was kind to me."

Darian nodded slowly.

She sighed. She had to say it now before she lost the courage. "How do I know I can trust you?"

He cocked an eyebrow.

"I mean, you were part of the Hāreef." She tried to make her voice sound as challenging as possible, but it came out as more of a squawk.

Darian laughed. "I . . . Look, you've got nothing to worry about."

Khadija crossed her arms.

"If it makes you feel better, I can drop you off at the nearest town."

"Why do you get to keep the balloon?"

He smirked. "Because it was my idea to steal it."

She scoffed. "Excuse me, but when you woke up this morning, how did you think you got here? Without me, you'd still be stuck with Vera." She paused. "If she hadn't already killed you by now."

His eyes sparkled. Khadija met his gaze with a stiff jaw. It was a stalemate.

Then Darian relented. "Can you fly?"

She chewed her lip to stop a smile from forming. "A little."

The day passed quickly, the awkwardness between them building with each passing hour until Khadija was sure it would weigh the balloon down. As much as she tried not to, her mind couldn't help but return to

Jacob. That familiar rage bubbled inside, but it simmered back down just as quickly as it had flared up. She could be angry all she wanted, but she could never change what was inside his head, and it was time she accepted that. Jacob was not Hassan. He was not a Ghadaean. He was nothing like her. No matter how much she wished to believe they could be similar, despite their differences in race, it was clear they were not. Hāri and Ghadaeans were poles apart. Her mouth soured. It sounded a lot like something Abba would say, but maybe he'd been right all along, and she'd been too naive to see it. Even after Hassan's and Ammi's deaths, she'd still refused to see what was blatantly in front of her. As Abba would say, she had a lot of growing up to do.

Khadija watched Darian stalk across the deck, his boots thumping loudly. This balloon was smaller than her previous one, so any semblance of privacy seemed impossible and Darian's pacing only served to remind her of that. There was something unsettling about his presence, as if he took up more space in the balloon than he should. He slumped himself down with the air of someone who felt comfortable, almost too comfortable. As if he didn't consider her a significant threat to him. As if he was perfectly in control of the situation and knew it. Khadija eyed him warily. She would not make the same mistake in befriending him as she had Jacob.

Darian glanced her way, and Khadija quickly hid Hassan's page from view, which she'd been staring at as if she could leap straight into the drawing if she thought hard enough. She pretended to busy herself with reorganizing their meager supplies.

Darian caught the motion. "What's that?"

She shrugged. "Nothing really. Just a piece of paper."

He hummed. "And what's on the piece of paper?"

There was no point lying. "Just a page from a book."

His eyebrows rose. "You can read?"

"A little. It's more from memory that I'm able to read it." She dropped her gaze, fidgeting with the buckles of her sandals.

"Who taught you to read?"

And just like that, her mind jumped at the first opportunity to shut the conversation down. Khadija crossed her arms. "Does it matter?"

He started at the coldness in her voice. Even Khadija was surprised by it too.

He threw his palms up. "Don't have to tell me if you don't want to." Khadija didn't respond. The silence between them grew. Darian started whistling to relieve some of the awkwardness. That just annoyed her further.

"So . . . any ideas what you'll do when we land?"

She shrugged. "I'll figure it out. On my own," she added.

Darian caught her tone and rose. At least that conversation was over. The less they spoke, the less he'd know about her. The less chance he'd have to stab her in the back like Jacob had. Darian unfolded the map and ran a hand across his chin, where a sprinkling of stubble was appearing. It gave him a ragged, almost feral appearance.

Heat rose to her cheeks. If only Abba could see her now, sharing a balloon with a hāri boy . . . again! He'd lose his last little tufts of hair in an instant—though he'd had no issue with her sharing a bed with that shoemaker, disguising it beneath the pretense of marriage, as if that somehow made the idea of it more palatable.

"The wind is pushing us south." Darian stabbed a finger on the map. "I was thinking we travel to Al-Shaam. It's the closest city now." He paused. "And I have some business I need to attend to there."

Khadija's mouth formed a ring. "*You* can read?"

Darian grinned. "I can."

Just like Ghadaean women, hāri were not permitted to read. That honor was exclusive to Ghadaean men. Whoever had taught him surely had some courage. "How?"

"Does it matter?" Darian chuckled and flashed her a wink. She pretended not to see it.

By late afternoon, the only sound was the ragged puffs of their breathing as they tried to handle the heat. Khadija's mind felt as if it had turned to liquid. Every movement caused her melted brain to slosh around her skull. She pressed her fingers to her temple. She was getting a migraine.

Darian attempted small talk with her throughout the day, most of which Khadija either blatantly ignored or shut down with one-word replies.

"Not much of a talker, are you?" he grunted.

Khadija said nothing.

"Bet you can't wait to be rid of me and be out there on your own." He inclined his head toward the horizon.

Guilt made her chew on the insides of her cheek. "It's nothing personal. I just prefer being alone."

"I get it. You trusted that boy and it backfired. You would be an idiot to make the same mistake twice." Darian pursed his lips. "And you don't strike me as an idiot." He paused, as if rearranging his next words in his mind before saying, "But you've got nothing to worry about. If I wanted to hurt you, I've had plenty of chances to."

He wasn't wrong. Darian could have hurled her over the edge while she slept, but perhaps he hadn't because it required two people to fly the balloon.

The mistrust on her face prompted Darian's next words. "If it makes you feel better, I'm not a terrorist. I never was."

Khadija let out a single hollow laugh. "Why do I find that so hard to believe?"

"It's true."

She twirled so that her back was to him as her eyes traced the fluffy outlines of the distant clouds. Darian shot to his feet and tailed her like a foul smell. "Your friend. The one who got left behind when we escaped Vera."

Khadija's brow creased.

"She was called Anam."

"How did you know—"

"She is Wāzeem." Darian paused. "I am Wāzeem."

She shook her head. That didn't make any sense.

"I was undercover. I'd been sent to gather information about the Hāreef, but after the nawab's death and Vera's plans to leave Intalyabad, I thought it best I leave before my cover was blown." He smiled wryly, and the motion caused a fluttering in Khadija's chest like it housed a tiny bird. Or perhaps it was the close proximity between them that made it suddenly difficult to breathe. "Thought I'd better bring you with me too. Couldn't leave you in that cage."

Khadija stepped back and studied him. She pictured Darian as a spy. She had to admit it suited him more than terrorism. "Why didn't you say anything before?"

He shrugged. "Would you have believed me before? Do you even believe me now?"

That question stumped her. "I don't know what I believe about you yet."

Darian's mouth twitched. "Well, you've got plenty of time to figure it out. It will be a few days before we arrive in Al-Shaam."

A part of her bristled with excitement. It was an overwhelming amount of freedom; it made her dizzy just thinking about it. The chance to finally reinvent herself. To be out there on her own, making her own decisions, having the freedom to do whatever, go wherever, be whomever she pleased. It was the same excitement that had preceded her arrival in Intalyabad, before that went spectacularly wrong—perhaps this time would be different.

But she was a girl. That thought was enough to slam her back down to reality. She could not work, read, write, or even own property. She was useless without a man. Maybe it would be better to admit defeat and return to Abba with her tail between her legs, and pray the shoemaker boy was still open to marrying her. Khadija threw her head back, squinting at the sky. Would she really do that? Condemn herself to a life spent indoors? Maybe before, she could have, but now that she'd had a taste of freedom, she'd always be craving more.

There was only one thing she was sure of: She was done involving herself with terrorists and protestors. From now on, life would be simple for her, if there was such a thing. Just her and the sky, like she'd always wanted.

"Can't wait," Khadija responded.

"You sure about that?" Darian's lips upturned. A crooked half smile. "It's a scary place, you know. You don't see many Ghadaean girls out there alone either. Too easy a target."

He was being patronizing. She clenched her jaw. "I'll manage."

"I'm sure you will." He grinned, clicking his tongue against his front teeth. "But I am curious. Why did you leave your home? Your family? How did you even come to meet Anam?"

Her silence didn't seem to faze him.

"And please explain to me where you managed to find that boy. What was his name?"

"Jacob," she breathed, as if even his name tasted poisonous now. She bristled. "So many questions. Am I really that interesting to you?"

Darian leaned in, his breath tickling the tip of her nose. "Very." He lingered there for a fraction longer than necessary before pulling back.

Khadija didn't breathe. Her heart was thrumming. She prayed Darian couldn't hear it. Khadija wasn't about to reveal all her secrets to him. Far from it. She'd give him only enough to stop him from talking, and nothing more. "We met in Sahli."

His eyes widened. They were the color of amber. The type of eyes you could lose yourself in if you weren't careful. "You mean the Sahli that burned to the ground? *That* Sahli?"

She nodded, reminded of dead hāri children and buildings being swallowed by green hellfire. She shuddered. "We were there when it happened."

Darian's face softened. "Your family?" His concern seemed genuine. Either that or he was a master performer.

Maybe it was the sincerity of his voice, or the richness of his eyes, or perhaps the heat messing with her head, but she started to feel herself opening up. After all, who knew how long they'd be floating around up here for? What harm was there in small talk? "Don't worry. I'm not from Sahli originally."

Darian audibly sighed. "Well, thank God for that."

"Jacob was though."

Darian leaned back on his elbows. "Now it makes sense. He lost someone, didn't he?"

Shame washed over her. She had no business telling Darian this. It wasn't her secret to tell. That didn't stop her from nodding. "Yes." She pictured William. How Jacob had clung to every word the older boy said. She imagined the loss, the grief, the pain.

For Jacob, it was still raw. Khadija had been a mess in the weeks following Hassan's and Ammi's deaths. Months even. It didn't excuse Jacob's behavior, not entirely, but it made a lot of sense. Part of her anger toward him died. Grief wreaked all kinds of havoc on the mind, she knew that firsthand. Of course Jacob was incapable of making sane decisions. And all it had taken was someone to prey on his vulnerabilities, sell him a dream of empty promises, and he'd snapped it up without question.

Darian was studying her. She could feel his gaze sweeping across her face. Her skin prickled. "That's a shame. I guess, being hāri, we're used to it by now." There was a fiery heat behind his words that made Khadija's cheeks tinge with guilt. "You're lucky you still have some family left."

She nodded, not daring herself to speak.

"Then why'd you leave them?" The accusation in his voice was spilling out.

I don't have to explain myself to you. Her face hardened. "I had my reasons." *Now back off.*

He chuckled. "Don't we all."

He was mocking her again. Khadija clenched her fists. He didn't know her well enough to mock her. "You think I should have stayed, do you?"

Darian's smile deepened. His eyes creased. He knew she was getting worked up. And he was enjoying it. She seethed. "Hey, I don't know your reasons, but I think I can guess. Something along the lines of an arranged marriage, am I right?"

Her eyes widened. How had he . . . ?

"No wedding ring, which is unusual for a girl your age." She glanced at her naked hand. "You Ghadaean girls are so predictable." He folded his arms, a smug smile gracing his lips.

"Proud, are you?" she hissed. Darian seemed to be an expert at riling her up, and right now she was furious. "You know, I think I've decided what I think of you now."

Darian edged closer. "Enlighten me."

"You're rude and arrogant. And I'm surprised this balloon is still in the air with your gigantic head weighing it down!" Then she rose, leaving Darian to gawk at her.

20

JACOB

Jacob watched another body being unceremoniously dumped into a pile. He covered his nose with his sleeve. Vera was in the center of it all, batting away hāri with an irritated flick of her wrist as they brought her drinks, something to eat, offered her a stool to sit on to rest her injured leg. "I'm fine," she snapped, leaning on her cane. She massaged her thigh.

The Wāzeem's raid had been more of a nuisance than anything else. The Hāreef had lost few in comparison to them, and now their bodies were being put to use. Despite everything, Jacob's chest felt lighter. At least Khadija had escaped.

Hāri parted as Caleb stormed into the cavern in a flurry of wings, the left one punctured. He shoved a figure forward, leaving a burned handprint against their leather armor.

It was Anam.

"Last one." His claws protracted. "I'll take care of it."

Jacob's throat closed up. Anam caught his eye with a look of pure hatred. He dropped his gaze, scalded. He hadn't realized she'd come too. Hadn't realized she would have Caleb's claws pressed to her neck, which wouldn't have been there if it hadn't been for him. Fresh guilt threatened to drown him.

Vera's cane clicked against stone as she limped over. "No. I have something else in mind for her."

Caleb flashed his pointed teeth. "Something . . . torturous, no doubt."

Vera winced as her knee buckled. She righted herself, leaning heavily on her cane as she looked Anam up and down. "You are an exorcist. I saw your trick with the flowers. Very clever." She grinned. "You are a good warrior too."

When Anam didn't respond, Vera smirked. "Not a fan of praise, I see." She snapped her fingers. "A talented fighter like yourself, it would be foolish of me to let you go to waste."

Anam's voice was like the peal of a bell as it rang across the cavern, deep but pure, not even the hint of a tremor. If she was afraid, she did not show it. "I would never work for you."

Vera hummed. "Oh, you don't need to tell me that. I already know you wouldn't." She tapped a nail to her chin. "The jinniya Queen Mardzma would take a liking to you. She has quite the appetite for the heart of a warrior."

"Are you sure that is wise, Ammi? Queen Bidhukh is our only queen. To involve another jinniya queen would suggest we are disloyal." Caleb hissed. "And it would be an insult to the queen of female warriors to present her with this . . . thing . . . this fake woman." He spat.

Anam's left eye twitched, but she remained otherwise unfazed by Caleb's strange comment. *A fake woman?* Jacob studied her. She seemed pretty real to him.

"You don't know the jinniya queen well at all if you think she will not be impressed by her. She is a fine warrior." She gestured at Anam like she was a slab of meat.

"Her!" Caleb scoffed. "That is not a her. That is an impostor. A clown in a costume."

Anam's teeth clicked together.

"Queen Bidhukh will not be happy when she hears of this!" Caleb narrowed his eyes and turned to leave. "You think it is as simple as offering Queen Mardzma a warrior's heart. You do not understand Al-Ghaib or the beings that live there like I do." He stormed out, leaving a fiery ash cloud in his wake. Red sparks floated in the air.

"Caleb!" Vera's face was etched in lines that made her look frailer. She turned to Anam. "Queen Mardzma will be impressed with you, I'm sure of it, and in exchange for your heart she'll grant us her jinniya army to command." Vera beckoned a hāri man over. "Lock her up. Take good care of her. We want her looking fit for a queen."

Anam was led away. She put up no fight, head held high, walking with the dignity of a queen and not a terrified prisoner. Jacob couldn't help but admire her, until he remembered he was the reason she was about to have her heart ripped out by a jinniya queen.

He batted the guilt away before it could fester, conjuring the flames inside of him to burn fiercely, turning his guilt to steam. This was the way it had to be. *It's us or them.* He'd have to get used to this. There would be many Anams, just as there would be many Khadijas. He could not sympathize with them all, not when they couldn't care less about him and his people.

"Ah, Sara." Vera's voice was clipped, her eyes focused on the passageway Caleb had stormed down. "Any news?"

Sara nodded briskly. "Since the nawab's death there's been widespread panic. The darkers are terrified of another attack."

Vera's eyes glimmered. "Excellent!"

An image of the nawab's corpse sprawled across the ground, the jinniya Queen Bidhukh feasting on the flesh, made Jacob shudder.

Sara scowled. "Tensions are at their highest. Many cities are refusing to allow hāri on the streets altogether. The darkers are killing off hāri left, right, and center." Her face twisted into a wicked smile.

Vera nodded, her mouth set in a firm line. She turned to Jacob. "It is unfortunate, of course." She placed a hand on her chest. "I more than anyone hate to see my people suffering, but oftentimes things must first get worse before they get better." She gestured for Sara to continue. "Go on."

"Our people have nowhere left to go, it seems. Nowhere is safe now."

Vera soaked up her words. She was silent for some time, clicking her tongue against her teeth, before she exclaimed, "This is exactly what we need!"

Jacob's brow furrowed. He failed to see how their people dying would solve things. If anything, Vera had just made things worse for them. It was as the nawab had said. His death had sparked widespread outrage among the Ghadaeans, and innocent hāri were bearing the brunt of her actions.

"We need our people to get angry. We need them riled up so that they'll do anything for change. We need them to suffer. Suffer to the point that they refuse to suffer any longer." Vera clasped her hands together, her lips upturned. "Then we channel their anger. Give them the opportunity to act on it while their anger is fresh. Wait too long, and the fear will start creeping in."

Jacob gulped. Change required sacrifice, of course, but he hadn't expected the sacrifice to include their own people. He chewed on the inside of his cheek. But then, what did he know? He wasn't a leader. If it was the only way, then it was the only way. Surely, in the long run, fewer hāri would die because of Vera's actions. Surely.

"Now, there are a few things I must discuss with Caleb." Vera's brows knitted together as her jade eyes once more flickered to the tunnel Caleb had departed down. "Why don't you go to the glass shop, Jacob? See if you're needed there."

Realizing he was being dismissed, Jacob hurried off down the tunnel, glad to be free of the cavern and all those bodies with their familiar faces. His footsteps padding in the dark seemed to match his own heart. Fast, irregular, stumbling every few yards. Lost in his own thoughts, he didn't pay much attention to the empty cages he passed until one of them whispered, "Jacob."

He jumped out of his skin. Jacob spun.

"So you are one of them." Anam sat cross-legged in the dirt, back perfectly straight.

He stuttered. *I don't have to explain myself to her.* It was none of her business what he chose to do.

"You choose them over the Wāzeem."

Heat fired up his throat. "I choose whatever is best for my people. I choose actual progress, not just empty promises."

"Is that what you think the Wāzeem are? Empty promises." Anam shook her head. She looked more disappointed than angry.

Jacob threw his hands in the air. "That protest." He scoffed. "The nawab wasn't even listening. He didn't care. What did you actually think that was going to achieve?"

Anam's voice was cold. "You think killing him was the better option?"

His words jumbled in his throat. "I—" He ran his hand through his fringe. "I didn't know about that, but at least now they've gotten the message."

"Which is?"

"They need to start taking hāri seriously."

Anam's dark eyes bored into him. "Have you seen what is happening to your people up there?" She pointed to the ceiling. "Tell me, how is this better? The Wāzeem were making progress. We were negotiating with those in power." She growled. "And you ruined all those years of hard work with a single reckless act."

Jacob ground his teeth. She was wrong. What progress could they have possibly made if the only audience they could get with the nawab was catching him leaving his morning prayers just to shout a few garbled sentences at him? That was not progress. "It's done now."

The corner of Anam's mouth twitched. "You are right. It is done." She sighed. "And now it is over, or at least for me. That is if the jinniya queen does not mind feasting on a fake woman." Her lips curled over her teeth.

Jacob dropped his head, fiddling with his sleeves. "What did Caleb mean by that?"

"It means"—Anam uncrossed her legs and began unlacing her boots—"I was not born female. Mardzma is the queen of *female* fighters." She shrugged. "My heart is probably worthless to her." Then she turned away, sinking into the shadows in the corner of her cell.

21

KHADIJA

There was something reassuring about being up in the air again, like it was the only place she felt truly safe. The swaying motion of the balloon calmed her, the silence, the moisture in the air that she could taste on the tip of her tongue like fresh rain. Khadija spent most of the time sketching, using the reverse side of the map when Darian wasn't squinting over it. She had to admit, he was a far more experienced balloonist, familiar with the purpose of each navigation tool and the numbers shown on the dials beside the burner, frequently consulting them before adjusting the ropes or dropping the altitude. But flying really was a two-person job, and Darian was often instructing her to feed the fire or spin the propeller while he studied the cloud movements for the fastest air current.

Despite his frequent instructions, they'd spoken little that day, a sticky awkwardness between them that clung to her skin.

The creak of the deck told her Darian had finished peering through the telescope at the ground and had joined her at the basket's edge. She didn't lift her head as he approached, eyes fixed on the horizon. Her reed pen scratched the parchment paper. For a moment, that was the only noise.

Darian whistled. "You're very good at that."

"Thank you." She traced the sweeping domes of the clouds, shading the underside of the ones heavy with rain, gliding the tip of the pen against the page with sharp flicks of her wrist as she drew the thinner, wispier clouds that had virtually no moisture remaining and were at risk of evaporating into the air.

A shadow appeared across the page as Darian leaned closer. She could feel him hovering by her neck. "As pretty as it is though, I may need to borrow the map."

"One second." Khadija's reed pen hovered above the page, thickening a line, adding a touch more shading, dotting the page to mimic the bumpy texture of the clouds. "OK. Done." She handed it back. "Don't smudge it."

Darian delicately flipped it over by the corner. "I'll try not to." A few seconds of silence passed as he studied the page before exhaling. "I wanted to apologize for earlier. I was rude before. I shouldn't have made that assumption about"—he gestured to the absent wedding band on her ring finger—"you."

Khadija picked at the black ink trapped beneath her nails. "It's fine. You were right anyway."

"That's . . ." he stuttered, "surprising."

"Surprising, how?"

Darian ran his hands across his scalp. "I just thought someone like you would already be married."

The way Darian said *you* made a nervous flutter build in the back of Khadija's throat. She quickly swallowed it down and folded her arms. "Is that what you thought?" There was a heat to her voice. "Maybe I'm not married because I don't *want* to be married."

Darian guffawed. "Isn't that all you Ghadaean girls care about? Marriage and babies."

Khadija growled. Just when she thought she might be able to get along with him, he had to say something like that. "It might surprise you to learn that we're not all the same, you know." She huffed. "I have no interest in marriage or babies."

Darian raised his palms in surrender. "You're right. Sorry, I—"

Khadija cut him off. There was no stopping her once she was sufficiently riled up. "I left because I refused to live the life that had been chosen for me. I wanted the freedom to choose my own path." She stabbed a finger at Darian's chest. "Sounds a lot like what you wanted when you chose to join the Wāzeem, doesn't it? The freedom to be more than what is expected of you, more than what people assume you're supposed to be."

"What did Anam tell you about the Wāzeem?"

She shrugged. "Not much. That you believe in equality for both races but only through nonviolent means." Khadija thought back to the disaster of the protest in Intalyabad, and she couldn't stop Jacob's earlier words from replaying in her mind. *Why would you want to break a system that suits you so well?* That system didn't suit her as well as Jacob thought, but at least that system wasn't designed to get her killed. Breaking it would surely mean deaths though, and that was the problem. Who would have to die for the system to crumble? Jacob seemed convinced it was every Ghadaean.

"And do you agree with that?"

"Of course . . ." She paused. "But I saw the Wāzeem protest. I don't think it achieved anything."

She expected Darian to argue his case. What she didn't expect was for him to say, "You're right. It didn't achieve anything. And now the nawab's dead."

She inhaled, gathering the courage to ask, "So why are we going to Al-Shaam?"

"Vera is planning her next attack on the Nawab of Al-Shaam. We have to warn the Wāzeem there. Help them protect the city."

Khadija pictured a world where all three nawabs lay dead, ruled instead by the Hāreef. She swallowed. The Ghadaeans would become the hāri, the hāri the Ghadaeans. The roles would be reversed and yet the world would remain the same.

"Don't worry. Once we arrive, you are free to do whatever you please. I wouldn't want to endanger someone who only half believes in our cause." There was a brittleness to his words that stung more than just her pride.

"That sounds best." Khadija snatched the map back. "I'll take that now." She resumed drawing.

Darian had sense enough to leave her to simmer down, busying himself with the balloon as the sky slowly darkened, unaware of the true effect his words had had on Khadija. Of course she believed in freedom for hāri people, now that her eyes had been opened to the true extent of their suffering. She wasn't a monster, but she knew how the world worked. It was a hopeless cause, even more hopeless thanks to the Hāreef and all they'd done in tarnishing the reputation of hāri people even further. It wasn't fair how an entire race of people could be judged by the extremist actions of a small minority, but life wasn't fair.

That last thought caused a heaviness in her limbs that she realized to be shame. Maybe Darian was right. She only half believed because, in spite of everything that had happened, she only half cared.

Khadija sighed and set down her reed pen, her eyes wandering to Darian. She'd done well in ignoring him for quite some time now. That was, until he picked up a gold disc with tiny symbols etched around the circumference and miniature cogs and mechanisms that reminded

Khadija of a clock. She'd always been curious what that device did. She peered over the edge of her page, careful not to make it obvious she was watching him as Darian began twisting the outer dials, frequently snapping his head up at the splattering of stars that were beginning to appear. He twisted it a few more turns before saying, "If you want to know what it does, all you have to do is ask."

Khadija quickly dropped her gaze. Her cheeks were flaming.

Darian rolled his eyes. "Come on. I'll show you."

Her pride tried to tug her back, but her curiosity got the better of her. Khadija approached.

"This is an astrolabe. It helps us track the position of the stars to determine latitude. We can then use this when referring to the map so that we follow the correct lines." He touched her wrist and twisted it so that the map flipped in her hands. "This is beautiful, by the way." His finger hovered over her recent sketch of the moon partially covered by clouds.

"Thank you," she breathed, skin tingling at his touch.

He traced his fingertip across the dotted lines of the map. "Latitude for north-to-south positioning. Longitude for east to west."

Khadija tried to mask the interest from her voice. "How do you know all this?"

Darian's eyes sparkled. He leaned in. Closer than he needed to. "I'll tell you if you tell me who taught you to read."

And just like that, her whole body jerked back to reality. "Never mind." She widened the space between them. "I'm tired." She plonked herself on the sanded oak bench that bordered the basket's interior and rested her head against the gold armrest, tiny pearls and gemstones digging into her cheek. She rolled over, though she knew she wouldn't sleep, not with him watching her.

* * *

The next morning, Khadija awoke first, having drifted into a light doze at some point during the night. Darian was splayed across the polished deck beside the sacks of rice and the mahogany armchair with the ornate arms that were carved into a falcon's beak. He was snoring loudly, his chest rising the way a balloon inflates as it breathes in air. Below, the ground was already transforming from lush green to pale gold as rolls of sweeping sand dunes stretched as far as the eye could see.

Khadija studied Darian's sleeping face, his dark brows, his sharp jaw, the high points of his cheeks where a shine of sweat made his skin glow like he'd been out in the rain. There was a flush to his neck where the sun was just beginning to leave its mark on his fair skin. She couldn't deny he was handsome, but that meant nothing, of course.

Her eyes lingered on his face for a fraction longer before her hands started to jitter, the artist in her screaming to be let out. She reached for the map, now mostly covered in clouds and ink marks, dipped her reed pen in the inkpot, and started to draw.

Darian awoke just as she was dotting his chin with the speckle of beard shadow. He growled the way a lazy tiger yawns in the sunshine and stretched his arms wide so that his tunic rode up, exposing a flash of pale skin. Khadija blushed.

"Morning, princess."

Her lips parted. Did he actually just . . . ? She seethed. That's it. He was going overboard.

Darian smirked, seemingly unaware of how close he was to plummeting toward the ground. He eyed the map resting on her lap.

Khadija quickly flipped it over, not caring if the ink smudged.

An amused smirk tickled his lips. "What were you drawing?"

"Nothing."

Darian hummed. "OK." He settled back on his heels. Khadija relaxed.

Then he pounced.

She snatched the map up, but Darian was quick, hand clamping on the opposite corner. "Let me see." His smirk deepened into a mischievous grin. He was clearly enjoying this.

"No." She tugged.

The paper crackled.

"Let go or it'll rip." He flicked the corner up, teasing a look at the other side. "Unless what you've drawn is worth spending the rest of your life stuck up here with me."

God, no amount of embarrassment was worth that! She flung the map at him. "Fine." She rose. "Laugh and I swear I'll send you over the edge."

Darian pressed his lips together to stop a smile from forming. He turned the map over. "It's . . ." His eyebrows rose. "It's me."

Khadija's skin was heating up. "Don't get excited. There's not much to draw up here other than clouds."

A smile was threatening to tug on the corners of Darian's lips. It only made her face feel like it was on fire. "I'm flattered you found me more interesting than clouds. Although is that really what you think my nose looks like?"

Khadija struggled to swallow her snort in time. "It smudged."

"Ah." His knees clicked as he rose. "Well, that's made my morning."

Her ears burned.

"Time for breakfast."

Khadija had expected him to toss her an orange and call it breakfast.

What she hadn't expected was for Darian to roll his sleeves up, sprinkle flour on the deck, and start kneading fresh dough, stretching it between his fingers until it was almost see-through.

He must have caught her staring because he said, "I worked in the kitchens, remember." He brushed each paratha with a generous layer of ghee and sprinkled the tops with carom seeds before toasting them on the balloon's burner. When the edges began to golden, he flipped one onto a plate and slid it across to her.

Khadija ripped off a corner. The dough was soft, flaky, and exactly how she liked it. "So you can be nice."

"On occasion." Darian tossed the next one over the fire so that the flames just licked the edges. "But it is extremely tiring and it's not something I do often."

She rolled her eyes. "So, we get there tomorrow?"

He nodded. "Just two more days with this." He gestured at himself. "Think you can manage?"

She hid her smirk in another mouthful of dough. "I'll try."

The day dragged on, though conversation flowed easier than it had the day before. The sun shone fiercely overhead, so bright Khadija was forced to keep her eyes firmly clamped shut for most of the day, or risk being blinded. Even with her eyes closed, the sun turned her world red. Darian's quick, shallow breaths and the creak of the ropes in the breeze were the only things to remind her she was in fact in a hot-air balloon and not the fiery pits of Hell. Though she doubted Hell could be much hotter than this. They were flying southwest through the Rajah Desert now, the air growing hotter with every passing hour.

Darian glugged some water, then pressed the water gourd into her hand. Her eyes snapped open.

"I think I'd prefer taking my chances with the Hāreef again over this," he said.

She lifted the water gourd to her lips. His cheeks were cherry red. She winced. A part of her knew she shouldn't. The less they knew about each other, the better. It was safer that way, but she couldn't deny her curiosity. What was Darian's story? He was like a prism that was only revealing one side to her.

"What was it like working undercover with the Hāreef?"

Darian propped himself on his elbows and met her gaze. "Let's just say I learned how far some people are willing to go, all in the name of revenge." His voice cut through the air like a knife. "And that grief is powerful. Vera's already lost everything dear to her. That makes her dangerous because she has nothing left to lose."

Khadija pictured the fiery ifrit Vera had called her son. "But she brought him back . . . sort of."

"That creature is far from the son she would have known." Darian shook his head. "It would have been much kinder to let him stay dead than to involve Queen Bidhukh in his resurrection."

Khadija's stomach convulsed as an image of the jinniya queen feasting on the nawab's corpse intruded her mind. "Why is Queen Bidhukh helping the Hāreef? What does she have to gain?"

Darian scratched his beard. "I'm still trying to work that one out. Why would she willingly give her jinn army to Vera? It just doesn't make sense!" He thumped his head. "She must have a motive. Jinn don't do anything for free."

He was right about that. Khadija's brows knitted together. "She said she needed the nawab's blood and that Vera would be seeing more of her now without having to use the mirror."

"Jinn can't freely cross into our realm unless the barrier between our world and Al-Ghaib is thin enough, which only happens at the point of death." Darian paced the deck. "When something weak dies, like an animal, only a weaker jinn can cross over. The stronger the jinn, the larger the death needed to bring them into our world. The nawab's death must've been powerful enough to enable Queen Bidhukh to cross over. He was a nawab. She is a queen. They were equals, so the balance was right. The mirror was likely a way to communicate before she could cross over." Darian dabbed his damp forehead with his fingers. "But why did she need his blood?"

"The nawabs have ruled this land for countless generations. Their blood is tied to this place," Khadija said. "To our world."

Darian nodded. "Maybe drinking his blood was enough to tie her to this realm, in the same way the nawab's blood ties him to his land." He faced her and shrugged.

It made sense. It made a lot of sense. A chill crept across her skin. "If the blood could tie her to this realm, she wouldn't need to wait until the point of death to cross over anymore." Khadija met Darian's eyes.

"She'd be able to cross over whenever." Darian stared into the orange depths of the balloon's burner and twisted the gas tap so that the fire roared to life.

"Maybe Queen Bidhukh isn't really helping the Hāreef at all." Her voice dropped to a whisper. "Maybe she's just using them to get to a greater prize . . . Ghadaea itself."

"If that's the case," he replied, "then we are all in even graver danger than I realized."

22

JACOB

The creak of the top bunk as Marcus clambered down awoke him. Jacob burrowed his fists in his eyes. Marcus always rose at dawn, and insisted Jacob did the same. "We've a long day ahead. Best get an early start."

Jacob groaned. As much as he found glassblowing a welcome reprieve from the chaos that had engulfed the tunnels as the Hāreef swiftly prepared to leave, packing supplies and disposing of anything too cumbersome to take, the glass shop was swamped with its own discord as Jacob, Marcus, and the other glassblowers fought to use up the last of their copper and brass. Jacob's fingertips were scalded and the skin of his cheeks raw from hours spent stooping over the furnace. The exorcists had been working day and night, he'd heard, filling up the glass vials they were churning out with jinn at an inhuman rate.

Jacob splashed his face in the dorm room's communal washbasin, tugged on yesterday's tunic he'd discarded in a crumpled heap on the floor, and followed Marcus to the glass shop. "Should be our last day of this." Marcus threw his head back.

Jacob forced a wan smile. His aching body reveled at the thought of not blowing glass for hours on end, and the chance to breathe in fresh air, see the sky again, which he hadn't since that one night out with Sara, who had made it very clear she didn't trust him. Her earlier words had been playing in his mind on a loop ever since. *When we leave in a few days, we won't be taking the workshop with us. Maybe we won't take you with us either.*

The thought of being left behind in Intalyabad, a city now descended into rampant chaos after the nawab's death, where soldiers were culling hāri in the streets, was his only motivator. He needed to prove he wasn't just a glassblower. He could be more than that. He'd be whatever the Hāreef needed him to be. Whatever William would have wanted him to be.

When the familiar smell of melted glass hit him, Jacob retrieved his tools and set to work. He dumped a crate of copper tableware into the furnace and watched it melt into a sticky puddle. He poured the amber liquid into molds and left them to set on the counter.

"We need more vial crates." Marcus coughed into his elbow and gestured to the last crisscrossed pallet they'd used to store the freshly blown vials. Jacob nodded and retreated into the tunnels, head down, counting his steps, waiting for the inevitable sting of Anam's dark eyes burning holes through his skull as he passed by her cage. He felt bad. Of course he did, but it was out of his control now. He hadn't forced her to attack the Hāreef. He'd given her a hint, but it was her decision to act upon it. She must have known the risks. As much as he tried to placate his guilt with reason, it still chewed at the back of his mind.

It's us or them, remember. There are no innocent Ghadaeans. His eyes flickered to where she sat, blending into the shadows.

"Come to harvest my heart, have you?"

Jacob winced. *Just walk on. Ignore her.*

"I have heard whispers the terrorists are leaving soon." Anam leaned her head against the bars. "And that spaces are limited. Will they think you useful enough to take with them?"

Jacob approached the bars. "It's got nothing to do with you."

"No." Anam tilted her head. "But if you were to get left behind, you would be left in quite a vulnerable position. Do you not agree?"

She was just trying to wind him up. And she was succeeding. "At least I won't have the Wāzeem to worry about," he sneered. "That's if there's any of you guys left." He straightened his shoulders, puffed out his chest, tried to give some semblance that he wasn't crumbling apart with guilt inside. Their bodies were now being used as jinn bait. Would they have still died if not for him? And what about their souls? What happened to the soul of a body that had been feasted upon by a jinn? The Ghadaeans believed it would not ascend to Heaven, forced to wander lost until Iblis dragged it to Hell. Jacob wasn't sure what he believed, only that he wouldn't want his own corpse to be food for hungry jinn. He pushed the image of Queen Bidhukh's pointed teeth ripping into the nawab's flesh from his mind before he gagged.

Anam saw right through his bravado. "We were not wiped out. It was a heavy blow, but we will recover." She shook her head. "We lost hāri too, you know. Your own people died as well."

He knew what she was trying to do, but he refused to succumb to her words. "They weren't loyal hāri if they sided with you."

"The world is not so black-and-white, Jacob. Good and bad. Hāri and Ghadaeans. Us and them. You cannot simply eradicate one race to preserve the lives of the other. That is not a solution."

His insides were heating up. Jacob's next words tasted like acid. "Then what is the solution? We've stood by while your people killed us for years, and what did that ever do for us!"

Anam sighed. "I am sorry for the way my people treat you."

Jacob's eyes rose to meet hers.

"Truly, I am. I know it is wrong what we do to you."

Her words doused the flames inside. "Then you understand why I want to change things."

"But sihr is not the answer."

Jacob growled. "Then what do you suggest we do? If we do nothing, then nothing changes. It doesn't matter where I go, I'll never be safe. I'll always be different. Always be hunted down just because of the color of my skin, but I guess you don't know what that feels like."

Anam soaked up his words. Seconds of silence stretched on until Jacob didn't think she would respond at all. "Actually I do. Maybe not because of the color of my skin, but I know what it feels like when your very existence, the very essence of who you are, something you cannot change about yourself no matter how hard you try, puts your life at risk." When Anam met his face it was like she was looking through him, delving deep inside his skull, seeing more of him than anyone had ever seen before. "I may not know what it feels like to live with the kind of anger and hatred, that thirst for vengeance that you have, but believe me, I know what it feels like to live in constant fear."

The type of fear that eats you up inside. The type of fear that makes it difficult to breathe, difficult to think. The type of fear that lingered at the corners of his vision, stuck to the back of his throat. That fear never went away. It ebbed and flowed like the tide, some days nothing more than a frightened whisper, and others a piercing scream, but it was always there. That was the fear Anam spoke of. If she knew that fear, then maybe she understood him better than he'd thought.

"Some people aren't happy with you dressing like . . . this?" He waved in her general direction.

A single bitter laugh escaped. "I am not a costume. I can no more take this off than you could tear your own skin off."

Jacob pictured it now, him clawing at his own skin until he was nothing but red. How many times had he wished to do that?

"It is much easier for me now since I joined the Wāzeem. They are far more accepting, but my old life was a different story." Anam shook her head. "My family were powerful people with a lot of gold and a lot of expectations for their son. They were training me to be the Nawab of Daevala's personal exorcist. Let's say they were more than just disappointed when they found out who I really was."

"Why are you telling me this?"

Anam brought her face closer so that her cheeks brushed the bars. Her next words were slow, smooth, like she wanted him to absorb every syllable. "If I were to kill every person who opposed me, there would be hardly anyone left."

Jacob sucked in a breath. He could see what she was doing. Sharing her pain in a bid to relate to him. But it wasn't that simple. "It's not the same thing."

"No. It is not." Anam's nails clicked against the bars. "I would have to kill far more people."

Footsteps slapping against stone made Jacob spring back from the cage like he'd been burned.

"Go." Anam sank back into the shadows. "You should not be seen talking to me."

He nodded and spun, putting just enough distance between him and Anam before Sara rounded the corner. Jacob froze, wiping his palms on his trousers. He couldn't look guiltier if he tried.

Sara's gaze flickered between him and the cage. Her eyes narrowed. "Hope I'm not interrupting anything?"

"J-just going to get more vial crates," he stuttered, and stumbled down the tunnel without a backward glance at Anam. Sara cocked her right eyebrow, the only one that hadn't been completely burned off. "Really. I'm heading that way too." She matched his speed, but while his footsteps were erratic, fumbling in the dark, hers were smooth and calculated. "I've been watching you," she said matter-of-factly.

Jacob swallowed, his throat like rice paper. "Watching me?"

"Oh yes! Ever since that night you returned without your cloak or the loot we stole, I've had my eye on you, wondering why you took so long. Where could you have possibly gone?" A wicked grin stretched across her face. "Why do you seem so interested in our prisoner?"

Jacob clamped his hands behind his back to still the tremor of his wrists.

Sara seemed to notice his shaking, and her smile deepened. "I've been meaning to ask you, what happened to Caleb's peri?"

"P-peri?"

"You know." She waved her hand. "The bird-lady Caleb was plucking the feathers off one by one."

He winced at her nonchalance.

"The Wāzeem attack, and then, *poof.*" She clicked her fingers. "The peri is gone. Along with that darker friend of yours . . . and one of our precious balloons." She rounded the corner and stopped behind the door where the vial crates, kitchenware, and other miscellaneous items were kept. The door had been left slightly ajar so that a faint white glow spilled across the rock floor.

She paused, expecting his answer, but when none came she thrust her face an inch from his. "I will find out what you're up to. Mark my words." Then Sara disappeared down the tunnel, her heels clicking against stone as they faded to nothing. Silence. Jacob let out a breath and approached the store cupboard, promising himself that for as long as he stayed with the Hāreef he'd keep well clear of Sara.

A crackle of a voice like lit kindling met his ears. "Despite my numerous attempts to dissuade her, she is convinced of involving Queen Mardzma."

He froze, hand hovering over the handle.

Another voice. This one deeper. "Is Queen Bidhukh's army not enough for her? She wants more power!" A growl that made the door hinges rattle. Jacob's eyes widened, and he stepped back. It was Caleb and the shaitan, Sakhr, conversing in a store cupboard, of all places.

"Mortals have always had a weakness for greed."

"My mother is not greedy, Sakhr, simply ill-informed. She is determined to win this battle for her people, but she does not understand Al-Ghaib, and certainly not the inner workings of jinn politics like we do."

"Well, perhaps you should inform her, and quickly," the shaitan snapped. "Your mother has no idea what our queen has already gifted her. She is ungrateful."

"Believe me, I have tried, but she doesn't understand the true power of the amulets Queen Bidhukh has blessed her with—and I certainly do not wish to tell her."

Jacob's hand shot to his amulet, thumb tracing over the mysterious green stone.

"No, you cannot. Do you understand the destruction that would be caused to our realm if that wretched stone is put back together again? If you do not stop her from this course of action soon, I will have to tell our queen."

"Of course I understand!" Caleb hissed. "You treat me as if I do not belong in Al-Ghaib. I am well aware what will happen if the Seal is restored, but my mother has only broken fragments, and she is content with that. Trust me, she does not have the power to restore Prophet Sulaiman's Seal."

"Indeed, only the most powerful jinn can restore that seal." Sakhr hummed. "Like Queen Mardzma, for instance. Do you see now? They must not strike an allegiance."

A rattling from within the cupboard sent Jacob darting down the tunnels just as the ifrit emerged, the tips of his skeletal wings trailing along the ground. Caleb's head whirled around, green eyes burning suspiciously into him.

Jacob flinched.

"What do you want, mortal boy?"

From where he stood, Jacob could feel the heat radiating off Caleb. He hastily jumped back, knocking his elbow against the store cupboard handle. "J-just getting a crate." He dipped into the cupboard and slammed the door shut, eyes glued to the sliver of red glowing beneath the door. Seconds stretched on before Caleb retreated. Jacob released his breath as welcoming darkness embraced him.

23

KHADIJA

The sky was violet-blushed indigo when the city of Al-Shaam came into view, its gold minarets jutting up from the horizon. The day had been long and difficult, and the heat and lack of oxygen that came with being so high up had caused a ringing to settle in her ears that refused to quiet. Khadija sighed with relief. "We made it."

Darian joined her at the basket's edge. "It'll be tricky entering the city."

"For you, maybe."

He chuckled, a crinkle of eyes and a flash of teeth. Then his face turned serious. "The Wāzeem could really use you."

She chewed her lip. He was right. A war was coming, and whether she liked it or not, that war would affect everyone regardless of race. If Vera killed another nawab, and if the jinniya Queen Bidhukh crossed over from Al-Ghaib with an army of jinn, there would be no Ghadaea to fight over.

But still something tugged her back. Was it fear, or a refusal to take responsibility? But if it wasn't her responsibility, then whose was it? She pictured Anam. She'd been fiercely loyal to the Wāzeem and it had cost her her life. Was Khadija willing to make the same sacrifice?

"You really think the Wāzeem has a chance at stopping the Hāreef?" She wasn't sure what she was searching for. Reassurance. A false sense of security. Either way, Darian refused to give it to her.

"I can't make any promises to you, Khadija. All I can say is that we have to at least try. Nothing is worse than not knowing what you could have done."

And that she understood perfectly. Khadija recalled the days spent watching the hot-air balloons from her bedroom window, longing for when she'd finally get to fly in one; if she hadn't taken that leap into the balloon when she did, she would have been left wondering for the rest of her life.

"OK." She faced Darian. "I'll help."

The smile that lit up Darian's face caused a fluttering in her chest as if her lungs were filled with butterflies.

Though night was swiftly approaching, the city was alive. Oil lamps flickered in all the windows. The streets bustled with movement. Darian steered the balloon toward the landing bay, where silk balloons were collapsing across the sand.

"They won't let you in." Khadija's breathing quickened at the sight of soldiers milling about the sand, reminded of the trouble Jacob had faced when they'd arrived in Intalyabad. After the nawab's death, it could only be worse for hāri now.

"I'll figure something out," Darian responded with a flick of his wrist. His nonchalance irritated her.

"No. I'm telling you, you won't even get past the gates. They'll lock you up." Her voice was breathy. "And as for me . . ." Last time, they'd seized the balloon as collateral for her lack of paperwork. This wasn't going to work. Her stomach twisted into a knot.

"It's all right. Calm down." Darian crouched by the trapdoor leading down to the little lavatory. The door swung open with a creak. "I was going to hide in here and slip out when I get the chance." A slow smirk spread across his lips. "You're welcome to join me in here, if you like."

Just when she was beginning to warm to him, he always found a way to cool her right back down. She rolled her eyes. "That's your plan!" She snorted. "They'll seize the balloon, you know." She rubbed her temples. "It's not going to work."

"Well, if you have any better ideas, then feel free to share." There was a hint of a challenge to his voice that made heat flood across her skin.

"You said you can write?"

A muscle in his neck twitched. "Perhaps."

She growled. The ground was getting closer. They really didn't have time for this. "Stop wasting time! Can you? Yes or no."

Darian's eyebrows shot to his hairline at her tone. Even she was surprised by herself. "Yes." He stretched the word out. Probably just to annoy her more. Khadija couldn't help but get the feeling Darian secretly enjoyed winding her up.

"Right." Khadija snatched up the map and tore off a strip that wasn't covered in her sketches.

Darian glared at her, wide-eyed.

She dipped the reed pen in the inkpot. "Write me a flight pass. It needs to say where I've traveled from." She tapped her chin. What else? She'd never seen one of these documents before and was unsure how detailed they needed to be. "It also needs to say I have permission to travel alone."

When Darian refused to take the pen, she thrust it in his palm, splattering ink across his tunic. "Hurry up!"

That snapped him into gear. Khadija watched, stunned, as he began gliding the tip of the pen across the page in a slow, looping text. "You traveled from Intalyabad. You're entering Al-Shaam because . . ." He glanced at her expectantly.

She chewed her lip. "It's no longer safe in Intalyabad after the nawab's death."

He scratched the pen along the parchment. "Makes sense. And why are you alone?"

"My husband . . . died." She shrugged.

"Need something better than that. You're not even dressed like a widow." His voice lowered so that she had to lean in to catch his next words. "Although I wouldn't put it past you."

Her jaw clicked.

"Your husband is a prominent noble from Intalyabad. He decided to stay to deal with the aftermath of the nawab's death." Darian scratched pen to paper. "He sent you away for your own safety as you are with child."

"Do we really need the last part?" She folded her arms.

"Makes you look more . . . vulnerable." Darian signed the bottom of the page with an elaborate signature.

Khadija peeked at the name, but the cursive handwriting made it difficult to decipher. "Is that a made-up name or a real person?"

"Oh, he's real, and he's rich. He's one of the nobles the Wāzeem were in discussion with about hāri rights." He paused. "Though I doubt he'd be willing to donate to our cause now. Trust me, the soldiers will give you no trouble once they read this." He blew on the ink and passed it to her. "And the balloon is grand enough to fool them."

Khadija nodded. The slip of paper instantly eased some of her fear. "And what about you?"

Darian kicked the trapdoor to the lavatory open. "I'll be down here if you need me."

Darian's note was enough to see Khadija through the gates. As soon as the basket grazed the sand, soldiers surrounded her, all with leering eyes and hungry smiles. One look at the signature at the bottom of the page, however, and she was whisked straight through without a backward glance while hāri men swiftly deflated the balloon and dragged it into a large storage hall where the other balloons were kept. She figured it would be easy enough for Darian to slip out and blend in with the other hāri.

It was in fact so easy, almost too easy, that as Khadija weaved through the crowd of people beneath the amber archway and into the city, Darian was already waiting for her on the other side, leaning against a wall with an amused smirk brushing his lips.

She made to go to him, but stopped a few feet short. It seemed to dawn on Darian too as he swiftly lowered his head, refusing her eye contact, as if she were the sun, too bright to look at. In that moment, they both suddenly remembered where they were, and what they were. They weren't in the balloon anymore, and he was hāri and she was Ghadaean.

Khadija sighed and glanced at the winding streets that gradually sloped upward, leading toward a magnificent golden palace topped with marble domes and minarets studded with rubies that reminded her of droplets of blood.

"There's still time to change your mind." Darian spoke without lifting his head.

It would be easy enough to allow the city to swallow her, and a part of her wished it would. But there was another part, one that had been steadily growing over the past few days. The part that, despite his arrogance, the tendency for his words to leave his lips while completely bypassing his brain, and his apparent delight in winding her up, made her crave his company, no matter how annoying. Company was better than being alone in an unfamiliar city.

Can you trust him? He could betray you just like Jacob did.

Maybe he would. Maybe the Wāzeem were just a disorganized bunch of hopeless optimists who had no real power or influence to change anything. Khadija straightened her shoulders. It was a risk worth taking. "Lead the way."

She didn't need to look at him to know Darian was grinning. He ducked down a twist and turn of narrow streets while Khadija followed, always maintaining a safe distance. Darian dipped into a tent with crates of rotten fruit outside, their squidgy flesh covered in flies. Khadija hesitated before following. Her eyes adjusted to the dim light. The tent was spacious but bare, save for a scattering of beaded cushions and a set of tabla drums in the corner beside a polished oud, its strings begging her fingers to glide across them. A Ghadaean woman knelt across the cushions, her henna-stained feet curled underneath herself. Her head jerked up as they entered, causing the gold hoops dangling from her ears to swing back and forth. Khadija eyed her earrings. They were the size of teacups and looked about as heavy too.

"Darian! What are you doing here?"

Khadija's tongue soured with something that tasted a lot like jealousy. Which was ridiculous, of course.

A beaded curtain rattled, and a Ghadaean man appeared. He was a similar age to Darian but with a shorter stature that almost made him appear unthreatening, save for his eyes. They were dark and piercing, and they were staring right at her.

"Darian! Who is this?"

Darian faced Khadija—the eye contact felt strange after the walk they'd just spent ignoring one another. "This is Khadija. She's come to help us."

All eyes fell on her as seconds of silence stretched on, before finally the woman said, "We could certainly use the help."

The tent absorbed her words.

Darian's face was grave. "At this point, we need all the help we can get. I overheard Vera's plans of assassinating the Nawab of Al-Shaam next. She will be here soon. We have to warn the city."

The woman's painted lips formed a grim line. "We expected as much but luckily we have some time still. Vera won't be arriving here first. She's been spotted traveling north to a village, apparently."

Darian furrowed his brow. "What village?"

"Qasrah."

Her breath clogged in her throat. Khadija's skin grew cold. *Abba.*

Time stopped. Mouths were moving, but their words were drowned out by the ringing in her ears. *I abandoned him. I left him there to die. It's all my fault.* Khadija squeezed her eyes shut, picturing Abba and his lopsided glasses trapped beneath rubble. Her head did a spin. She reached out for the nearest arm to steady herself.

It was Darian who kept her upright. Khadija focused on her breathing.

"What's wrong?"

Her skin started to catch alight, fire traveling up her limbs, acid pooling in her stomach. *I have to do something. I have to save him.*

"My abba." Her voice was barely a whisper. "I hurt Vera, so now she's trying to hurt me."

Darian's eyes widened. His head darted to the Ghadaean couple. "I—" he stuttered. "I'm so sorry, Khadija."

But she didn't want him to be sorry. Sorry didn't change anything. Sorry wouldn't save Abba. "I have to go."

"Darian." The man clamped a hand on Darian's shoulder. "We still need to warn the city. We must begin preparing for an attack."

Darian shrugged out of his grip. "I know, Zaid, but—"

"The Council will want details about your time with the Hāreef."

Darian ran a hand across his scalp. His next words sounded like he'd swallowed gravel. "I know, it's just—"

Zaid's expression was stern. "Then you know what needs to be done. A city of people takes priority over a little village." His eyes flickered to Khadija, only briefly. "I am sorry about your abba, but it is probably already too late for him."

No. She refused to believe that. Fire scalded her insides, traveling up her throat, setting her tongue ablaze.

Darian couldn't face her. "We have to stop Vera before it's too late. Before what happened in Sahli . . . and now Qasrah happens here." He sighed. "You understand, right, Khadija?"

Oh, she understood. She understood that he had his priorities and she had hers, and now that they no longer aligned, it was time to part ways.

When she didn't immediately respond, Darian's fingertips brushed her elbow. The action was gentle, tender, but its edges were tinged with fear. Khadija flinched and drew back. "Then stay, but I have to go."

The woman shook her head, hoops swaying from side to side. "It would be dangerous, and she has a head start. By time you get there . . ." Her voice trailed off.

Khadija tried to empty her ears of the woman's doubts.

"Stay here with us, Khadija. The Wāzeem needs you." Darian lowered his voice so only she could catch his next words. "And I need you." There was a desperation in his eyes she'd never seen before.

She sucked in a breath. His words began a fluttering in her stomach like a hundred butterflies all coming alive at once.

But this wasn't about what *he* needed. It was about what *she* needed.

And just like that, all the butterflies died.

"My abba needs me more." Khadija made for the tent flap. Darian blocked her path. She shot him a look of fire that caused him to flinch.

"How will you even get there? You can't fly a balloon on your own."

"And why not?"

His words stumbled. "It's . . . it's dark out. At least wait until morning."

The more time she wasted the less chance Abba stood. No. She had to leave now, with or without Darian. "I'm going." She slipped past him and ducked through the tent flap. "There's nothing you can do to stop me." Khadija stepped into the night.

A rustle of fabric from behind, and then Darian was hovering by her ear. "The soldiers may not let you have your balloon back."

She marched ahead, heedless of his doubts. He was rambling. She could tell. Nervousness leaked from his voice, making him spout anything to convince her to stay. A part of her ached to know why, but she stomped it down before it could fester into a distraction. She had to keep her mind clear. Focus only on Abba.

"Qasrah is a long way from here."

She increased her speed. Darian jogged alongside her.

"And the balloon is low on supplies."

She spun. "Anything else, or is that all?" Her chest was hammering. "Why do you care what I do?"

Darian pressed his lips together. His voice was so soft it was barely a whisper. She didn't know boys could speak so softly. "Because I care." He reached his hand out. Khadija studied the lines gracing his palms, the pinkish tinge to his skin, the thin sheen of sweat. But she let it hang there until Darian's arm fell to his side. He sighed. "I can't stop you from going, and I can't go with you."

She nodded, not daring to meet his eyes in case it were to release the churning mess of mixed-up emotions inside. She'd unravel them later. Not now. "I'm not asking you to."

He resumed walking. "Come on, then." He turned down a street. "Least I can do is get you in the air."

A small smile graced her lips.

The streets were mostly empty, but they often had to duck behind a stall or squeeze into the gap between buildings as soldiers patrolled the streets, stinking of tobacco and liquor. The large hall that housed all the balloons was boarded up now, two soldiers guarding the entrance. Darian tugged her behind a low wall. "I'll distract them while you get the balloon."

Khadija's brow creased. That wouldn't work. "No. I'll distract them. You get the balloon." She rose.

He tugged her down. "Are you insane?!"

Possibly. But time was running out. Every second she wasted could be a second too long for Abba. "Who is more of a distraction? Me or you?" That brought a smirk tickling the corner of his lips. She rolled her eyes. "Never mind."

"Just be careful."

Khadija sucked in a breath. If she waited any longer, her courage would falter. Her sandals smacked against the sandstone. She shrieked.

The soldiers stood at attention, fumbling for their spears in the dark. "Are you OK, miss?"

"My husband." Khadija pressed a palm to her chest and fake wheezed. "Hāri are trying to rob him. Please! He needs help."

That got their attention. There was only one thing that tempted a soldier more than a girl in the dark, and that was the possibility of spilling hāri blood.

"Where are they?"

Khadija pointed into the night. "In the market. Please. Hurry!"

The soldiers clattered off without a backward glance. It was only when their metal boots smacking the ground were a hum in the distance that Khadija felt Darian near. "That was . . . impressive."

"Thanks." She fumbled with the padlock. "Now how do we get in?"

Darian crouched beside the lock. "I need something sharp, like a—" He clicked his fingers.

Khadija swiftly plucked a hairpin from her hijab. "Like this?"

"Perfect!"

A few agonizing minutes passed where Khadija had to fight the urge to scream for him to hurry up, and the lock hit the ground with a clang. Darian faced her, sporting a smug grin.

They combed through the line of balloons in relative silence before Khadija caught the shimmering gold panels of their balloon. "It's here."

"Why don't you take this one instead?" Darian had his hands on his hips, admiring a balloon that she could only describe as an actual sunset. She gasped, fingertips aching to glide across the painted silk that had been stained wine red and blood orange, ending in a dash of sunflower yellow along the edges of the material that bordered the balloon hoop. Along the seams of each panel, feathers had been interwoven with the stitching so that, once airborne, she imagined the balloon could be mistaken for a bird.

"It's small enough for you to fly on your own, and it's got more gas canisters. Should be enough to get you there." He paused. "And back. If you're coming back."

Was she coming back? She hadn't thought that far. His words hung in the air like a heavy fog. "I—"

"Please come back, Khadija." His eyes shone in the dark. "Bring your abba with you . . . if, you know . . ." He fiddled with his wrists.

She sighed. There was no use making empty promises. "You really want me to help the Wāzeem." She reached for the sunset balloon's wicker basket. Darian grabbed the other end.

"I mean . . . yes. You're smart and resourceful. We could use you."

Khadija was glad for the darkness to hide the pink tinge appearing across her cheeks. They dragged the balloon out into the night and stretched the material along the sand. "The Wāzeem mean a lot to you."

Darian hopped into the basket to light the burner. "I wouldn't be here if it wasn't for them." Sparks lit up the night as the burner roared to life. "They were there when I needed them."

Khadija spun the propeller, forcing hot air into the balloon. "I still find the whole idea of the Wāzeem a little hard to believe. Like, I want to believe that it can work." Her breathing became ragged as the propeller gained speed. "But you're talking about changing the very foundation that our society is built upon. I just don't think it's feasible. Not in our lifetime, anyway."

It felt easier voicing her doubts in the dark for some reason. Darian hummed, taking his time to answer. "Maybe society needs to crumble. Maybe there's too much wrong in the world for it to be put right." Darian grasped the balloon's material and started to flap.

Khadija grabbed the other end of the balloon. "Breaking society would mean chaos. It would mean a lot of deaths."

Darian's breathing grew heavier. "There's already chaos, Khadija. Too many have already been lost." The pain in his voice was leaking out.

"Who have you lost?"

Darian exhaled, the air leaving his lips all at once like a balloon that had just burst. "I had a younger sister who was half-Ghadaean."

Whatever she'd been expecting Darian to say, it certainly wasn't that. The balloon was almost full now, lifting its mighty head toward the stars. Darian secured the rope to a post.

"My mother was attacked by soldiers one night, and she fell pregnant with her." Darian's gaze was fixed on the glowing balloon. "We both adored her. She was completely unaware of the reality of what her existence meant." His words turned bitter. "She was shunned by both hāri and Ghadaeans, like she was stuck between a war she knew nothing about." He swallowed. "We kept her hidden for as long as we could." His breathing hitched. Darian stiffened. Khadija wished he'd stop talking so she wouldn't have to hear the words she knew came next. "But the soldiers got her." Khadija winced. Everyone had a Hassan, a life that had been snatched away too soon, and that seemed to be the heart of this war. It wasn't hāri against Ghadaeans. It was grief against revenge.

"I was supposed to watch her." Darian's voice sounded distant like it was coming from underwater, as if he was drowning in his own loss, his head unable to break through the surface. "But she kept whining. She was hungry." His face contorted. "All I did was turn my back on her for five minutes." His head lowered. "And she was gone."

Khadija couldn't speak. There were no words for that.

"My mother was never the same after. She sank into this dark place like she was this empty shell of a person. She wandered off one night, and I never saw her again." Darian's knuckles protruded as he curled his fingers around the balloon's fabric. "I always wondered how she could do that when I needed her." He shook his head. "I felt like I lost them both, and I blamed myself for years. That's why I joined the Wāzeem. At first, it was merely for survival. They clothed me, fed me, gave me a purpose." Darian exhaled. "I don't know where I'd be if they hadn't been there for me." He looked her dead in the eyes. Khadija shifted uncomfortably, unused to the raw honesty of Darian's words. "They gave my life meaning again, and for that, I'll always be grateful."

She was stunned into silence. The atmosphere reeked of pain and guilt and shame, so heavy with it, she didn't think they'd ever get the balloon in the air.

"So." Darian straightened up, as if shutting the door on the downpour of misery he'd just unleashed. "If society can justify the death of a child, then trust me, that society has already descended into chaos."

And Khadija felt that. She felt that hard. All those years she'd lived with her grief, allowed it to swallow her, to chew her up, eat away at her insides, and spit her out, this mess of twisted limbs that she'd spend the rest of her life failing to put back to how it was. "I lost my mother and brother." She didn't know why she was telling him this. Why it even mattered if she'd probably never see him again. "They were killed by hāri."

Darian moved to stand before her. He was close. So close she couldn't breathe deeply without their bodies brushing together. Her breathing grew shallow.

Darian's fingertips grazed her wrists. "I'm sorry. That must have been . . . there aren't even words for it." His breath tickled her nose. "I will always hate soldiers. Always detest every soldier I meet." His voice twisted into something bitter and cruel. It didn't suit him. "My question is, do you hate us?" He bit his lip. "Do you hate me?"

Tears prickled the corners of her vision. Khadija squeezed her eyes shut, swallowing the thickness in her throat that stole all her air away and yet expected her to scream. Without opening her eyes, she responded, "No. I don't hate you."

Then something pressed against her lips.

Darian's lips. Her eyes shot open. They were soft and warm and full of all the unspoken words that hung between them, and Khadija allowed herself to melt into it. He kissed her top lip, then her bottom lip, his mouth moving slower, deeper, stealing all the pain inside of her and tossing it into the night. Khadija brought her hands to his neck, brushing her fingertips up the sides of his face, feeling the smooth skin beneath them. In the dark it was just skin. It was not an outfit or a piece of armor. It was not something to be worn or something to hide behind. It was not a freedom flag flying in the wind or a ticket to a better life. It was not a guarantee of oppression or a promise of privilege. It was human skin. That's all it was because that was all they were: human.

Khadija's cheeks were wet before she could stop it. Her salty tears merged with their kiss. Darian kissed her slower, each kiss longer than the last. He broke away and rested his forehead against hers, kissing each of her eyelids. "You should go."

Her lips were tingling and swollen, and Khadija didn't trust herself to speak. "I will . . . try to come back." That was all she could promise him. She leaned against the basket and swung her legs over.

Darian's hands were shaking as he fiddled with the rope. He stole one last look at her. "Please come back." Then he released her into the air.

Khadija floated upward, Darian's face shrinking until the night swallowed her so that she could see only the amber glow of the balloon's fire and the silver speckle of stars.

24

JACOB

"Last vial," Marcus declared to exhausted whoops from the other hāri glassblowers. Marcus nudged him. "Hear what I said, Jacob? It's the last bloody one."

Jacob managed a meek smile as Marcus popped the delicate copper glass into the last remaining slot in the vial crate. Then he unceremoniously tossed his blowpipe and chisel to the floor. "Never blowing glass again, me," Marcus grumbled.

They had finally used up the last of their copper and brass, and though his aching body was relieved at no longer having to blow glass for twelve hours a day, Jacob couldn't shake the rising trepidation that seemed stuck to his skin like maggots clinging to a carcass. What now? Marcus hadn't stopped blabbing about being asked to accompany Vera when they eventually left in the hot-air balloons. But he was handy with a sword. The others, Jacob wasn't sure about, only that numbers were limited and Vera was being highly selective of who she wished to bring.

Would she bring him when he could offer her nothing? Well, nothing except a strong suspicion that her son was scheming against her. Jacob hadn't returned to the store cupboard since, for fear he'd bump into the ifrit. He was keeping something from his own mother, something about the amulets that could potentially prove her downfall if she allied with the jinniya Queen Mardzma as she intended. Jacob traced his finger over the green iris of his amulet—the eye of Bidhukh. This stone was significant, so significant Queen Bidhukh had sent her shaitan, Sakhr, to remind Caleb of the need to keep his silence.

And what was the Seal of Sulaiman? So many questions whirred around his skull over the past few days he thought his head would explode with them. He needed answers, but where to get them? Jacob mindlessly followed Marcus and the other hāri as they left the workshop.

"Think we've earned ourselves a drink," Marcus boomed, and jabbed an elbow in Jacob's ribs. "You coming, Jacob?"

Jacob shook his head. "Think I'd rather go back to bed," he mumbled to an onslaught of snickers from the other glassblowers.

"Good lad—you're too young for it anyway," Marcus chuckled. He ruffled Jacob's hair and disappeared down the tunnel with the rest.

Jacob waited until their voices melted into silence before removing the amulet William had given him. The emerald-green iris swirled like trapped mist in the center of the necklace. He studied it, slotting the gemstone between his molars, attempting to pry it from the silver amulet with his nails. Caleb had said to Sakhr that Vera possessed only broken fragments, useless if not put back together.

He knew he shouldn't. When it came to sihr, Jacob preferred to leave well enough alone, but this wasn't quite sihr. This was something, probably the only thing, he was good at. Jacob was stumbling back through the tunnel toward the workshop before he could stop himself.

The door creaked open, the dying orange glow of the furnace

sending his shadow rippling across the ceiling. Jacob placed the amulet on the workbench, retrieved Marcus's chisel, and, stealing a moment to fully absorb what he was about to do, slammed the chisel against the stone. It popped out of its silver casing as smoothly as a boiled egg from its shell. Jacob held the gemstone to the light, twirling it between his fingers. One of its edges was jagged, as if it had been hastily snapped apart. Jacob approached the furnace, retrieved a mold, and slipped the green stone into the fire.

Now all he had to do was wait. He chewed his lip, hoping he hadn't just made an amateur's mistake. Most gemstones were exposed to heat only to alter their color, and it was only the precious gems used mainly in jewelry craft that could be melted down, but at extreme heat. If this stone could indeed melt, it would take a while. Jacob softly shut the door to the workshop behind him.

It was time for some answers to his questions, and as much as he hated to admit it, there was only one person he knew of to ask. Jacob reached Anam's cage, squinting for the lump of her figure in the dark.

"You should not be here."

Jacob's eyes searched for the voice in the gloom. There she was, leaning against the rock wall, back perfectly straight.

"If someone sees you—"

"You used to be an exorcist, right?"

Anam leaned in, allowing the candlelight to illuminate her features. "Back in my old life, I was, but I was a different person then. Now I prefer simply banishing jinn back to Al-Ghaib instead of attempting to trap them." She cocked her head to the side. "Why do you ask? Does Vera not have enough exorcists?"

His tongue stumbled over his sentence. How to word it without giving her too much information? What to say without it appearing like he was having doubts? He didn't doubt the Hāreef's mission, not at all. Of course hāri should be liberated, but sihr and jinniya queens had never quite sat right with him. And if Vera's own ifrit son was playing her for a fool, he needed to know. If the Hāreef were simply cannon fodder for Queen Bidhukh's ulterior motives, then he wasn't about to lose his life for a jinn.

"I just wanted to ask you something."

Anam shuffled toward the bars. "Something you cannot ask the other exorcists?" She raised an eyebrow.

He growled. "Just tell me what the Seal of Sulaiman is."

Anam rocked back on her heels. "Why would you ask about that?"

Jacob shrugged. "I just overheard it being mentioned."

Anam didn't look convinced. "I doubt you would have heard Sulaiman's name being tossed around idly when he is feared by all jinn." At his quizzical look, she continued. "Sulaiman was the prophet gifted with the Seal of Sulaiman, which granted him command over humans, beasts, and all creatures of Al-Ghaib."

"So where is this seal?"

"Gone." Anam threw her hands in the air. "Lost. The story goes that a shaitan stole the Seal from the Prophet Sulaiman and, with it, impersonated him to seize control over the jinn realm. The demon went unnoticed for forty days before the prophet Sulaiman trapped the demon and threw him to the sea." Anam's forehead creased. "It is not known what happened to the Seal, but most believe it was either broken, or perhaps lost at sea as well."

Jacob's heart was pounding. *Lost at sea.* The sea was Queen Bidhukh's territory. Perhaps she had retrieved the Seal, broken but still powerful, and gifted its fragments to the Hāreef to command her jinn army. He shook his head. Surely this was all myth and legend. "But that's just a story, right?"

Anam laughed. "Everything is just a story. You and I are just a story."

He rolled his eyes, then asked, "What happened to the demon? Did he stay trapped?"

"Possibly, but I doubt it." Anam rapped her nails against the iron bars. "Sakhr was a crafty shaitan. I am sure he found a way to free himself."

Jacob stiffened. "The shaitan was Sakhr," he breathed.

In seconds, Anam's face grew serious. "You have met this demon."

"He is here. He works for Queen Bidhukh." Jacob wasn't sure why he was telling Anam this. Why any of it mattered when she was trapped in a cage, destined to have her heart ripped out by Queen Mardzma.

"Vera is a pawn." Anam's voice sliced through his thoughts. "The Hāreef are simply pawns in a game played by jinn, that much is clear to me."

"We're not—"

"Come on, Jacob. Use that brain of yours." Anam shut down his protests. "Jinn do not care about mortal affairs. Would you care about the color of a beetle's shell?" Anam scoffed. "Blue, green, black. The color is irrelevant if all you intend to do is crush it."

Jacob thought back to Queen Bidhukh ripping the flesh from the nawab's bones, and the Wāzeem's bodies, both hāri and Ghadaean, used as bait for the exorcists to fill the glass vials he had crafted. Jacob felt sick. Anam was right—the jinniya queen never cared about hāri at all. Only the Hāreef were not pawns. They weren't even worthy of a place on the playing board. Whatever game Queen Bidhukh was playing, it was for her own gain.

Anam's gaze flickered across his drawn cheeks. "You have made a mistake."

Jacob didn't trust himself to speak. He nodded.

"There is still time to fix this."

How could things possibly be put back the way they were? The Nawab of Intalyabad was dead, hāri were being punished for Vera's crimes, and the Hāreef were preparing to leave with a jinn army. There was no way out of this mess regardless, and Jacob would be kidding himself if he thought he had any power or influence to make a difference.

"How?"

Anam's fingers curled around the bars. "You could start by helping me out of here."

Jacob chewed his lip. There was no going back from this. He eyed the rusted keyhole. "I don't know where they keep the key."

"Then break the lock."

His pulse was beginning to quicken. Jacob smeared his clammy hands on his pant legs. "If Vera finds out—"

Anam slammed her palm against the iron. Jacob recoiled. Everything about Anam screamed control, from her purposeful movements to the rich tenor of her voice, so to see her lose her composure startled him. "You are wasting time! Pick a side and stick with it," she growled.

He nodded. "I'll . . . get something to break the lock." He fled down the tunnel. Jacob encountered no one on his journey to the workshop—no doubt the rest of the Hāreef were either furiously packing or executing their last-ditch attempts at impressing Vera in hope she'd bring them with her.

The deep grumbling from the furnace as he entered the workshop reminded Jacob of a giant beast clearing its throat. He snatched Marcus's chisel off the workbench and made to leave when the dancing flames yanked him back. Jacob donned an oversized pair of blackened gloves and retrieved his mold.

The green stone rattled, completely untouched. That couldn't be right. Jacob carefully placed the stone in the center of his thick glove. Not even a slight alteration in color. He closed his palm around it, expecting to feel the itchy heat through his glove, but nothing. Jacob tugged off his glove and, knowing he was insane for even attempting this, picked up the stone with his bare fingers.

It wasn't even warm. *Impossible!*

But then, it wasn't an ordinary stone, was it? He knew that now. He'd have to unravel his confused mess of thoughts later. Jacob stuffed the gemstone in his pocket and left the workshop with Marcus's chisel shoved up his tunic.

As he neared Anam's cage, the scrape of the cage door opening caused him to stumble. The chisel clattered to the floor.

"Who's there?" a familiar voice snapped.

Sara.

Jacob swiftly kicked the chisel into the shadows, glad its movement was muffled by the sand.

"Oh, it's you." Sara nudged Anam forward with her blade pressed against her neck. "Always turning up where you're not supposed to be. If I were you, I'd slink back to your workshop now. Save the embarrassment." She smirked. "Vera isn't going to bring you."

Jacob's eyes darted between Sara's twisted grin and Anam's stonelike expression, as if she'd swept the emotion from her face as simply as sweeping dust under a rug.

Sara wiggled her fingers. "Bye, new boy." She made off with Anam.

"No! Wait." Jacob jogged up to her. "Vera *is* going to bring me."

"Really! And why's that?" Sara's voice was thick with condescension as they wove through the twists and turns of tunnels to the large cavern where Vera had slit the nawab's throat on the first day he'd arrived. Not even a week ago, and already it felt like a bad dream.

Voices bounced across the ceiling as they emerged into the cavern, which was brimming with hāri. Jacob stood on his tiptoes to catch a glimpse of the red streak of hair standing in the center on a pedestal. Vera raised her crisp white glove, and a hush befell the crowd. "I thank you all from the bottom of my heart"—she pressed a hand to her chest—"for your loyalty and servitude. If I could take you all with me, I would, but alas, spaces are limited for this next phase. I need only the best." She flashed her pearl-white teeth to the audience. "Who will I bring? You decide."

The crowd burst to life then, everyone eager to impress. It reminded Jacob of the first time he'd met Vera in the poppy fields in Sahli, where she'd expected him to put on a performance to prove his worth to her. Hāri were either donning weapons and twirling them above their heads in a bid to impress, or smashing vials and using their amulets to command jinn to dance.

Sara chuckled. "Still think you stand a chance?" She forced a path through the knots of people, dragging Anam by the ropes binding her wrists. Hāri jeered and spat, so that by time Anam stood before Vera, globs of spit were running down her cheeks. Still her head remained high. Jacob pushed his way to the front of the crowd.

"Ah, my warrior heart." Vera gestured to Sara. "Take her to the balloons."

Sara nodded and turned, then abruptly yelped as Caleb appeared in a crackle of jinn fire, blocking her path with his extended wings. "Ammi!"

Conversations died mid-sentence, all heads turned to the ifrit.

"Queen Bidhukh does not approve of you striking this allegiance. Stop this foolishness. Now!" A flurry of sparks sprayed from his lips.

Vera jumped back. "Caleb. I thought you understood why—"

"I thought you were merely ignorant. But now I understand: You are greedy."

Vera gasped.

"Power-hungry." Caleb rounded on his mother, the sharp points of his wings scraping against the floor. "I have told you again and again why you cannot do this, and still you will not listen."

Vera retreated, her palms raised. "Caleb, please. Stop this! This—this isn't you," she stuttered. "I'm only thinking of what's best for our people."

Caleb bared his fangs. "Our people need only Queen Bidhukh and no one else."

Vera tripped over her words. "Yes. Of course, and I am so grateful for all she's done to help us. I'm just covering all angles here." Her tongue darted across her upper lip, where a shine of sweat had appeared. "Queen Mardzma is a marid. If we earn her favor, maybe she will grant us a wish—"

Caleb's palms burst into green jinn fire. "Then do so at your own peril, Ammi, but remember this: Queen Bidhukh created me; she is as much my mother as you are."

Vera recoiled as if his words had stung her.

Caleb continued. "You gave me my first life, but she gave me my second."

"Caleb. Wait!"

The ifrit erupted into a violent emerald flame and was gone. Vera hid the tremble of her jaw with a hand clamped to her mouth. Seconds passed, and then like a switch being flicked, she regained her composure. "Well, don't just stand about! We leave in an hour. I want the amulets back from anyone who is not coming." She snapped at Sara, "Bring her to my balloon." Vera jutted her chin toward Anam and stormed out of the cavern with Sara hot on her heels, towing a stone-faced Anam in the direction of the balloon cavern. Jacob trailed them. If there was any hope of saving Anam, he needed to get on Vera's balloon.

Jacob swallowed his nerves and floundered after Vera. "V-Vera."

She didn't bother turning.

"I have to tell you something."

Her footsteps smacked the stone impatiently. Her head whirled around. "What?"

This was the only thing he could offer her. "I think Caleb—"

"Don't!" Her shriek stung deep inside his ears. Jacob retreated. "I don't want to hear it."

But he needed her to. It was his only chance at earning a ticket aboard her balloon. "I overheard Sakhr and Caleb talking about the Seal of Sulaiman." His words were a jumbled mess but they froze Vera in place. "Sakhr said Caleb wasn't supposed to tell you—"

"Seal of Sulaiman," she whispered, and then her face twisted into something poisonous. "That demon thinks he can turn my own son against me!" She dug her nails into Jacob's shoulder. "Tell me everything you heard."

Jacob's brain felt like a deflated balloon by the time Vera had finished probing him with questions. She'd worn him down until he'd finally cracked open like a shelled pistachio. He'd told her all he'd heard, repeated it until she was satisfied, and only then had she agreed to bring him with her. Jacob threw himself on the deck and glanced at the balloon's crisscrossed ropes above his head.

After days spent underground, it was a relief for Jacob to be up in the open air again. Space was exceedingly tight, however, with Jacob forced to sleep curled up between teetering stacks of crates all rattling with glass vials. Since Khadija had stolen one of the Hāreef's balloons, they were carrying more than they should across the remaining nine balloons. The balloon was full of many faces he didn't recognize, and the extra weight made their progress slow.

Jacob's gaze shifted from the burner, a constant roaring flame since they'd ascended to accommodate the weight, to Anam shoved between sacks of lentils. He desperately needed to speak to her, figure out a way to free her, but with so many of the Hāreet aboard, he didn't dare. Instead, Jacob could merely watch her fend off constant jeers from the other passengers with nothing but a face of stone.

"How long until we arrive?"

Sara twisted the gas tap a fraction. "Three days."

Vera elbowed Sara out of the way and rotated the gas tap until the balloon squealed in protest. "We'll get there in two." She sauntered off.

Vera's impatience was putting everyone on edge. She hadn't told him where they were heading, but by the faint blue streak of the Ravi River below, he reckoned they were flying northeast, though he couldn't imagine why. With no hope of speaking to Anam, there was nothing to do but sleep away the day, and so Jacob curled up on the deck and succumbed to the rocking motions of the balloon.

He awoke to a hand wrapped around his throat. Jacob started.

"Tell me again what you heard." Vera was crouched over him, her nails digging into his neck. There was a wild look to her eyes, emphasized by the purple bruises of her eye sockets, as if she'd forgotten what sleep was entirely. "There must be more."

Jacob shifted up onto his elbows. He'd already told her everything he knew. "Sakhr said the Seal of Sulaiman was broken. The pieces are the amulets Queen Bidhukh gave you." He rubbed the sleep from his eyes. "And that only the most powerful jinn could restore it, like Queen Mardzma."

Vera removed her hand from his throat and ran it through the knotted clumps of her hair. "But no jinn would dare restore it." She paused. "Not willingly, anyway."

Jacob's gaze flickered from her cracked lips to her crumpled cloak. It seemed Caleb's absence was already beginning to show.

"My son does not wish me to offer a warrior's heart to Queen Mardzma." Vera glanced at Anam, who was sat cross-legged with her head lolled back against the basket. Most would have assumed her sleeping, but Jacob reckoned Anam wasn't the type to allow her guard to slip, even for a moment, in the presence of her enemies.

"But even if I were to do so and earn her favor, Queen Mardzma would never willingly restore the Seal." Vera gnawed her chapped lips until a drop of blood appeared. "Willingly." She repeated the word, over and over, as if tasting it on her tongue, before finally shaking her head. "They are afraid that if I contact Queen Mardzma, I will restore the Seal and gain control over Al-Ghaib." She shook her head. "But I have no interest in Al-Ghaib. I am not going to waste a marid's wish on restoring the Seal." She was thinking out loud, almost as if Jacob wasn't there.

"What is a marid?" he ventured when she didn't continue.

"A marid is a wish-granting jinn. Their magic is so powerful they can wish even the most impossible into existence, but they don't give out their wishes for free. Most marid are forced, trapped in vessels and made to grant wishes in exchange for their freedom."

Jacob nodded. The more he learned about jinn, the more he wanted nothing to do with them. "What would you wish for?"

Vera's mouth contorted into a snarl. "I'd wish for my Caleb back, of course . . . as a human. Not that monster Queen Bidhukh has turned him into." She rose abruptly and descended on the balloon's burner, releasing another furious shriek of gas.

Was this what sinking into madness looked like? Grief had swallowed Vera whole, chewed her up, and spat out a congealed mess studded with teeth marks. She would do anything for her son, Jacob realized. He glanced at the other hāri in the balloon, most now fumbling awake as the first rays of dawn turned the sky pale orange like the flesh of a cantaloupe melon. They were all expendable to Vera. The Hāreef's mission was not, first and foremost, liberating hāri people. That came second. It was reuniting Vera with her son.

That was the thought burning at the forefront of his mind as he drifted back to sleep, dozing through the following day as clouds sailed across the sky and the sun burned down. He couldn't watch a jinniya queen rip Anam's heart out. But what could he do? When night fell, he slept, but even his dreams were filled with his attempts at rescuing Anam.

An elbow sinking into his ribs snapped Jacob from his dreams. Sara smirked, the burned skin around her neck tightening like taut leather. "I heard you were from Sahli."

He nodded, following Sara's finger toward the horizon. His breath caught in his throat. Jacob rose and staggered toward the edge, fingers curling around the basket.

And there it was. What was left of it. Charred buildings smiled at him with broken windows like missing teeth, surrounded by blackened fields, with no signs of the purple poppies that had once circled the village. The air above Sahli felt stagnant, not even the whisper of life. It had been burned to the ground. He pictured William's body down there still lying where he'd left him in the opium fields, a red stain across his tunic, empty eyes gazing up at the sky. He slammed his fist against the wicker basket.

Vera clapped her hands, and all eyes in the balloon turned to her. "I want everyone to take a good look at what those darkers did to our people." Her lips curled into a sneer. "Innocent families. Children. Remember the mercy that was denied them. Now it is time to make our voices heard." Vera's words rang out like the chime of a copper bell. "The darkers are about to learn that we will no longer accept their mistreatment." She tapped her foot against the teetering stack of crates filled with glass vials, all swirling with the black smoke of trapped jinn. "Soon they'll know who is really the superior race."

Murmurs spread across the group like a hungry flame. Jacob could feel its heat passing over his skin.

Vera threw her gloved fist in the air. "We are hāri. We do not burn easily!" She was the electric storm cloud and the rest of them brittle firewood. Her words were the spark that caused them all to burst into flames, and then they were chanting, stomping their feet, punching the air.

But this time, Jacob didn't ignite.

* * *

Another two days in the air they spent before a town appeared on the horizon with the rising sun, its bone-colored buildings and beaded tents fluttering in the breeze. Jacob couldn't shake the dread clinging to his skin. The village looked peaceful. Innocent. Unaware of what was to come. Vera licked her lips and addressed the balloon. "Everyone pick a crate. On my count, we drop." She flashed her teeth. "And then the fun begins."

Bile rose up his throat. Jacob could feel the blood in his ears. He pictured the type of people who lived down there. Ghadaeans and their families, children. Hāri would be down there too. Guilt soured his tongue. He couldn't say for certain that every single Ghadaean down there was guilty of some form of hāri mistreatment. Did they deserve to die along with the rest of them?

His gaze wandered to Anam, her back as rigid as a board, her dark eyes locked on him. Did she deserve to die?

The answer burned at the back of his throat. *No.*

A whoop from the edge of the balloon stole his attention as the first crate was released. Everyone rushed to watch it drop. It seemed to fall forever before finally smashing against a flat-roofed building in a shatter of glass and a twist of smoke. The hāri cheered and the other balloons followed suit, dropping their crates over the edge.

They sank to the ground like lead balloons, raining down over market stalls and shattering at people's doorsteps. The village swirled, obscured in smoke as the jinn took shape, and then carnage. Jinn the shape of snakes slithering through open windows while wolves made of smoke with emerald eyes ripped tents to shreds. Jinniya pranced through the streets, blowing kisses that sprouted green hellfire from their lips, setting buildings ablaze. And then screams. Screams of pure terror. Jacob backed away from the edge.

The crackle of green flames devouring brittle timber and the sharp sting of smoke reached them even from up there. Vera cackled. The village stood no chance at all. Jacob's world started to spin, screams mixing with the jeers and yells of delight as the other hāri watched the village burn. How could they enjoy this, watching bright green flames lick away at brown skin? How could they find the justice in this, hearing the piercing screams before they were abruptly cut off by a jinn sinking its teeth into flesh? This was not vengeance. This was mindless violence hidden beneath the pretense of justice. What use was fighting against oppression and violence with more oppression and violence? That wasn't the answer; it was merely altering the reflection in the mirror.

Jacob staggered, clawing at his throat, which felt like it was wrapped in barbed wire. He hadn't wanted this at all. He'd wanted change, a better life, not a senseless slaughter. And that's when it clicked, as Vera dropped another crate over the edge, eyes sparkling as it burst meters from a shoemaker's stall before carnage ensued, that this had nothing to do with equality. Vera didn't want hāri to be equal to Ghadaeans. She wanted hāri to *be* the Ghadaeans.

His head did a spin. He couldn't breathe. Jacob grabbed a rope for support.

"What's wrong, Jacob?" Sara sneered. "Aren't squeamish, are you?"

When Jacob refused to answer, she scoffed. "Knew Vera was making a mistake by bringing you. You make friends with darkers." She threw a look of pure hate in Anam's direction. "Well, I hope you don't have any friends in Qasrah."

His heart thudded to a stop. Time stood still, suspended, before a bloodcurdling scream yanked him back to the present. He covered his mouth with his hand.

This was Khadija's village.

Vera's voice sliced through his thoughts. "Ready to finish off the job?" she asked to a muddle of cheers and raucous applause. "It's time to land."

25

KHADIJA

The memory of Darian's kiss was the only thing tethering her to the ground as the clouds threatened to whisk her away. His navigation lessons on their journey to Al-Shaam had proved invaluable, where he'd gone through each navigation device in turn, reciting what it did until Khadija could repeat his words back to him with near perfection.

The more she busied herself with the balloon, the less time her mind had to wonder about all the ways Abba could be lying dead right now. When she wasn't checking the burner, adjusting the ropes, or dropping the altitude, Khadija jittered on the deck, biting her nails as guilt flooded her insides. Abba had only her to rely on, and she'd left him in a heartbeat. The man of the family was always to blame for the wrong-doings of his children. Leaving him had been selfish. She smacked her fist against the basket until tears pricked her eyes. He'd never have even been in this situation if she'd just stayed in her bedroom where she belonged. Khadija bit her tongue to stop the tears from escaping. Crying wouldn't help Abba now. She pictured him all alone in that house with nothing but empty bedrooms. Grief seemed to seep out of the walls in that house. Ammi's old shoes. Hassan's notebooks full of drawings that she knew Abba kept in a drawer, stealing glances at them every evening. Even Talia's bedroom reeked of loss, and her sister wasn't even dead.

Khadija pictured the blade sinking into Vera's thigh. Revenge. That's what this was. Abba was being made to pay for her recklessness with his life. Khadija allowed that single thought to consume her, letting it set her skin ablaze.

Vera wouldn't get away with this. If anything were to happen to Abba, she'd make Vera pay.

It took all night and another two days. The painted silk above her head was a living, breathing, flying piece of art. In an attempt to distract herself, Khadija sketched every inch of it, using the leftover water from boiling her supply of beetroots to re-create the balloon's vivid purple sunset as it suffused into orange and yellow.

The Ravi River appeared in the distance along with the blackened remains of what was once Sahli. She fed the fire, urging the balloon onward. Would Qasrah look the same? Her home was likely already reduced to ash and cinders. She tugged on a rope to drop the altitude and catch a swifter air current. The cool breeze carried her across the sky. At this speed, she reckoned she'd arrive in a few hours.

Khadija shoved a fist into her abdomen to stifle the rising nausea. Hopefully she wasn't too late.

The sun hung low and heavy in the sky when Khadija caught sight of a spiral of smoke twisting into the air. Bits of brick and rubble dotted the pale grass, and the ground was strewn with broken beams and ripped sheets. She was too late.

He's gone. Abba's dead.

No. She didn't know that yet. He could still be alive . . . but how? How could he have survived this? Her lips quivered. She'd come all this way. She wasn't going to give up now. Khadija eyed the little figures pulling one another out from underneath collapsed buildings. Pictures of Abba lying facedown in the dirt scorched her mind. Or with his legs trapped beneath a pile of bricks. Or a knife protruding from his chest.

No. Stop it!

Nine balloons were tethered to the ground, figures in white cloaks milling around beside them. She had nothing. No weapon. No means to stop them. Nothing but a smoldering rage to watch them all burn.

Khadija tugged on a rope, and the balloon descended. She'd have to be smart about this. There was no room for recklessness. She killed the fire, steering the balloon toward a mango grove. This was a rescue mission, not an act of revenge. As the basket hit the ground, she quickly caught the fabric as it crumpled, and then she was out of the balloon in a flash, head snapping from left to right. Her vision was blurry with tears. Khadija furiously wiped her eyes and steadied her breathing. She needed to think. With all the buildings reduced to rubble, it was difficult to know exactly where in Qasrah she was. She scanned the wreckage, searching for landmarks, familiar places, something to help her get her bearings. Where was her house from here?

But her eyes kept focusing on the bodies. Everywhere. Bodies sprawled across the ground, jinn feasting on flesh. Most had been licked to bones.

Her home. Her life. Her childhood. All gone.

Vera had done this.

She walked in a daze, swerving around shattered glass as she followed the crowd. Faces covered in ash and dust were making their way to what she recognized as the soldiers' barracks in the center of the village: the only building that remained standing. As Khadija neared, the metallic smell of blood and guttural groans made her stomach churn. The barracks reeked of death. Should she look for Abba there? Would she want Abba to be in there among all the dying and the dead? She took a breath. What choice did she have?

Khadija approached the barracks, slotting into line behind limping women, and men with worryingly still children in their arms, all pushing and shoving as they tried to slip through the bottleneck forming at the doorway. She weaved her way through and entered, wrinkling her nose at the smell of alcohol and disinfectant. Rows and rows of cots were lined up on the ground. Women hurried back and forth, cutting up fresh bandages and making herbal poultices in mortar and pestles. Her eyes adjusted to the dim light as Khadija scanned faces, so many faces, praying for that familiar shine of a bald head and that crooked pair of glasses. *Where are you, Abba?*

"Khadija?"

She turned her head.

"Khadija! Is it really you?"

There he was. Sitting on the ground, knees curled to his chest, pressing a bandage to his forehead.

Abba.

He looked the same, with his long beard speckled with gray and white, and his thick glasses that sat a little lopsided on the tip of his nose, but then he also looked so much older and frailer. There was a nasty graze on his knee and a cut above his eyebrow, but he appeared otherwise unhurt.

Abba's eyes widened so much that if not for his glasses they probably would've popped out of his head and rolled across the ground. "You came back!" He squeezed her so tight she couldn't breathe.

"Of course." She fought back tears but they kept coming freely. Abba just held her. Everything was OK again. Everything would be fine now.

Abba drew her at arm's length and scrutinized her. Suddenly Khadija felt self-conscious, like a scared little girl afraid to meet her father's gaze. She read the question on his face. The betrayal in his eyes. The hurt was fresh. Her head lowered in shame.

"Why did you leave me, beti?" Abba's shoulders slumped like they'd been carrying the weight of the world for years. "You stole a balloon. You dishonored me." Every word was a slap to the face. Her head grew steadily lower. She supposed Abba was going to have this conversation now, and there was clearly no stopping him. She knew she deserved every word.

"I haven't seen you in nearly two weeks. You could've been dead for all I knew!"

Khadija bit her tongue. He was right. She'd been stupid, reckless, selfish. She'd put him in danger. She'd put the whole village in danger. Her mouth soured. How many had died because of her? "I'm sorry, Abba. I never meant to make you suffer."

Abba crossed his arms. "You are not a little girl anymore, Khadija."

She knew that. Of course she knew that, but it didn't stop her from breaking down in tears. "I was just tired of being your puppet, Abba! I couldn't have married Abdel and you know it. I would have been miserable!"

"But you would have been safe." Abba removed his glasses and massaged his temple. "Why couldn't you just be more like your sister, hmm? Talia never complained, and now look. She is happily married."

It always came down to that. The measure of a girl's worth was determined by her obedience, her ability to not make herself a nuisance. After all, girls were the hāri of the Ghadaeans. Khadija rose to her feet and patted her eyes with her scarf. "It might look that way, but you don't know that for certain. She could be suffering."

Abba shook his head fiercely. "I would never allow my daughter to suffer—"

"*I'm* suffering!" Khadija shouted. Nearby heads turned, then swiftly looked away. "All those years you kept me in the house, I was suffering. Could you not see that? Or was all you cared about marrying me off so you could impress the neighbors? What about what I wanted? Did that not matter to you?" Khadija had torn her heart out now, laid it on the ground for all to see. "Why can't you just accept me for who I am?"

Abba wiped his glasses on his kurta. "I'm sorry if I made you feel that way, Khadija. I've only ever wanted to protect you, to keep you safe." His voice shook. The pain in his next words was so raw, a fresh set of tears graced her cheeks. "I'm getting old. You need a husband who can provide for you, not some . . . old man." He gestured at himself and shut his eyes. "I can't lose any more of my family, beti. My heart won't allow it." A single tear escaped.

There was something truly heartbreaking about seeing a parent cry. Khadija's throat ached. She didn't think she'd ever seen Abba cry. She'd heard it, stifled sobs behind closed doors, but never like this. Khadija went to Abba, curling her hand in his. "Marrying me off isn't the answer. You'd never see me. I'd be like Talia. How would you know I was safe?"

Abba couldn't meet her eyes. "Faith, I guess. Just like a part of me knew I would see you again. Every day when I pray, I pray only for you and Talia, for your safety, even if that means I never see you again. It is enough knowing you both are safe."

Khadija knew Abba put a huge amount of confidence in prayer. For her, it was less so. Something she did when she didn't know what else to do. "You need to stop putting so much pressure on yourself, Abba. My safety isn't just your responsibility. It's mine too."

Abba cocked his head to the side like that had never occurred to him. "But I am your father—"

"And I am my own person. You can't possibly take all responsibility for my safety unless you plan on keeping me constantly under your watch." She laughed softly then. "Or locked in my bedroom."

Abba dipped his head. "I hope you realize I never did that to punish you."

"I know, Abba." Khadija squeezed his hand and helped him to his feet. "You've looked after me your whole life. Let me look after you now."

Abba brushed the dust from his shirt and cupped her cheek. "OK, beti."

Her chest felt tight, as if a hundred birds were trapped inside trying to escape all at once. Had Abba just agreed with her about something?

"Do you know who did this, beti?"

Her voice was hoarse from all the dust. "The Hāreef, Abba."

"Hāri," he spat. "Vermin! They're still outside. It's not safe for us to leave the building." He shivered. "And they use sihr. I saw them." He closed his eyes. "There was this one, a woman with red hair."

Khadija swallowed. Vera. Her blood boiled.

Abba began muttering prayers under his breath. "The woman. She said she would do this again." He started rocking. "She said she'd keep doing this until there were none of us left to burn."

Khadija's stomach dropped. She pictured the wreckage outside. No. This couldn't happen again. "What exactly did she say, Abba?"

Abba sighed. "She said she would kill the nawabs next. All of them. One by one." He shook his head. "Burn their cities to the ground."

Khadija paled.

Abba met her eyes. He looked so small, so fragile, his clothes covered in blood and dust. "She called us darkers, beti. What does that mean?"

Khadija had no words for him. She rubbed his arms.

Abba held his head in his hands. "She told her jinn to destroy our home. She must have thought me dead, but I hid under the stairs." His wrists shook. "It's almost like she was looking for me, beti. But how could she be looking for me?"

"I—" What could she say? Tell him this was all her fault. That she'd gotten on the wrong side of a terrorist and now they'd spend the rest of their lives fleeing demons and jinn.

"I have a balloon, Abba. I can get us out of here."

Abba shook his head. "It's not safe, beti."

"We can't stay here."

"I'd rather die in here than get eaten alive by the jinn out there!"

Khadija bit her tongue. The survivors had barricaded themselves in the barracks, using upturned tables and broken beams to block the windows, but it was only a matter of time before the jinn's appetite for human flesh brought them to the barracks' door. The Hāreef wouldn't even have to lift a finger, just watch as jinn tore their limbs apart. Or perhaps they'd set fire to the building and watch them burn to slow, agonizing deaths. She wasn't sure what was worse, only that they had to get out of there somehow.

"There must be a back entrance somewhere." Her head whipped around.

Abba stilled her with a hand on her wrist. "It is too late, Khadija."

"It's not too late." She jumped to her feet and attempted to haul Abba up, but he turned to dead weight in her hands.

"Khadija. Please!" he snapped, swatting at her hands.

"We aren't giving up, Abba! We can make a run for it—"

A windowpane shattered. The whole room froze, everyone held their breath at once, all eyes on the broken window partially blocked by only a single mahogany coffee table. No one screamed. No one dared make a noise.

Then the jinn poured in. Khadija yanked Abba to his feet. "Run!" She followed the crowd, all making for the door, until people began pushing in the opposite direction. She dug her nails into Abba's elbow and tugged him back just as a jinniya appeared in the doorway, a leery smile showing her bloodstained teeth.

Abba threw his hands over his face. "Khadija!"

Her head snapped around, searching all the windows and doors. Jinn the shape of cats were climbing the walls before pouncing, transforming into vicious dogs midair to sink their teeth into people's ankles. The jinniya pranced into the room in a swirl of black petticoats and set the curtain drapes ablaze. The room instantly turned black and green.

Khadija retreated until her back hit the wall, yanking Abba with her. An orange flicker of fire caught her eye from the fireplace, contained within an iron grate. It was the only iron she could find. "Stay here, Abba."

He yelled after her, but Khadija kept running, swiping a roll of bandages off a table and furiously wrapping them around her palms until she was encased in linen mittens. She sprinted toward the fireplace, swerving a snake as it lashed out at her. She stumbled but kept running, eyes locked on the orange flame as she aimed a kick at the grate, dislodging it and knocking the coals free where they scattered across the rug and set it alight. Her heart was hammering. She braced herself, then snatched the iron grate up. For a few seconds she felt nothing, and then the bandages started to heat up. Khadija ran back to Abba, brandishing the iron grate like a shield. She tugged Abba to the nearest blocked window.

"Move the table!"

Something black shot out from the corner of her vision. Khadija shrieked and brought the iron grate to her face. A jinn smacked the bars with a furious hiss and hit the floor, leaving a smear of inky black blood. Like copper and brass, iron wounded jinn, but only the most inferior ones. She pictured Anam's copper whip as she'd fended off jinn crows in Intalyabad. She swallowed the lump in her throat. If only Anam were here now.

"Hurry, Abba."

Abba groaned as he leaned his weight against the upturned table. Khadija planted a foot on the polished wood and pushed. The table squealed against the floor tiles.

"Stand back, Abba."

Abba ducked and covered his eyes as Khadija struck the windowpane with the iron grate. It shattered. The bandages were really starting to heat up now, her palms itching with a furious heat. "Go!"

Abba's knees creaked as he swung his legs over the window ledge and dropped to the ground with a thud. Khadija followed, blocking a crow with the grate as it nose-dived for her. The jinn squawked and retreated in a flurry of fallen feathers.

And then they were both out and running fiercely.

There was a line of white cloaks up ahead. She skidded. They were standing there, not even bothering to attack. There was no need for the Hāreef to attack when they had the jinn to do their bidding. Their laughter carried across the breeze, bitter and shrill as they cheered, punching the air, wolf whistling at one another, eyes glimmering as they watched the village burn. They all had their hands clasped to their necks where identical amulets with an emerald-green stone hung.

Her insides flared white hot. She didn't think she could hate them any more than she did now.

But they had weapons and jinn, and she had an iron grate and an old man hanging on her elbow. Khadija pulled Abba toward a row of collapsed houses, hopping over the debris. Abba stumbled. She went down with him, almost knocking her front teeth on a cracked kitchen sink.

Heavy breathing. Her head whirled around, thinking it was Abba, but his mouth was clamped shut, face-to-face on the floor with a boy in a white cloak.

"Terrorist!" Abba sprang back and attempted to pull her with him, but Khadija was locked into place, completely frozen, her skin suddenly so cold that even the hot grate in her palms felt like a lump of freezing iron.

"Jacob."

No. It couldn't be him. He couldn't have done this. But one look at those terrified eyes, pupils blown wide with fear, and then she was slamming the grate down. Jacob yelled and ducked just as the iron grate put a dent in the wall right where his head had been. He jumped to his feet, palms facing her. "Khadija. Please. Wait!"

"You did this!" Her throat felt raw, as if she'd swallowed a jar of nails.

His face crumpled. "I didn't want to. I didn't know she'd do this." His bottom jaw was trembling so violently it made his words shaky. "This has all been a mistake."

She shook her head. No. He didn't get to cry. Not when so many had died because of his mistake.

Abba pulled on her elbow. "You know this boy, beti?"

Khadija glanced at Jacob as his shoulders rocked with furious sobbing. "No. I don't know who he is. Not anymore." She turned.

"Wait!" Jacob wiped his nose on his sleeve. "Please. We have to save Anam."

Her breathing hitched. "Anam's alive?"

"For now." He pointed to a black balloon embroidered with silver leopards and baby elephants made out of pearls; it was hovering a few feet above the ground, tethered by a single rope. "She's tied up in Vera's balloon. We have to free her before Vera sacrifices her to Queen Mardzma."

Queen Mardzma. The jinniya queen who sent her jinn to kidnap Princess Malika in Hassan's book. *That* jinniya queen?

Abba retrieved a broomstick and waved it at Jacob like a sword. "The boy practices sihr! Leave him, Khadija."

Jacob turned to her with pleading eyes bluer than the sky at midday above the clouds, where time didn't seem to exist. "Please. I know what I did was wrong. Unforgivable. But you have to trust me now—"

She scoffed. "Why would I ever trust you again?"

Jacob winced at her words. "B-because," he stuttered. "Because Anam will die if you don't . . . and I don't want her to die."

"Khadija." Abba stabbed the broomstick at Jacob's chest. "Forget this boy. He's speaking nonsense. We must go."

But seeing Jacob drowning in his own guilt and shame, Khadija knew he was telling the truth. "I'm sorry, Abba, but we have to do this."

"Pah! He is a deceiver, Khadija, and still you trust him. His kind killed your mother and brother," Abba spat. "Or don't you care?"

Jacob's lips parted, eyes flickering to hers. She stiffened as if Abba had just slipped a blade through the gap between her shoulder blades. Her gaze fell to Jacob cowering in the corner, all his bravado, his hatred, his anger stripped back to leave only fear: the same fear she'd seen in the boy in the glass shop who had smashed a vase over Munir's head to protect her. That was the boy begging for her help now. Not Jacob the liar, or Jacob the terrorist. This was Jacob the boy who had saved her life and helped her fly a balloon.

Khadija faced Abba. "But *he* didn't kill them, Abba. You cannot blame them all." She turned to Jacob. "Let's go," she said, throwing her head back at Abba. "Hide here, Abba. We'll come back for you."

Abba yelled. He cursed. He screamed. He kicked the cracked kitchen sink until the ceramic shattered and turned his foot bloody, but still Khadija did not turn. She and Jacob weaved through the rubble, eyes fixed on the black balloon. The rest of the Hāreef had abandoned the balloon for front-row seats as the barracks burned. There were only two figures guarding it, but the red streak of hair escaping from beneath a white hood of one was enough to make Khadija's lungs feel like they were full of ice crystals. It was Vera.

"Vera's plan was to kill enough people to get Queen Mardzma's attention," Jacob said.

Khadija watched as Vera held a silver hand mirror inches from her face. It reminded her of the mirror Vera had used to speak to Queen Bidhukh before she'd been summoned.

"She wants to summon Queen Mardzma and offer Anam's heart to her in exchange for a wish."

Khadija paled. "So, what's the plan?"

Jacob narrowed his eyes. "I'll distract Vera while you free Anam."

Khadija supposed they didn't have time for anything more complicated than that. "OK."

Jacob made to leave when she stopped him with a hand on his forearm. "Be careful."

"I will." His blond eyelashes were wet as he faced her. "And I am sorry, Khadija. For everything." Then he pelted toward Vera before Khadija could yank him back.

26

JACOB

His sandals smacked the ground as Jacob made for Vera and Sara at full force, desperately concocting a story to draw both of them away from the balloon. Sara saw him coming. "What is it, new boy?" Her fingers teased the hilt of her blade.

Before he could speak, a flash of furious heat from behind made his neck prickle. Sara screamed and drew her blade, but Vera shoved her aside. "Caleb!"

Jacob whirled around.

Caleb was standing with his wings outstretched in a scorched circle, his green eyes locked on Vera. "Stop this now, Ammi! Before it's too late."

Vera hugged the silver mirror to her chest. "But I'm only doing this for you! I'm asking for a wish from Queen Mardzma for you, not the Hāreef. Don't you want to be human again? To be alive?"

Caleb growled. "Why? So I can go back to being weak, powerless, afraid of what those darkers will do to me? *No.*" His roar made the balloon's fabric flutter. "What kind of a life is that?" Then Caleb lashed out with his talons, slicing the balloon's rope.

The balloon began to ascend, whisking Anam into the sky.

"No!" Vera leaped for the rope, catching its frayed edge at the last moment and dragging it back to the ground.

Caleb bared his teeth. "Then you have made your choice. Queen Bidhukh will take her jinn army back, and you will have no hope of conquering Al-Shaam without her." The burned circle in the grass surrounding him flared to life with green jinn fire.

"Wait!" Vera thrust the rope into Sara's hand and stumbled forward. "You're right. I've made a mistake. Please, Caleb. Let me fix this." Again, Jacob was struck by how afraid she was of Caleb—and of losing him.

The flames encircling Caleb died down. "You will have to beg for her forgiveness."

"Of course."

"Then I will speak to her." Jinn fire enveloped Caleb before he was gone, leaving only burned grass in his place. Vera ran a hand across her brow, her fingers jittering slightly.

"So *that's* your plan. Traitor!"

Vera whirled around as Sara raised her sword arm, a look of incredulousness on her face. "What did you call me?" Her words were poisonous.

Sara stood her ground. "You heard me! All this time you led us to believe that you had the best interests of our people in mind." Sara sent a ball of spit flying in Vera's direction. "Instead you plan on wasting Queen Mardzma's wish on that beast you call a son!"

Sara's words were lost to Vera's roar. Blades whirled through the air inches from Sara's cheek. Sara staggered, and the balloon's rope slipped from her fingers. Jacob lunged for it. "You've gone mad! You're not fit to lead our people." Sara angled her blade to block Vera's next strike.

Jacob backed away as the two women circled each other, his grip so tight against the balloon's rope that his knuckles were white.

"You call my son a beast!" Vera lashed out in a flurry of strikes that had Sara ducking and diving to escape the blows. "Have you seen yourself?" A bitter laugh escaped her lips.

A deep growl reverberated in Sara's chest. She pounced. Vera and Sara collapsed in a heap and rolled across the grass. Sara fought her way on top and smashed her elbow down on Vera's nose. Blood sprayed the ground. Sara pressed her knee to Vera's neck and fumbled for her blade.

Footsteps trampled across the grass. Jacob lifted his head.

It was Khadija with her father in tow. "We need to leave—now!"

Jacob's eyes flickered to Vera and Sara locked in a furious dance of fists and flying kicks. He nodded.

"Anam," Khadija called up to the balloon, and Anam's face appeared as she frantically chewed on the ropes binding her wrists.

"Khadija. Come quickly!"

Jacob held the balloon steady as Khadija climbed in. When she reached the top she flung her arms around Anam's neck before peering down at her father. "Come on, Abba."

Jacob could feel the heat of Khadija's father's gaze as he offered his hand to the older man, but the urgency of their situation was stronger than his hatred—and Khadija's abba gripped his hand and allowed Jacob to bundle him into Khadija's waiting arms. Then Khadija leaned over the basket. "Your turn, Jacob. Climb!"

A shriek made his head snap around as Vera planted her blade in Sara's side. One strike was all it took, and Sara crumpled in a pile of white cloth that was rapidly staining red. Vera spat on the body. "Serves you right." She crouched to clean the blade and rose, her eyes murderous, her nostrils bloodied, and her crimson hair wild as she faced him. Jacob's throat twisted into a knot.

He glanced up at Khadija, her eyes wide with fear, and in that fleeting moment it was like they finally managed to shed all those layers of misunderstanding that hung heavy between them, leaving only their mutual fear. Because that's all it was. That's all it had ever been: his fear that had driven him to act in ways that he shouldn't have. Her fear of him and what he'd become. Fear that drove them both in opposite directions now, as he released her to the sky.

Vera's face contorted. "What have you done, Jacob?"

He craned his neck back, catching a final glimpse of the balloon before it shrank to the size of a bird. They'd escaped. He let the knowledge wash over him. It didn't matter what happened to him now. As long as they were safe, then he had managed to undo at least some of the wrong that he had caused. With that thought, he made his peace. "I let them go," he said. "I won't let you sacrifice Anam for a wish."

"You idiot!"

"No, Ammi." Their heads whirled around as Caleb reappeared in a flash of green fire. He stepped between them. "The boy is wise. He's proven his loyalty to Queen Bidhukh by refusing to allow you to ally with Queen Mardzma." He shot Vera a glare. "Just as you promised me."

Jacob nodded slowly, attempting to disguise his surprise.

Vera swallowed her protest and wiped her bloody nose on her sleeve. "Yes, of course."

"Good." Caleb surveyed Qasrah's ruins. "We've wasted enough time here. We leave for Al-Shaam. Immediately. Prepare the balloons."

Vera's next words were lost as Caleb flexed his wings and launched himself into the sky. She turned to him, and Jacob prepared himself for her wrath. Instead she simply said, "Round everyone up. We're leaving now."

They were forced to leave some members of the Hāreef behind due to the loss of the black balloon—the journey would already be slow because of the number of fighters aboard—but Caleb insisted Jacob accompany the group bound for Al-Shaam.

"You understand the bigger picture," he rasped quietly in that voice that reminded Jacob of hungry flames devouring brittle firewood. A voice that was also full of cunning and manipulation, he realized as the balloon took flight. So unlike his lesser counterparts that seemed focused only on bloodshed, Caleb was a jinn with his own agenda. "Not like the rest of these sheep." Caleb gestured scornfully at the Hāreef, busy attending to the balloon. "All they want is mindless violence."

Jacob could only nod, and pray Caleb's sudden interest in him would work in his favor. It was a stroke of sheer luck that Caleb had seen his role in assisting Anam and Khadija's escape as a sign of loyalty, and Jacob wasn't about to correct the ifrit. Ropes creaked above his head as the balloon made steady progress across the sky. Pictures of Qasrah aflame scorched the back of his eyelids. He couldn't let it happen again. He couldn't allow more blood to stain his hands, but there wasn't much he could do but wait and pray they never arrived in Al-Shaam. Pray that Khadija and Anam had flown to safety and not headed directly toward a war zone as he suspected. Prayer, as if *that* had ever served him before.

"They are ungrateful!" Caleb spat. "Unworthy of Queen Bidhukh's gifts."

Jacob instinctively squeezed the green gemstone in his pocket that he'd pried from William's amulet. "Then perhaps they should return them," he suggested. Without the stones, the Hāreef would be unable to command the jinn army.

Caleb's wicked smirk made Jacob's stomach shrivel to the size of a date kernel. "That is not a bad idea. And as for my mother, she's sworn her loyalty . . . for now. But I know the temptation to earn Queen Mardzma's wish still remains." The ifrit rounded on him. "I have two tasks for you, human boy. See them as a chance to prove your loyalty to our queen."

"O-OK," he stuttered.

Caleb leaned in, his fiery breath scorching the tip of Jacob's ears. "First, bring me the silver mirror my mother uses to contact Queen Mardzma. She won't be needing that now." He tapped a curved talon to his chin. "And second, I want you to steal the amulets."

Jacob choked out a gasp. "Me?"

"Yes, you! It *was* your idea after all." Caleb's gaze drifted over the rest of the Hāreef with murder in his eyes. "Imagine the look on their faces when they discover the jinn army they had put their hopes in cannot distinguish between them and the Ghadaeans in Al-Shaam."

Jacob stiffened. With his words, Caleb had revealed his true self. He was a hāri no more, and saw no issue with guaranteeing the Hāreef's demise.

Caleb rose, causing the balloon to tilt sharply. "Get it done, human boy," he snapped. "Or pay the price of failure."

Jacob swallowed, knowing it would be foolish to question an ifrit's command. He surveyed the remaining faces in the balloon. The Hāreef's previous energy as they'd watched Qasrah burn had long been extinguished, replaced with a solemnity at the members they'd left behind, and a tension that was close to snapping point the closer they got to Al-Shaam. How was he supposed to convince them to give up their amulets, their only reassurance that the jinn army wouldn't turn on them? He chewed his nails. No matter what he said, they wouldn't believe him. He had lived among them barely even a week. Confined mostly to the glass workshop, he'd failed to make any meaningful impression on anyone other than Marcus. And Sara—but Vera had left her body sprawled on the grass in Qasrah. Her most loyal member, and Vera had hacked her down without hesitation. It only reinforced the lengths Vera would go to for her son.

Vera had distanced herself from the group since they'd ascended, and everyone knew well enough to avoid her. Jacob watched her lean over the basket's edge, her hair whipping around her like red storm clouds. Would she keep the mirror on her person? If so, he had no hope of getting it either, and certainly no chance of claiming her amulet. Jacob watched Caleb loop through the darkening sky, leaving a trail of ash and sparks. He knew he would not accept anything less than success. Unless Jacob intended to plummet toward the ground, he'd have to carry out the ifrit's wishes somehow.

Marcus glanced his way then, and he must have noticed the worry knitting Jacob's brows together as Marcus waved him over. "Come eat, Jacob, while it's still hot."

Jacob approached the circle, slotting into place beside Marcus and a hāri woman he didn't recognize. A plate of pilau appeared in front of him, and only then did Jacob become aware of how hungry he was. His stomach growled, eliciting a chuckle from Marcus as he polished off his plate of rice in seconds and eagerly asked for more.

"Slow down. We've got to make this food last until we get there."

"Sorry." Jacob dabbed his mouth on his sleeve. The fierce ache in his stomach had receded enough for him to glance around the circle at the other faces, all gazing intently at him. He shifted nervously.

"What were you talking about with . . . him?" Marcus inclined his head toward Caleb, now only a pair of black wings in the distance.

"Erm . . ." This could be his chance to obtain their amulets. If only he was good at lying. His eyes flickered to Vera, out of earshot, then Jacob opened his mouth, allowing the lies to pour from his lips. "He said he was impressed with everyone and that he'd never seen a town burned to the ground so quickly."

Smug grins spread among the group. Jacob swiftly disguised his horror at their reaction. "And that he expects the same in Al-Shaam."

Murmurs traveled around the circle. "But Qasrah is a village and Al-Shaam is a city, and there are less of us," a man he vaguely recognized said to a flurry of agreement.

And that's when it finally clicked into place. "He's aware of that, which is why he wants to give you all a very special gift."

Excited whispers passed through the group. "Gift! What gift will he give us?"

Jacob straightened up and addressed his audience. "He wants to enchant your amulets so that they are more powerful. You'll be able to control even the most superior jinn that way."

By the gleeful grins spreading across the Häreef's faces, Jacob knew he'd said the right thing. "Well, it's about time," Marcus murmured beside him. "I'm tired of crows and snakes. If we plan on taking a city, we're going to need far stronger jinn."

Jacob nodded. "Caleb agrees. If you just give me your amulets, he'll enchant them for you." He paused, eyes resting on the other seven balloons drifting in the distance. "Spread the word to the other balloons and bring me everyone's amulets if you can. I'll give them to Caleb."

Jacob had expected at least some resistance, suspicious glances, not the eager way in which the Hāreef removed their amulets and flung them toward him. Jacob scooped them up and shoved the load in his pockets before his head whipped around to Vera, still gazing at the night sky with empty eyes.

Now, how to get her mirror?

Once supper was over, most of the Hāreef retired to their separate bed rolls. Jacob sat cross-legged on the rough linen, refusing to lie down with so many amulets digging into his thighs, but he didn't dare remove them from his pockets. He leaned his head against the basket, allowing the lulling motions of the balloon to soothe him. It was only as his eyelids were beginning to droop that a sharp whisper dragged him back from sleep.

"Jacob."

His eyes snapped open.

"Jacob."

He scanned the sleeping figures. That's when Vera stepped into the light, green eyes fixed on him. He swallowed. Had she noticed the amulets weighing down his pockets? His hands shifted guiltily to his sides.

She waved him over, and Jacob had no choice but to follow, rising slowly in an attempt to stifle the jingle of the amulets in his pockets. He joined her at the other end of the balloon.

"You and Caleb seem to be getting along well. I saw you talking earlier."

Up close, the exhaustion dulling her skin was striking against her bright hair, and the shadows deepening her eye sockets gave her a haunted look. "I always knew you two would get along. He used to be quite like you . . . when he was alive." That last part was barely a breath on the night breeze, but it held so much pain that even the fire in the burner receded, the flames threatening to die. "Always crafting things, always collecting bits of junk and saving them in the hope they'd be useful later." The corners of her lips upturned a fraction. "He was a quiet boy, and most people thought him stupid because of it, but he was far from that." She sighed, her shoulders deflating, then she turned to him. "Is it wrong to want that same boy back instead of this . . . creature?" Her eyes fell to the outline of Caleb's wings.

And Jacob couldn't help but shake his head. There was no timeline when it came to grief, no point where the loss was finally forgotten, love severed upon the moment of death. He thought of William and how his absence was a gaping hole in his side where the only relief was to fill his mind with so much noise to distract him from it. Would that be his life, living each day jumping from one activity to another, searching for his new distraction? Did it ever end? "It's not wrong to miss him. But . . . you've gotten him back, haven't you?"

Vera slammed her fist against the basket. Jacob recoiled. "It's just . . . he's so different now. Al-Ghaib has changed him. Queen Bidhukh has changed him." She ran a palm across her drawn cheeks. "Queen Mardzma was my only hope of getting that same boy back. A real boy. Alive. Human. *My* son—not *hers.*" She dipped inside her cloak to reveal the silver hand mirror. "But now I have nothing to offer her." She held the mirror over the edge.

"Wait!" Jacob's hand hovered over the mirror. Caleb had told Jacob to bring the mirror to him; he couldn't risk Vera destroying it.

Vera raised an eyebrow. “You don’t think I should give up just yet?” Her gaze returned once more to Caleb, and her fingers tightened around the mirror. “Maybe you’re right. I would travel to the depths of Hell for my son. I would raze an entire city just to make him smile. I would spill the blood of every last darker so that the world will finally be safe for him.” She pushed her shoulders back and stuck out her jaw, and Jacob could only watch as the old Vera returned to life. “I will find another way to impress Queen Mardzma. Even if I have to burn every city in Ghadaea to the ground. She will grant me a wish. I will get my Caleb back.”

Jacob studied her, stunned. Vera was like a pendulum that swung back and forth between grief and rage, and right now she had caught alight. She slipped the mirror into his hand. The cold silver made him flinch. “I can’t let Caleb see me with this. So, I need you to keep it safe for me. I can trust you, can’t I?”

Jacob nodded dumbly. Then she spun in a whirl of white material, leaving him alone at the edge of the basket.

27

KHADIJA

The last Khadija saw of Jacob was the top of his head shrinking from view as he faced off with Vera and her ifrit. She bit her lip, because if she didn't she'd scream. He'd sacrificed himself for them. He'd thought himself evil, irredeemable, so that his only chance of atonement for his crimes was death. And she'd let him die. The hole in her heart, the hole she'd spent years trying to stuff with things, anything, so that she could function began to stretch, grow, until it was a bottomless pit in her chest sucking everything inside it. Khadija wailed.

"What's wrong, beti?" Abba was by her side. "Are you hurt?"

She was, but not in the way he knew. Not in a way she could possibly explain. Anam brushed her fingertips. Khadija spun and buried her face in Anam's shoulder. "He was a good boy," she sobbed. "He wasn't evil. He was misled." Tears overcame her so that it became impossible to form words.

"I know." Anam stroked her back. "There was good in his heart."

It was the memory of that good inside Jacob, the good that Vera had feasted upon, snatched from him, replaced with her poison, that drove her. With Anam's help, they steered the black balloon in the direction of Al-Shaam, and all the while Abba stared at her wide-eyed. At first, he'd snap at her whenever she reached for a rope. "Are you sure that's the right one, beti?" he'd ask while peering at the ground. The first time she tugged on the rope to open the parachute vent, causing the balloon to suddenly drop and catch a faster wind current, Abba shrieked louder than she'd ever heard. They flew two days in the balloon before she finally earned his trust, and then he could only marvel, gasping each time she spun the propeller or fed the flames. "How did you learn all this, beti?"

"I learned some of it myself." She paused. "And the rest I was taught."

Abba stuttered. "But . . ." He rubbed his beard. "What man would teach you to fly?"

"A hāri one, of course."

That elicited a hiss from Abba, though he had sense enough not to question her further. It was as evening of the third day in the balloon approached that Anam's patience finally snapped. "We're traveling too slow. Al-Shaam will be in flames by the time we arrive." Her boot thumped the deck. "Vera has a jinn army. She is too powerful." Her shoulders fell. "I fear we are merely flying toward our deaths."

Abba, who was slumped on the deck attempting to sleep, stiffened at her words. Any mention of jinn would send him into a fit of violent shaking so that Khadija and Anam had to make sure to lower their voices whenever the Hāreef were mentioned.

Anam groaned. She was always so controlled, so put together, and she was crumbling before Khadija's eyes. Had the Hāreef done that to her, the same way they'd chipped away at Jacob, bit by bit, piece by piece, until he was reduced to nothing? Her skin prickled with heat. They couldn't give up now. They'd come too far, lost too much, to give up now. "Al-Shaam has been warned, and they will have the Wāzeem's aid. Besides, surely we have at least slowed Vera down by taking one of her balloons." She gestured at the swaths of black material that blended into the night. "There's still some hope."

It was the way Anam looked at her that made her cheeks blush and her shoulders curl in on themselves. Perhaps she was being naive. But even false hope was better than giving up entirely.

"The Wāzeem do not have the numbers to tip the balance. I am sorry, Khadija. I do not know how to make this situation better—"

"It's not up to you to make this better." Khadija joined her at the edge, staring out into the dark. "I'm asking you not to give up just yet."

"But—"

"Stop," Khadija said. Her eyes traced the silver globe of the full moon, so close she could reach out and pluck it from the sky. "Let's just focus on getting to Al-Shaam. One step at a time."

Anam's exhale tickled the tip of Khadija's nose. "OK, Khadija." She turned the gas tap so that the orange flames crackled to life, but the night air was still, and despite feeding the burner and adjusting the altitude they could not find a wind current. They were merely floating, only a whisper of wind giving them any inclination that they were moving at all. Anam was right. They'd never get there like this.

Khadija groaned. All they needed was a breath of wind, a flock of birds to pull them along, even a swarm of winged ifrits if it made their progress quicker. Her eyes traced the silvery outline of the moon.

Or perhaps one pair of wings was all they needed. A peri's wings. Her fingers curled around the basket's edge. It was worth a shot.

"Tahmina," Khadija cried out into the night. Anam was staring at her as if she'd finally lost it. Khadija called again. "We need your help."

Her voice died on the night air. Her eyes furiously searched the blackness, hoping, praying for the silvery glow of the peri's wings to grace the sky. "Tahmina!"

Nothing. This was stupid. Khadija sank to the deck, curling her arms around her knees. That's when Anam sprang to life. "Wait. I see something!"

A slice of silver lit up the deck. Khadija jumped to her feet just as the beating of wings reached her ears. And there she was, the peri hovering a few feet above her head, her opalescent feathers gleaming in the firelight.

"Tahmina," she gasped. Even in such a short amount of time, her mind had already begun to forget how beautiful the creature was. Tahmina fixed her lilac eyes on her and smiled, her teeth shining like pearls in the darkness. Khadija could only gape in awe of her.

Abba's elbow thumping the deck as he jolted awake seemed to break the spell. "Khadija." His head twisted toward Tahmina, and then his eyes almost popped out of their sockets. "Oh my goodness!"

Abba's reaction elicited a chuckle from Tahmina, the sound like wind chimes. "It is good to see you again."

"Khadija." Anam tugged on her sleeve, mouth forming a ring, eyes glued to the peri. Khadija slipped out of Anam's grip and approached Tahmina.

"I was wondering if you could help us."

Tahmina fluttered down to the deck. "You helped me in my time of need. I would gladly return the favor." She ruffled the silver crown of feathers gracing her slender neck, no evidence remaining of how Vera's ifrit had cruelly plucked them from her skin. "If I am capable of it."

"Can you pull the balloon?"

Tahmina's silver brows creased.

"We need to get to Al-Shaam as quickly as possible."

Tahmina glanced at the material above their heads and hummed, "I could try." Her wings flickered to life as she sprang into the night and grasped a rope. The balloon creaked in protest. At first, it seemed to make no difference at all, and Khadija's insides quivered with doubt until a fresh breeze brushed her skin. The balloon began to pick up speed.

"I think it is working."

Khadija stared into the night, now lit with the silvery glow of the peri as they headed for Al-Shaam. They would make it. Darian was counting on her.

It was dawn by the time curved domes and minarets jutted into view, the buildings covered in spidery marble veins and mosaic tiles that sparkled beneath the blazing amber of the rising sun like they were ready to catch fire. Khadija could only gasp. Tahmina had taken them almost to the city's gates, only fading with the night's disappearance, and the promise to do all she could to aid their fight against the Hāreef.

"I did not think we would make it in time." Anam tugged on a rope, the air shifted, and they started to drop. Khadija's stomach began doing backflips as they sank, landing heavily in a cloud of dust beside a cluster of balloons of various colors, shapes, and sizes. Al-Shaam was still standing, for now. Soldiers with orange turbans and gold spears milled about atop the walls while hāri tended to the balloons. They'd landed just outside the city's walls. From the ground, they loomed above her, so high she had to crane her neck back to glimpse the tops of them.

Soldiers surrounded them. Khadija clenched her jaw to prevent her fear from showing. Anam immediately took the lead and approached the basket's edge, much to the confused glances and raised eyebrows of the soldiers. That's when Abba sprang to life. His knees creaked like the hinges of a door in desperate need of oiling as he beat Anam to the edge.

"Good morning, sir." The nearest soldier wagged a finger at Khadija and Anam. "Who are you traveling with, and what is your reason for entering Al-Shaam?"

As the words spilled from Abba's lips as smoothly as if he'd rehearsed them, Khadija was reminded of the days back when Ammi and Hassan were still alive and Abba had bristled with confidence. He'd always been a social butterfly, chatting with the neighbors, turning down wedding invites and the celebrations of the births of babies because he hadn't the time to attend so many. Khadija had forgotten what he looked like when he smiled, never mind the sound of his laugh. Slowly, before her eyes, the butterfly's wings were returning.

"These two girls are my daughters." He patted Khadija's and Anam's heads in turn. "They are both getting married today. It's been quite a hectic couple of days organizing two weddings at such short notice." Abba chuckled and rubbed his beard.

"I can imagine." The soldier waved them through. "Well, enjoy the weddings, sir."

And it was as easy as that. They were seen through the gates without so much as a double glance, serving to only prove to Khadija just how easy the world was for a Ghadaean man.

When the soldiers were out of earshot, Khadija rounded on her father. "Abba!"

"Do you think I was convincing enough?" He fiddled with the tassel on his topi.

"Enough? You made it look so easy!"

A slow half smile spread across his face. "Next time you plan on stealing a balloon, beti, you should take me with you."

Khadija could only bite her lip to stop a grin forming. "OK, Abba."

Anam led the way through cobbled streets made from bits of marble and colored glass that twinkled in the sunlight. The streets were only just coming to life this early in the morning. At each person they passed, Anam frowned. "I thought the Wāzeem had already warned the city about the Hāreef. People should not be in the streets. They should be barricading themselves in their homes." Her mouth was a thin line.

"Perhaps they did and no one believed them," Khadija murmured.

"That is likely." Anam powered ahead. "We must hurry." They clambered up another steep set of stairs cut into the sandstone, all while Abba complained about the heat and how dusty the air was, until Anam's face lit up. "Finally. I thought I would never find it." She approached a house, while Khadija and Abba stopped to catch their breath.

Anam knocked, the curtains fluttered, and then the door swung open to reveal Zaid, the Ghadaean man Khadija had first met with Ruqaiya, who appeared to be his wife. He was dressed head to toe in armor a size too big for him so that his metal shoulders consumed the width of the doorway. "Anam!" He pressed a palm to his polished breastplate. "It is so good to see you again."

Anam smiled. "I hope I have not missed the action."

"You're just in time." Zaid waved them inside. The room was bursting with activity as members of the Wāzeem pored over detailed maps of the city or sat cross-legged sharpening copper-tipped arrowheads. Everywhere, gongs, wind chimes, and other elaborate symbols to ward off the jinn hung off curtain rails and dangled out of windows. Khadija scanned faces, searching in vain for that one face she was aching to see.

"Ruqaiya." Anam's gaze was fixed on the woman with hoops dangling from her ears.

"Anam!" Ruqaiya enveloped her in a hug. "We thought the worst." Her made-up eyes flickered to her. "Khadija. You came back." She faced Abba and respectfully dipped her head. "And this must be your father."

Khadija nodded, surprised Ruqaiya had remembered her after their brief meeting. Her eyes fell to the crates against the far wall, brimming with freshly cut flowers, their stems knotted together. She furrowed her brow.

Anam followed her gaze. "For the jinn," she explained. "They cannot cross an unbroken chain of flowers."

"Jinn." Abba rubbed his elbows. "Khadija. I don't like this. It is too dangerous."

Khadija's lips parted, unable to string together the words to explain, before Zaid swiftly introduced himself to Abba and led him to a table with a selection of sweetmeats and spiced chai, momentarily disappearing before returning with a plush footstool for Abba's aching feet. It was enough to transform Abba's frown and silence his questions. Khadija rolled her eyes. Her father was a simple man at heart.

"Have you seen Darian?"

Ruqaiya's smile caused a flush to creep across Khadija's neck. "He is in discussion with the Wāzeem's Council. You should join them, Anam. You are, after all, the Council's best third."

Anam grinned and eagerly disappeared to join her remaining Council members, leaving Khadija to sit with her abba and nibble on pink ladoos until Zaid waved her over.

"The Hāreef could arrive at any moment. The city isn't safe. We've tried to warn the soldiers, but they only laughed in our faces. We've been reduced to going door to door, warning individuals. The ones who did believe us have been evacuated to the tunnels beneath the city." Zaid's eyes didn't lift from the map he was bent over. "Ruqaiya will be going there soon. You should go as well, Khadija."

Her shoulders stiffened. She hadn't come all this way to hide. "I want to help."

Zaid cocked his head to the side. "There is nothing cowardly about it. You have proven your bravery just by showing up here."

But she hadn't come to flaunt her courage. Khadija's next words were sharp. "Have you met Vera?"

Zaid shook his head.

"Well, I have. I've seen firsthand what she can do. I want to help stop her."

Zaid sighed. "Can you fight? Can you wield a sword?" Her silence said everything. "Then what exactly will you do, Khadija?"

Heat rose to her cheeks. "I won't sit and merely do nothing!"

If Zaid had been surprised by her outspokenness, he didn't show it, but then Zaid didn't strike her as a typical Ghadaean man. It was Ruqaiya who broke the silence. "If she wants to help, then let her. We need all the help we can get."

"We'd be sending her to her death."

"Then allow her to tend to the wounded." Ruqaiya rested a hand on Zaid's arm. "Let her help, Zaid."

Zaid finally relented. "Fine. Get her ready." With that, he rolled up his map and left the house.

Something passed briefly over Ruqaiya's face before it was gone, replaced by a smile. "Well, I suppose you'll need a weapon." She pulled back the beaded curtain at the end of the hallway to reveal a table covered with all manner of armor and weapons. Copper arrows were lined up and spears were laid out, their tips freshly sharpened. Beside them was a selection of pendants, talismans, and trinkets to ward off the jinn, their colorful glass twinkling in the light. "Take your pick."

Khadija traced her fingertips over the nearest spear. She had never even held one. Maybe Zaid was right. What use would she be? The little voice in her head readied its tongue to scold her, but Khadija batted it away and swallowed the self-doubt before it had chance to shatter her resolve. *I have to do something. I've come this far. It can't all be for nothing.*

Ruqaiya left her alone. "Let me know if you need any help," she called from the other room.

Khadija slipped her kameez over her head and replaced it with a thin cotton tunic and a breastplate. Her fingers shook as she tightened the buckles. This was really happening. She steadied her breathing, images of Qasrah's destruction scorching the back of her eyelids. She was willing to do anything in her power to prevent Al-Shaam from befalling the same fate. She donned a pair of shalwar pants and long boots, retied her scarf so that it was tight, and then she grabbed a dagger and a scimitar, testing their weight against her wrist. The metal felt cold and unfamiliar. Khadija chose a simple gold talisman etched with a delicate scripture. A prayer to ward off the jinn. Its words were so intricate she had to bring the talisman an inch from her face to admire it. She clipped the chain around her neck and hid the talisman beneath her tunic. Whether it would protect her against a jinn army was another thing, but just the feel of the jewelry against her skin was reassuring.

She looked down at herself. Such a stark contrast from the girl who'd stolen a hot-air balloon a few weeks ago. Now she felt like one of the warriors from Hassan's book. Khadija's hands flew to her kameez, retrieving the single folded page, its edges blackened to a crisp. She slipped it up her sleeve. Now she was ready. She could do this. Her whole life she had been waiting for this moment. The moment to prove her worth. Not to anyone else but to herself.

I am not simply an ornament to lock away indoors, placed on the window ledge to admire life from the safety of a house. I am so much more.

Khadija straightened up, her limbs buzzing with newfound energy. She reemerged through the curtain. Ruqaiya looked her up and down from beneath her thick eyelashes and beamed. "It suits you."

When Abba caught sight of her, his eyebrows shot to his hairline and he sprang to his feet, knocking over the footstool. "And just where do you think you're going dressed like that, Khadija?"

She rolled her eyes. "I'll only be helping the wounded, Abba."

"You most certainly will not!" Heads were turning. "It's far too dangerous."

"Everything is dangerous, Abba! We're in the middle of a war," she snapped. That silenced him. Khadija steered him away to a corner where their voices wouldn't carry, but when she opened her mouth to argue her case, no words escaped. She reckoned she was tired. Tired of explaining herself, tired of being ignored, overruled, proving herself to someone who would never see the real her.

As this realization flickered across her face, her posture deflated, her eyes sinking to the floor. That seemed to bother Abba more than her earlier outburst. He sighed, rubbing the dents caused by his glasses on the bridge of his nose. "I suppose I can't stop you, can I?"

Her silence made him chuckle. He cupped her cheek. "You are so much like your ammi, you know, only she was better at pretending to listen to me." He laughed the type of laugh that made his shoulders bounce up and down and the skin around his eyes crease. She hadn't seen him laugh like that in so long. "You are even braver than her. You don't bother to pretend."

And then Khadija was giggling too, throwing her head back. Abba placed a palm on the wall to steady himself, the laughter making him wheeze until they were both doubled over, struggling to breathe, tears streaming. In that moment, Abba didn't just feel like her father anymore. He felt like her friend.

"Do what you must, Khadija, just please be safe." Then Abba returned to his seat.

Khadija's skin was glowing. Finally she had her abba's blessing. As she rounded the corner, her shoulder struck something hard and metal. Khadija stumbled back. "I'm so sorry—"

"Wouldn't be the first time you've pushed me."

That voice did inexplicable things to her heart. Her eyes traveled up to his face, now framed by a sweeping fringe that covered his forehead the way ocean waves curl across the shoreline. Her tongue suddenly felt like it was made of wool. "Darian."

He leaned in, so close it took all her restraint not to brush her fingertips against his. "I see your father has made himself at home." He gestured to where Abba had already garnered a crowd as he reenacted their recent balloon flight to Al-Shaam, with some embellishments, of course.

A pause, enough for the sticky awkwardness to start creeping in.

Darian was the first to speak. "I'm sorry I couldn't come with you."

"It's—"

"It's not fine. It's not OK." Darian's eyes were fixed on a spot a few inches to the right of her. It was strange seeing someone as confident as Darian suddenly unable to meet her eyes. "I should have been there for you and I wasn't."

Khadija swallowed. She would be lying if she said it hadn't stung when he'd refused to accompany her, but it would also be unfair to expect his priorities to align with hers. "You had to prepare the city for Vera's army. It wasn't like you were doing nothing."

Darian scoffed. "We might as well have done nothing with all the good that's done."

Her face darkened. The city barely stood a chance against a jinn army as it was, but if the soldiers were too lazy to defend the walls, Al-Shaam would most certainly fall.

"I'm glad your father is safe. You have no idea how glad I am."

She cast her gaze to Abba as he flapped his arms in an attempt to mimic how Tahmina had pulled the balloon across the sky. "It was something I had to do on my own anyway."

He nodded. "I've always got that impression of you—that you're used to doing things on your own."

She didn't even need to answer. Her face said it all. That was what years spent alone in her bedroom had done to her.

Darian's eyes finally found hers. "But you don't have to do everything on your own anymore. The Wāzeem are like a family to me, and we rely on each other." He hooked his hand in hers and tugged her to him. "I want you to be able to rely on me."

How she wished to melt into his words. He made it sound so easy, like sinking backward into a fragranced pool, if only she had the courage to allow herself to fall. Khadija worried at her bottom lip, struggling for the words. The way Darian stood in front of her with that wicked gaze that both set her skin alight and made her insides melt, and the crooked half smile that tugged on the corners of his mouth, was making it impossible to think.

Then, as Darian pressed his lips to hers, she didn't need to think anymore. This kiss was quick and desperate, full of all the longing and unspoken words over the past few days. When they finally broke apart, Khadija was breathless and her senses muddled by the taste of Darian still lingering on her tongue.

28

JACOB

When the gold-tipped minarets of Al-Shaam appeared across the horizon, the Hāreef broke out into cheers. Jacob's stomach knotted with dread. What now? His pockets still rattled with the weight of the Hāreef's amulets—he had virtually all of them thanks to Marcus rallying around the other balloons—but his anxiety at having lied to them, and the subsequent destruction that would befall them, was heavier. Jacob had fended off questions all morning as the Hāreef in his balloon asked for their amulets back.

"He's still not finished with them. You'll get them soon. Ask Caleb if you have a problem with that." His response had been met by scowls, but luckily no one had the nerve to approach the ifrit directly. And luckily for Jacob, Caleb had simply gestured with a flick of his wrist that Jacob stash the amulets in a barrel, without so much as a glance at them. Switching the amulets for a sack of coal had been easy enough. He prayed Caleb wouldn't think to check the barrel.

As for Vera's mirror . . . the polished surface was cool against his bare skin where Jacob had shoved it up his tunic. Caleb had demanded it earlier, and though Jacob knew it would be easier to relinquish the mirror, that hadn't stopped him from uttering the lie that Vera had tossed it overboard—news that had certainly pleased the ifrit. He'd kept the mirror, largely because the opportunity of a wish from Queen Mardzma was too tempting to pass up. Jacob had seen Vera's army, and he knew with a sinking feeling in his gut that Al-Shaam did not stand a chance. A wish was the only hope the city had of surviving, if only he could figure out what else would please the jinniya queen other than Anam's heart.

Vera upturned an empty crate and leaped onto it so that she stood head and shoulders above everyone else. "Are you ready for justice to be served?"

Hāri whistled. The balloon swayed with the stomping of too many pairs of feet. Seven balloons hovered nearby, close enough to hear her voice carry across the still air.

"Are you ready for the dawn of a new age? An age where we are the ones on top and they are at the bottom?" She jabbed her finger in the direction of Al-Shaam. The Hāreef roared and brandished their weapons. "That day has come. The darkers will learn just what we are capable of, and they will regret ever treating us this way."

The balloon erupted into curses and slurs.

Vera took her time scanning the balloons, a sneer prickling her lips, crimson hair dancing in the breeze. She enjoyed putting on a show, rallying up a crowd, having them cling to every word she spoke. She raised her gloved palm to silence the crowd. Her next words were so soft the balloon tilted sharply as everyone leaned in.

"And we will give them no mercy."

Bile made Jacob's tongue taste bitter.

They approached the city walls. Vera dropped the first crate and brandished her amulet. A flock of jinn crows rose up from the glass shards and dived toward the walls, where archers dozed in the sunshine.

Unloaded ballistae were lined up, pointing uselessly at the sun. The city was built for battle and yet ill-prepared for war.

Al-Shaam could not even fathom the carnage that was to come as more crates plummeted toward the ground and jinn appeared from the fragments. The swarm of crows with emerald eyes descended on the walls, knocking the spears from the soldiers' hands, pecking at their eyes. Confused shouts carried across the air, soldiers toppling over the walls like falling leaves.

Vera smiled. The balloon was safe to land.

A hot breeze tickled Jacob's face as they swiftly dropped altitude, sinking into powdery sand as the material crumpled above their heads. The Hāreef swiftly assembled on the ground a good distance from the newly emerged jinn army. Jacob slotted into their ranks, hands clutching the amulets in his pockets, afraid the creatures would turn on the Hāreef instantly and expose his deception. Instead, as Caleb landed beside Vera, the jinn army obediently turned their gaze to the ifrit as they awaited his command. Caleb strode toward them, his taloned feet causing no footprints. "Queen Bidhukh expects bloodshed. Only when enough blood has been spilled will she grace us with her arrival. It is time to burn this city as you did Qasrah. Do not disappoint her."

Caleb launched into the air, his powerful wings sending a scorching breeze toward them. The Hāreef raised their arms against the spray of sand. Jacob watched as Caleb flew toward the golden arch of the main gates. A few remaining archers fired, but their arrows passed through the ifrit and planted uselessly in the sand. Caleb clapped, green sparks erupting from his fingers, as a torrent of jinn fire shot toward the main gate. The gold was indeed pure, because it melted like sugar, the bolts sealing the city curling in on themselves. Within minutes, the gate was clear. Caleb landed in a swirl of dust and strode into the city.

With Caleb a good distance away, the jinn army's loyalty began to falter, their emerald eyes flicking toward the Hāreef as hungry grins lit up their wicked faces. The Hāreef shrank back, tightening their circle.

"We've got no amulets," Marcus grumbled at Jacob's side as his hand rested on his sword's hilt.

Jacob swallowed drily as a jinn wolf up ahead emitted a low growl that seemed to disturb the sand at his feet. The jinn leaned back on its haunches and pounced.

The Hāreef shrieked. Vera swore and revealed her amulet. The wolf fell back in line. She rounded on the group, fifty or so members all expecting her to lead them to victory. If only they knew Vera's true motives. "We're wasting time!" she shouted, marching ahead. "To the palace!"

The Hāreef followed Vera through the melted hole that had once been the city's gate and into Al-Shaam. Jacob squinted at the golden dunes in the distance, rising up behind a palace constructed entirely of gold and white marble with ruby-topped domes and minarets that stretched higher than most balloons. If Vera couldn't offer Queen Mardzma Anam's heart, perhaps the heart of a nawab would work instead . . .

The streets were a bloodbath. The soldiers had quickly realized their steel-tipped arrows and gold-plated swords and pikes had no effect on the jinn. Dozens of these weapons lay discarded on the ground. It was only the lead bullets from their matchlock firearms that wounded the creatures, but they were only suited for close range, and for the most inferior jinn. There was a pile of bodies littering the city's entrance, jinn and jinniya clamoring over each other for a taste. Soldiers had taken refuge in nearby buildings, firing stray bullets into the swarm.

They didn't stand a chance.

Marcus clamped a hand on Jacob's shoulder and steered him away. "Best not to look." He pointed to the winding stairway the Hāreef were clambering up. "Keep your eyes on the palace, and stay close to me. You'll be all right."

Marcus's words dulled his rising nausea as they darted up the stairway and through a series of narrow streets. Screams erupted from doorways and market stalls as merchants hastily ducked behind upturned tables and customers fled inside, barricading their doors with crates and barrels. Soldiers thundered through the streets in a jumbled mess of swords and spears, but none paid much heed to the Hāreef—hāri obviously not worthy of attention—instead hurrying for the main gate and the swarm of jinn spilling into the city. A cloud of smoke descended over the city as green flames licked up the buildings on the main street. Jacob spluttered and covered his mouth with his sleeve.

The back streets had now long since emptied, terrified eyes watching from the relative safety of their windows. Shopping bags and even the odd shoe lay abandoned. Vera breezed ahead, her eyes fixed only on the carnelian-studded domes of the nawab's palace. Even with her obvious limp caused by her injured thigh, she kept a swift pace that caused the rest of the Hāreef to pant as they kept speed. Jacob's hood was soon stuck to his neck.

Then she stopped abruptly, and the rest of them followed suit.

"What is it?" Marcus asked.

Vera massaged her thigh, head snapping left and right. Then she drew her sword. "We are not alone."

No sooner had the words left her lips than a spear lanced through the air. Marcus sliced it in half before it sank into Vera's neck. "Ambush!" he shouted.

Arrows were flying from all directions. Everyone dropped to the ground. Jacob quickly ducked behind a crate of lemons and curled his knees to his chest. His heart was banging against his ribs. The Hāreef were thrashing their swords wildly, everyone forming a ring around Vera as they became locked in combat with hāri and Ghadaean fighters that could only be the Wāzeem. Vera's eyes rested on him as she carved a path through the bodies and sprinted toward him. "The mirror. Give it to me!"

She snatched at his cloak, but a wave of arrows sent Jacob flattening himself against the sand and halted her movements. When it was safe to rise, Jacob glimpsed Vera's bloodred hair disappear into the maze of streets toward the palace.

She'd left them. Easily. Without question. Without even a backward glance. Vera's absence caused a state of panic among the Hāreef, who spun around in confusion, hacking at anything that came their way. Jacob emerged from behind the crate and promptly tripped over the nearest body. His face hit the sand. Jacob coughed up a mouthful and rubbed the grit from his eyelashes.

What he saw caused a stabbing in his chest as if he'd swallowed a handful of nails. He choked.

Marcus. Arrows studded his back. His eyes were glazed over in a permanent state of fear.

A wrangled sob escaped Jacob. The glassblower had been kind to him, and that kindness had made it easy for Jacob to overlook Marcus's affiliation with the Hāreef. Perhaps, like him, Marcus had been led astray, manipulated by Vera's words. Perhaps they all had, he thought as he glanced at the growing pile of bodies. Maybe they could have been saved if only he'd tried hard enough, their rage used for good instead of to inflict revenge. Jacob couldn't shake off the feeling that he had failed them.

A familiar face was twirling in the center of the fray, blade a blur like it was an extension of their arm, a metal limb.

Anam!

He rose, scanning the remaining Hāreef. A hāri man roared and tackled Anam to the ground, causing her extra metal limb to detach. The man planted a fist on her jaw. Anam sank her boot into his ribs, then made a scramble for the blade, but the man yanked her back.

Jacob made a dash for it, eyes fixed on the glint of the sword's hilt as he swerved around fighters engaged in combat. "Anam!" he shouted.

Anam faced him. He kicked the sword her way and she snatched it up, eyes burning—not with a wicked flame that sparks brilliantly before smoldering, having licked away at everything around it that burns, but a controlled fire, the type of fire with a purpose, the type that only burns when it needs to, and then burns furiously and without mercy.

Anam slipped the blade into the man's side. He convulsed, a trickle of blood escaped his lips, and his head hit the sand. Jacob could only stare with both amazement and repulsion at how swiftly Anam had stolen a life.

Anam seized his arm and pointed at the street ahead. "The marquee. Go!" She elbowed a freedom fighter—no, a terrorist, that's what they were. That's what they had always been, excusing their violence under the label of justice. But there was nothing to justify attacking a city with its guard down, slaughtering its civilians in the streets. He knew that now.

Jacob started running.

"And take that ridiculous cloak off!" Anam called after him.

29

KHADIJA

Earlier, the streets had been busier than she would have liked as Khadija accompanied the Wāzeem, passing families returning from the market with crates of peaches, and children towing goats with droopy ears. They had been warned and still they did not listen. Atop the walls, soldiers lounged in the heat, spears hanging idly by their sides. Darian shook his head and tutted. "There is nothing we can do for them now. They've made their choice."

Their eyes met as she traced the dark circles under Darian's eyes that looked like purple bruises. Her jaw jittered slightly. Darian caught the motion.

"Nervous?"

"A little," she breathed.

He nodded. "Remember, you already faced Vera in Intalyabad. That's more than most of the Wāzeem can say."

His words loosened the coil of rope tangled around her stomach so that she no longer felt like throwing up. She pictured Qasrah, a smoking mess of charred buildings, and the insides of her throat began to burn. Vera would pay today for what she had done. Khadija would make sure of that.

They walked in silence toward the main square, where the Wāzeem had erected blockades that children were eagerly climbing. Zaid shooed them away. "Go back to your parents and tell them to hide. Quickly, before the jinn kill you!" That sent the children scattering in gales of laughter while their parents turned their noses up with disapproval at the sight of hāri and Ghadaeans walking the streets side by side. Khadija couldn't help but feel slightly silly dressed head to toe in armor while people milled about with shopping bags. Perhaps it was the calm before the storm, and yet a shred of hope began to blossom. Maybe they'd made a mistake. Maybe there would be no battle today.

"Good work, Zaid." Darian thumped him on the shoulder. "Really got the message across."

"They are all stupid, and it will cost them their lives." Zaid dragged a blockade aside and joined the Wāzeem's ranks assembled in the square. A striped marquee fluttered in the morning breeze, surrounded by an unbroken chain of flowers. Khadija stared at their flimsy stems. Would they really hold back a jinn army?

As they entered the marquee, Khadija eyed the empty beds, the rolls of linen bandages, the crates of herbs and tinctures. The air smelled faintly of mint and sage leaves. Zaid pushed his way through the crowd gathered inside with an air of authority. Here was a mix of Ghadaeans and hāri, both races readying themselves to fight side by side, as one. Equals. She couldn't help but be amazed.

Zaid greeted an older Ghadaean woman, short in stature and with a plumpness that was only emphasized by how tightly she'd pinned her hijab around her neck. "Khadija." He beckoned her over. "This is Jameela. You'll be helping her. Make sure she has everything she needs," he said before melting into the crowd.

•

Jameela nodded, face stern, like she wasn't too pleased by the prospect of babysitting her. Khadija chanced a small smile. Jameela simply huffed and resumed her task without bothering to offer Khadija any instruction.

"I'll check back on you in a few hours." Darian hovered by her shoulder. For a while they simply stared, taking each other in, burning the other's image across their eyelids. She sighed, eyes falling to the copper sword at Darian's hip. He would be up front with Zaid, Anam, and the rest of the Wāzeem's fighters. She prickled with shame at how safe she'd be in comparison, but she pushed the thoughts from her mind before they could fester. She would still be of use, which was better than hiding away in the tunnels with Abba.

Her tongue felt stiff in her mouth, unable to conjure all the words she wished to say, so that all she was capable of uttering was "OK."

Then Darian pressed his lips to her forehead. The action was brief, too brief, a quick brush of skin that left her aching to yank him back, and then he was gone.

Jameela shoved a spool of thread and a pack of needles into her hands before she'd had time to properly recover. "Thread these so they're ready." Khadija shook herself back to reality, letting all thoughts of Darian and Abba slip from her mind. She needed to focus. She regarded the pack of twenty or so needles, all with tiny eyes that looked frustratingly fiddly. She gritted her teeth. This was going to be a long morning.

It was. As the morning crept into the afternoon, the tent emptied as fighters claimed their positions around the city. It took all of Khadija's willpower not to scream at Jameela as she ordered her around. After Khadija had threaded the needles, Jameela instructed her to cut the linen into strips. All this Khadija did without complaint, even when

Jameela insisted she start over. "Those strips are far too small," she snapped. "Cut them bigger. Big bandages for big wounds!" She sauntered off, leaving Khadija cursing under her breath. Still, it felt good to do something with her hands, even if it was only preparing bandages. It took her mind off other things.

A loud bang made the ground shake. Khadija jumped to attention. A glass bottle slipped from Jameela's fingers. She swore, then turned to her, eyes wide.

"Get ready. The Hāreef are here."

Screams, far too close for her liking, had Khadija steadying herself on a tent pole. All she saw of the soldiers atop the walls in the distance were orange uniforms slowly being engulfed by green fire. Black shapes danced across the walls, flickering in the sunlight. She squinted, at first mistaking them for shadows, and then she gulped, mouth suddenly dry. They weren't shadows. They were *jinn*.

Soldiers shrieked and plunged to the sand below as jinn scaled the walls, fifty, maybe even a hundred of them. Jameela joined her at the tent flap, furiously grinding herbs in a mortar and pestle until they resembled a green mush. "We cannot win this." The older woman faced her and clasped a pendant around her neck, eyes glazed with fear. She began reciting prayers.

Khadija hugged her elbows to her chest. "We must."

A swarm of crows stole her attention. The green fire was spreading rapidly, licking away at the gates. The gold started to crumple. She could feel her heart rising steadily up her throat. Khadija swallowed it down.

Then, like a house of cards, the main gate collapsed and a flurry of jinn flooded into the city. Khadija instinctively drew her scimitar, not knowing quite what to do with it. The metal felt clumsy in her sweaty palms. She eyed the Wāzeem's fighters positioned ahead, trying to pick out Darian among them.

This was it. There was no going back now. It was time to put an end to Vera. She faced Jameela, who regarded her sword with skepticism, but she didn't instruct her to put it away. Jinn flooded the streets like spilled coffee followed by the shrieks of children as people tripped over one another in a panic. The square emptied within seconds, and soon Khadija could no longer make out the orange uniforms of the soldiers, only a mounting pile of bodies at the gate's entrance. Jinn and jinniya charged through the streets, scaling walls, hopping from building to building, brushing their fingertips along washing lines and setting them ablaze. The streets were clogged with smoke and the glitter of green eyes.

Then the jinn reached the ranks of the Wāzeem. Khadija's ears were ringing. Her breath grew shallow. It was a bloodbath; even with the Wāzeem's copper swords and brass-tipped arrows, there were too many jinn. The jinn were too quick, the jinniya too bloodthirsty as they sank their teeth into flesh, painted the streets red.

The Wāzeem quickly started falling back, making for the marquee at full force, leaving trails of fresh blood across the sand. But the flowers held, sending the jinn reeling, unable to enter the marquee. Khadija stepped out of the way as the first few wounded appeared. Jameela snapped into gear. "Get them in the beds."

Khadija steered a hāri man with a deep gash across his cheek to the nearest bed and looked to Jameela for her next instruction, but she was busy elevating a Ghadaean woman's leg that bore teeth marks. The hāri man groaned, eyes rolling back. Khadija pressed a bandage to his face. The man moaned. Her hands were covered in blood. She retched.

A tap on her shoulder made Khadija spin. A Ghadaean man was

hunched over the bed with his hands to his abdomen, trying to keep his guts from spilling out. Blood splattered the floor. Khadija left the hāri man and tended to the Ghadaean, as she pressed on his stomach. The man cried out, but she maintained a firm pressure, watching his chest rise and fall, up and down, weak, unsteady, until it fell a final time and never rose again. The man was still.

Outside, fighters and jinn were colliding in a furious dance of spears and swords. Boots trampled across the chain of flowers as the Wāzeem retreated.

That was when the stems snapped.

Then there were too many bodies, too much blood. The tent spun. Colored blobs spotted Khadija's vision. Blood and screams and green eyes blurred together. Her ears started ringing. Louder. Sharper. Her throat tightened.

Just breathe. She fought to control her breathing. *Be brave.*

Jameela shrieked. Khadija's head snapped up just as a man-shaped jinn appeared at the marquee's entrance.

"Khadija!" Jameela screamed.

Khadija had no time to think. She readied her copper blade and charged, but her footwork was clumsy, her aim amateurish, and the jinn easily twirled out of reach like a shadow being chased by the afternoon sun.

Khadija readied to strike again when a flash of metal sliced the jinn in two. It erupted into a coil of smoke, leaving Zaid in its place.

He was propping up a jittering Darian.

Khadija's heart thudded to a stop. "Is he OK?"

In response, Darian let out a hiss that barely sounded human. His limbs spasmed. Zaid hurled him onto an empty bed as Darian's eyes began to roll back and forth in their sockets like marbles.

"What happened to him?" Her eyes traced over Darian's face, which was covered in a sheen of sweat. She studied the way his lips curled over his teeth, how the veins in his neck were protruding, and with a sinking feeling in her stomach, she knew what this was.

"A jinn possession. It—" Zaid raked his nails across the back of his neck. "It just . . . stepped inside of him."

Her skin went cold. No. Not now. Not this soon. Not when they'd barely had a chance to feed the hungry spark that had erupted between them. They deserved longer. She needed more time.

Jameela pressed two fingers to Darian's neck, then furiously snatched her hand back. "His skin is on fire," she yelped, and unclasped the pendant from her neck, pressing it to Darian's forehead. Khadija heard skin sizzle. When Jameela snatched the pendant back, a red ring was burned into Darian's skin.

Darian hissed again, this time the noise sounding distinctly more inhuman. He began to thrash on the bed.

"Tie him down!" Zaid barked.

Khadija swiftly clamped Darian's flailing limbs to the bed while Jameela wound thick rope around his torso. Darian fought against his restraints. When his eyes flickered open, Khadija searched in vain for any remnants of the boy she knew in his amber eyes, but she couldn't mistake the green tinge of his irises. She bit her tongue to stifle the scream clawing its way up her throat.

"We need an exorcist," she said.

"There must be something we can do. Some prayer." Zaid looked to Jameela with pleading eyes.

She dashed his hope with a shake of her head. "Sometimes charms and pendants are enough to exorcise a weak jinn, but this . . ." She trailed off. "This case is severe. I'm not sure if Darian even understands who he is anymore."

No. Khadija refused to believe that. There had to be a part of him, no matter how small, that still remained, and she was determined to dig it out of him. Khadija rushed to Darian's side and placed her palms on both sides of his head to force him still. Touching his skin was like picking up a kettle with her bare hands. "Darian. Look at me." Her voice cracked. "Can you understand me? Say something. Please."

Darian bared his teeth and snapped at her fingers. She snatched her hands back.

"It's chaos out there." Zaid gestured to the open tent flap, where more Wāzeem were piling in. Those at the front were crouched in the sand, furiously trying to repair the broken flower chain.

All the beds were now occupied with the wounded. Jameela rushed off to attend to a woman covered in burns while Khadija hovered by Darian's bedside. The ropes were beginning to fray where the force of Darian's struggles had worn them thin as they rubbed against the bedframe.

She had to try. She wasn't going to give up on him. "Come on, Darian!" She shook him again. That only caused the rope to burst into green flames. Khadija yelped, scrambling for a sheet to smother him. The flames licked away at Darian's skin, but he gave no indication that it pained him as he rose, the ropes dropping to shreds at his feet. He made a grab for her neck.

"Darian!"

Zaid swiftly tackled him to the ground and pressed his knee to Darian's chest. "I can't hold him down much longer!"

Khadija pushed her way through the crowd to the front of the tent. The flower chain had been repaired and was keeping back a wolf that growled a few inches behind. "I need some flowers."

A hāri woman sliced the wolf's head clean off. "There's some broken ones there." She nudged a pile of wilted stems with her foot. "Not sure what use they'll be."

But Khadija had already scooped up the flowers and was racing back to Darian, swiftly knotting them. The first few snapped. She grimaced. The ring she made was barely larger than a serving platter. It would only work if Zaid got Darian to stand.

Darian sank an elbow into Zaid's ribs. His eyes were a vivid green now. Zaid backed away with his palms raised. More Wāzeem circled Darian. He growled, a gray tinge spreading across his face as if he'd been bathed in charcoal dust. What would happen when the jinn had fully consumed him, wiping away all remnants of the boy she'd known? What would happen to Darian, to his laugh, his smile, his soul? Where would he go, and more important, would she ever be able to bring him back from there? Khadija tightened her grip on her ring of flowers.

Darian lunged for her. Zaid quickly pinned his arms behind his back. "Hurry, Khadija."

Khadija threw the ring over Darian's head. As soon as the ring hit the floor, Darian stood to attention and hissed at the flowers by his feet, but he didn't move.

There wasn't even a moment to breathe as the screeching of jinn crows from outside the tent drew Zaid's attention. "Watch Darian," he instructed before disappearing outside, swerving around the figure barging into the tent and dragging a boy with a familiar face. It was Anam, pushing her way toward Khadija, pulling Jacob behind her.

30

JACOB

"Jacob!"

The sound of her voice had him frozen to the spot. A pair of arms wrapped fiercely around him and squeezed all the air from his lungs.

"I thought you were dead." Despite all the commotion in the tent, Khadija spoke softly. So softly he had to read her lips.

He shrugged, the corners of his mouth upturning. "Still standing."

When she didn't respond, Jacob fiddled with his shirtsleeve, too scared to meet her gaze. "I am sorry. I should never have listened to Vera. I should never have done all those things."

Khadija pressed her lips into a thin line.

"I just want to make this right. I want to stop her."

"I know, Jacob. I understand." A weight lifted off Jacob's chest. She understood. He did not have her forgiveness yet—he knew that—but this was the first step.

Khadija turned to Anam. "Darian needs your help." She gestured to the young hāri man Jacob remembered from when Khadija had freed the peri. He was standing in the center of a circle of flowers, his irises glowing a vivid green.

"He is possessed." Anam rushed over, eyeing the flimsy flower chain at his feet. "That will not hold forever."

"Can you get the jinn out of him?" There was a desperation to Khadija's voice Jacob hadn't heard before. His gaze fell to the tent flap, where fighters were hacking down crows before their beaks could pierce the material. His stomach churned with dread. There was no winning this, he realized, only prolonging their inevitable deaths. Unless . . . His hands flew to the bulge of his pockets where the Hāreef's amulets rattled. He delved into his pocket and produced the smooth green stone that he'd pried from William's amulet. Jacob twirled it around and around as he studied it, still marveling at how, despite being heated in the furnace, the stone remained flawless.

But could he command jinn with it? During his lessons with Marcus, he had struggled to command even the simplest of creatures.

Anam's firm voice sliced through his thoughts as she gained command of the tent. "I need flowers steeped in fresh water, and honey."

While Khadija hurried off to gather the supplies, Jacob stole himself away to the far side of the tent and pulled Vera's silver hand mirror out from under his shirt. Maybe there was something else he could do. He stared at its polished surface. He was met only with his own reflection. His eyes flickered from the green stone, to the mirror, and back to the stone. What could he offer Queen Mardzma in exchange for her help? Not Anam's heart, that's for sure.

When Khadija returned with the supplies, Anam laid down her copper whip and rolled up her sleeves. She now neared Darian with the same wariness as an animal tamer approaching a circus tiger. "Jacob." She snapped her fingers. He quickly shoved the mirror and William's stone back into his clothes and rushed to her side.

Anam dug into the satchel strapped across her chest and pulled out a set of brass bells. She pressed the bells into his palms. Jacob rang them carefully. The larger one elicited a deep hum, while the smaller bell a high-pitched chime. Darian roared and clamped his hands over his ears.

Khadija held a bowl with yellow flower heads bobbing on its surface. In her other hand was a sticky jar of honey.

"OK, I need you both to listen very carefully." Anam's eyes swept across him and Khadija. "Jacob, I need you to ring the bells. Keep a steady rhythm, and do not stop until I tell you to."

Jacob nodded, fingers tightening around the brass handles.

"Khadija, when I say, I want you to pour the water over Darian. Make sure he is covered completely."

Khadija nodded briskly.

"OK." Anam unscrewed the honey and scooped out a dollop, smearing it across her hands and up her forearms until her brown skin shone with an amber stickiness. "The honey will allow me to touch his skin, albeit briefly," she explained. "Jinn are wicked, bitter creatures, and show an aversion toward anything sweet, like flowers, for instance."

"And honey," Jacob breathed.

"Exactly." Anam took her position behind Darian, her palms hovering beside his head. "Now, Jacob."

Jacob rang the bells, one after the other, a monotonous rhythm that had Darian hissing in response.

"Pour the water, Khadija."

Khadija tipped the bowl over Darian's head. Darian shrieked, the water sizzling as it struck his skin before erupting into curls of steam. Anam pressed her hands to his forehead.

"I command you to leave this vessel!"

Darian thrashed his head, but Anam's grip remained strong.

"Leave this soul that is too pure for your wicked touch."

Sparks of jinn fire were erupting from Darian's lips. Anam grabbed his jaw and yanked it open. "Leave this body. You are not welcome here!" Her voice reached a crescendo that dwarfed the ringing of Jacob's bells. Anam's head snapped around. "Stop, Jacob."

Jacob curled his fists over the bells.

All eyes were glued to Darian as his face contorted, a silent war etched across his features. Then a waterfall of black mist spilled from his mouth, pooling by his feet, stretching and growing until a man made of smoke stood before them with two emerald eyes.

The jinn vaulted for Anam.

"Anam!" Jacob yelled, just as Anam's copper whip crackled to life, licking a line across the jinn's torso. The jinn's scream was like the squeal of pressurized gas igniting, and then the jinn crumpled in a severed heap of smoke and dissolved into nothing.

Khadija rushed toward Darian with her arms extended.

"Wait." Anam held her back. She leaned over Darian, who lay collapsed in the ring of flowers, his chest rising and falling erratically. His eyes were clamped shut, sweat pooling in the hollow of his neck. "Darian?" At Anam's voice, his eyelids fluttered open, and a collective wave of relief washed over the tent at his amber eyes, no longer tinged green. Anam released a breath. "It worked."

Then Khadija sank into him. "Darian. Can you hear me?"

A moan reverberated in his chest.

"He must rest. He will be very weak," Anam said.

Together, Anam and Khadija steered Darian to a bed. Khadija pressed her lips to his forehead, the relief on her face clear to see. "Rest now," she whispered, then faced Jacob, and enveloped him in a hug. "Thank you." She squeezed him so tightly that Jacob felt his spine click.

Khadija released him and embraced Anam. "Thank you, so much."

Anam peeled Khadija's fingers from around her waist. "We still have a battle waiting for us." She stormed toward the tent flap. Bodies parted to make way for Anam as she once more returned to the fray.

Khadija's face was etched with worry. "I don't know how much longer the Wāzeem can go on like this." She gestured to the fighters piling up at the entrance with wounds that a Ghadaean lady was furiously trying to patch up before they returned to battle, only to retreat again with even graver injuries. It was a constant cycle of blood and death, each time with fewer fighters returning.

At this rate, there would be no Wāzeem left come sundown. Jacob pulled the mirror out from under his shirt.

"What are you doing?" Khadija hovered over him. "What is that?"

"This is how Vera planned to speak to Queen Mardzma," he said quietly.

"You're not thinking of involving her, are you?"

He spun to face Khadija. "As soon as enough blood has been spilled, Queen Bidhukh will arrive, and then we'll have no hope of winning this. That's if we're not already dead by then."

"What makes you think Queen Mardzma will help us? She could kill us all too." Khadija folded her arms and thrust out her jaw.

There was that possibility, of course. She could see his calling upon her as an insult and lash out in anger. Was it worth the risk? He still didn't know what he'd offer that Queen Mardzma would be willing to exchange for a wish either. "What other options do we have?"

That silenced Khadija as she digested his words before finally uttering, “She is the queen of female warriors.” Khadija tapped her chin. “She would love nothing more than witnessing a battle.”

“Maybe we show her one, then.” Jacob made for the tent flap, Khadija trailing him like a shadow.

“Do you even know how to call upon her?”

That, he did not. As Jacob peeled the tent flap aside, the sour sting of smoke and burned flesh assaulted his nostrils. The edges of the sky were tinged orange with the gradual descent of the sun, and the market square was littered with bodies and broken arrowheads. The Wāzeem were locked in a tight circle, Anam’s whip in the heart of it as she lashed out at crows and wolves, reducing them to a puddle of mist. Jacob inched forward when a hand on his elbow yanked him back.

“Stay behind the flowers.” Khadija pointed to the trampled flower chain by his feet.

Jacob positioned the mirror so that it was facing the action. “Here goes nothing.”

“I don’t like this idea.” She shook her head. “Queen Mardzma is a mistress of trickery, and she always gets what she wants. At least, that’s what the books say.”

Jacob couldn’t help but chuckle then. “This isn’t a book, Khadija.”

“I know that,” she snapped. “But still, we should be very careful about accepting any deal she offers us—that’s if she offers us anything.”

He nodded and sucked in a breath. What he was about to do would either save them or guarantee their deaths. He squeezed the silver handle until his knuckles were bone white. “Queen Mardzma.” His voice was swallowed by the clanging of swords outside.

“Louder,” Khadija instructed.

“Queen Mardzma! We wish to speak to you.” They stared at the mirror's surface, waiting for their reflections to morph into the image of the jinniya queen.

Only his face glared back at him. He huffed. This wasn't going to work.

"Oh, give it here." Khadija snatched the mirror from him and said in a voice as clear and pure as copper bells, "Queen Mardzma. I wish to speak to you." No sooner had the words left her lips than their reflection rippled like a pebble dipping below the surface of a pond.

A face the color of pewter and two jade-green eyes started to appear.

31

KHADIJA

Hassan's storybook, Khadija realized, had obviously been illustrated by a man with its depiction of a voluptuous Queen Mardzma with dark hair spilling over her shoulders and dressed in too-tight armor that barely contained her exaggerated bust. The face that met them looked like it had been carved from pure iron. Instead of the delicate features from the storybook, Queen Mardzma's skin was etched with battle scars and pockmarked with puncture wounds so that she resembled the surface of an old, scratched coin. Her hijab was twisted tightly around her head and appeared sopping wet, red lines dripping down her neck and pooling in her collarbone as if she had soaked the material in the blood of her victims. Khadija's stomach constricted.

"Who dares to call upon me!" Her voice was like the boom of a soldier's musket.

Khadija struggled to remain hold of the mirror as the finger-bone earrings dangling from Queen Mardzma's earlobes rattled. "I—I . . . we—"

"You are not a warrior! You insult the very name of battle with that sword you have so clumsily strapped to your belt." Queen Mardzma bared her teeth, filed to points, and raised her bloodstained spear. "Give me one reason why I should not slit your throat and watch you bleed."

Her throat closed. Khadija spluttered. This was a terrible idea. Her grip loosened on the mirror's handle, ready to send Queen Mardzma smashing against the ground, when the jinniya queen's eyes glittered. "Is that the sounds of battle I hear?" Her tongue darted across her lips. "Show me."

Khadija swiftly spun the mirror, glad to be free of Queen Mardzma's glare. The jinniya queen purred. "How I love spilled blood, but these are men fighting, and I do not care much for men."

Khadija wet her tongue, readying herself to speak, but her teeth refused to stop chattering. "There are women among them," she managed. She anxiously searched the Wāzeem's remaining fighters for any women still standing. That's when her eyes rested on Anam, her copper whip twirling over her head.

"Now there is a real warrior." Queen Mardzma's voice crackled with giddy excitement. "I will only speak to her."

When Khadija flipped the mirror back, only her reflection met her. She thrust the mirror toward Jacob and shoved her hands in her armpits to stop them from jittering. "We shouldn't have done that."

Shrieks sounded from behind. Jacob and Khadija spun around, mouths parting in horror at the green flames licking at the tent material. The Wāzeem rushed to smother the fire, but this was jinn fire and spread rapidly. In seconds, the tent was filled with smoke, fire licking away at the tent poles and causing the fabric to crumple.

"Darian!" Khadija dived toward the flames. Jacob yanked her back.

"Everyone out!" Jameela cried, swiftly rounding up the wounded, grabbing what supplies and poultices she could carry.

But there was no sign of Darian.

Khadija made another lunge for the burning tent. "Khadija, it's too dangerous!" Jacob shouted.

She wrestled out of his grip. "Darian!" She drew in a breath until her lungs were bursting and barreled into the fiery tent, ignoring Jacob's hand attempting to snatch her back.

Smoke made her eyes water. Her vision was blurred with gray and green. The air was too hot to breathe. "Darian," she spluttered.

A hand squeezed her arm. Khadija jumped.

"It's me," Darian croaked. He was leaning heavily on a tent pole, sweat dripping down the sides of his neck. Khadija's gaze hurried over him. "Are you hurt?"

He shook his head and doubled over as a fit of coughing consumed him.

Khadija flung his arm over her shoulders and wrapped her hands around his waist. "Come on!" She spun, the motion sending stabbing pains shooting through her skull as she desperately searched for their escape.

"There." Darian pointed to where Jacob's face suddenly appeared through the smoke as he held the tent flap open.

"Khadija!"

They allowed Jacob's voice to guide them as they limped toward the exit just as the marquee's pointed ceiling folded in on itself. Jacob tugged her forearm, and she collapsed in the street, nose streaming, chest fighting for clean air.

Darian's weight shifted, allowing her to stand. "Are you OK?" His voice was raw like he'd swallowed hot coals, but his eyes were that same glowing amber that she could lose herself in. "What did I miss?"

Khadija scanned the square, eyes attempting to adjust to the gloom. The sky had almost entirely darkened now, and the jinn reveled in the night, their only distinguishable feature being their vivid green eyes. Soldiers occupied most of the nearby buildings, firing brass-tipped arrows into the fray, while the Wāzeem's remaining numbers attempted to drive the jinn toward the center of the square and surround them, but the jinn moved far easier under the cover of night.

"We need to regroup." Darian marched toward the action.

"You're not going anywhere." She tugged him back. "You need to rest."

That elicited a wry smile from Darian. "I'll rest when I'm dead."

She winced. Maybe it was useless continuing as if they stood a chance at winning. Maybe it was best to make her peace and accept their fates. She pictured Abba alone in the tunnels, his head dipped in prayer. Come morning, he'd be met only by her charred body. That's if he survived the night.

She pushed images of her own funeral from her mind. No. She refused to let it end like this, but Queen Mardzma had been their only hope, and she had been adamant she would speak only to Anam. Khadija didn't like the idea of involving Anam in Queen Mardzma's games. It was one thing risking her own life, but another entirely to risk someone else's.

Darian nudged her and inclined his head to where Zaid was whirling around the battlefield. "I have to help him." He limped off, decapitating a snake and dodging a crow as it beelined toward him. His movements were slower than she remembered, and it wasn't long before a jinn the shape of a wild cat threw him off balance. He landed heavily in the sand.

"Darian!" Khadija rushed forward when Anam's whip licked the cat in two. The jinn melted into the air.

Anam yanked Darian upright. "It is good to see you back on your feet . . . sort of." Anam's dark eyes were blown wide, the muscles in her neck twitching as adrenaline coursed through her.

Darian flashed her a grateful smile, shot one last glance at Khadija, then hurried unsteadily to Zaid's side.

Anam was about to return to the fray when she clocked the mirror in Jacob's hands. She frowned. "You tried to contact Al-Ghaib."

"We spoke to Queen Mardzma," Khadija mumbled.

"It was a mistake, anyway." Jacob attempted to hide the mirror.

But Anam's jaw was set. "What did she say?"

"It doesn't matter," Khadija interjected. "She won't help us. We're on our own."

Anam cocked her head to the side and studied her. Khadija hated how easy she was to read.

"Tell me what she said."

Khadija sighed. "She said she'd only speak to you."

Anam hummed, coiling her whip around her wrist absentmindedly. After a long pause, she said, "Then I will speak with her."

Khadija shook her head. "You don't have to—"

Anam silenced her with her palm. "It might be the only hope we have left." She gestured to the battlefield. "At this rate, we will not last the night."

Jacob's cheeks drained of their color. "But we don't know what she wants from you. She might hurt you."

Anam chuckled. "This is a battle. It is a sacrifice I am more than willing to make." Anam unpeeled Jacob's fingers from the mirror's handle and, before either of them could stop her, spoke in a voice as deep and rich as a brass instrument. "Queen Mardzma. It is me, Anam. You wish to speak to me."

The reflection in the mirror swirled, and then Queen Mardzma's face appeared. "Anam." Queen Mardzma elongated the name, as if tasting it on her tongue. "So you are the warrior. Tell me, do you enjoy spilling the blood of your enemies?"

Khadija struggled to hide her revulsion at Queen Mardzma's bloodlust. It took all her restraint not to snatch the mirror from Anam and send it hurling toward the ground.

"I spill blood only when it is necessary."

Queen Mardzma stroked the tip of her spear. "You fight with great skill, but also control. You do not allow rage to cloud your judgment." She tilted her head, causing a red streak of blood to drip down the side of her cheek. "I like that. I could train you to be better. Join me and my ranks of jinniya."

No. She refused to allow Anam to make that sort of a sacrifice. Khadija kicked Anam's shins and mimed, "No."

If Anam had read her lips, she gave no indication. "I will if you grant me a wish." Her words hung in the air like a lead bullet.

"What are you doing?" Khadija hissed. "This is insane!"

Queen Mardzma's eyes narrowed. "Foolish mortal! You think I would throw away a wish that easily? You will have to do far more than that to earn a wish from me."

"Then name your price" was Anam's response.

"Anam, please," Khadija whispered. She'd already lost Anam once. She couldn't lose her again. "We'll find another way."

Anam locked eyes with her, and Khadija frantically searched her face for an ounce of fear, a flicker of uncertainty. All she was met with was Anam's cold, hard resolve. There was no talking her out of this.

"This is the only way, Khadija."

Queen Mardzma grinned. "Compete in a duel with one of my best fighters. If you win, I will grant you your wish."

"Don't—"

"Agreed." The word dangled above their heads. For a few seconds, Khadija could only stand there with her jaw slack. There was no taking the word back.

Anam had just agreed to her own death.

Queen Mardzma raised an eyebrow. "You agree without even hearing the consequences if you lose."

"I will not lose."

That elicited a chuckle like the scraping of steel swords. "Spoken like a true warrior. I will send my jinniya to fetch you. You may bring one companion to Al-Ghaib, preferably one with a strong stomach, as they will be scrubbing your bloodstains off my floors." With that, the image of Queen Mardzma dissolved.

Everyone was too stunned to speak. A duel! With what creature? Anam was a fierce warrior, but she was still human. Could she really expect to win against a powerful jinniya, or perhaps an ifrit, or a demon? Whatever Queen Mardzma had planned, Khadija knew with a sinking dread that it would not be a fair fight.

"You shouldn't have agreed without knowing what you'll be up against." Jacob held his head in his hands.

Khadija bit her lip. It was clear trying to convince Anam otherwise would be in vain. They may as well return her to the battlefield unarmed. At least it would be a less gruesome death. Her eyes scanned over the Wāzeem's fighters, now less than twenty. The rest were lined up in a row on the ground as Jameela furiously tended to the wounded, whispering prayers for the dead.

"But if you do win . . ." Jacob dug into his pockets and produced a cluster of amulets with a luminous green stone in the center. "You should wish for her to restore the Seal of Sulaiman."

Anam's lips parted with awe. "How did you get these?" She sifted through the knot of necklaces. "It this every amulet the Hāreef possess?"

"More or less." Jacob shrugged.

Anam nodded and tucked the amulets into the satchel across her chest. "It is worth a try."

Khadija had heard stories of the Seal before, a talisman that had the power to command all jinn. Anam would have some audacity asking a jinniya queen to restore it. "That's assuming you win—"

Anam rested her hands on her shoulders. "I will win this. All I ask is that you do not give up hope."

Hearing Khadija's own words echoed back to her did nothing to calm the tightening in her chest, as if her lungs had forgotten how to deflate. It was foolish for Anam to even make such a promise. "And if you don't win?"

Anam sighed. "Then you will have to scrub my bloodstains off Queen Mardzma's floor."

Khadija paled. Jacob puffed out his chest. "I'll go with you."

"You cannot. No boy or man can enter Queen Mardzma's kingdom," Anam explained. "It has to be Khadija."

Her stomach convulsed. She was going to have to travel with Anam to Al-Ghaib, witness her duel with whatever twisted creature Queen Mardzma had planned, and ultimately watch her die. She took a breath.

Could she do it? Khadija swallowed her fear before it could fester. It was Anam who was actually laying down her life. All Khadija had to do was watch, but even that seemed an impossible task. "OK."

A green ring of fire materialized on the ground. Everyone leaped back as a jinniya appeared in the flames, this one far more substantial than the shadowy creatures in Vera's army. This jinniya had a thick braid dangling past her waist and a curved bow that, on closer inspection, appeared to be made of bone. Khadija gulped.

"Queen Mardzma is expecting you, Anam," the jinniya said in a wary voice like the crackling of kindling.

Anam slipped her hand in Khadija's and gave it a squeeze. "Are you ready?"

She scanned the fighters for Darian, catching a glimpse of him battling back-to-back with Zaid. She shot Jacob a final look, saw the mix of fear and guilt on his face, then nodded. Together, she and Anam stepped into the ring of jinn fire.

At first, nothing. Then the heat hit her. It was like thrusting herself into the depths of a hot-air balloon's burner. Khadija buckled, the fierce burning spreading across her skin. She shrieked. Flames enveloped her, turning her vision green. Every fiber in her being was throbbing, pleading for the burning to stop. She dug her nails into Anam's hand.

The jinn fire abruptly receded. Khadija staggered forward and collapsed into soft sand. Her limbs refused to stop shaking. When she looked up, the battle and Al-Shaam were no more.

Khadija pushed herself shakily to her feet. She and Anam stood in the middle of the desert on an overcast day, with clouds tinged green. Sand dunes stretched as far as the eye could see in every direction. Ahead was a gazebo made of wrought iron where a ring of green fire crackled. It was surrounded by a roaring crowd of jinniya, and in the distance was the faint green smudge of a palace fashioned from emerald and jade with spiraling staircases hugging its towers.

Beneath the gazebo stood Queen Mardzma.

So this was Al-Ghaib, the jinn's parallel realm. Anam faced her, and Khadija caught the slight jitter to her jaw. She was afraid. Khadija wasn't sure why she had assumed Anam didn't feel fear. Perhaps it was how swiftly she'd offered up her life. Now knowing Anam had done so in spite of her fear made Khadija's cheeks burn with shame. For Anam, she would be strong. *She* would show no fear.

Khadija pulled Anam in for a hug. "You will win this. I believe in you."

The fear in Anam's eyes softened slightly as she returned the embrace.

"Come forth, challenger, and meet your opponent," Queen Mardzma barked to wild yells and the thudding of swords against shields from her jinniya audience. With their fingers still interlocked, Khadija and Anam approached the ring. Jinniya parted for them until they reached the flames. That's when Anam twisted her hand free of Khadija's grip.

The flames died down to a smolder, allowing Anam to step into the ring, where she was met by cackles from the jinniya crowd.

Queen Mardzma raised her spear for silence. Seeing her through a mirror was one thing, but being in the presence of a jinniya queen was quite another. Queen Mardzma was over seven feet tall, was dressed head to toe in steel, and carried a double-ended spear, one end sharpened to a needle-thin point, the other end serrated as if intended to cut through bone.

As Anam entered the ring, Queen Mardzma's green eyes glittered.

"Now, for your opponent." The crowd erupted into cheers. "My finest warrior. Princess Malika!"

Khadija's breathing hitched as a girl who looked to be of a similar age to Anam emerged from the crowd. But she wasn't of a similar age, was she? This was the Princess Malika from Hassan's storybook, the one who was abducted by Queen Mardzma and ruthlessly trained to become one of her best warriors. This was the warrior Anam would have to duel.

How was that possible? The story was hundreds of years old.

Khadija studied the princess; her complexion was not the charcoal gray of the other jinniya but a pale gold like the distant sand dunes. She appeared to still be human. How she had survived so long in Al-Ghaib was a mystery, though it only served to show how powerful Queen Mardzma's magic could be if she could keep a human alive in Al-Ghaib for centuries.

Princess Malika stepped into the ring, and Queen Mardzma raised her hand for silence. "The rules are simple. If Princess Malika wins, Anam will join my ranks of jinniya, where she will remain under my command for all eternity." Queen Mardzma's wine-colored lips curled into a smirk. "Or until I tire of her."

Khadija chewed on the insides of her cheek. Would she be able to leave Al-Ghaib knowing Anam was trapped here forever? Somehow, that seemed a worse fate than death.

"If Anam wins, I will grant her one wish." Queen Mardzma's words were met by excited whistles from the audience. Queen Mardzma thumped her spear in the sand. "Fighters. Approach!"

It seemed to take an age for Anam to traverse the ring until she stood before Princess Malika. Princess Malika dipped her head. Though there was nothing she wore that identified her as royalty, there was a regal air to her demeanor that only served to make her more intimidating. Anam inclined her head in return.

"Ready your weapons."

Metal grated as both drew their swords. At almost three feet long, Princess Malika's blade had the advantage of reach over Anam's, the metal an insidious black. The princess wielded the sword with both hands, knees already bent, poised to strike. Anam's blade was far smaller in comparison, but it was light enough for her to use one-handed, and hopefully that would give her the advantage of speed.

Khadija's heart was in her throat. Queen Mardzma took her place on the sidelines. *Please, Anam. Please win this!*

"Fight!"

Princess Malika's long sword veered for Anam's knees. Anam cleared it and struck a blow at Princess Malika's side, but the princess twirled out of reach at the last second, smashing her elbow into Anam's nose. Anam staggered.

And so it began. Khadija bit her lip, eyes flicking back and forth between them. They exchanged blows, ducking, diving, spinning around the ring in a blur of arms and legs. Princess Malika brought her blade down on Anam's shoulder, the tip just grazing flesh before Anam managed to sidestep and parry the blow, sending the princess stumbling across the sand. It was a battle of gaining ground, both Anam and the princess attempting to dominate as much of the ring as possible while simultaneously driving their opponent toward the green flames of the outer edge. Anam's ankles came close to being licked by jinn fire before she swiftly rolled, knocking Princess Malika off balance with the hilt of her sword. Princess Malika retaliated with a fist that connected with Anam's jaw.

The blows were coming faster, growing less coordinated and more desperate. Anam's neck was slick with sweat, her footwork no longer as deliberate as it had been. But Princess Malika also appeared to be tiring—Khadija could tell by the slight tremble of her forearms as she fought to keep her heavy blade in the air.

Come on, Anam! You can win this.

Steel clanged as their swords connected, over and over. For every strike of Princess Malika's, the jinniya audience erupted into whistles and cries of delight that only served to goad the princess further. Anam's composure was faltering—Khadija could tell by the puff of her cheeks and the permanent crease to her brows. All she needed was for Princess Malika to make just one mistake, and Anam would have her, but the princess fought ruthlessly, her aim flawless.

Anam overextended her arm in an attempt to pierce Princess Malika's thigh, and in that fleeting second, managed to leave her left side exposed. Princess Malika saw her opportunity to slide her blade across Anam's abdomen in one long streak.

"No!" Khadija pressed her fist into her side as if it were her stomach that had been sliced.

The sand turned red at Anam's feet. Anam sank to her knees, hugging her arm to her torso, her other arm swinging wildly in an attempt to fend Princess Malika off. The crowd roared. Their taunts spurred the princess forward. She aimed a quick succession of blows that left Anam flat on her back, scrambling for her blade.

Khadija pressed her hand to her throat, hating to watch and yet not daring to take her eyes off the two of them. Princess Malika lacerated Anam's sword arm from wrist to elbow. Anam hissed and retreated. More sand was painted red.

Princess Malika struck again, a smile gracing her lips. She was enjoying this, her arrogance leading her to make much bolder moves. Anam had gone on the defensive as she struggled to her feet, her back hunched, refusing to fall for Princess Malika's taunts as she skipped and spun around her. Anam's gaze remained calculated, studying the princess's footwork, waiting for her opportunity.

And then she had it. When Princess Malika raised her sword, rather than bring it down in a quick jab, she took a long, low sweep. Anam swerved and knocked her off balance, finishing with the tip of her blade pointed at the princess's throat.

For a moment, nobody breathed. Nobody could quite comprehend what had just happened.

"What?!" Queen Mardzma spluttered. "How?"

Princess Malika retreated, rubbing the part of her neck where Anam's sword had been, as if she couldn't quite believe it either.

Had Anam won?

Anam staggered out of the ring, nursing her injured side. Khadija rushed forward as Anam collapsed into her arms. Her whole body was shaking, her hands sticky with blood. "Make the wish," Anam whispered, before her eyes rolled back.

Khadija faced the queen. All eyes were upon her. She cleared her throat. "Anam would like to make her wish."

Queen Mardzma lifted her chin, daring her to speak. "Go ahead." Her voice crackled with heat. "But be careful what you wish for."

Here goes nothing, Khadija thought. "She wishes for you to restore the Prophet Sulaiman's Seal." She reached into Anam's satchel and thrust the amulets forward.

The jinniya hissed. Queen Mardzma recoiled, the finger-bone earrings swinging wildly from her earlobes. "I will do no such thing!"

Khadija swallowed; her throat felt like sandpaper. "A deal is a deal," she said, keeping her voice steady.

A vein bulged in Queen Mardzma's neck. The queen shot her a look of burning loathing and peered at the amulets in Khadija's hands. Then her eyes gleamed. "I cannot. You do not even have all the pieces to restore the Seal fully. Make another wish."

Khadija bit her lip, forcing down her panic, trying to focus on what else she should wish for and not the fact that Anam was bleeding out in her arms. "Then use what we have to create the most powerful weapon against jinn that you can."

Queen Mardzma eyed her. Khadija held her gaze. "You will regret asking me to do this, mortal." She waved her hand, and the stones popped out of their amulets and rolled across the sand of their own accord. Queen Mardzma launched a green fireball at the stones, where they melted like spun sugar and re-formed before her eyes into a solid bar. A click of Queen Mardzma's fingers, and the solid bar morphed into a bright green blade.

"There, your weapon." The queen's eyes were heavy with disgust.

Khadija hesitantly picked it up, testing the weight in her hand as she supported Anam with her other arm. It felt warm from the heat of the jinn fire, incredibly light and completely transparent—like it was made of glass. Her lips parted.

"Now, leave this realm." Queen Mardzma's palms were alight as she sent a torrent of jinn fire hurtling toward her and Anam. Khadija braced herself as green flames engulfed her.

32

JACOB

Jacob gnawed at the inside of his cheek and thrust his hand in his pocket. His fingers curled around the cool surface of William's stone. He should have relinquished it to Anam with the rest of the Hāreef's amulets, and yet he couldn't bear to part with it. Jacob cursed. How could the Seal of Sulaiman be restored if pieces were missing? He thought of Vera's amulet, which he had been unable to collect as well. He'd sent Anam to her death, and it would all be for nothing. Jacob squeezed the stone so hard it hurt. But there was no calling Anam back from the jinn realm now. All that remained was to wait.

Ahead, fighters and jinn collided, but the Wāzeem were tiring, and in the past ten minutes, they'd lost four more. How much longer were Anam and Khadija going to take? That's if they ever came back, but he couldn't think that. Not now.

Darian had retreated from the fray and was allowing Jameela to tend to a wound on his arm. With his elbow bound, he approached. "Here." He unsheathed a dagger from his belt and passed it to Jacob.

Jacob couldn't hide the relief from his face. "Thanks." The blade was barely longer than the length of his palm, but just the feel of the weapon in his hand was reassuring. Seconds passed, neither knowing how to smash through the wall of ice that stood between them. He sighed. "The first time we met wasn't the best . . ."

Darian shot him a side-eye. "You mean when we were trying to save the peri. The one that had been tortured," he added coldly.

Jacob winced. "I didn't torture her!"

"You sided with the people that did though. That makes you just as bad."

Heat simmered in the back of his throat. Jacob swallowed it down. "You're right. I know I was wrong. I just want to make things right again."

Darian nodded, eyes surveying the pandemonium ahead. "Everyone makes mistakes." He paused. "Your willingness to fix your mistakes is what matters. Restoring the Seal of Sulaiman was all your idea."

Jacob chewed on his lip. It was his idea, but Anam was the one laying down her life for it. If she died, Jacob would be responsible for the death of the Wāzeem's best fighter, and it would all be for nothing. "I hope she wins."

"I hope so too."

No sooner had the words left Darian's lips than a ring of green fire flared to life before them. Jacob shielded his eyes from the blaze. When the jinn fire died down, Khadija staggered beneath Anam's weight and dropped to her knees.

"Khadija! Anam!" Darian rushed forward, slipping Anam's limp arms around his shoulders and dragging her to the side.

"Is she . . ." Jacob broke off mid-sentence, afraid to utter the words aloud. Anam's eyes were screwed shut, her hand pressed to a deep gash that sliced right across her abdomen and was oozing dark, sticky blood.

Her chest was barely rising, stopping every few seconds, so that each breath looked like her last.

"Jameela!" Khadija beckoned the Ghadaean lady over, who had been tending to an ever-growing line of bodies, not all of them moving. Jacob couldn't help but notice the insipid cast to Khadija's skin, like she'd just bathed in ash. Is that what Al-Ghaib did to mortals? Anam's was similar, a dull graying of her skin, as if the brief time she'd spent in the jinn realm had already sucked some of the life from her.

"My goodness." Jameela's eyes scanned over Anam. Then she snapped into gear. She pressed her palms into Anam's side, eliciting a moan from Anam. Blood seeped through her fingers. "I'll take it from here."

Khadija collapsed in the sand.

"What happened?" Darian planted his hands on Khadija's shoulders to stop her shaking.

"She won." Khadija removed a bright green blade from her waist.

Jacob's jaw dropped open. "Is that what I think it is?"

Khadija nodded. "It's the Seal of Sulaiman—or as much of it as we had. A weapon against jinn."

Anam had done it! How, he couldn't even comprehend. Jacob's hand curled around the hilt of the green blade. It was unbelievably light in his grip, almost completely transparent like glass and polished perfectly smooth. It glittered like a shard of pure jinn fire. He gasped. "Now we can send the jinn back to Al-Ghaib."

Amber light bathed the market. Everyone's heads lifted. A blood-orange balloon studded with rubies and opals that could have only come from the nawab's personal balloon collection was hovering, its basket grazing the sand. Jacob watched as Vera's head appeared at the basket's edge, her blade pressed to the throat of none other than the Nawab of Al-Shaam. He was older than the Nawab of Intalyabad had been, with a long, graying beard, its edges a brilliant orange where they'd been dipped in henna. Instead of a crown adorning his head he wore a simple white topi.

Jacob gasped. Even without her Hāreef, Vera had infiltrated the palace and captured the nawab single-handedly. The last remaining amulet glittered green around her neck. She scowled at the Wāzeem.

"Surrender! The fight is over, the nawab has fallen!" Her voice rose above the clanging of swords. "Lay down your weapons!"

But her command only served to send a fresh wave of energy through the Wāzeem's ranks. Darian raised his sword. The Wāzeem charged. "Protect the nawab at all costs!" Zaid shouted, leading the fray as fighters sprang to life.

That's when a pair of wings as black as midnight descended, blocking Vera and the nawab from view. Jacob gulped.

Caleb.

The ifrit hissed and fought with impossible speed, and though copper arrows pierced his wings and brass spears pelted down from above, he continued to fight as if their weapons were only a drizzle of rain against his charcoal skin.

Jacob glanced down at Khadija, still curled in the sand as if her legs were refusing to work. "Do you know how to use it?" she said, her eyes fixed on the glittering sword in Jacob's hand.

He twirled the crystal shard so that it caught the light as if it were about to burst into flames. "I—I—"

Caleb's roar, like a clap of thunder, stole his attention. "Come forth, my queen. Come forth and feast on the flesh of royalty."

A shadow spread across the ground, stretching, swirling until it stood on two feet: a jinniya with eyes like sea moss and a skirt with ocean-foam edges. Everyone in the market square reeled back, fighting ceased.

A white spark appeared by Queen Bidhukh's side, so bright it was hard to look at, and then the shaitan, Sakhr, materialized.

The jinniya queen took her time surveying the destruction before her. What she saw apparently pleased her as she flashed a pair of razor-sharp teeth. "You have done well, Caleb." Her voice was like crashing waves. Her eyes glittered as she faced the Nawab of Al-Shaam in the balloon, his gold sherwani covered in blood and sand. "I am impressed."

Vera fumbled in the balloon, a hand reaching for the burner as if to fire it up and escape into the clouds, but Queen Bidhukh was too fast. She yanked the basket with one hand and dragged it to the ground. Vera and the nawab toppled out, Vera barely managing to land on her feet. When Vera regained her composure, her expression was torn between outrage and confusion as she forced the nawab up and held him close like a war trophy.

Because the nawab was supposed to have been Vera's gift to Queen Mardzma in exchange for a wish, Jacob realized. Not Queen Bidhukh's next meal.

Queen Bidhukh grasped the nawab by his hair, which immediately started to smoke, and wrenched him out of Vera's grip. "Once I have feasted on his flesh, my power in this mortal plane will grow. I will be one step closer to establishing my new kingdom."

Jacob ground his teeth together; he and Anam had been right: conquering the mortal world had been the jinniya queen's plan this whole time. The Hāreef had merely been pawns and Caleb her loyal subject from day one. He'd chosen her, his new mother, over the one who had sacrificed everything to bring him back to life.

Vera staggered forward. "Caleb? What's going on?"

Caleb's talons sank into polished wood with a crunch as he perched on the balloon's basket. "This is how it must be, Ammi. Think, with a jinn realm in the mortal plane we will never have to worry about the darkers again."

Vera's lips quivered. "But . . . what about our people? How can you guarantee their safety if the world is teeming with jinn?!" Her voice had turned shrill.

Jacob felt a hand squeeze his elbow as Khadija used him to pull herself to her feet. "Use the blade now while they're distracted," she whispered urgently.

He nodded. Jacob brandished the crystal sword, sucked in a breath, and entered the fray, picking his way across the square as he swerved around members of the Wāzeem all glued to the sight of the jinniya queen before them. He made it halfway across the square, Khadija trailing him with her own sword drawn, before Queen Bidhukh's gaze fell upon him, causing a sloshing in his stomach as if he'd swallowed the ocean: Jacob thought he'd be violently sick.

The queen's emerald eyes darted from his face to the green blade in his hand. "He holds the Prophet Sulaiman's Seal!" She flung the nawab away like a rag doll.

All heads turned to Jacob; it was as if everyone in the square had inhaled at once. Time stopped. Jacob froze. Then, as the blood rushed to his head and the ringing in his ears turned to a furious pounding that matched his racing heart, he readied his tongue. "I command you—"

Queen Bidhukh's roar, which sounded like thunderous waves striking the shoreline, drowned his words. "Mardzma has restored it. But how?" She rounded on Vera, and her palms burst aflame. "You traitor! I gifted you the amulets to control my jinn army and instead you fashion a weapon to use against me!" Every jinn in the market hissed. Jacob could feel the queen's rage shaking the ground, making every bone in his body thrum with her fury. His grip tightened on the handle.

"No. There's been a mistake." Vera swiftly retreated, putting the deflated balloon between herself and the jinniya queen. "I never offered—" Her words were cut off as she stumbled over a fallen spear. She crawled backward. "I was never granted a wish. I swear it!"

Caleb lunged. "You never listen! No matter how many times I warned you." He seized Vera's wrists, causing her white cloak to instantly blacken. Vera screamed at the flames traveling up her sleeves before she was tossed aside, where she disappeared from view.

His own mother! If the ifrit could do that to his own mother, what would he do to the rest of them?

That's when Jacob saw his moment. He brandished his sword high, thinking back to how William had first commanded a jinn with nothing but his amulet and the power of his voice. Jacob filled his lungs, allowing his body to be consumed with all the fear, all the hate, all the rage he'd ever felt. All the pain caused by the injustice of how his people were treated. He thought of Vera's empty promises of a better life. Khadija's friendship despite their differences. Anam's unwavering faith in his redemption, which had led her to sacrifice herself. And William, doing all he could to protect Jacob, even up until his dying breath.

"I command you to return to Al-Ghaib!" His voice, which usually stumbled and shook, was as clear as the call to prayer.

For a moment, his words faded on the next breeze with seemingly no effect. Then every jinn in the square began to screech. One by one, jinn melted into the floor. Queen Bidhukh's jinn dissolved before their eyes until only the Wāzeem were left.

Jacob gasped.

"You've done it," Khadija breathed beside him.

But three creatures still remained: Caleb, Sakhr, and Queen Bidhukh—the three of them too powerful for his incomplete Seal of Sulaiman to banish.

Queen Bidhukh's glare pierced straight to his heart. His chest convulsed. "The boy. Kill the boy!"

Caleb lurched toward him. Khadija yanked Jacob out of the way before Caleb's talons could lacerate his side. "Traitor!" Caleb struck again, causing Jacob to stumble back.

Khadija tugged him up. "Run, Jacob!"

He didn't need to think. Jacob pelted across the sand. Fighters circled him, bodies pressed tightly around Jacob, shielding him from view. Darian's face appeared. "Why didn't it work on them?" he panted.

"Maybe it has to touch them." Jacob winced as Caleb sent two fighters flying with a flick of his wing. "They're too powerful to simply be commanded away. Maybe that's why Queen Mardzma made it into a sword. So that it can be used like one." Jacob's mind whirred, and then he held out the weapon. "Except, I don't know how to use it."

Darian's jaw set. He accepted the blade from Jacob, his fingers flexing around the glowing green hilt. "Then let's finish this." Darian raised the blade and charged toward the queen.

Sakhr blocked his path. Darian struck. Sakhr twirled and aimed a swipe at Darian's neck. Darian dropped low and attempted to pierce the shaitan's knees. Sakhr shoved a boot in Darian's chest. He groaned and rolled over.

"Darian!" Zaid stormed ahead, tossing his blade to the side. "Over here."

Darian hurled the Seal of Sulaiman to Zaid and sprang back as the tip of Sakhr's white-hot blade sank into the ground where his head had been only moments before. Darian and Zaid then engaged in a furious dance with Sakhr as the two passed the green sword back and forth between each other, each trying and failing to take a swipe at the shaitan.

A wing struck Zaid off balance as Caleb joined the fray. Zaid stumbled forward, arm extended, the tip of the green sword nicking Sakhr's forearm. A sharp shriek made them both stagger as Sakhr clamped a palm over the ash-white bloodstain erupting from his arm. Murder blazed in the shaitan's eyes. "I tried and failed to obtain the Seal once before, and it cost me my freedom." His horned head turned to face his queen. "I will not make the same mistake again." No sooner had the words left his lips than Sakhr erupted into a furious white-hot flame.

Jacob cupped his palms over his eyes, momentarily blinded. When he dared open his eyes again, his vision was spotted with black blobs, and Sakhr was gone. Queen Bidhukh's crown of fish bones and shark teeth burst into flame. "Aargh! Can nobody be trusted?"

Caleb landed at the jinniya queen's feet. "You can trust me, my queen. I will not fail you." The ifrit launched into the air, raining green fireballs upon the Wāzeem. Fighters dived for cover. Jacob hit the ground, watching in horror as Zaid's left arm caught alight. He yelled and hurled the sword to Darian, who caught it and spun, eyes locking on Queen Bidhukh. He charged.

Queen Bidhukh saw him coming. "Think you can defeat me? I am the daughter of Iblis." With a click of her fingers, a vortex of sand appeared in Darian's path, throwing him off balance. Another snap of her fingers and she was encased in a protective sheet of water that defied all logic.

Khadija dragged Jacob to his feet. "We have to help him." She raced ahead with her sword drawn. Jacob staggered after her.

Darian was darting left and right, searching in vain for an opening in the wall of water. Jacob and Khadija joined his side, the three of them circling the jinniya queen, who smirked and goaded them, her face blurred by the water surrounding her. She was untouchable. Jacob skidded to a halt, eyes flashing to Darian and the green glint of his sword. That's when an idea occurred to him.

He rummaged into his pocket to produce William's bright green stone. He'd been too afraid to part with it before. Too afraid to relinquish the last thing William had ever given him. But now Jacob stretched his arm back. He understood the gift's true purpose. Jacob hurled the stone at the queen. It passed through the water, knocking her straight in the eye.

Queen Bidhukh howled. The water sloshed against the paving stones. Darian saw his moment and seized it.

A piercing scream split the air in half. Queen Bidhukh flung Darian to the side, the glass sword protruding from her abdomen. She roared. The sound caused the sand around them to flare up as if they'd been caught in a spontaneous sandstorm. Jacob quickly covered his eyes.

Queen Bidhukh yanked the sword free, pressing her palm to the inky-black blood that was erupting from her stomach and pooling at her feet. "Foolish mortal," she hissed, and hurled the sword away, where it smashed against the pavestones. "You may have banished me to Al-Ghaib, but I will return." She keeled over. "And I will be sure to make every living moment of your pathetic life a misery," she rasped. Already, her form was flickering, her body fading into the air like mist. She staggered forward and reached for Darian's collar, yanking him to his feet.

And then the jinniya queen plunged her fist into Darian's heart.

"No!" Khadija screamed.

Queen Bidhukh's hand passed through Darian's chest as if she'd dipped it in a body of water, and in her palm was a pulsing, beating heart made of smoke. Darian dropped to the ground, hands flying to his chest searching for a wound, but not even a drop of blood stained his tunic.

Queen Bidhukh smirked. "I do not feast on such inferior flesh." She crushed Darian's heart in her palm. "Instead, I've stolen something better." She dropped to her knees, black blood gushing freely now as she erupted into a tendril of smoke and was gone, leaving Darian spluttering in the sand, surrounded by shards of the glass sword.

33

KHADIJA

All the air left her lungs. Khadija's scream was so raw that, for a moment, she didn't recognize her own voice. She rushed to Darian's side, tears obscuring her vision.

"I'm OK. I'm fine." Darian thumped his chest and erupted into a fit of coughing.

"But . . . she took your heart," she spluttered. She wasn't quite sure what she'd seen, only that Darian ought to be dead. But he wasn't. There wasn't even a wound. She buried her face in his neck.

Darian's chuckle was like the beating of a bird's wings within his chest. "How could she take it when it belongs to you?" he whispered.

Khadija brought her lips to his. Their kiss blurred everything around them into nonexistence. It stole all her fear, her pain, her grief, and tossed it into the night. Left her so empty she became weightless. Airborne. Free.

"Khadija, watch out!" Jacob yelled as a pair of wings slammed into her. Khadija skidded across the ground.

The ifrit roared, sparks spraying from his lips. "My queen!" A ball of jinn fire hurtled toward them. Darian quickly shoved Khadija free of the flames and rolled to the side, but the ifrit's fire licked his leg. Darian yelped and thrashed his leg in an attempt to smother the flames.

Caleb descended on them, his charcoal skin glowing silver in the light of the moon, his face twisted in savage rage. The sword was shattered. Their only weapon against Caleb lost. There was no stopping him now, Khadija realized with a sinking dread as she braced for his impact. This was how it would end.

Then there was a harmony like the sigh of a sea brushing the shoreline. The beating of wings. Khadija's head lifted just as a shimmer of pearlescent feathers came into view. "Tahmina," she gasped.

The peri circled the ifrit, her soft voice morphing into a shattering scream that was louder and more powerful than anything she'd ever heard. Khadija's palms flew to her ears.

Tahmina slashed the ifrit's cheek with her talons. The ifrit screeched and took flight, and Tahmina followed, her lilac eyes burning with vengeance. She twirled out of reach of Caleb's next strike and clamped her talons around the tip of the ifrit's wing. She yanked, tearing the thin membrane of his wing. Caleb howled.

Khadija threw her head back, trying to make sense of the frenzy of wings knotted above her before glancing back at Darian, who was lying dangerously still. That's when she noticed a swirl of red hair crouched beside the deflated balloon, locked in a scuffle: Vera and the nawab. Vera had managed to overpower the nawab, sending him crashing to the ground. She pressed his cheek against the pavestones and brought her knife to his neck. "I *will* get my wish from Queen Mardzma!"

The next moments seemed to unravel in slow motion as Khadija fumbled for her sword and charged toward Vera. Vera spun at the last second, teasing her to follow as she dipped behind the empty balloon carcass, shielded from view of the market square.

Khadija yanked the nawab to his feet. "Run." She pushed him away and swerved around the deflated balloon with Jacob by her side, his dagger poised for attack. Vera's face contorted into a snarl at the sight of him, her crimson hair spilling down her back like a river of blood. "It was *you* who wished for the Seal of Sulaiman." Her eyes narrowed. "You *betrayed* me, Jacob! There's nothing I hate more than traitors." She spat on the ground, unsheathed another sword from her belt, and brandished the twin blades. "Now give me back my mirror."

"No." Jacob struck, but Vera easily blocked his attack, sending his dagger flying out of his hands. She swung again. Jacob ducked and retreated as Vera sliced through the air. "We could've been such good friends, you and I." Her lips curled over her teeth. "We could've liberated our people, ended their suffering—just like William wanted."

Khadija furiously searched for an opening to strike but Vera was too quick.

"You're wrong!" Jacob screamed. "William never wanted this."

Vera threw her head back, her two swords hanging limply by her sides like steel limbs. "You obviously didn't know your friend very well, then. Too busy making friends with their kind instead." She spat in Khadija's direction. "Now you'll watch her die." Vera spun and reared her swords back, bringing them down on Khadija.

Khadija lunged out of Vera's path and landed unsteadily on her feet. Vera approached, scraping her two swords against each other, creating little sparks along the metal. "I've been meaning to ask, have you been home recently?" She purred. "You should consider paying Qasrah a visit. It is very . . . different from when you were last there."

Khadija's skin seared. Burned. Scalded. Fire spread through her veins.

Vera giggled and staggered forward, an obvious limp to her gait. "You'll pay for this." She squeezed her injured thigh. "I'll make you pay." She readied her twin blades.

Vera charged. Khadija's fingers flexed against the hilt of her weapon. Pictures of Qasrah flashed across her mind. All the deaths. All the lives lost because of this woman. Rage consumed her.

She saw red.

Khadija swung. Vera attempted to sidestep her attack, but the tip of Khadija's blade managed to pierce her shoulder. Vera howled.

"Ammi!"

A rush of hot air scorched Khadija's face as the ifrit descended on her. He knocked her aside with his talons, which dripped silver with Tahmina's blood. Khadija's heart clenched as she furiously searched the sky for any sign of the peri, until Caleb vaulted for her and knocked her sword from her hands. "I will avenge my queen!" Caleb yelled.

Khadija escaped being lacerated by his talons by mere inches.

"Khadija!" Her head whipped around just as Jacob launched something in the air toward her.

Something twirled above her. Something that shimmered and glowed a brilliant green. Khadija leaped for it, catching a crystal shard of the broken sword.

Out of nowhere, Vera's blades slashed down, and Khadija could only react by angling the shard to block before Vera's swords shredded her to ribbons. The tip snapped off and fell at her feet. She stared at her blunt fragment in horror.

"See, Caleb. See how I will always protect you. Not like that queen of yours you worship." Vera's blades veered down again, and Khadija blocked with what remained of her crystal shard. It shattered.

Vera was hysterical. "I am your true mother!" She turned to her ifrit and thumped her chest.

Light glinted off the point of the crystal shard lying discarded in the sand, and Khadija moved to snatch it up, but the ifrit was faster. His hand curled around her neck. Khadija shrieked as her skin exploded with pain. She thrashed her arms, her skin blistering at his touch. The ifrit squeezed tighter. Khadija screamed and spasmed.

A pressure was mounting in her ears, a high-pitched ringing that threatened to burst her eardrums as her fingers began to tingle, then throb. Her limbs screamed for oxygen. The world grew dimmer. The only thing she could focus on was the glitter of the green-eyed ifrit.

Jacob's voice called her name, faint, distant, from another life. A green flash at the corners of her vision, something sharp and cold beside her fingertips. Khadija's fingers closed around the crystal shard. It slit her palm open.

She thrust it into the ifrit's heart. The ifrit's howl was like the scream of gas igniting. He tossed her away.

Vera screamed. Khadija rolled to the side as Vera lunged for her son, trying to hold him together, but the ifrit was withering away. Khadija could see right through him now. He was fading into the air.

"No! Don't leave me!" Vera clawed at her son, and her white gloves burst into flames.

The ifrit clutched his mother's wrists. Fire licked at Vera's cloak. Her skin began to blister, and her red hair caught fire. Vera shrieked and tried to pry the ifrit from her. She went up in flames, a brilliant green jinn fire, so bright that Khadija had to shield her eyes. They dissolved into a puddle of smoke and were gone.

Khadija pressed a hand to the raw skin of her neck. It was over. Vera was gone. She had paid the ultimate price for love. With that thought, pain turned her world black.

EPILOGUE

"I think she's waking up." Muffled voices overhead. Khadija's eyelashes fluttered open.

The first thing she knew was pain, hot and furious at her throat like she'd swallowed pure fire. Khadija's face contorted.

"Here. Drink." Cool liquid graced her lips. It was Jameela.

Khadija blinked back tears as colors came into focus. She was in an infirmary of some kind, bay windows occupying the walls so that sunlight turned the room amber. All the beds were full, and nurses padded softly between the wounded. Where was she?

A familiar face appeared. "Khadija! Are you OK?" Jacob's voice was filled with fear. He visibly flinched as his eyes traced over her neck.

Khadija lifted a hand to her throat. Jameela slapped her hand away. "Don't touch it!"

She swallowed. Her voice sounded burned. "Vera—"

"Gone. They're all gone." Jacob perched on the end of her bed and squeezed her hand, as if checking she was really alive. "We won, Khadija. It's over." The relief was leaking out of his voice.

"Darian—"

Jacob's gaze fell to the bed on her right where Darian lay bundled beneath swaths of blankets. "Is he OK?" she asked anxiously.

"No need to worry about him." Jameela rose to tend to the patient on her left, who Khadija realized was Anam. "Or her," Jameela added. "They are both doing just fine."

Khadija allowed Jameela's words to wash over her, and then she settled back down among the pillows as memories of the battle flashed across her mind. She tried to make sense of it at first, but when the images grew so fast they blurred into one another, she gave up and glanced out the window at the bright gold coin of the sun and the distant balloons floating toward the clouds. The sight instantly calmed her.

As Jameela busied herself with the other patients, Jacob nudged her elbow, his face erupting into a grin. "I heard the nawab's on his way. He wants to thank you in person for saving his life."

No sooner had the words left his lips than the door to the infirmary swung open with a sigh, and a face appeared. One she was aching to see. Khadija attempted to smile, but the delicate skin around her neck seared with pain. She settled for shifting herself up onto her elbows in an attempt to appear less incapacitated.

"Khadija." Abba hurried over and threw his arms around her, careful not to touch her neck. She tried to remember the last time her father had shown his affection so brazenly, but couldn't. He kissed the top of her hijab.

She prepared herself for his scolding. What she didn't expect was him to utter, "My daughter. A warrior!" His eyes glittered.

"You're not angry?" She couldn't quite believe what she was hearing.

"Angry that my daughter risked her life to save this city?" He rubbed his temples. "I'm furious! I'm shocked. Amazed." Abba cupped her cheek. "And I am proud."

Khadija glowed with his praise.

Abba turned to Jacob then, and his lips curled with disgust, tongue ready to utter the slur that he was so used to saying, until something seemed to stop him. A long pause, and then Abba did something she would never in a thousand years have ever predicted.

He stretched his hand out to Jacob. "You fought alongside my daughter. You are a brave boy."

Jacob's mouth fell open as he took Abba's hand and shook it. Then he was grinning from ear to ear. "Thank you, sir."

A collective gasp from the rest of the room had the three of them whirling around as a figure appeared in a crisp white sherwani bordered with gold trim; on his head was a white topi.

"The nawab!" Abba jumped to his feet and furiously smoothed out the creases in his shalwar before urging his daughter to do the same. Khadija knew she no doubt looked dreadful, but the most she could manage was to rub the gunk from her eyes as the nawab approached.

The nawab padded over. His face was stern, his posture demanding; even the brush of his slippers against the floor tiles whispered of his stature. When he reached her bedside, Khadija swiftly dipped her head, not daring to meet his gaze.

"Oh, come now! I should be the one afraid to meet the eyes of a warrior like you." The nawab chuckled. "Khadija, is it?"

She could only nod dumbly as the nawab pulled up a chair, batting away nurses as they appeared with trays laden with biscuits and steaming pots of tea. When his dark eyes faced her, his expression was sincere. "I would like to personally thank you for saving not just my life, but the lives of my people in Al-Shaam."

It was an overwhelming gesture and yet she couldn't bring herself to accept it. Khadija shook her head. "They deserve your thanks too." She nodded toward Jacob, and Anam and Darian in the beds on either side. "And them." She thrust her head in the direction of the other wounded lying in the infirmary.

Khadija felt Abba stiffen beside her at her outspokenness, but there was no use holding her tongue now. She met the nawab's stare with a steady gaze.

The nawab nodded, twirling the end of his henna-stained beard. "Then they will be appropriately rewarded." His eyes flickered to Jacob, a hint of repulsion marring his features before he returned to her. "But I am here to discuss your reward. Such courage cannot go unacknowledged. It is common for me to reward my soldiers with medals of bravery and honorable titles." He hummed. "But you are not a soldier, and I struggle to see what a girl would do with such things." He twirled the ruby ring around his forefinger absentmindedly. "I have never formally congratulated a woman before. I do not know what an appropriate gift would be."

"A husband," Abba blurted.

Khadija glared at him.

"I mean"—he fumbled over his next words—"if that is what she wants."

She rolled her eyes. "I don't want a husband, Abba."

He sighed. "No, I suppose not."

"What about wealth? I could make you and your family very rich." The nawab smiled.

Khadija considered it. Definitely the way Abba perked up and rubbed his palms together had her almost uttering her acceptance, until she realized with a sinking feeling that what use was gold when she, as a woman, would never actually own it? It would be Abba's gold, which she would forever keep having to ask his permission to spend. She didn't doubt that Abba would allow her access to it, but then came other hurdles. She could not own property, open a business, travel the world without a document granting her permission. Wealth was useless without the power to use it, and she realized that all along, that's all she'd wanted. Power.

"I want to be able to do as I please."

The nawab's brow creased with confusion.

"I want to make my own decisions, go wherever I want to, without the barriers." She glanced at Jacob, saw the eagerness in his eyes, and then added, "I want that for all of us."

The nawab scratched his chin. "And how do I gift you something so intangible?" His eyebrows rose in a challenge.

And she knew exactly how. The thing that embodied both power and freedom. The thing she'd spent every day of her life wishing she had. Khadija's next words rolled off the tip of her tongue.

"Give me a hot-air balloon."

Acknowledgments

I began writing *Rebel of Fire and Flight* in the summer of 2018; after numerous dead-end jobs had me convinced I was unemployable, I decided the only way to boost my bruised ego was to sit down and do something I was actually good at. This was the result. It's been a crazy couple of years. In that time, this book has survived a business degree, a pandemic, three lockdowns, countless rewrites, and two pregnancies—yes, I have two under two . . . send help! Amid so much change, *Rebel of Fire and Flight* has been my constant, something I can dip in and out of when the world gets too much, and though writing a novel is very much a lonely endeavor, there is still a long list of names that this book would simply not exist without.

Lucy Irvine, my incredible agent, for seeing the potential in the utter mess of my original manuscript and helping me polish it into something worth reading! A huge thank-you to Tim Bates and Kimberley Chambers for arranging the Kickstart Prize for underrepresented writers, which provided me with a way into an industry I had wrongly assumed I had no hope of being a part of. The amazing teams at Peters Fraser + Dunlop and Chicken House for championing *Rebel of Fire and Flight* through many months of editing. Rachel Hickman, Jazz Bartlett Love, Esther Waller, Elinor Bagenal, Rachel Leyshon, and Sarah Wallis-Newman—such a brilliant bunch with so much passion for *Rebel of Fire and Flight* right from the start. A special thank-you to Barry Cunningham, who, despite being one of the nicest people to ever grace my Zoom calls, will probably always scare me purely for being one of the biggest names in publishing—though I blame myself for searching for you on Wikipedia! My editor, Kesia Lupo, for channeling all your energy and excitement into *Rebel of Fire and Flight*. It's been such an incredible experience working with you as the story has evolved, largely due to your creative input and ability to understand what I am trying to say even when I have no clue!

Thank you to Jenni Chappelle and the wonderful RevPit community for your input on a very rough and messy first draft, without which *Rebel of Fire and Flight* could have well flown off in an entirely different direction. To all the lovely writers of Twitter for providing a wealth of knowledge, support, and, at times, a safe place to scream as I navigated the roller coaster of a ride that is getting a book published.

My Aunty Shahnaz, for seeing my writing potential before even I was aware of it and encouraging me to pursue my dream of being an author. My parents, for the countless trips to bookstores and libraries growing up, and my brother, Hamza, for answering all my ridiculous questions about the aerodynamics of a hot-air balloon!

And finally, Reg, my husband, for being my support system, for encouraging me to follow my dreams and for being there to listen through all my periods of doubt. For someone who doesn't even read books, and will probably never read this book either, you've never once complained when I needed someone to bounce my crazy ideas off of. And don't worry, you will get your commission for that one sentence you helped me write!

Author's Note

When I first sat down to write *Rebel of Fire and Flight*, my intention was to produce not the book that you have before you but simply something that would quell my obsession for things that fly. As I delved into the fantasy of flight, the weightlessness of being airborne, and the sense of disconnection with the world below, I wondered if it was as easy as discarding one's problems on the ground and jumping in a balloon. As a teenager, my own escapist desires would have me craving the opportunity to drop everything and quite literally float away in the same way Khadija and Jacob flee the problems in their own lives—Jacob's battle with racism, and Khadija's struggle with misogyny and gender inequality. However, both characters soon come to realize that, like everything that ascends, they must come down eventually, where their problems still remain.

This book is a battle of two things: identity and loneliness. It is as much a journey to find one's place in the world as it is a longing for acceptance and companionship—both increasingly relevant in today's world.

The spotlight has been shone on bigotry and prejudice, racism in particular, around the globe in recent years. Many of us have grown up to be so conditioned to such things, to expect them in our daily lives, that to see these forms of hate exposed for their ugliness is both liberating and has been a long time coming. When people become hardwired to accept something as normal, quite often they become blind to it.

This is a book that may make a lot of people feel uncomfortable with its discussion of terrorism, extremism, and racism, drawn mainly from my own experiences with Islamophobia. Growing up as a British Pakistani and a Muslim, I often felt this constant need to apologize. As the news became saturated with Islamic extremists, I found myself feeling almost partly responsible for the violent acts of other Muslims. This guilt, partnered with frequent taunts of being told to go back home, meant that I, a second-generation Muslim born in Britain, felt that I did not and most likely would never belong. My childhood was a constant questioning of my own identity being British but sadly never British enough.

It took a long time for me to accept that bigotry comes from a place of fear and often cannot be reasoned with, and that there are good and bad people in the world, irrespective of religion, race, class, or gender. I belong to a group of people, but I am by no means responsible for anyone's actions within that group except my own. I remember when I heard the news that my brother's classmate had fled to Syria to join ISIS, and the shock that followed from everyone who knew him. It was unexpected, completely out of character, and I could not help but wonder, what would push a person to extremism? And once they had tipped over the edge, was there any hope of bringing them back? I believe there are many push-and-pull factors of radicalization, and while these will never be an excuse to justify violence, my hope with this book is to show that the world is not so black-and-white, and that people are often the product of their environment and life experiences. In short, hate breeds hate; however, I hope to show with *Rebel of Fire and Flight* that love and friendship can and do prevail.